GANGSTER JAZZ

Also by Tom Ardies

Kosygin is Coming (aka Russian Roulette)
In a Lady's Service
Palm Springs

The Charlie Sparrow Series

Their Man in the White House
This Suitcase is Going to Explode
Pandemic

As Jack Trolley

Balboa Firefly
Manila Time
Juarez Justice
La Jolla Spindrift

As Richard O'Brien

Storming Heaven
By Friends Betrayed (aka Gangster Jazz)

GANGSTER JAZZ

TOM ARDIES

ISBN-13: 978-1-952138-98-0

Previously published as *By Friends Betrayed* by Richard O'Brien

Published by
Cutting Edge Books
PO Box 8212
Calabasas, CA 91372
www.cuttingedgebooks.com

NEBRASKA

CHAPTER 1

He woke up screaming. His heart was pounding madly and his nightclothes were soaked with sweat. For a long moment he thought he was still in France, in the hospital at Vendeuil-Caply, but then the bedroom door opened and it was his mother's face that shimmered in the yellow lamplight, not Nurse Burton's. Was that possible?

Yes, God, please, he prayed. The lamp moved closer, etching the room with eerie shadows, and he still wasn't sure if the nightmare was over. Sometimes everything got all mixed up. His father would be with him in the trenches and his brother too. The world would be coming to an end and they would be talking about the weather, wondering if it would rain in time to save the corn crop, and then the order would come to attack, and then .... But it was over, wasn't it?

Please, he prayed. The lamp moved closer and the flickering light finally brought him the peace he wanted. He was awake and the war was over and he was back home in Nebraska. He had all the proof he needed in what he saw in his mother's eyes. The concern and bewilderment that had been his homecoming gifts to her.

Wordlessly, she stared at him, the lamp trembling in her hand. She had nothing to say anymore; no words left to express her grief. She just wanted to make sure that he was alive, that was all. Satisfied, she turned away, taking the swaying shadows with her. The door pulled shut and the room was inky black again.

Greg Meister closed his eyes against the darkness. He hadn't spoken either—what was there to say?—and so he didn't resent his mother's silence. They had come to a kind of understanding about these wordless encounters in the terror of his nights. Her expressions of concern and his false reassurances had ceased long ago. It was senseless to voice them.

Two years and they had finally reached an understanding, their *only* understanding, Meister thought. He kept his eyes closed with an effort, trying to go back to sleep, but he knew that it was useless. The nightmare was too fresh in his mind, too vivid.

It was always the same nightmare and it always started the same way, with that May morning when he arrived on the Western Front, in a wagonload of replacements for M Company, Twenty-eighth Regiment, First United States Infantry Division.

Right from the start, nobody liked him. He was too much the farm boy, a country hick with the hay sticking out of his ears and his big hands sticking out of his sleeves. He didn't fit, either in his uniform or with the rest of the men. He didn't belong.

Not even John Crain liked him at first. Crain, in temporary command, waiting for a new captain to take over the company, threatened to have him shot for breaking that bastard Reardon's jaw. Crain couldn't understand about the teasing, that Reardon had called him a sissy, a bookworm.

Nothing went right until Phipps took command and they moved back to Maison-Tuilerie to rehearse for the attack on Cantigny. There he had proved himself, tossing grenades better than any other man in the company, so accurate that Sergeant Truggs called him the best damn grenade man on the Western Front. This after he had already established himself as perhaps the best card player.

If he still didn't belong, at least he was respected, but by then it was too late. They were back in the Picardy sector and it was time for the assault on Cantigny. They were back in the trenches getting ready to die, and he still didn't have anyone he could call a friend.

He didn't want to go. It was no way to die, alone in an army of your countrymen, and he might have bolted, except for Crain.

It was strange, because Crain still wasn't sure about him. To Crain, the bloodied veteran, he was still just a poor dumb doughboy, a lost puppy with hands too big for the rest of him.

Yet, in that moment of truth, waiting for their artillery to destroy Cantigny, waiting to lead the first American offensive of the war, Crain had paused to pat him reassuringly on the shoulder and had accepted the offer of a cigarette.

Somehow, that made all the difference, a small sign of regard, an acknowledgment that he existed. He had wanted to say, "Listen, for a millionaire's son, you're a bit all right yourself, Lieutenant." And he had wanted to confess that he had been afraid and that he wasn't anymore, but the roar of the guns wouldn't permit it.

They drowned him out, denying any last expression of his humanity—was this why only his father and brother ever talked in the nightmares?—and then there wasn't any time left at all. The tempo of the guns changed and the barrage began to roll before them, the curtain of deadly fire no longer landing on the village but exactly one hundred meters beyond their forward trenches.

It was time—the bad part, the part that made him wake up screaming—and what made it so vivid was that it had all been rehearsed in the peaceful countryside near Maison-Tuilerie. The barrage first, then the twelve French tanks, and then the men ….

Phipps climbing over the top of the trench. Crain following the captain and signaling for his own men to follow him. They begin walking toward the outskirts of Cantigny, burdened by their packs and shovels.

Every two minutes the barrage lifts to advance another hundred meters. The chatter of Hotchkiss machine guns intersperses with the hiccupping fire of the French Chauchats.

It's all as rehearsed, and then suddenly they are walking through the gates of hell. German mortar shells begin to explode among them. Phipps is hit first, his right leg torn off and flung away like a bent stick. Sellers is next, hit in the stomach, and then Rhone, screaming that he is blind.

Crain leads them on relentlessly. When at last they reach the village, they are running at high port, their bayonets fixed. The taste of their comrades' blood is in their mouths and they kill the enemy indiscriminately. Aging, half-starved men, emaciated, hollowcheeked boys. They club them, bayonet them and smash them to gore in a wild, almost joyous, blood bath.

The most efficient killer is a gangling recruit too big for his uniform. No one escapes the awful anger suddenly unleashed within him. Swooping down like an avenging angel, huge hands monstrously large on his Springfield, he uses the rifle first as a pike, then as a club, a smooth controlled movement he learned scything wheat in Nebraska....

Meister opened his eyes. It was always the same nightmare and it always ended the same way—in the German trench where he discovered, to his everlasting dismay, that he was *good* at it, good at killing.

Cursing softly—would God ever forgive him?—he fumbled for his cigarettes, lit one and sat smoking in the dark. He knew he wouldn't go back to sleep now. He never did after one of the nightmares.

The memory couldn't be blotted out. The only thing that ever helped was to remind himself that he also did one thing worthwhile in the war; he saved John Crain's life.

That had happened the same day, late in the afternoon, when the Germans, backed by their artillery, threatened to overrun the positions M Company had secured at dawn. One of the German machine guns somehow sneaked in deadly close. It was raking a field of fire over the entire company front.

With Meister's reputation—best grenade man on the Western Front—Crain ordered him to take the gun out, but he couldn't throw a grenade anymore. He had been hit in the shoulder by a shell splinter.

Instead, he'd passed the grenade to Crain and the lieutenant had thrown it. Then, anxious to make sure the machine gun had been silenced for good, he went to investigate. One of the German gunners was dead. The other got off two shots with his Luger before Crain killed him.

Crain went down, hit in the stomach and the shoulder, screaming with pain. Meister had to go get him. He had no choice. It was his fault; he hadn't thrown the grenade. So he had gone after Crain. With his good arm he had pulled him out of that muddy hole, managed to drape him over his back and made a last crazy run through hell.

Where had he found the courage?

Smoking in bed, waiting endlessly for the dawn, Meister still wasn't sure, but he was glad he had. It helped atone. Not much, perhaps, but some.

And, as it turned out, it was his last chance. He had been hit bad, worse than he thought, and spent a long period of convalescence—the whole summer—in the hospital at Vendeuil-Caply.

Meister sighed, remembering. He'd belonged there, a cripple just like the rest of the patients, his right arm in a cast that held it at a right angle from his shoulder, the elbow bent and his hand directly in front of his face.

No trouble making friends either. Hal Rosen needed a friend. He had lost three fingers of his left hand and the dream of becoming a concert pianist.

Pop Fagan needed a friend. Dosed with gas—dichlorodiethyl sulfide, a poison he couldn't even pronounce—the young Negro had been taken out of the lines with lung corrosion, his lifelong ambition, to blow trumpet with a jazz band, destroyed.

Meister could commiserate with them. He had wanted to play baseball, but he would never throw a ball again, or at least not hard and straight.

And John Crain? Well, it seemed he needed a friend, too. Besides being shot, he'd been hit in the leg with a hot shell fragment and the wound had become infected. The doctors had done their best, but he'd been left with a slight limp. After he had said his thanks to Meister—"You probably saved my life"—he hung around, an officer and a gentleman, consorting with the ranks.

Meister smiled, stubbing out his cigarette. He reached immediately for another. Crain had had an ulterior motive. He wanted the Luger, the one he had been shot with, for a souvenir, and Meister wasn't about to give it up. He had claimed it from the German machine gunner's death grip before starting that crazy run through hell with Crain on his back. It was his, his only prize of war, earned and taken, and he was damned if he was going to hand it over to Lieutenant John Crain.

Meister lit the fresh cigarette, still smiling. Did Crain know that he would get the Luger eventually? Probably not, and it really couldn't have mattered all that much to him, because nothing else did. Crain wanted to do just two things at Vendeuil-Caply: get drunk and listen to Pop Fagan play the guitar, his substitute for the trumpet he could no longer play.

The four of them would meet in the hospital basement, John Crain, Pop Fagan, Hal Rosen and Meister. Fagan supplied the whiskey—he could get *anything*, that boy. Crain paid for it and drank most of it.

Crain had made a toast at the first meeting. "Gentlemen, I give you the good Dr. Wilson, who's making the whole goddamn world safe for democracy. Here's to Thomas Woodrow, who's fighting a war to end all wars." Long, dramatic pause. Then, "Stupid son of a bitch."

At the time, Meister had thought the comment was treasonous, and he had said as much. He might even have done something about it if he hadn't been too drunk to stand up.

Remembering, Meister felt better. Those were good times. The killing was over for him and he was safe with his fellow cripples, drinking whiskey and listening to Pop Fagan's magic guitar and spouting nonsense, all of them.

They were each of them sure that they had things figured out. Crain said he was never going to worry again. The world had changed forever and there was nothing he could do about it. He was going to go home and indulge himself in the American dream. He was going to have all the money and fun and good times he could get.

Hal Rosen, on the other hand, whom Crain called a Bolshevik, was sure there was going to be a revolution. It had already started in Russia and it was going to sweep the world. "The workers had been pushed too far," he'd said. Somehow, it sounded like he had been pushed too far, too.

Pop Fagan was just going to play the guitar for whoever wanted to listen. He said it was white folks who had made up democracy for themselves. Making it safe or dangerous wasn't going to make any difference to him, no way.

Of the four of them, Meister had been the most certain of his future, he remembered. At their last meeting in the hospital boiler room he had made a solemn speech about it. He told them he intended to return to Nebraska. He said he was going to finish college and then get married.

He could remember his exact words: "I've seen France. Now I want to go home and get things back to normal, the way they were before all this started."

Of all of them, he had been the most certain—and the most wrong. He sat in the dark and smoked his cigarettes and waited for the dawn.

With morning's first light, marked by a rooster's uncertain crow, the small farmhouse stirred and came alive. Oil lamps glowed at the windows. A white thread of smoke climbed from the chimney.

A short time later, more quickly than one would expect, a tall, heavily muscled man emerged from the back door, pausing to button his mackinaw against the bitter cold. He breathed cautiously, a kind of test, getting used to it, and there was a white puff when he exhaled. He stamped his feet, waiting.

The door behind him opened again and a boy of about fifteen quickly joined him. In all but weight—there were fifty pounds missing—he was almost an exact duplicate of the man. Six feet tall, grim-visaged, hardened by toil. He also wore similar clothes, a checkered mackinaw, dark blue overalls, rubber boots. A felt cap with earflaps to fight the cold.

The man gave no indication that the boy had joined him. He continued to button his mackinaw, blowing on his fingers to keep them warm, the white puffs of breath so regular that they seemed to be coming from a machine. The task completed, he stamped his feet, waiting.

The boy turned up his collar and moved closer to him. They stood huddled together in the chill.

"Do you think he'll come?" the boy asked.

The man didn't answer. He was staring across a flat, snow-covered field to where a line of cottonwoods, mottled sticks stripped of their leaves, marked the bank of the river and the end of his property.

That far, he seemed to be thinking, settling the boundaries in his mind. He had two hundred thirty acres, most of them flat, all of them rich, that had provided, until recently, everything he wanted. In return for his toil, the land gave him food and shelter, clothing and warmth. It did so with precarious uncertainty, but it still provided. It was good land … God's land. Work it and it would provide.

"I could ask him …"

"No," the man said. In fifty years of life, almost all of it spent in the fields, he had never resented a single sacrifice for wife, children or country. Now, however, he wondered. The war had done something totally unexpected. Though it had returned his older son physically whole, it had kept a strange, persistent hold on him.

The man shook his head, unable to comprehend what had happened, unwilling to question the Almighty. He pulled down his cap and stepped off the stoop into the new day's fresh mantle of snow.

"What about Greg?" the boy inquired.

"Forget him," the man said gruffly. He led the way across the field to the barn, fists jammed into his mackinaw pockets, shoulders hunched into the wind.

He couldn't wait forever. There were forty cows to be milked.

Inside the house, Pauline Meister glanced out the kitchen window, watching the two figures trudging through the snow. Their progress was marked by a single line of footprints, her husband leading the way, her youngest son following.

Following in his footsteps, she thought, the words coming to mind unbidden, and she also thought how drastically her world had been altered. Before, there had been three in that line, all making the same imprint, sharing it. Her three men, together. Then, without warning, without explanation or reason, Greg had been … what, plucked out?

Yes, that was the word, it suited; it fit the imagery that haunted her these days, the imagery of a divine hand reaching down from heaven. Unlike her husband, Pauline Meister had begun, however reluctantly, to question God. It was so unfair. He shouldn't give and then take away.

She had always been so sure about her boys, both of them. Donna, her only daughter and the baby of the family, had been a wayward child from the beginning, lost in dreams and fantasies, conversing with playmates not present. Pauline Meister had come to observe the child with a kind of awe—was she really from the same family?—and was used to fearing for her future. At ten she was already a beauty and her willfulness was beginning to get out of hand.

But Greg, her first-born? He had never caused any trouble. He was a joy, all a mother could ask for, tall and strong and intelligent, handsome in his special way. Until the war, until He took him away, Greg had been the perfect son.

Flushing at her blasphemy, Pauline Meister turned from the window, busying herself at the oilcloth-covered table. She cleared away the dirty dishes and left the one clean setting. Even if the boy wouldn't work, he still had to eat, she thought. She put another stick of wood in the stove and refilled the kettle. She pulled a cast-iron frying pan from the warming oven and filled it with thick slices of bacon.

She was a well-organized woman and she didn't like to make two breakfasts, but this morning she was determined that he eat something. A cigarette was not the way to start anyone's day.

Also, no matter who objected, she was going to sit him down this morning and they were going to have a good, long talk. This nonsense had gone on long enough. He was going to have to see a doctor, that's all there was to it.

Such resolve was not usual to her nature. Unlike her husband, who was built like a farm animal, tanned hide pulled over taut muscle, she was a frail creature with a soft white body. Her plain, open face was unmarked by the sun, and in January she wore the same print dress that had served her in July. Her place was in the home and she stayed there. She kept busy with her work. She didn't argue. She seldom offered a comment.

It was said in town that Pauline Meister did not wring her hands only because her husband had forbidden her to do so. Normally, she held her tongue until he was out of the room, partly out of respect, partly because he considered her speech to be idle chatter.

Even so, she had done more to shape their children than her husband, and this was especially true of Greg. It was she who had gotten him interested in books and made him apply to the university. It was she who wrote to him every day when he was wounded. And it was she who, when he came home from the war, took the lamp in when he screamed.

After all that, she couldn't stop now. If Warren Meister had given up, Pauline Meister hadn't. If her husband didn't want to talk about it anymore, she did.

She glanced out the window again. Father and son, now tiny dots in the distance, disappeared into the barn, barely visible itself, a white blur against the grey of the landscape.

She took a deep breath and steeled herself for the ordeal ahead. For the first time in her marriage, she was going to disobey her husband's express wishes, which were to trust in God.

Greg Meister entered the kitchen looking like he was still back in the trenches. He hadn't washed and his hair was uncombed and a black stubble covered his jaw. Behind his steel-rimmed glasses his eyes were puffed from lack of sleep.

It was with regret that he saw his mother waiting. He wanted to have the stove's warmth to himself. The nightmare always left him drained. Any activity, even idle conversation, was more of a burden than he cared to bear. Besides, his nerves were raw. The slightest thing would touch him off.

He was going to complain, but something about her warned him to be careful. She seemed to have gathered herself, become larger by sheer force of will, and there was a look in her pale-blue eyes that he had previously seen only in his father's, and then only on rare occasions.

He hoped she hadn't chosen now, of all times, to try to lecture him. If she had, she was going to get a lecture back, and he didn't want to hurt her. She cried so easily, drawing from an endless reservoir. She cried for all of them, the whole family.

Please, not this morning, he thought. But he had the terrible feeling that an argument was unavoidable and that it was going to get out of hand. He somehow knew that they were going to say things that were better left unsaid. A break was coming, permanent, irreversible. The kitchen was heavy with its foreshadowing.

"Morning," he said, the word sounding more like a statement of fact than a greeting. Perfunctorily, he brushed his lips against his mother's cheek, then moved to the table like a man in a trance. He took a chair opposite the setting that had been left for him and patted his pockets for his cigarettes.

Pauline Meister watched in dismay. "Can't you at least wait till you have your tea?" she asked.

"Huh?" He pretended not to understand.

"Before you have a cigarette."

"Oh." He considered that briefly, the cigarette looking hardly bigger than a toothpick in his huge hand. Then, expression unchanged, he committed the cigarette to his mouth. He lit it and inhaled deeply and blew out a long stream of smoke. "No," he told her, not even trying to be polite.

She turned away, but not before he saw the look on her face. He had just sat down and he had hurt her already. He told himself he ought to apologize, but the words wouldn't come. He wanted to get up and walk away, but he didn't have the strength. He found himself smoking and waiting again, this time for the inevitable.

"They at it already?" he asked, trying to change the subject. "They" were his father and brother, and he knew as well as she did that they were in the barn, but at least it was something else to talk about besides his smoking.

She nodded and moved the pan of bacon over the stove's firebox. "Yes," she answered carefully, and then, unable to stop herself, she blurted out the rest. "They could use your help, you know."

God, it is coming, he thought. She wanted it. She was determined to have it. Involuntarily, he looked out toward the barn, picturing his father and brother there, bent beneath the cows. "They've done it without me before."

"I know."

"All the time I was away."

"I know."

"So what difference does it make?" he demanded, still staring at the barn. His father was doing what he wanted to do. His father was a farmer and farmers milked cows and planted corn and talked about the weather. When he first came home, his father had questioned him for ten minutes about the war and then he had spent two hours informing him about crops and cows. "I don't want any breakfast ... and what difference does it make?"

"You're supposed to be part of the family."

"Am I?"

"Aren't you?"

He looked away from the window. No, not anymore, he thought. He had come home to strangers and he had been living with them for two years. "I'm not sure."

"I see." With an effort, she turned to confront him, the tears shimmering in her eyes. Her face was stiff and white. All the blood seemed to have left it. "Greg ... how can you say that?"

"Easy."

"Greg, please." She raised thin hands, outstretched, pleading. "You've changed so much. You're not the boy I knew. You're not the same."

He came up out of his chair. In the next second, he was screaming at her, his face contorted. "That's not the problem!" he shouted. "The trouble is, you *haven't* changed—*you are the same!*"

The words struck her like a physical blow. Shaken, she backed away, staring at him in disbelief.

For what seemed an eternity, they stood rigid, facing each other as if frozen in time. Then the back door opened and Warren Meister came in, followed by young Tommy. He looked from one to the other.

"What's going on here?" he asked.

"Nothing," his wife said.

Greg Meister looked into his mother's eyes. They were cold and dry; she had no tears left for him. Finally, he had used them all up.

CHAPTER 2

The farm was in what some people liked to call the heartland of America. It sat in a pie-shaped wedge between the Platte River and a dirt road that had once been a part of the Oregon Trail.

The Platte, a long, straight ribbon, flowed eighty miles east to the Mississippi and Omaha. The dirt road led two miles west to a town called Bellville.

Omaha, that winter of 1920, was already a major rail, trade, insurance and food processing center in one of the country's largest livestock markets.

Bellville was a very small town. There was the Bellville Trust & Warranty—otherwise known as the bank—a Sears, a general store, a farm supply, a stable, a gas pump, a law office, a few shops, two hotels with restaurants and two churches, one Methodist, the other Lutheran. There was a schoolhouse on a rise and a cemetery farther off on another. There was also a railroad line and the inevitable row of granaries and a bridge across the Platte.

Three hundred families, hard-working, God-fearing, lived in the town and on the surrounding farms that were among the first claimed under the Homestead Act of 1862. Most of them were of European ancestry, particularly German.

The soil was good, a rich, black vegetable mold over equally rich silt and sandy loams, and it was noted for its fertility in growing corn, wheat and grain sorghums. Corn, the favored crop, yielded an average thirty-four bushels per acre.

There wasn't enough rain, but it fell at the right time—seven-tenths of it in the growing season—and most of it stayed. There was almost no run-off. Even in times of drought, a farmer could subsist. There was a seemingly inexhaustible supply of ground water, and one had to dig only fifteen to twenty feet to reach it.

The summers were hot and dry. The sun seemed to shine perpetually in a cloudless sky. If there was a long period without rain, the wind, when it came from the south, from the Gulf of Mexico, could bring disaster. It would be so hot that in a day or two it would shrivel and ruin the crops in its path. Such calamities were, however, uncommon.

The winters were cold and bleak. The snow drifted high on the unbroken prairie. The prevailing wind came out of the northwest then and it was constant. The average velocity was ten miles an hour.

Nature was not very grand. The only native trees were the elms and cottonwoods along the Platte. Still, the place had a certain glory in the summer, the com high in the fields and the sunflowers, relentless weeds, growing in myriads. They lined the roads in yellow bands from horizon to horizon. They enclosed the broken fields and choked the waste places.

The Platte had a glory of its own. In the spring it was magnificent, the herald of the annual awakening. In the summer, its volume greatly shrunk, it was still the constant of the year's cycle, maintaining a remarkably straight course and even gradient across the length of Nebraska. A broad, shallow, sluggish stream flowed through interlacing channels among sandbars it had earlier heaped athwart its course. The stream might diminish, but it would never die.

Over all was a peace and tranquillity peculiar to the rural America of the Great Plains. Fifty years before, the dirt road had been a kind of highway, clogged with thousands of wagon trains in the mass migration to Oregon, California and Utah. Now there was just the local traffic, sleighs in winter and wagons in summer, and sometimes an uncertain car. Progress, as defined eighty miles away in bustling Omaha, was coming very, very slowly to tiny Bellville.

On the blustery March night that Greg Meister rode into Bellville astride a sullen plow horse named Kaiser—his father's one joke—the town was exactly as he had always remembered it.

It hadn't changed, in any substantial, meaningful way, since he had first laid eyes on it as a child. It looked the same as it had when he went to the university. It looked the same as it had when he joined the army. It looked the same as it had when he was invalided back from the war.

Now, another two years later, it still hadn't changed. Like the farm, like his parents and his brother and sister, Bellville seemed to be frozen in time. It wouldn't, couldn't change. It would always be small, plain, serene Bellville.

Greg Meister once dreamed of it being just this way. In the trenches outside Cantigny, in the hospital at Vendeuil-Caply, at Number One Base Hospital in New York, even in Harlem, celebrating the Armistice, that dream was what had sustained him.

He wanted to be back home then, to be working the fields again with his father and brother, to have his mother's love and his sister's adoration. He wanted to start building for the future. He wanted to court and marry his childhood sweetheart. He wanted to have a family of his own. He wanted his life to center around this small, plain, serene town.

Once he had had a dream. Now he had only nightmares.

Meister couldn't understand what had happened to wreak such a change in his hopes and aspirations. The war, the discovery of the savagery within him, the shrapnel that had ruined his shoulder and denied him the pleasure and possible fortune of professional baseball—none of that was a satisfactory explanation.

It was something else. Somewhere, somehow, something else had touched his life and forever altered his perception of what he wanted.

Six weeks before, after his violent clash with his mother, he had vowed that he would change. But slowly, inexorably, the malaise had taken hold again.

Everything around him seemed rigid, blind, set. Before, he had thought of his father as steady, but now he just saw him as plodding. His mother, whom he once thought happy in her place, he now saw as trapped. Tommy's devotion to the family and the farm annoyed him. Donna's fantasies, once amusing, were now silly.

Even Kathy Jenkins, the girl he had loved, or at least thought he had, seemed impossible. He had regarded her as cultured. Now she was the epitome of small-town life.

Greg Meister's whole world had been turned upside down and he couldn't get it right again. While he knew what he didn't want, he couldn't figure out what he did want, and so all he had was his disillusionment. Somewhere, somehow, something had cut him adrift and failed to throw him a life line. The one thing that kept him precariously afloat was a part of Bellville that had been denied to him before the war. The room upstairs at Sim's Café.

Kaiser—so named, Warren Meister said, because he needed his rump kicked—headed for Sim's with no need of guidance from his rider. He knew the route well.

The café was located in a two-story red-brick building on the wrong side of town, a block back of Main Street. It shared its unpaved stretch of road with a pawnshop, a secondhand store, an empty shed that had been condemned as a firetrap, and Ah Sung's Chinese laundry. It did not have a reputation for good food.

The proprietor, Sim Zukowski, a short, dark, fat man who traded happy insults with all who entered, was both cook and dishwasher. His wife, Helena, who looked as if she should have been an empress, was waitress, cashier and janitor. Together they managed to eke out a modest subsistence … until Prohibition.

With the emergence of the Noble Experiment, business at Sim's took a decided turn for the better. After six o'clock, when the sign in the door was turned around to read "Closed," a man could buy a drink at Sim's. In the card room upstairs, he could have a whole bottle if he wanted it.

Unlike the food, the whiskey was good; some even considered it excellent. Daniel Everett, Omaha's newly famous moonshiner, courted as far away as Chicago, always saw to it that an ample supply first went to his good friend Sim Zukowski. Helena Zukowski took to wearing a fox stole.

Greg Meister liked to drink Sim's whiskey. Mostly, though, he liked to play cards. In the two years since his return from the war, he had become one of the regulars in a garish living room with floral wallpaper that had been converted into a gambling den for—in the opinion of some—the low lifes of Bellville.

Actually, the regulars were a mix. There was Art Miller, eighty-six years old and practically a founding father. He was a real estate dealer who still kept active, despite his advanced years, and who considered himself the driving force behind Bellville's growth and development.

"Towns are like wheelbarrows," Art Miller was fond of saying. "You never see one going anywhere unless someone is pushing it." The "someone" meant him, of course, and everyone was too polite—a concession to his age—to point out that the Bellville wheelbarrow hadn't moved in years.

Among the other regulars, Ben Taylor, the bank president, was as substantial a citizen as could be found in the town. So was Mack Watt, who owned the general store.

Henry Untermeyer, on the other hand, hadn't been known to work a full day in his life, and Willie Thiessen, despite early promise, hadn't amounted to a hill of beans either. He was a store clerk, when everybody thought he'd be sitting on the Supreme Court.

They were a mix, their only common denominator a taste for whiskey and cards, and none of them especially good with the latter. The only sharps in their midst were Meister and Jack Delaney.

Black-eyed, black-mustached, Delaney dressed the part for his own and the others' amusement, wearing a sharply tailored frock coat and a vest hand-painted with hunting scenes. A diamond stud, a fake, decorated the front of his ruffled shirt, and he carried a massive gold watch.

Delaney was so lucky that he was carefully watched for the possibility of cheating. Willie Thiessen was once moved to remind him what happened when the steamboat *Constitution* blew up on the Mississippi: "A dozen passengers were scalded to death, including a professional gambler—who was buried separately." Delaney just laughed and pocketed his winnings and went home to his wife and his wood yard.

On the March night that Greg Meister rode into Bellville on Kaiser, none of the other regulars were expecting him. He had not been around for six weeks. His prolonged absence had been accepted with a certain equanimity—in cards, nobody needs a winner—and it was suspected that Warren Meister had at long last laid down the law to his oldest son.

Had they known Greg was coming, there would have been room for him at the regulars' table. Bob Taylor, as peaceful as he was prosperous, would not have invited Edgar Roth, who was Richard Jenkins' new law clerk. And Henry Untermeyer, who had a loose tongue, wouldn't have drunk so much so quickly.

An uneasy silence greeted Greg when he entered the room. It was brief, lasting hardly more than a few seconds, but he was acutely aware of it. So were the men seated at the table. They eyed him warily.

Ben Taylor reddened. "Oh, hello, Greg," he said, putting his cards aside. "We weren't expecting you." He looked at the young man who sat in the chair that Meister normally occupied. "You haven't been around for a while."

"No," Greg said. He took off his cap and stuck it in his jacket pocket, feeling awkward. It was a private game, seven the limit, and kibitzers weren't invited. There wasn't an extra chair.

"You want a drink?" Henry Untermeyer asked. Instead of a glass, he kept a bottle on the table, pulling at it straight.

"No," Meister said again, but then he changed his mind. It would be ridiculous for him to just turn around and stomp out. "I mean yes, why not?" He moved around the table and accepted the bottle from Untermeyer. "Thanks."

They were all watching him. He wiped off the top of the bottle and raised it to his lips. "Cheers."

"Cheers," Untermeyer said. His face was flushed and he seemed somchow expectant.

Meister took a long, deep drink of the whiskey. It burned going down, flooding him with its warmth. The awkward feeling was gone when he handed the bottle back. For the first time he looked at the young man who was sitting in his chair.

"Have you met Edgar Roth?" Ben Taylor asked, picking up his cards, a signal that the game should resume.

Meister shook his head. "No."

Edgar Roth regarded him evenly. "How do you do?"

"I'm all right," said Meister, staring back at him. Had he been asked to render a judgment before the war, before New York, Meister would have dismissed Roth as a city slicker, not up to much. He had that smooth look about him, all brushed and combed and manicured. If not for the thick swirl of cigar smoke, you could probably have smelled his cologne. Still, beneath the veneer there was substance, an aura of breeding and confidence and, possibly, money. Roth's steady blue-eyed gaze suggested that he didn't have to worry about too much.

"Whose bet?" Mack Watt wanted to know.

For answer, Roth threw in a dollar chip. The others followed suit, none dropping out. It was early in the hand. They were playing seven-card stud and had only one card up.

Delaney, the dealer, flicked cards all around, his hands as fast as his steamboat-gambler clothes. “Read ’em and weep, gentlemen. The queen has the bet.” Then, to Meister: “What have you been doing, lad?”

“Nothing,” Meister said.

“Nothing,” Delaney repeated. He dug an elbow into Untermeyer. “Henry, look out, you’ve got competition.”

Willie Thiessen, who had the queen, bet the dollar this time, and again they all stayed. The pace of the game quickened. Meister was forgotten on the sidelines, the turn of the cards more interesting.

He stood watching the young man in his chair. Edgar Roth was about his age, twenty-five, perhaps a bit younger, and physically more formidable than he appeared at first glance. The well-tailored business suit hid a powerful, thickset body. His round head was so oversized, the steady blue eyes so deep-set that it seemed they could only look one way, forward. The wide mouth had a determined cast to it. Cologne or not, Meister decided, Roth was not someone to be challenged needlessly.

As the deal progressed, the cards began to fall in a pattern, the high going to Roth and Untermeyer. By the sixth card the others had dropped out. Roth had two aces showing; Untermeyer had two kings.

The bet remained the same, each put in a dollar chip. Neither raised.

“Down and dirty,” said Delaney.

Meister moved behind Untermeyer, watching as, with drunken deliberation, Henry lifted his last card. It was a king.

Mack Watt was instantly impatient. “Whose bet?”

“Mine,” Edgar Roth said. He pushed five dollars into the pot.

Untermeyer took a long pull at his bottle. "Five, huh?" He showed his hole card to Meister. "Would you believe there's more?"

"Bet," Mack Watt complained.

Untermeyer pushed all of his chips into the center of the table. It amounted to about fifty dollars.

"Hey," Ben Taylor said, casting a paternal look at young Roth, whom he had invited at the request of his good friend Richard Jenkins. Jenkins had asked that the boy be "introduced" to the game. He had not asked that he be fleeced.

"There's no limit," Willie Thiessen said. This was true, but in point of fact the game's largest bet ever—and it had required a loan—had been twenty dollars.

Edgar Roth reached into his suit pocket and removed a smart black billfold. He extracted five crisp ten-dollar bills that appeared to have just been withdrawn from Ben Taylor's Bellville Trust & Warranty. He laid them atop Henry Untermeyer's pile of chips. "I think that should do it," he said quietly.

Henry Untermeyer took another long pull on his bottle. He fingered his hole card, lifting the edge of it, confirming that it was still a king. Then, his hand cupped so that no one else could see them, not even Meister, he checked his first two down cards.

Meister tried to reconstruct the deal. He couldn't remember seeing any other kings out. Was it possible that Untermeyer had four?

"I'd like to borrow some money," Untermeyer announced, as if in confirmation. "Fifty dollars."

The request was met with the same kind of uneasy silence that had greeted Meister's unexpected arrival. It was a lot of money for the times; young Roth was new to the game, Untermeyer was drunk. The other men looked to Ben Taylor.

"I don't think that would be wise," Ben Taylor said.

Untermeyer looked around the table, polling each man separately, accepting their silence as answer. He reached to flip over his cards. "The hell with the lot of you!"

Greg Meister's huge hand was suddenly covering Henry's. "You're covered. Make the bet."

"Fifty dollars?" Edgar Roth asked. His round face showed no emotion.

Meister nodded. He had it in his pocket, exactly fifty dollars. He released Untermeyer's hand, not knowing why he had done it. Henry Untermeyer turned over his cards. He showed four kings. Laughing, he started to reach for the pot, but then Meister's huge hand was on his again, the grip so tight it made him cry out with pain.

"Four aces," Edgar Roth said.

Meister was staring at Roth's cards. He couldn't believe the aces were really there. He hadn't given such a possibility the slightest consideration.

Roth pulled in the pot, his steady blue eyes fixed on Meister. He sat waiting.

"Pay him," Untermeyer told Meister, angrily twisting out of his grip. "He's taken everything else. Why shouldn't he take your money?"

Meister had his hand in his pocket before the words registered. His fist had already closed around the money. "I beg your pardon?" he said dumbly.

Untermeyer was rubbing his throbbing wrist. "You big dumb ox! You don't know he's taken your girl?"

Meister looked at Edgar Roth, seeing him suddenly through a red haze. "Is that right?"

Roth's steady gaze never faltered. "I didn't know you were engaged."

"Damn you!" Meister was across the table, reaching for Roth's throat. Startled, Roth fell backward, dragging Meister with him. The table's felt cloth followed in the tangle of Meister's legs. Cards, chips and money went flying.

The others scrambled for safety as Meister and Roth rolled on the floor, two mad dogs now, viciously pommeling each other.

Meister fought like a man possessed. His right fist pounded relentlessly into Roth's face. He had reduced it to a bloody pulp when Roth finally screamed for mercy.

The cry came just as Meister was about to deliver a last, crushing blow. His huge fist shuddered, a hammer he could barely restrain. Then, realizing the damage he'd already caused, he pushed Roth away and struggled to his feet. He, too, had been savaged. One eye was closed and his lower lip was split. His jacket and shirt were bloody and torn.

He stood uncertainly, looking at the circle of shocked, disbelieving faces. "Sorry," he muttered, and then he was gone.

"God in heaven," Ben Taylor said. He knelt beside Roth.

Art Miller followed Meister to the door and watched his unsteady progress down the stairs. He hadn't seen a fight like that in his whole life. He told himself the town was getting better all the time.

His brother Tommy was awake when Greg Meister got home late that night, smelling of iodine and too much whiskey. The boy stared bug-eyed when Greg entered the circle of light cast by the lamp hanging over the stove.

"Jumping jiggers!" Tommy exclaimed. "What happened to you?"

"Shush, you'll wake your mother," Meister told him. He looked into the pot, confirming it was cocoa. "What are you doing up anyway? You're supposed to be asleep."

"I don't know," Tommy said. "I've just been feeling unsettled. You get that way sometimes, don't you?"

Meister looked at him with his one good eye. Yes, he thought, but not you, you lucky stiff. Normally, Tommy slept like a stone. The boy had the bedroom next to his, the wall the thickness of a board, open at the top for ventilation. Yet when Greg screamed in the night, it was his mother who came, from the other side of the house, not Tommy. "Sometimes."

Tommy looked away. "It doesn't matter."

"What?"

"What happened ... you don't have to tell me." Good, Meister thought. Briefly, he put a hand on the boy's shoulder, the only show of affection he was able to give him now. Before, when Tommy was small, he would tousle his hair, give him wild piggyback rides, swing him screaming through the air. Now there was barely an inch difference in their heights.

"You want some cocoa?"

"No."

"You're going to have a beaut shiner."

"Yes."

Meister went into his bedroom and closed the door. He settled back on the bed, not bothering to remove his boots. He ached so much, he'd never manage it, he thought. It had been a long, cold ride back home aboard Kaiser. If Sim Zukowski hadn't given him the bottle, he might not have made it. He might have pitched off into the snow and frozen to death.

The Zukowskis were his kind of people, he thought. When he came downstairs after the fight, they didn't ask any questions. They seemed to know what had happened and they also seemed to approve. They got him out of there slick and smooth. Iodine for his cuts and a bottle for the road. Damages? They'd worry about that later.

Meister took a careful sip from the bottle and wondered what he owed them. Not too much, probably. One card table and maybe a couple of chairs. What worried him was that he might be asked to pay doctor bills. Edgar Roth was a lawyer—well, a law clerk, anyway—and he might file suit.

If he did and it was successful? Meister didn't want to think about that. He hadn't held a real job in almost two years. For money he had relied on the poker games at Sim's, and if anybody wanted a sure bet, they could give ten to one Meister wouldn't be welcome there anymore. Sim just owned the place; he didn't make the rules. The regulars did that, and the one firm rule was against brawling.

No, he wouldn't be playing there again, Meister told himself. The easy money was over. Farewell, so long and good-bye. Which left him with—what?

Meister took another careful sip of whiskey and added up his worldly wealth: the fifty dollars in his pocket, another fifty or so in the trunk at the foot of his bed, two hundred in a savings account at the Bellville Trust & Warranty. Altogether, three hundred dollars, give or take a couple. Not much of a stake.

There was a soft knock on the door. Tommy entered, bearing two steaming cups of cocoa. "I thought you might change your mind," he said in explanation.

Meister almost sent him away. But his brother's look, hopeful and yet wary, made that suddenly impossible.

"Sure," he said. "It's just what I need." He put his bottle of whiskey on the floor and made room for the cup of cocoa on the night table. He shifted his feet so that Tommy could sit at the foot of the bed. "Why don't you stay awhile? It's a long time since we had a talk."

Tommy hesitated. Although he had wanted such an invitation, he wasn't certain he should accept it. He looked at the whiskey bottle, checking the contents' level.

"Don't worry. It's medicinal only," Greg told him. "I'm not planning on a party."

Tommy sat down on the bed. He took a sip of his cocoa, eyes watchful over the rim of the cup. "I'm not worried."

Liar, Meister thought. Of all the members of his family, it was Tommy he had hurt the most because he was the most vulnerable. Tommy used to idolize him—Greg was his big brother and the best baseball player in the county and maybe the whole state. He mussed his hair and he gave him piggyback rides.

"You okay?"

"Sure," Meister said, now lying himself. His kid brother used to look at him with pride shining in his eyes. Now there was always that wary look and, worse, sometimes fear.

Meister hated himself when he saw that. It was his fault. He had imposed his disillusionment on his brother. He had purposely shattered the boy's dream world, alarming him with high tales of war, women and drunkenness.

Tommy didn't want the disillusionment. Yet, the less the boy wanted of it, the more Meister tried to impose it on him—on all of his family, for that matter. It was a disease he carried and that he had to spread.

Idol? Not anymore. In the boy's eyes he had become a badgering, sometimes drunk critter, spreading unhappiness. He had become something to be wary of, to fear.

"How did you get it?" asked Tommy.

Meister felt his face. "The eye?"

"Yes."

"A fight."

"Who with?"

"Nobody special," Meister said. "Just—just a loudmouth, that's all."

"Oh," Tommy said. He took another sip of cocoa. "You never used to fight."

Meister looked at him. That had sounded like an accusation, and besides, it wasn't true. He tried to smile, his cracked lip burning. "You mean you don't remember me and Jim Deeley?"

Tommy nodded. "Sure, but that was kid stuff."

"Really?" Meister remembered it differently. He had had Jim Deeley down in the schoolyard, locked in a full nelson, and he wouldn't let him up until he promised to shake hands. The reason he'd done that was because he feared Jim Deeley might kill him otherwise when he got loose. There were a number of others in the schoolyard who apparently shared that idea. It was supper time, yet no one had gone home. "I don't even think you were there then, too young."

"I wasn't, but I remember what you were fighting about. Glue."

Meister laughed. Actually, it was paste. They were going to build a kite and they had mixed a flour paste. Jim Deeley, showing off, ate it. All of it. The whole bowl. "Then what about Jack Giesbrecht?"

"The same thing, kid stuff."

"Clancy Loringer?"

"The same thing."

"That Italian kid—what was his name? Romeo Jacobucci?"

"The same thing."

"Kid stuff?"

"Yes!" Tommy said defiantly.

Meister looked at his brother. For some reason the boy was suddenly angry, tears shimmering in his eyes. "Hey," Greg said, baffled. "What's got into you?"

Tommy was off the bed. "You used to let them up."

"Let them up?"

"Yes, you'd get them down and you'd hold them there until they agreed to shake hands and then you'd let them up. You wouldn't hurt them."

Meister was lost for an answer. It was true. He'd had his share of fights, but they didn't amount to much and they never lasted long. He would just lock his opponents in a full nelson and wait until they'd rather be friends. "How do you know I didn't let—?" He stopped, not wanting to say the name, thinking that Tommy might have heard something at school about Kathy Jenkins and Edgar Roth. It was, after all, a small town.

"The loudmouth?"

"Yes, the loudmouth. How do you know I didn't let him up?"

"Did you?" Tommy asked.

"No," Meister admitted, and he wondered why he had asked the question. He never let anyone up anymore. He ground them all down—Tommy, his parents, Kathy... even himself. "No, I didn't, Tommy."

"I didn't think so," Tommy said. He finished the last of his cocoa, the wariness gone now as he looked over the rim of the cup. "Well, I ought to be getting to bed."

Meister searched his brother's eyes. There was nothing, just an empty stare. He's stopped caring, Meister thought. His disillusionment is complete.

"Good night."

"Good night," Meister said. He turned away, reaching for the lamp, quickly blowing it out. In his own eyes, he could feel tears starting, a flood that he seemed to have been holding back forever.

Tommy's voice came out of the darkness. "Are you going to see Kathy anymore?"

Kathy? Meister could barely speak. The tears were burning his face now. "Why do you ask?"

"I was just wondering."

"So am I," Greg Meister said. "So am I."

CHAPTER 3

Kathy Jenkins, her mother often said, was as pretty as the corn was high, and no one was inclined to argue. Her father called her an angel. There was some doubt about that.

The girl—actually, a young woman now—did project a childish innocence that made one think of an angel. She had an angel's face, shining and cherubic, framed by honey-blonde hair so fine it looked celestial.

Inside that pretty head, however, were thoughts no angel would dare harbor. Kathy Jenkins dreamed of becoming a movie star. When she closed her clear blue eyes she saw herself in Hollywood.

Also—and again this was something denied proper angels—Kathy Jenkins dreamed of having a husband, specifically Greg Meister. She could close her eyes and see herself in his strong arms. She could imagine him making love to her.

That she could spin both dreams at the same time was a mark of her sweet and innocent confidence. It really never occurred to her that one dream might conflict with the other.

Her father teased her about this and about her shoulder blades sticking out. Wings, he called them, and sometimes he imagined, just as she herself did, that one bright and shining morning she was sure to fly away on them to the glories she so richly deserved. If—and this was a big if—she could get settled once and for all about Greg Meister.

Richard Jenkins prided himself on being a patient man. Being a lawyer, he also liked to see things resolved, and his experience had taught him that compromise was an essential part of that.

For two years he had sat patiently by and watched his beautiful daughter pine away over Greg Meister. Of late it had become apparent, to him anyway, that the childhood sweethearts were not going to get married after all. Greg's calls at the house had become less and less frequent. Kathy would go for days without mentioning him.

To settle the matter, to get it resolved, Richard Jenkins had introduced Kathy to his new law clerk, Edgar Roth. He had invited the young man home to dinner several times. He had suggested that they might like to go to the high-school concert together. He had provided the tickets.

Kathy had not objected. Like her father, her own patience was wearing thin and she saw no harm in attending a school concert with Edgar Roth. He was personable and pleasant. He worked for her father and he was new in town and ought to get acquainted. If she could help, why not?

If something more ever came of the innocent relationship, it would only be because Greg Meister, the fool, didn't sit up and take notice.

That, at any rate, had been the scenario, a screenplay worthy of her first starring role in Hollywood. She had been devastated when nothing went according to script.

The concert was followed by a movie and later by a dance. Edgar Roth proved to be not quite as pleasant as she first thought. And Greg Meister, the fool, instead of taking notice, had remained totally ignorant of everything, disappearing from sight for weeks.

Kathy Jenkins buried her face in her tear-stained pillow. The whole thing was like a bad dream, she thought, sobbing. *Nothing* had gone as planned. Without even bothering to talk to her, Greg Meister had flown into an awful, frightening rage. Edgar Roth had been savagely beaten. Sim's card room was a shambles and so was her world.

All of Bellville, she was sure, was talking about it. Her shame was such that she could not leave the house. The way she felt, she'd never be able to leave it. She'd never be able to fly away on her angel wings.

And it was all Greg Meister's fault. She would never speak to him again.

Never.

He could come crawling on his hands and knees, pleading for forgiveness, begging that she marry him. None of that would make the slightest difference. She would never speak to him again.

Her mother knocked on the bedroom door.

"Go away," Kathy sobbed.

"Kate, listen to me," Margaret Jenkins said. "There is a young man here, and I really do think you should see him."

Kathy buried her face deeper into her pillow. If it was Edgar Roth, she couldn't bear to look at him. Her father said he had been brutally beaten, and she knew, deep in her heart, that she was partly to blame. "No!"

"Kate," her mother said softly. "It's Greg."

Greg? Kathy sat up. Greg Meister in this house? Her first reaction was that he had his nerve! Her second thought was how she looked. She'd been crying all day. "No," she repeated, the tears coming again. How could her mother be so stupid? "I can't let him see me this way!"

"Young lady," her mother persisted. "Let me assure you, whatever you've managed to do to yourself in there, he looks a lot worse than you do.'"

Kathy's heart seemed to skip a beat. Her father had made no mention of Greg being hurt. The way he had told it, quoting Ben Taylor, it was only Edgar—taken by surprise and given no chance. Not that she cared one way or the other. "I told you, I don't want to see him!"

"Well, he's seeing you, like it or not, young lady. I want you in the parlor in five minutes. Otherwise he has my permission to break down this door."

"What?"

"You heard me."

Margaret Jenkins, who prided herself on being a no-nonsense woman, turned abruptly and went back downstairs. Greg Meister, standing in the hall with cap in hand, had heard every word.

"I," she informed him, getting her own hat and coat, "am going out. I'm sure you young people have lots to talk about. You'll be more comfortable if you can do it in private." She looked at her watch. "Mr. Jenkins comes home at six o'clock sharp. A word to the wise."

"Thank you," Meister mumbled. His lower lip was still sore and it was painful for him to speak.

"And another thing, you really ought to get something for that eye."

"Thank you."

"God, what a mess."

With that, Margaret Jenkins was gone, purse clutched firmly under her arm, intent on buying something she didn't need. It was her way of coping when she got mad at her husband.

Greg Meister went into the parlor and sat down to wait. It was a large, comfortable, oak-paneled room with beamed ceilings and a red-brick fireplace, the walls lined with photographs and paintings of three generations of the Jenkins family.

As a boy he had often sat waiting on the same overstuffed leather couch, marveling at the almost overwhelming display of linear pride. In his own family, his mother kept a picture of her mother—a faded tintype in a small locket—and everybody else was represented only by scrawled signatures in the family Bible. The photos on his father's side had been lost, so his mother said, in the move West. Greg suspected that they might have been purposely set aside and that it had something to do with religion and church. But he had no proof and it had soon ceased to matter.

The Jenkins' genealogy had always seemed capable of holding up both ends in a union with Kathy. The men, according to the photos and paintings, had all been handsome, well-bred and prosperous. Their women had been stunningly beautiful.

Meister, studying them now with his good eye, decided that he hadn't been wrong there. They were just as impressive as ever. His mistake—and he still wasn't sure it *was* a mistake—had been in his evaluation of Kathy.

All through school he had kept Kathy Jenkins on a pedestal, the only girl in the world for him. She had remained there during his two years at the university and the eighteen months he had spent overseas. Not once had he ever faltered in the sureness of his love and devotion. She was Kathy, beautiful, glorious, marvelous Kathy, and he had wanted nothing more than to come home and claim her as his bride.

It was true that he had known other women. In Paris, before they sent him to the front, he had slept with a barmaid, and in New York, while recuperating at Number One Base Hospital, there had been frequent forays with John Crain after ladies of easy virtue.

In New York he had also felt the pangs of an unrequited, impossible love. Meeting John Crain's sister Tandy, a child goddess, the heart had fallen out of him. He had been hopelessly, irreversibly stricken.

But he had realized from the start that it was impossible and as soon as he was released from the hospital, caught the first train home. Though she looked like a woman, Tandy was a child, only sixteen. Besides, she was a millionaire's daughter. That made her a world—and a breed—apart.

He had known that and he had put the foolish infatuation aside and come home determined to marry Kathy. Nothing had really changed . . . or had it?

Greg Meister shook his head helplessly. Despite his good intentions, something had gone terribly, terribly wrong. Their reunion—a day he had wanted to cherish as the happiest in his life—had somehow degenerated into a fumbling disaster.

That had also occurred in this room. Margaret and Richard Jenkins had gone out for the evening. Their first time together in two years, a young man and his girl probably could use a little privacy, Margaret Jenkins had said. She'd also announced the probable time of their return.

At first everything was as before. She was his Kathy, his beautiful, glorious, marvelous Kate. Her lips were as sweet as ever and her soft body pressed against him passionately, promising all he had dreamed of in the horror of the trenches.

Gently he had opened her dress, cupping her breasts in his hands, putting his lips to the soft full wonder of them . . . . Suddenly, she had stiffened.

"Greg—*don't!*" she had cried, pushing his hands away. He had stared at her, surprised to find her crying, wondering if he had somehow hurt her.

"What's wrong?" he had asked. She had told him, weeping, "I don't want to go too far."

Too far? God, Greg Meister thought, staring now at his big hands. Did she really think he could come back from the war and not expect to hold her? Did she honestly believe that he would not want and need to have her?

He had come home and he had *needed* her, and she had pushed him away.

The denial had left him feeling lost and empty. Why had he come home to this? During his time away, he had become a man and he had expected to find in Kathy a woman, not a silly, naive girl. He could respect innocence, but not nonsense.

It was never the same between them after that. Without fulfillment he came to question his love for her. Hurt, confused, she became more guarded. They had grown further and further apart.

And now this. He wouldn't claim her for his wife, yet he had practically killed a man for trying to court her.

Greg Meister clenched his hands. Damn! All his life she had been his girl. He should sweep her up, carry her away. He knew she would marry him if he asked. A hundred times he had almost done so, but then she would spoil the moment, making some silly statement in her honey-cake drawl. And he would ask himself the same question: Why had he come home to this?

Why this? He knew the answer. He came home because he was *supposed* to come home. It was his obligation and his duty.

But that didn't mean he had to stay.

Upstairs, Kathy examined herself in her mirror, despairing of ever looking presentable. She had washed her face and combed her hair and put on her favorite dress, and still she was a positive disaster, she thought.

Her eyes were bloodshot and her nose was as bright and shiny as a Christmas tree bauble.

In desperation she applied a touch of rouge to her cheeks, thinking that it might help if she was all the same color. Rouge was forbidden by her father. Only hussies used it, he said. But now it was coming out of hiding to stay. She wasn't going to worry about what her father thought anymore. He'd interfered too much already. Look at all the trouble he'd caused!

From now on, she vowed, she was going to be her own woman. If it took wearing rouge to get Greg Meister, she was going to do it. Whatever it took, she was going to do it.

"Yes, that's correct, young lady," she told herself, mimicking her no-nonsense mother. "Whatever it takes."

It was the first time she had given voice to the thought and it made her feel better. She managed a smile and pulled herself erect, her breasts swelling the front of her dress. She decided that she might pass muster, after all.

Kathy licked her lips to make them glisten. "Go get your man," she told herself.

This change in her had not come abruptly. It had been a gradual process over the long winter. In her heart she knew she was losing Greg Meister and she knew why. Part of it was the rigid moral code that had been drilled into her since puberty. "Nice girls keep their pants on," was the way her mother had put it the first time, making her turn red as a beet. "You'll get in trouble if you don't."

The warning had hardly been necessary. In the hopeless puppy love that she and Greg shared, they held hands, and that was all. The stolen kisses didn't come until the last year in high school. They both wanted it that way. When he married her, she was to be as pure as the day he first laid eyes on her. When he took her as his wife, it was to be with the permission and approval of God.

Later, though, when Greg went to the university, his attitude changed. He would come home on vacation frustrated and unhappy. It was going to take him four years to get his degree and find a job. That was a long time to wait, he would tell her pointedly, the stolen kisses more passionate.

Her only defense then was her innocence. She'd act the child, saying something foolish, her affected drawl more pronounced. She'd pretend she was a movie star—Miss Proper Goodie guarding her virtue until the proper time—and she would pretend to be shocked by his impatience. "Why, Greg Meister! I do declare! The things you say sometimes! What's a poor girl to think?"

It worked—at least for a while. He would sigh and look hurt and become sullen, but he never made a real issue of it. Quickly enough he'd be his old self again, happy in her company. He'd tease her out of baby talk—it was he who had nicknamed her Proper Goodie—and they would find their pleasures in other things. There were long walks on summer evenings, sleigh rides in the winter snow. Through all the seasons they found time to be together, and they found the strength to wait.

The only really bad time was when he received his orders to go overseas. Then, when there was the chance that he'd be killed, the chance that she would never see him again, she almost succumbed. Almost, but she didn't. "If we've waited this long," she'd said, taking his hands. "You understand? I want to wait and I *will* be waiting, Greg. I'm your girl and I love you and I will wait for you."

No honey-dripping drawl, just the plain truth. He had accepted it. He had held her tightly and kissed her deeply and gone bravely off to war. In a way, she was what he was fighting for. The fact that she was waiting was what gave him strength.

And then?

Kathy hesitated at the top of the stairs, remembering the mistake she had made, vowing not to make it again. When Greg came home he was almost like a stranger. He had changed so much. She had needed time and he didn't seem to understand that. She wanted time to get to know him again, to make certain that he was her Greg, the boy she loved.

That's all she had wanted, just a bit of time, and she was sure that he would have given it to her if only she'd had the good sense to ask. Instead, like a child, she'd retreated to the sanctuary of Miss Proper Goodie, pretending shock and foolish innocence.

No wonder he'd been hurt and angry. If you loved someone, promises must be kept. She had said that she'd be waiting when he returned and they had both known, in the passion of their parting embrace, exactly what she had meant. She would be waiting—and he wouldn't have to wait any longer.

Remembering, Kathy blinked back more tears, unable to believe that she had acted in such a manner. What was the poor man to think? Weeping, she had pushed him away, as if she didn't want him. Yes, she could have told him. Yes, with all my heart. Just give me time, my darling. Just give me a bit more time....

Time? She sniffed and laughed bitterly. There wasn't any left. Time had run out, two years of it wasted. And she was to blame, playing the innocent schoolgirl who no longer existed. She was a woman now, a grown, passionate, head-over-heels-in-love woman.

Greg Meister, the man she loved, the man she had always loved, was waiting downstairs to take her into his arms. Greg still loved her—he had almost killed another man to prove it—and now he had come to claim her.

She knew exactly what he was going to say. "Kate, I love you," he was going to tell her. "I want you and I need you." And she knew exactly what *she* was going to say. Whatever he asked, her answer would be, "Yes."

She started down the stairs to get her man.

Greg Meister felt a lump come to his throat when Kathy entered the room. He had never seen her look more beautiful. The fact that she had been crying made no impression on him. She was radiant, glowing with a strength and purpose and expectation totally new to her. This was all that he saw.

He got to his feet uncertainly. "Hello," he said, baffled by the transformation. The last time he had seen her, he had despaired of her ever growing up. Now, by a process unknown to him, maturity had been accomplished. Some magic had touched her and made her a woman.

"Hello, Greg," Kathy greeted. She was shocked at the sight of him, the closed eye a purple welt, the lower lip split. Her first impulse was to run to him, to cradle his poor head, but she held herself back. She would wait. "Please... sit down."

"Uh, no thank you," he said, staring at her. He wondered what had finally brought out the woman in her, if it had been

Edgar Roth. That thought made him see blood again. He told himself he'd better get it done, get out of there. "I just came to apologize."

Kathy sat in a chair opposite the couch. "About Edgar? I know, my father told me. He said there had been—" She looked up at him, trying her best to smile, to set him at ease. "I'd rather that you told me what happened."

"No, not about him," Meister said. "I came to apologize to you. I'm sorry I've acted so badly and I'm sorry I've hurt you. I don't know what's wrong." He paused, shaking his head. "The whole time I've been back, I've been a sorehead, that's all. It's my fault. Things aren't the same—not the way I remembered them—and I just can't adjust to it."

"If it's about Edgar—" Kathy started to say again. As always, she had rehearsed her lines and it was terribly important that she get to say what she wanted to at exactly the right time. She didn't want to make any mistakes.

"Him?" Meister felt his puffed eye, wishing now that he'd landed that last blow. "I told you, he doesn't matter. Whether you've been seeing him or not, it's not important. I don't want to know. Either way..." Again he shook his head. "What I'm trying to say is that I'm leaving and it's not your fault. And it's not because of Edgar Roth. I'm leaving because I'm not happy here."

"Leaving?" The word flew from her lips like a cry of pain.

"Yes. I'm sorry, but that's how it is. I'm not happy and I doubt I ever will be. There's no sense staying any longer."

She stared at him in shock and disbelief. "Leaving? I don't understand. For how long? Where will you go? What will you do?"

"To New York. I've got a friend there. John Crain. The guy I told you about? He should be able to get a job for me."

New York? Kathy couldn't believe what she was hearing. If they went anywhere it would be Hollywood. If they went anywhere, it would be together. No, no, she thought. He wasn't saying this. It couldn't be true. Her eyes filled with tears. "But what about me?"

Meister shrugged helplessly. "I said I'm sorry."

"Sorry?" She stared at him. He meant it, she realized. He really meant it. He was going to leave.

Meister shrugged again. He didn't know what else to say.

"Greg, for God's sake," she sobbed. She tried to get up, to go to him, but there was no strength in her. She fell back, drained, helpless. "You said you loved me. We were going to get married. That was understood."

Meister looked into her tear-filled eyes. Briefly, when she had entered the room, he had caught a glimpse of a woman there, the woman he wanted, the woman for the man he had become. Now that woman was gone.

"I'm sorry," he said again. "I really am sorry."

On the way out he paused in the hall to drop an envelope on a mahogany side table. It was addressed to Edgar Roth, Esq., and it contained fifty dollars.

A gentleman never welshed on a bet. Greg Meister pulled the door shut behind him, closing off his old life, beginning a new one.

NEW YORK

CHAPTER 4

F. Scott Fitzgerald, raising a glass of bathtub gin in its honor, christened it the Jazz Age. The name stuck, but so did a lot of others. It also would become known as the Roaring Twenties, the Golden Age, the New Era, the Get-Rich-Quick Era, the Era of Wonderful Nonsense and the Lawless Decade.

The last, if not the most popular, was perhaps the most appropriate. Many laws were to crumble during the vibrant and tumultuous years from the Armistice to Repeal. Criminal laws, moral laws, civil laws, social laws, political laws, religious laws—all manner of laws would be tested and flouted and many would be forever put aside.

At war's end a freedom won had become a freedom to do as one pleased, be it personally or nationally, and the throwing off of old shackles had brought a maelstrom of change.

With the Armistice, Woodrow Wilson may have promised that America—by sober, friendly counsel, by material aid—would assist in the establishment of just democracy throughout the world. He may have won over the League of Nations at Versailles, but his own nation wanted none of that. It was isolationist now, tired of Europe and its bickerings and bloodletting, distrustful of entangling alliances. Wilson had been defeated in the election and there was an America-first president now, Warren Gamaliel Harding.

The war was over, and the wartime honeymoon between labor and capital was over, too. The dollar was suddenly worth half of what it had been in the prewar economy. Everything cost more, especially the basics: food, clothing, shelter. Housing was short, rents sky-high. Millions of men had hit the streets to support their demands for higher pay to meet ever-increasing inflation. There had been thousands of strikes across the Nation, hitting steel, the railroads, the building industry, the meatpackers, the garment trade, even the Boston Police Department. Only federal intervention had finally broken labor's back. Woodrow Wilson's Attorney General Alexander Mitchell Palmer, the "Fighting Quaker," doomed a national coal strike by improper application of the wartime food-and-fuel control act, then whipped up anti-union sentiment with the Red specter.

The Kaiser defeated, there had been a new menace, the Bolsheviks. The anti-Red hysteria, fueled by a handful of fanatics and bomb throwers, had been boundless. Civil liberties had been trampled into dust in the mass roundup of suspected subversives staged by Palmer. Political prisoners had been thrown behind bars by the thousands. Now, come December, the army transport *Buford*—"the Soviet Ark"—was to sail out of New York with some two hundred fifty hastily deported Russians.

The prim morality of the pre-1914 world had been discarded. The process of emancipation for women was a revolution in progress. Not only did they have the vote, but they had the will to be equal, to dress and to do as they pleased. The flapper was on the scene, raring to go, ready for anything. Wealthy young women were bobbing their hair, wearing short skirts, using lipstick, smoking cigarettes and—Prohibition be damned!—drinking cocktails.

The automobile was changing the pattern of both courtship and morals, providing unchaperoned mobility, and everybody wanted a car now, even the poor. It was the new priority. You couldn't go to town in a bathtub.

Sometimes it seemed everything was new. Radio invented one day, psychiatry the next. The theory of relativity rapidly followed by mahjong. Sometimes it seemed like a new dawning in the arts—the stage at its most compelling, the movies getting better every day, a wave of important literature flooding the bookstores. Who could ever exceed Barrymore, Chaplin and Mary Pickford, or Fitzgerald, Eugene O'Neill, Sinclair Lewis, Sherwood Anderson and H.L. Mencken?

The Nation churned. If there were doubts and fears, there was also hope. The economy was starting to turn around, jobs were becoming more plentiful and there were many roads to sudden riches, especially along the pavements of Wall Street.

If there were mistakes and excesses, there was remorse. There was a clamor for the release of political prisoners, the Wobblies, and the pardon of jailed socialist leader Eugene Debs.

If there were the poor, there was also John D. Rockefeller, who had by now given $75,000,000 to charity. The Ku Klux Klan was at work in the South and there were race riots in Chicago and Washington, but everybody loved Louis Armstrong. If there were villains, there were also heroes. Babe Ruth was going to be the new home run king.

Of all the tumult, of all the change, the easiest to get caught up in was the lawlessness, in the street or at the highest levels of government. Prohibition, which was supposed to bring peace, happiness, prosperity and salvation, was instead spawning a powerful crime empire. Warren Gamaliel Harding, who had promised to put America first, was putting himself and his friends first, heading the most corrupt administration to ever hold sway in Washington.

The Jazz Age? Yes. But the Lawless Decade, too. Some would carefully plan to be a part of it. Others, whatever their intentions, would be simply swept up by it.

Greg Meister was only dimly aware of all this. He knew little of the changes that were taking place and had given scant thought to the probable upheaval that lay ahead. In his disillusionment he had virtually isolated himself from the rest of the world, not wishing to know about the things he could not be a part of.

It had been easy to turn inward in Bellville. The farm had no telephone, let alone that newest fad, radio. The weekly newspaper, which came by mail, dealt mostly with agriculture. Days, even weeks might pass before the family heard news of importance. When they did hear, that was soon enough, for it never had any direct bearing on their lives.

Denied involvement, Meister had taken refuge in his books, preferring history to current events. On his infrequent visits to town, he would barely glance through the daily newspaper, if at all. He heard enough—more than enough, he thought—through barbershop gossip and the running commentary that came with the poker game at Sim's.

So it was that Greg Meister arrived in New York an innocent, ready for anything and prepared for nothing. He knew he had two hundred dollars in his wallet, knew he had to get a job very quickly. And he knew more about ancient Rome than he did about the era of Warren Gamaliel Harding.

Standing in the middle of Grand Central Station, far from home and alone in a sea of humanity, he had a feeling of déjà vu. He had been in the same sort of situation before, arriving on the Western Front. Here he was, and he didn't fit.

For an instant he considered turning back. Thousands of people were swarming through the concourse, all seemingly with a destination in mind. They had a clear purpose, a goal. He just had a stupid dream, that somehow things would be better here.

And if not—?

Meister hesitated, feeling very much like he'd felt waiting for the order to attack Cantigny. He didn't want to venture into the unknown alone. Again he thought of going back, and then he felt a hand on his shoulder, turned and saw John Crain.

"Greg Meister!" Crain was smiling broadly. "Welcome to New York, you ninny."

Meister stood staring at him. He couldn't believe they were beginning again this way, Crain materializing at the moment of truth, bringing reassurance. If he had a flair for the dramatic, Greg thought wryly, he'd offer him a cigarette.

"Well?" Crain demanded. "Are you going to just stand there, or are you going to shake hands?" He had removed his glove and was waiting. "You haven't changed a bit, you know that? Still as slow as ever!"

"What are you doing here?" Meister managed to ask. He put down his suitcase and gripped the extended hand, harder than intended, making Crain wince.

"And still as strong," Crain complained, laughing. "I got your letter, what do you think I'm doing here? You said you'd be arriving today, but you didn't say what train. I've been here since morning!"

Meister reddened. "I didn't expect you to meet me."

"Obviously," Crain said good-naturedly. "Otherwise you'd have told me what train and what time. I must have searched ten thousand faces, do you realize that? What's worse, I've approached several dozen strange men!"

"When I wrote, I didn't know what train . . . ." Meister said, glancing around uncomfortably. He wasn't used to so many people at such close quarters, and he imagined them all listening and laughing at the farm boy.

"Then why didn't you phone?" Crain demanded, amused by Meister's discomfort. "Or haven't they got phones in Nebraska?"

Meister didn't know what to say. He hadn't telephoned for the same reason that he had written so late, just a couple of days before his planned arrival, giving no opportunity for a reply before he left. He didn't want to give Crain time to say, "No, don't come." For the same reason he didn't identify what train he'd be on and what time. If John Crain didn't want to resume the friendship after two years, he'd have an out. They'd both have one.

"I planned to phone you when I got here," Meister said, which was the truth. "I didn't want to bother you until I got settled. Then, if you had any ideas about a job, you might be able to help me." He bent to retrieve his suitcases. "That's why I wrote, so you'd have a chance to think about it, all right?"

"God," Crain said, "what a convoluted mind." He pulled one of the suitcases away from Meister. "You haven't changed one iota. You think so much, you arrive at sixteen different conclusions, none of them right. Also, you worry too much. Another thing, you don't know who your friends are."

Meister started to protest. He wasn't quite sure that he agreed with all that.

"I've already got you a job, or the promise of one, or at least the promise of a recommendation," Crain said. "You have an 'audience' with my father tomorrow, and don't think it didn't pain me to arrange it, chum. So, show your appreciation."

"Well—uh—thanks," Meister stammered. The last thing he had expected was help from Nelson Crain. He had met John's father only once and, as he recalled it, hadn't exactly made a favorable impression. Besides, John and Nelson Crain were at odds. "You're sure that's okay?"

"Of course it's okay. Come on," Crain said, starting off, carrying the suitcase.

"Where are we going?"

"To catch the shuttle," Crain shouted over his shoulder. "We're going to Times Square. We'll eat and then I'm going to take you on the town. If you show enough respect and appreciation, I might even get you a woman."

Meister felt himself blushing again. He wasn't imagining it now. People *were* listening and laughing.

"Come on!" Crain shouted. "You're in the big city now."

Meister hefted his suitcase and hurried after him. He still wasn't sure of much, but one thing was settled: He did have a friend.

Two hours later they sat across from each other at a littered table in a small lunchroom off Broadway. They had eaten, they had toasted each other's health—in tea, the strongest thing available there—and they had brought each other up to date, in colorful if spare detail, on what they had and had not been doing with their lives since being mustered out of the army.

Meister, his initial uncertainty overcome, had poured out everything. His disillusionment with life on the farm, the gulf between himself and his family, his inability to pick up where he had left off with Kathy Jenkins, the terrible nightmares that haunted him with the reminder of how good he had been as a killer.

John Crain had a similar story. He had been unable to reconcile his differences with his millionaire father. Left to his own devices, he had taken the only job that interested him and paid enough, smuggling whiskey out of Canada. That had turned into a disaster when police stopped him on a return run, wounding his driver as they fled in a hail of bullets. Lying low, he took the job of peacekeeper and general factotum at his boss's private club, Farley's. When they ordered him to make the run to Canada again, he quit, went to work at the New York Stock Exchange. He had met a girl, he told Meister, Nadine Berns—the sister of his wounded driver, Sid Berns—and fallen madly in love. That had turned out to be still another disaster. Now he was out of work and at loose ends and damn glad to see an old friend—even a ninny from Nebraska.

Meister had the feeling that Crain hadn't told all and didn't want to. He had said very little about Nadine Berns, had been vague about his problems at Farley's, and had been strangely silent when their mutual souvenir, the Luger, was mentioned.

Still, Meister thought, not everyone enjoyed mourning a lost love, and smuggling whiskey wasn't something everybody would talk about either. The Luger? Well, after his own long account of his nightmares and the guilt he suffered, it was only natural to avoid the subject of guns and killing.

But except for his reluctance to share every secret, John Crain was the man Meister remembered, the same hell-raising, happy-go-lucky character, determined to have all the fun and good times he could get and damn the expense. He was still set on somehow making a fortune of his own—and still living on his father's dole.

"What are you grinning about?" Crain wanted to know.

"Oh, I don't know," said Meister. "How much alike we are, I guess."

Crain's benevolent expression changed immediately. "Us? How the hell do you figure that?"

Meister laughed. In truth it would have been hard to find two men more varied in appearance, background, position and outlook. Crain—stocky, muscular, handsome—was every inch the urbane, city-bred gentleman. He wore his well-tailored suit as if he'd been born with it and his prep school tie like a banner. Poise and assurance radiated from his blue-green eyes. He was a comer and he was going places—if he ever settled down.

As for himself? A mess, Meister thought. Try as he might, he couldn't get the hang of looking sophisticated, not even acceptable. He was gangling, awkward, too tall and too thin. His clothes hung on him as if they'd been draped on a scarecrow. Even when new they somehow became instantly out of fashion.

Though he wasn't ugly, no one had ever called him handsome. His expression wouldn't permit that. He appeared, by his own appraisal, to be perpetually bewildered. Doubt, not self-assurance, showed in the eyes behind the steel-rimmed glasses.

Crain was still waiting for an explanation. "Well?"

"I mean, we're both drifting," Meister tried to explain, gesturing with his huge hands, another difference that marked them. For a man, Crain had small hands, scrubbed and manicured, suited for counting money. "We're both kind of lost and we're both searching for—I don't know—for something."

"For the same street paved with gold?" Crain suggested. looking relieved.

"Yes." Meister agreed, "but not both up from the same gutter."

They stared at each other for a moment. There, I've said it, Meister thought. He imagined that Crain, by his look of relief, was glad to have it settled.

"Let's get out of here," Crain said. The moment over, he was his old boisterous self. "If it's a search we're embarking on, I intend for us to be properly provisioned—meaning you." He called for the check and reached for his wallet. "How much money have you got?"

"I'll get it," Meister offered, reaching for the check. Crain shook his head. "I mean, altogether. You said you had a stake. How much?"

"Two hundred dollars."

Crain raised his eyebrows. "That's a *stake*?" He made it sound like lunch money. "Lord save us, you do need a job, don't you? Otherwise you're going to starve to death."

"I had three hundred," Meister said defensively, "but I owed that fifty I lost at poker—"

"To Roth, the guy you beat up?"

"Yes, and then there was the train fare and I had to buy this suit."

Crain was laughing now. "You *had* to buy that suit?"

"Yes, in Omaha," Meister replied, failing to get the joke.

"It shows."

"What?"

"Nothing," Crain said, amused. He got his wallet open and his money out, shoving a fistful of bills at the hovering waitress. "You see this man?" he told her. "If he ever comes in again, don't serve him a drink, understand? He's a minor, and I'm his guardian."

For the rest of that day Meister felt just like that, a minor in the care of John Crain. Any idea of "seeing the town" was forgotten. Instead, Crain took him on a shopping spree—that was the only term for it, Meister thought—for what amounted to almost a whole new wardrobe.

The serviceable wool suit purchased in Omaha would not do in New York, or at least not in the better circles, Crain insisted. In New York a man's suit had to have a certain style and flair—much like his own, as it turned out—and it was a shame there wasn't time to have it tailored.

Other items were equally at fault. Meister's shirt had the wrong collar and the sleeves weren't long enough. The tie was too colorful. Hand-painted with the assault on Cantigny? Crain wondered. The shoes looked too much like boots: "What are they, the boxes they came in?" Crain inquired.

A hat, a wide-brimmed fedora, replaced Meister's felt cap, and his woolen mittens, though he had really had no intention of wearing them, were thrown away and leather gloves substituted. The plain cotton handkerchief in his suit pocket was replaced by one bearing a monogrammed "M." His thick farm socks were retired in favor of thin socks with clocks on the side which required garters to hold them up.

By the time he was done over, Meister wasn't sure if any improvement had actually been accomplished. Yes, he looked more stylish, but he also looked even more uncomfortable.

"You'll get used to it," Crain assured him, as if reading his mind. "After all, it's quite a jump—"

Meister looked at John Crain's smiling face in the wardrobe mirror at Vicar's, the fashionable men's store.

"From overalls," Crain finished.

The next project involved finding a place for Meister to stay. In this Crain proved to be less expert. Initially confident, he soon had to admit that "suitable digs"—his term—were unconscionably expensive. Meister could never afford any of the apartments in the list of upper West Side addresses Crain had prepared in advance. Even Crain's own apparently generous allowance would have been sorely strained if not depleted.

In the end, darkness falling, Meister had been obliged to take command, leading them to the lower East Side. There, on Essex, just above Delancey, responding to a crudely lettered "To Let" sign, they had settled on a one-room, cold-water, third-floor walk-up.

Meister was satisfied. Though small, it served its purpose. There was a narrow cot that doubled as a couch, a table and two chairs, a wardrobe for his clothes. There was a gas burner, a sink, an icebox, and a cupboard with a few dishes, pans and utensils. Down the hall, the landlady assured them, was a toilet and a tub, shared by only tenants on the third floor.

Crain was appalled. He sat down on the cot, tired and frustrated, totally at a loss. The place was a disaster, nothing whatsoever to commend it, yet a wasted afternoon had proved there was no alternative. West Side digs required West Side money.

"What's the matter?" Meister asked.

Everything, Crain seemed about to say, but he held his tongue. He looked around, as if trying to find something, anything, positive about it. "It's, uh, a little barren, don't you think?"

Meister put a suitcase on the table and started to unpack. "It will do."

Crain wasn't convinced. "How are you ever going to bring a girl here?"

"A girl?"

"Yes, a girl," said Crain. He moved his hands, indicating what a girl looked like with full breasts and ample hips. "What's a girl going to think if you bring her to a place like this?"

Meister resumed his unpacking. "I wasn't planning to bring a girl here."

"You weren't?"

"No."

Crain took a deep breath, exhaled noisily. "Well, that settles that."

Meister eyed him. Crain's woebegone expression indicated more than just sympathy for a friend's penurious plight. "Do you take your girls home?"

"Me?" Crain snorted. "Oh, sure. Can't you just see me doing that? 'Hello, Mother, this is Poopsie. We'd prefer not to be disturbed tonight and would you mind very much bringing up breakfast at eight?' "

Meister didn't laugh. "Then where do you take your girls?"

"Me?"

"That's right, you. That girl you told me about, Nadine Berns. the one you were in love with, where did you take her?"

Crain hesitated. "The Ritz," he said softly, as if the admission were painful to him.

"Ah, the Ritz," Meister said, laughing now. He had a stack of underwear he was going to put in the wardrobe. Instead, he threw the pile at Crain, draping him with it. "*Now* I understand."

Crain pretended innocence, but his neck, red at the collar, gave him away. He sheepishly removed the underwear. "What?"

"Aren't you the sly one?" Meister grinned. "All those apartments this afternoon, the right address, swank. We weren't looking for one to suit me. We were looking for one to suit you!"

Crain said nothing, handing the underwear back. His neck was getting redder.

"Don't deny it," Meister told him. He took back the underwear, ready to rag him some more, but then he saw the extent of Crain's embarrassment. "Hey! I'm just kidding!"

Crain still didn't reply. He had the look of a thief caught red-handed.

"John, listen. I understand, you know? Your father's house is like my dad's farm. Big as it is, there's no room. You can't do what you want if it's not yours."

Crain nodded, not necessarily in agreement but indicating that he had heard.

"This place—" Meister looked around, seeing it from a new perspective now, through Crain's eyes. "What the hell can I tell you? You're a friend and you'll always be welcome, and I just wish it was the Ritz."

"It doesn't have to be," Crain said. He stood up, his composure suddenly recovered, grinning as he tossed a last suit of underwear at Meister. "Take a nincompoop out of Nebraska and in just one day he starts getting uppity. The horseshit isn't off his boots and already he's worrying about where he should put 'em."

Meister was caught off guard by the abrupt change of mood. He stood holding his things, not sure of what to say, if anything.

"This place is fine," Crain assured him. "It's a place to stay, and what the hell else do you need?" He surveyed the room again, this time more favorably. "I tell you what, we'll use it as base, okay? From here we'll venture forth, reconnoitering. And if we get lucky..."

"We'll take 'em to the Ritz?" Meister suggested, feeling better.

"Definitely." Once again Crain was his old boisterous self. "We'll take them to the Ritz—and there'll be mints on the pillows."

Greg Meister had no trouble going to sleep that night. He literally fell into bed, exhausted by the day's events and by the long train ride from Nebraska. Mixed with that physical exhaustion was an inner peace he had not known since his return home from the war.

He no longer doubted John Crain's friendship. Crain had erased any doubt by showing up at Grand Central. Only a true friend would take the trouble of meeting every train, only a true friend would take him shopping for the right clothes and spend the rest of the day trying to find him an apartment, albeit with an ulterior motive.

Meister smiled, remembering Crain's crestfallen look when he realized that it actually cost money, a lot of money, to rent a swank apartment. What was even funnier was Crain's discovery that any sort of shared love nest was out of the question. Crain had led a quest for Valhalla and been detoured to a fleabag.

What a joke! Who, then, was the nincompoop?

Both of them. They were a pair, Meister decided. He didn't care that Crain had had another reason for helping him find a place to live. Ulterior motives were part of John Crain's make-up. They came with the man, like it or not, and they were not necessarily bad. They were simply hidden—at least, he tried to hide them—and good things could come of them.

The Luger was a good example. Meister felt certain that Crain's initial purpose in consorting with the ranks at the hospital at Vendeuil-Caply had been simply to try and get hold of the gun. Crain wanted it—he asked for it—and he hung around when Meister refused to give it to him, hoping for a change of mind. That a bond should grow from this—the friendship shared by himself, Crain, Pop Fagan and Hal Rosen—was purely coincidental.

The end result, that's what counted. It might work that way again, Meister thought. Crain's original inten was to find a place to take a girl once in a while, he realized. But maybe Crain would understand that a decent apartment wasn't really all that expensive if the expenses were shared. If the two of them got together, fifty-fifty, they could rent something acceptable. Maybe even two bedrooms with a bath, in a good neighborhood. Then they both could invite all the girls they wanted.

It wasn't a bad idea, and if he'd had any kind of money at the moment, Meister would have suggested it. As a matter of fact, he'd rather expected just such a proposal from Crain. There obviously was no way Meister could afford such rents alone, so why bother to look if it wasn't with the idea of sharing?

Meister shook his head. The only explanation he could think of was that John Crain, sheltered from the facts of economic life in his family's mansion, really hadn't had the slightest clue about what one paid for rent these days on Riverside Drive. It had been a simple case of the blind leading the blind.

Who's the nincompoop? Meister wondered again. He drifted off to sleep certain that he had the best friend he could ever hope for in John Crain. John's occasional puzzling behavior, his reluctance to confide all . . . what did any of that matter? Forget it, Meister told himself. You're in New York. You're starting a new life. You're going to get a job and you're not going to starve to death.

He fell asleep and there was no nightmare.

On the other side of New York, in an upstairs bedroom of the huge brick house at 14 Washington Square, John Crain was still awake, unable to find the peace Greg Meister had.

The day had not gone at all as he had hoped or expected. When Meister's letter had arrived, Crain had grabbed for it like a drowning man lunging for a life preserver. He saw it as the fates granting him another reprieve from death. Meister had saved his life before. Might he not do so again?

Besides being a friend, Meister was the best damn soldier he had ever met, a skilled, relentless, awesome destroyer. Thus Crain had gone to Grand Central looking for both—a friend and a killer. What kept him awake was the knowledge that he had found only a friend.

Greg Meister had left his murderous instincts in France. Now he only sought peace, to get a job and to live a normal life, to be free of the nightmares of his bloody battlefield exploits.

To ask him to kill again? No, that was impossible, out of the question. Anyway, his answer would be no.

Crain had slowly come to realize this as the day had progressed. The plans he had made—to take an apartment together, to use it as a base of operations, to go up against the underworld on its own terms—all that had to be abandoned. Meister, unfortunately, wasn't to be his salvation. That left—who?

Crain tossed restlessly. Two weeks before, he had shot and killed bootlegger Tony Capullo, his boss at Farley's. Now he was the target of one of Capullo's friends, a hoodlum named Scarface Al Brown. Brown was a cold-blooded gun for hire—he already had three murders to his credit—and the word on the street was that he had sworn revenge for Capullo's death.

There was no way to reason with a hoodlum like Brown. To explain that there had been justification, that it was self-defense, would only make him laugh—supposing he took the time to listen. The only way to deal with a man like Brown was to kill him first.

The only way, Crain thought, and he couldn't do it himself. He had neither the stomach nor the experience. He had been in a drunken stupor when he shot Capullo. Tracking Al Brown, he'd have to be cold sober, fully aware of what he was doing. When he pulled the trigger it would have to be a conscious, premeditated act, the act of a skilled killer.

John Crain struggled in the grip of growing fear and desperation. Meister could not help him. For a killer, he had to look elsewhere, and it was going to require connections and it was going to cost money.

He knew of only one other person who might be able to help him.

His father.

CHAPTER 5

Nelson Crain, the crafty, bullheaded Irishman singled out for this salvation, arose the next morning blissfully unaware of the burden about to be thrust upon him. He had forgotten all about his promise to arrange a job for Greg Meister. He had no idea—not the slightest inkling—of the danger stalking his son.

If one dared ask, Nelson Crain's excuse, bluntly stated, would have been that he was too busy. His mind was occupied with stock transactions, business deals, corporate mergers and political connections. He had no time to find work for a country bumpkin or keep track of a willfully wayward son. He was, in brief, too busy making money.

Money, along with the comfort, status and power it could buy, fueled Nelson Crain's inexhaustible drive. First generation Irish, raised in poverty, he was a self-made man who had let nothing stand in his way, especially his origins. The "Mc" in his name had been dropped long ago, cast aside like his shanty relatives, like the forgotten friends of his youth. For him the past ceased to exist. He knew only the present, and the promise of an even richer future.

The war had been good to him. He had made millions manufacturing uniforms and knapsacks. He had made millions more through shrewd investments on the stock market.

Equally important, he had made a lot of new and powerful business friends, among them Harry Sinclair, one of the world's richest oil men. This had led to even more influential connections within the new Harding administration. He had attended

President Harding's inauguration in March, he had been a personal guest of the president at the White House, and he had gotten cozy—very cozy, indeed, he thought—with Harding's new attorney general, Harry Daugherty.

Nelson Crain had high hopes for the Harding administration. He had picked Harding as his man the moment he read newspaper reports of the candidate's speech to a meeting of the Ohio Society. It was fine to idealize, Harding had said, but before attempting the miracle of old-world stabilization, wasn't it practical to make sure our own house was in order?

Others would call it the selfishness of nationality. Warren Gamaliel Harding called it an inspiration to patriotic devotion: "To safeguard America first. To stabilize America first. To prosper America first."

Nelson Crain liked the word "prosper." After all, if America prospered, *he* prospered.

It was that simple and, the way things were going, that sure. Harding's cabinet choices had been brilliant. Secretary of the Treasury Andrew Mellon was, with Rockefeller and Ford, one of the three wealthiest men in America. He was a banker whose investments included steel, railroads, utilities, waterpower, coal, oil and insurance. Hell, he owned it all, so who knew better what was good for the country?

Secretary of Commerce Herbert Hoover believed that taxes should be cut, interest rates should be lowered and people should fend for themselves, though banks needed federal aid. Who could argue with that?

And Attorney General Daugherty? Well, there was a gentleman, Nelson Crain thought. He and Harry Sinclair were going to make a great deal of money as a result of their acquaintanceship with Harry M. Daugherty. They were going to make many more millions of dollars. They were going to *prosper.*

"Why the smile, buy a bankrupt railroad?"

Nelson Crain came out of his reverie. The teasing comment had been made by his wife, Sandra, the one possession he perhaps loved more than money. He could never fault her gentle chiding. The same remark from someone else would have brought down his ire. In her case it only served to broaden his smile, in loving anticipation now, not greed.

"No," he told her, putting his account books aside. "The truth is . . ." He hesitated, wondering how much he should reveal, for she had no head for business and was easily bored by it. "I was thinking of buying some oil wells."

Sandra Crain cocked an eyebrow. "Oil wells? That sounds awfully stuffy somehow. Why don't you buy something interesting for a change?"

"Such as?" He rose from his desk and crossed his study to meet her, taking possession of a breakfast tray, kissing her on the cheek.

She considered for a long moment, frowning in supposed concentration, then pretending to be inspired. "How about me?"

Nelson Crain laughed and kissed her properly. Sandra Crain, the former Sandra J. Harper of the Harpers of Hyde Park, could not have been purchased for any price. A tall, slim, dark beauty with flashing blue-green eyes, she'd had her choice of any number of husbands, many of them already rich. That she had chosen Nelson Crain, a rough Irishman with only the obsession to be rich, was a puzzle to her family, her other suitors and sometimes even to herself. It was also a puzzle to Nelson Crain.

"You're a wonder, you know that?" he said.

"I know," she answered, smiling sweetly. "And so are you."

Together they went to a small alcove with French windows that overlooked the back garden. Its original purpose had been to serve as a kind of sun room, but Sandra Crain had turned it into a breakfast nook, the one place she could trap her husband in the morning. It contained a small table and two chairs and that was all. No one else could join them there, not that anyone ever thought of doing so. It was private, reserved.

Nelson Crain put the silver breakfast tray on the table and whisked away a linen napkin, revealing, as he had expected, only coffee, boiled eggs and dry toast.

"Again?" he moaned.

"Forever," his wife said. She sat down, glancing significantly at his ample waistline. "Or until you get rid of some of that."

Nelson Crain didn't need the reminder. Once he had been built like his son, stocky and muscular. Lately he had begun to look like a wayward butterball. He had trouble fitting into his chair in the small alcove. "Yes," he said contritely.

Sandra Crain smiled. It was a continuing battle that she was determined to win. "For a treat, there's marmalade."

Nelson Crain brightened at that prospect. He liked his pleasures, however small. He also knew that his wife was right, that he must lose some weight. He had lost a number of corpulent friends in recent years, heavy in their caskets. A return to moderation was in order.

And, in addition to staving off the reaper, he owed it to his wife, he thought. She had kept her trim figure through almost thirty years of marriage. She was still the slim, elegant, wondrously beautiful creature whose hand he had won. The streaks of grey in her hair only served to complement her innate grace and refinement.

He loved her dearly. Within reason, he would do anything for her. It was, from his point of view, the perfect marriage, an inspired combination of show horse and dray. She brought the breeding; he provided the drive.

Initially, the marriage had seemed to be a mistake. He had thought he was winning status by marrying her. Instead he had only won a reminder of his lowly position in the complex world of social slights and affronts. He could visit the Harpers of Hyde Park, but he would never be accepted there.

Also, she had seemed aloof at first, treating him with what he took to be snobbishness. Later, however, he realized that it was only a calculated distance. Before she could give her all, she had to come to know him, just as he had to understand her.

With that understanding had come both a deep love and an inner serenity. The marriage had been no mistake. On its foundation, Nelson Crain was building a new dynasty, separate and apart from the Harpers of Hyde Park. The Crain dynasty would have far more than mere respectability and status. It would also have immense wealth and power.

His beautiful wife, married for the wrong reason, kept for all the right ones, was a key to that now. Sandra Crain, with her background, breeding, charm and beauty, had instantly won the friendship and confidence of President Harding's wife, Florence, whom everyone called the Duchess. It was a friendship that Sandra was cultivating—not for the sake of business, she had no head for that—simply because the Washington social whirl fascinated her. So, to a degree, did the Duchess.

The inspired combination, Nelson Crain thought again. Rough, tough, wily, he could handle Attorney General Daugherty. Well-bred, socially connected. without guile, his wife—even unknowingly—could sway the Duchess. That accomplished, was Warren Gamaliel Harding far behind?

"You're *sure* you haven't bought a bankrupt railroad?"

"No, no," Nelson Crain quickly assured his wife, embarrassed that he had again drifted off into his imaginary counting house. "I was just thinking. . . ." He paused, trying to pick something that would account for the smile. "Why don't we just pack up and spend the weekend at Wicklow?"

"Wicklow?" Sandra Crain considered the idea, sorely tempted. The Newport country estate, which they had completed only last year, was one of her favorite places. "That's a marvelous idea, but don't you think you're rushing the season, darling? It's barely April."

"It's the middle of April," Nelson Crain corrected her. Having concocted the proposed trip out of thin air, he was anxious that it have some credence, however shaky.

"Well, it's not July," Sandra Crain said, making up her mind. Wicklow was for the summer. "Besides, aren't you forgetting something?"

"What?"

"John's friend, the one from Nebraska. Greg Meister."

"What about him?"

"You said you'd recommend him for a job."

Nelson Crain paused, marmalade-piled toast halfway to his mouth. "I did?"

"You certainly did. Also, you set an appointment for him. This afternoon at three o'clock."

Nelson Crain shook his head. "Cancel it. I'll see the lad some other time."

Gently but firmly, Sandra Crain took hold of her husband's hand, denying him the last precious bite of toast. "Darling, you promised. He's just in from the country. Some wretched farm by the sound of it, and hardly a dollar to his name from what I understand."

"Then why didn't he stay on the farm?"

"How do I know? Probably because it *is* wretched."

Nelson Crain grunted, tried again for the last bite of toast, but his wife's hand held firm.

"Nelson, listen to me," she said. "He's a nice boy. Don't you remember him? I do. I want you to help him if only for John's sake."

Nelson Crain's face clouded at the mention of his son. He put the toast aside, his appetite gone. Why must she spoil breakfast by asking a favor for that layabout? he wondered. The boy—no, the man, for that's what he was, or at least what he should be—the man didn't deserve any favors. Except for overseeing some of the construction of Wicklow, John Crain hadn't done a worthwhile thing since his return from the war. Instead of settling down, he had hung around doing God knows what at that gin mill, Farley's. When he finally got a job at the Stock Exchange, he had only played at it. Now, without explanation, he had quit. He had once shown some honest ambition and direction, but now he wanted it easy, the easier the better. Easy times, easy money, easy girls. Any prospect of orderly behavior had been blown out of his character in the trenches. Now his only goal was to live life to the hilt and damn the consequences—damn his father.

"I want you to see Greg Meister, and afterwards I want you to talk to John," his wife was saying. "He worries me. He's been walking around like a condemned man since he quit the Exchange. He doesn't look right. He's not himself."

No, the hell with him, Nelson Crain wanted to say, but he felt his wife's hand on his, asking the favor not for John but rather for herself. He nodded acquiescence. He loved her dearly. Within reason, there was nothing he would not do for her.

The house at 14 Washington Square was even more impressive than Greg Meister remembered. Four stories high, square and solid, it seemed more like a fortress than a home, and perhaps it was meant to be both, Meister thought. Nelson Crain kept his treasures here. Fine furnishings, period pieces, rare books, works of art.

Standing on the front stoop in his fashionable new suit, hand poised at the brass knocker, Meister felt strangely ill at ease, as if he had come as a thief. He told himself that was ridiculous. He wanted none of Nelson Crain's treasures. What he wanted, pure and simple, was a job. Yet the feeling persisted. Deep within him, some voice of conscience, muffled till now, had escaped its prison. Liar, it was softly calling. Liar, Meister.

Was he? No, damn it. He had come this far and he wasn't turning back. He lifted the knocker, banging it decisively. A moment later the door was flung open, the nagging voice of conscience drowned out in a flurry of greetings.

"Mister Greg!" Sadie Fagan cried. "It sure is good to see you! My, oh my, it's been a long time, and you sure have grown some, filled out!" Her dark eyes were sparkling with unrestrained joy as she took his hat and gloves. "And a new suit! Don't you look smart in it!"

"Hello, nincompoop," John Crain said from behind her. "Welcome to home and hearth." He hurried forward to shake hands, then took the hat and gloves from Sadie. "I'll handle these. You go find Father. And remember, after this, you're not supposed to kiss our guests, no matter how handsome."

Meister grinned at Sadie, wishing they *could* kiss. Pop Fagan's young wife was one of his favorite people, always full of life, vibrant. "Hello, Sadie," he beamed. "It's good to see you too." He looked at John Crain. "Though why she's still here is beyond me. There must be better things to do than pick up after you."

The petite young Negress took this as her cue to go find Nelson Crain. With a grin, she curtsied, then hurried away, black and white uniform shaking in all the right places.

The two men watched her go with open admiration. Pop Fagan, bless him, had got lucky there. He had married her when he was fifteen, she only thirteen. They had a baby daughter, Eleanora. Meister tried to recall her age. Almost six? He wondered if she was still living with cousins in Baltimore.

When the Armistice was declared, Meister and Crain had gone celebrating in Harlem and found Pop Fagan there, playing guitar with McKinney's Cotton Pickers. Sadie was in New York, too, but not the baby, not yet, and Sadie was looking for a job to help make ends meet. Ergo, another maid for the big house on Washington Square. A very attractive one.

"That reminds me," Meister said, turning to Crain. "How is Pop? You get to see him much?"

Crain shrugged. "Not lately. Guess he's on the road." He put Meister's hat and gloves on a sideboard and led the way toward the library. "We'll wait in here, okay? And I suppose you could use a drink."

The long hall, richly carpeted with an exquisite Oriental masterpiece, led past an ornate Louis XV console table flanked by matching chairs. Beyond, through an open double door, the library waited like a scholar's paradise, its high walls lined to the ceiling with leather-bound books.

Meister entered in awe, but quickly checked his enthusiasm. The first and last time he had been here, he had slid a volume away from its companions and opened it only to find the leaves uncut. He had wondered if this magnificent library was all decoration, little more than wallpaper bought by the yard. He hadn't found out then; he didn't want to now.

Crain pushed a walnut panel and a section of books swung away from the wall to reveal a fully stocked bar. "What will it be?"

"Scotch, please," Meister told him. He settled into a deep, luxuriously soft chair, resisting the temptation to examine one of the books. "With just a bit of ice." Crain nodded. He chose Dunbar's Special and poured a double shot.

"God," Meister said, impressed. The Eighteenth Amendment had been in effect for almost a year. "You've still got some of that left?"

"Private stock," said Crain, grinning. He peered under the bar. "Four more bottles, and when they're gone—?" As if suddenly aware of impending disaster, he poured a double shot for himself, although he really preferred rye. "A stupid law."

Meister couldn't quarrel with that. He got up, accepting his drink, raising the glass in toast. "What'll it be?"

John Crain thought for a moment. Suddenly, without warning, his face was like a dead man's, eyes cold and vacant. "To me," he said, staring blankly into his drink. "No future, no memory."

Meister frowned. What the hell was that supposed to mean? He was going to ask, but then Nelson Crain was in the room, his presence, like his voice, overwhelming.

"Johnny!" he cried. "I'll take one of those too—whatever you've got going." A stouter, livelier, more pugnacious version of his only son, he pushed between them with almost swaggering confidence. "You must be Meister."

"Yes," Meister admitted.

"Didn't recognize you at first without your sling." Nelson Crain waited for his drink to be passed to him. "Last time you were here you had a sling on your arm, didn't you?"

"Yes."

"How's the arm now?"

"Actually, it was my shoulder," Meister said, wondering why he was making that distinction. Nelson Crain's blunt manner struck him as bordering on rudeness. There had been no greeting other than the confirmation of his identity.

"Well, how's your shoulder, then?" Nelson Crain said, shooting a questioning glance at his son. What's this you've dragged in? he seemed to be asking. Someone else to argue with me?

"It's fine," Meister said. "I can even shake hands now." With deliberate slowness, he transferred his glass to his left hand, then extended his right. He looked Nelson Crain directly in the eye. "How are you, sir?"

The older man stared back. For an instant, a hard, demanding look showed in his eyes. Then it was gone.

"I'm all right," Nelson Crain decided. He shook hands, taking a better look at Meister, a thoughtful, careful appraisal. "The country's finally getting back on the track. We're headed the right way."

"Business as usual," John Crain put in. It was the first time he had spoken since his father had entered the room.

"Yes," Nelson Crain said, ignoring him. He was still studying Meister, as if trying to make up his mind. "Johnny tells me you're looking for a job."

Meister nodded. "Yes, I am."

"What experience have you had?"

"Nothing much," Meister admitted. "Two years of university. Then, like John here, it was off to the war."

"Yes," Nelson Crain said impatiently. "But what have you been doing since then? Back in Nebraska, isn't it?"

"Farm work."

"No job?"

Meister shook his head. Nelson Crain made farm work sound shiftless, but Meister wasn't inclined to argue. In truth, he hadn't even worked on the farm, just done as little as he could get away with.

"Well," Nelson Crain said, "that's not much of a resume." He took a long pull on his drink, swirling the whiskey in his mouth, hard eyes still on Meister. By the time he had finished swallowing, he had made up his mind. "You'll have to start at the bottom."

Meister gave a little shrug. "I had expected that. It's where I am."

"Yes," Nelson Crain said, but he wasn't being rude now, merely agreeable. "I was talking to Jack Morgan the other day. He could use somebody like you. You're big enough."

Meister was speechless for a moment. Even for him, a student of historic conquests, not modern-day lootings, the name Morgan held a special magic. "J.P. Morgan?"

"Junior," Nelson Crain said, a trace of contempt in his voice. "Poor Jack, presiding over the dismantling of old Pierpont's empire and convinced that he's doing a proper job of it. But then . . ." He looked at his son, then quickly glanced away. "You interested?"

"What would I be doing?"

"Does it matter?"

"Yes."

Nelson Crain paused for another careful appraisal of Meister. "Going from A to B," he said finally. "He's looking for a messenger, somebody he can trust." There was another pause. "Johnny says you can handle yourself. Is that true?"

"Yes."

"All right, then. I'll set up an appointment for you. No promises, but if you haven't got a jail record, you should be working by next week." He raised his glass in a toast, looking at his son again, not Meister. "Here's to work!"

"To work," Meister repeated. He hadn't said he was interested, but that didn't matter. It was, obviously, the only recommendation being offered and he ought to be grateful. The House of Morgan, whatever some people might think of it, wasn't a bad place to start.

"To work," John Crain said. It didn't sound like he meant it.

Meister glanced over at him, troubled by his friend's dispirited, almost sullen, behavior. Cheer up, will you? Meister thought. It's me who's got to work.

He was going to make some comment when a woman's cheery voice, echoing their toast, stopped him.

"Work? You mean it's all settled?"

Meister turned toward the door. Sandra Crain was standing on the threshold, her glowing beauty seeming to bring a light to the room, infusing it with her presence, a far better rebuke to dark moods than any Meister could think to offer.

"Good," she said. "I seem to have arrived at just the right moment, after all the business talk is done." She came forward, smiling in welcome, her quiet confidence the very antithesis of her husband's brash swagger. "How are you, Greg? It's good to see you again."

"Thank you," Meister said, and meant it. There was a quality about Sandra Crain that Meister had never encountered in any other woman. She had the kind of style that set her apart.

Sandra Crain kissed her husband on the cheek, then her son, squeezing their hands at the same time.

Then she turned back to Meister. "Well? Are you going to tell me about it?"

"I'm fixing him up with Jack Morgan," Nelson Crain answered.

"Oh?" Sandra Crain was still looking at Meister. She directed the question at him. "With what position?"

"Messenger boy," Nelson Crain said bluntly.

Meister didn't hear, or if he did, it didn't register. Nothing would for the next few minutes. It would all be remembered later as a blur, a hopeless, helpless, glorious blend of disjointed phrases and imagery.

Tandy Crain was at the door of the library. She was dressed in a camel hair coat and matching tam, waiting politely for an opportunity to say good-bye.

John Crain was the first to acknowledge her presence. "Hi, Sis!" he called. "Come say hello. You remember this character?"

Then, for Meister, everything became a jumble.

"Yes, I think so. You're Greg, aren't you? Hello again …"

"Hello …"

"Darling, where's your scarf? There's a howling wind out there," Sandra Crain chided her daughter.

"Mother! I'm already bundled beyond reason. They'll put me in the mail if I so much as add a string."

"Where are you going?"

"Father, must you always ask that question? I'm going out."

"Say good-bye to Greg, then."

"Good-bye, Greg."

"Good-bye …"

A smile and a wave and she was gone.

The next thing Greg Meister knew, he, too, was leaving, ushered out in a similar flurry of good-byes. J. P. Morgan's business card was the only sure evidence that he had ever been inside 14 Washington Square.

Instinctively, without conscious decision, he started down the street, headed for a trolley stop. All he could think of was Tandy Crain.

If her mother's beauty glowed, hers was radiant. It shone like the very heavens. She was, as he had remembered her, an incredibly beautiful creature. He was rendered speechless by her mere presence. It was as before, the first time he had ever seen her. He was in love.

When he reached the corner, he stopped and looked back, wondering why he had waited so long to return, why he had never been able to admit the truth to himself.

Admit it now, he told himself. You came as a thief to that fortress, Greg Meister. You came to find and to take Nelson Crain's greatest treasure. You came, as you always knew you must, to steal his daughter.

Nelson Crain was watching Meister from one of the library windows. His face clouded when he saw him stop and look back. "How well do you know that lad?" he asked his son.

"Greg Meister?"

Nelson Crain's gaze shifted momentarily, picking out his son's reflection, flawed and twisted, in the thick panes of the French window. "Who else did we just have in here?"

"I know him well enough," John Crain said. "I told you, he was in my platoon and he saved my life."

Nelson Crain watched until Meister turned and continued on down the street. Then he swung around, facing his son. "Yes, but can you trust him?"

John Crain laughed. "What the hell are you talking about?"

"Ah, Johnny." He finished his drink and started toward the bar to make another. "You're not as bright as you should be, do you know that? There's something lacking since the war. You don't think like you used to. You're not as quick. You don't—"

"Please you in any way?"

Nelson Crain didn't answer. He paused briefly, as if out of step, then quickly resumed his stride. He found the bottle of Dunbar's Special and filled his glass. He swallowed half the drink in one gulp.

"Your mother thinks I ought to talk to you," he said finally, fortified by the liquor. "I'm ready if you are."

No answer, on the grounds that it might incriminate me, John Crain thought bitterly. He stared into the bottom of his own empty glass. There was no answer there, either.

As his father had done, he went to the bar, refilling to the brim. He was going to toss it down, but then he changed his mind. What he needed more was a clear head.

"Goddamn, what's the matter with you?" his father exploded.

John Crain put his drink aside. "I've—I've killed a man," he said softly.

Nelson Crain's face turned white. He sagged, holding onto the bar for support. "What?"

"I've killed a man," John Crain repeated, making no move to go to his father. If nothing else, he thought, the admission had gained him Nelson Crain's full attention. "Tony Capullo, the man I worked for at Farley's."

"One of your gangster friends?" he asked in a harsh, rasping whisper.

"He wasn't a friend. I just worked for him. He was my employer."

"A gangster," Nelson Crain maintained, not to be denied. "How the hell did it happen?" He still looked stunned.

"I shot him."

"Why, for God's sake?" he demanded.

"He was going to kill a friend."

"Another gangster?"

John Crain didn't reply. There wasn't any use arguing. In his father's mind, Sid Berns, a poor Jewish kid scrambling for a few bucks, running whiskey to help keep his family fed, would fall into the category of gangster.

"You damned idiot!" Nelson Crain shouted. A raw, livid rage had replaced disbelief. "Who else knows about this?"

"It doesn't matter. I did the police a favor, and everybody at Farley's too. They all hated the bastard."

"Except *who*?" Nelson Crain demanded. "You're afraid of someone, or you wouldn't be telling me this."

John Crain hesitated. He wasn't a coward. He had proved that in the war. But he could feel himself sweating now, the stink of fear upon him, filling his nostrils.

"Who?"

"I wish I knew," he said. "I just know the name. Al Brown. He's a hired gun and he was a friend of Tony's. He's supposed to be coming after me."

"A gangster?"

"Yes, damn it, a gangster," John Crain said resignedly. "A mobster ... and how do I stop him? That takes money, doesn't it?"

"Hell, that's what you want from me? A hired gun to kill a hired gun?"

John Crain kept his eyes averted. His hands were shaking. "You helped me before."

Nelson Crain stood staring at his son, the rage subsiding and a heavy sorrow rushing in after it, falling upon him. Its weight was more than he could bear. "Not again, Johnny. This time you're on your own."

John Crain looked into his father's face and saw his determined look. It was true, he thought. The verdict was final. There was no appeal.

He turned away and, without another word, left the room.

Nelson Crain took his whiskey over to the window. He stood looking out to where he had last seen Greg Meister. He made a vow to himself, fire in his eyes, fed by a new fury. He wasn't even thinking of his son.

I may have lost Johnny, he thought, but I'm not about to lose my daughter.

CHAPTER 6

In the spring a young man's fancy may turn to thoughts of love, but come summer, if that love is still unrequited, his thoughts can just as easily turn to morose brooding.

This had happened to Greg Meister.

It was a hot, humid, sweltering summer, and Meister was seriously considering a return to Nebraska. He was lonely and homesick and all his grand dreams were in a shambles.

The job at J.P. Morgan & Company was exactly as Nelson Crain had described it. He was a messenger boy, going from A to B. Although he was carrying extremely important documents and large sums of money, in a very short time he was bored. He was the equivalent of a postman, except he worked harder and got paid less. He had been hired at the whopping salary of thirty cents an hour. He wasn't expecting a raise.

Opportunity for advancement appeared slimmer with each passing day. He'd met with Jack Morgan only once, on the morning he had been hired.

There had been a brief encounter in the Morgan Library, resplendent with its Renaissance ceiling from Lucca, its red brocade walls from the Chigi Palace in Rome and its awe-inspiring portrait of J. Pierpont Morgan.

Even in death, the House of Morgan's founder was more vital than his son, a huge, portly plutocrat with a grotesque nose, dressed in a velvet-collared overcoat and a huge silk hat.

Jack Morgan, though he had his father's build, was a couth gentleman by comparison, very English in his manner. He had made a brief, prepared speech on the House of Morgan, noting that it had saved the gold standard in America for Grover Cleveland, the credit of Wall Street for Theodore Roosevelt and, quite possibly, since it had been banker for the Allied cause, the world for everybody. He had quoted some of the wisdom of his father, concluding with his favorite: "You can do business with anyone, but you can only sail a boat with a gentleman." And he had suggested that the future held great promise for any young man so fortunate as to become associated, in whatever capacity, with the House of Morgan.

Then Meister had been sent away to report to a man named Davison, who sent him to a man named Lamont, who sent him to a third man named Fisher. He ran errands for Fisher and, since Fisher hadn't been promoted in thirty years, he saw little prospect of taking Fisher's position, not that he wished to.

In a three-story limestone building at Broad and Wall Streets, the financial center of the United States, Meister worked for J.P. Morgan & Company, the most powerful nexus of capitalism in the world, and as long as he did he would probably have trouble paying his rent.

Some job.

John Crain had proved an even greater disappointment. Meister had seen almost nothing of him since the visit to 14 Washington Square.

For some inexplicable reason, Crain made no attempt to maintain their friendship and sometimes gave the impression that he would just as soon end it. Messages were not returned. Appointments were not kept.

When they did get together, Crain was depressed and uncommunicative, easily irritated and quick to find some excuse to leave. He was never his old self, never lively, boisterous, eager for a good time. He was more like a man under a death sentence, looking over his shoulder for the fall of some phantom guillotine only he knew about.

The transformation was so sudden and complete that Meister suspected Crain's initially warm greeting had been all an act. John Crain, he thought, had given it the old college try, attempting to renew their friendship because he owed him one for saving his life.

Crain had tried and it hadn't worked. Now he was wriggling out of it as best he could. If there was some other explanation, Crain hadn't chosen to confide in him. And that only made it worse, because if you didn't have a man's confidence, you had nothing.

Maybe nothing real had ever existed between them, Meister thought. Maybe he had just imagined it. Maybe it was just wishful thinking. Palling around with a millionaire's son.

And what of Tandy? Meister didn't even want to think about her. If ever there was a lost cause, a hopeless quest, a doomed prospect, it was in his thinking he might ever win the love of Tandy Crain.

There had been no opportunity to see her again. The Crains had failed to issue a second invitation to him. John Crain only shrugged absently when Meister inquired about her. There wasn't the slightest indication from any quarter that she might be interested in him. Without it he could hardly come calling, ask her out on a date.

Finally, in desperation, he had gone to Washington Square, hoping to "accidentally" meet her on her way to or from home. Like a fool, like a stupid, idiotic, lovesick fool, he had stood around on street corners night after night waiting for a chance meeting. And when it happened, she didn't even recognize him!

Meister turned red with embarrassment whenever he recalled that indignity. Tandy Crain had suddenly appeared out of the darkness, that wonderful, radiant glow about her, and he had stood transfixed, mesmerized while she passed him by, showing no sign of recognition. She had passed without speaking and he had been unable to utter a word.

Fool! Meister thought, the word that finally came to his lips long after she had gone.

He had gone back to the same corner on other nights, hoping to see her again, to be given a chance to speak, to explain, but she never passed that way again. It was as if she knew he might be waiting and was avoiding him.

Fool! Why did he stay in New York? Why did he torture himself? His job was a dead end ... John Crain no longer wanted to be friends ... Tandy had gone away for the summer to Wicklow ... what was left?

He had awakened that July morning in such a despairing mood that he had almost started packing. He had pulled his suitcases out from under the bed, thinking there was nothing to keep him here and there never would be, when he saw the ticket he'd pinned on the wall the week before.

It was for a ten-dollar seat at the Dempsey-Carpentier fight and it was one of a pair he had bought at a reduced price from a fellow messenger at the House of Morgan. The other ticket he had mailed to John Crain at 14 Washington Square.

"Lucked out," his accompanying note had said. "Some sorry bastard's wife won't let him go. Got this for nothing and another one too. If you can make it, see you at the fight! Meister."

John Crain had been given one last chance. He could take it or leave it. If he didn't show, the friendship was over. So was a fool's quest.

Greg Meister would be going home.

Meister wasn't a fight fan. He preferred baseball, avidly following the career of Babe Ruth, the game's new idol, who that summer was leading the American League in batting, ahead of the veteran Ty Cobb.

Yet, Jack Dempsey, the Manassa Mauler, was an intriguing figure, and it was with an increasing sense of anticipation that Meister arrived at Boyles' Thirty Acres in Jersey City.

For the past several weeks, the newspapers had been full of what was being hailed as the "Battle of the Century," Dempsey versus the French champion, Georges Carpentier. It was Dempsey's first defense of his heavyweight title, the title he had won two years before from Jess Willard. A sellout crowd was predicted, boxing's first million-dollar gate.

Here was history in the making and it was easy to get caught up in the spirit of the thing. Quite apart from his hope of seeing John Crain, Meister was intent on seeing the match, and he was also intent on getting down a bet.

Popular sentiment favored Carpentier. He had served his country gallantly during the war while Dempsey, an ex-hobo, had barely escaped conviction in a trial for draft evasion. George Bernard Shaw called Carpentier "the greatest boxer in the world," on the strength of his victory over the English champion Joe Beckett.

Meister, however, was inclined to side with a less prejudiced authority, Nat Fleischer. Fleischer said Dempsey had it all—the punch of Sullivan, the speed of Corbett, the cunning of Johnson and the strength of Jeffries.

There was also Dempsey's ring record. He had come up fast, knocking out Fred Fulton and "Battling" Levinsky, and it had taken him just three rounds to dispose of Willard, a giant who outweighed him by almost sixty pounds and had a five-inch advantage in reach. Willard hadn't been able to come out for the fourth round.

If he got the chance, he'd bet on Dempsey, Meister decided. He was anxious to recoup some of the losses of his last wager, the fifty dollars he'd thrown away on Henry Untermeyer's four kings.

Boyles' Thirty Acres, a vast wooden soup bowl, was filled to the brim. From the topmost bleachers to ringside, it was a solid sea of humanity, the largest crowd ever gathered for a prizefight. More than ninety thousand had come to view this pale, New World version of a Colosseum spectacle. The gate, announced later, exceeded $1,600,000.

Meister had never seen so many people in one place before. Pushing through the crowd, he was glad he had a reserved-seat ticket, for there was hardly even standing room left.

Latecomers were being directed to the rim of the arena. Meister doubted that the match could even be seen from that distance. The ring would be the size of a postage stamp.

Finally, reaching his section, he searched for John Crain, but there was no sign of him. He climbed up the aisle, locating his row and his seat, but still there was no sign of Crain.

That shit, he thought, the disappointment stabbing through him even though he had tried to prepare himself for it. He stood in the aisle for a long moment, again alone in a crowd.

"Move it, will you, buddy?" someone yelled.

"Fuck you," Meister replied, to no one in particular.

Angry now, he pushed roughly down the row, not caring about anyone he jostled in the process. He took possession of his seat, took out his cigarettes and quickly lit one. If he didn't calm down, somebody was going to get bopped, and it wasn't going to be in the ring.

He took a long drag, pulling the smoke deep into his lungs, exhaling slowly. That shit. He was more angry with himself than with John Crain. He had put himself into this situation.

"You got another one of those?"

Meister turned. The question had been asked by the man on his left, a man sitting—Meister suddenly realized—in the seat reserved for John Crain.

Actually, he wasn't much more than a boy, eighteen at the most, Meister guessed. The dark, knowing eyes were the only sign of maturity. They gave no indication that he was aware of occupying someone else's seat.

"A cigarette? You got another one?"

Meister was momentarily at a loss. He'd been aware, coming down the row, of only one empty seat, but had assumed it was just a matter of shifting over. Now he realized that that wasn't possible; there were no spaces left along the row.

"I think there's been a mistake," he said finally, anger welling up in him again. "I bought that seat for a friend of mine. Can I see your ticket?"

"Sure," the youth said. He pulled a stub out of his pocket and passed it over.

Meister checked it against his own. It was one number off, which made it the other half of the pair he had bought, the ticket that he mailed to John Crain. Which meant what? Crain had scalped it?

He started to get up, the fight forgotten, his only desire to find John Crain and beat the hell out of him.

"I'm Sid Berns," the young man said, taking the ticket stub back. "John couldn't make it." He paused, as if considering adding something more, but then let it go at that. "I guess you're Meister, huh?"

Sid Berns? Meister stared at him, trying to place the name. Then he remembered Crain saying his girl's name was Berns, and that she had a brother. Sid Berns had been Crain's partner, the kid shot on the whiskey run from Canada.

"Why the hell didn't you say so?" Meister demanded.

"You didn't give me a chance." He waited for Meister to sit back, then helped himself to a cigarette that still hadn't been offered to him. "You've got a temper, huh?"

Meister didn't say anything. He was still trying to control what indeed was a temper. He couldn't understand what had made him fly off that way, except everything suddenly seemed to be at stake—his friendship with John Crain, whether he stayed in New York, whether he should try again to see Tandy. And it all seemed to hinge on one stupid fight ticket.

"John said you did," Sid Berns was saying, lighting up. "A real tiger when you got mad." He turned away, looking down into the ring where the announcer was now climbing through the ropes. "Who do you think is gonna win?"

Meister still didn't answer. He ground his own cigarette out where he had dropped it when he'd been about to rush away.

"Me, I like Dempsey," Sid Berns said. "If you want my opinion, this ain't gonna last long."

"No argument," Meister said, finally responding. He had, he decided, no quarrel with Sid Berns, and he might profit from studying him. Berns was a tight package of raw energy. But he had it firmly under control. When released, it would be at his bidding, and then only in the amounts required. Somewhere—in the slums, probably—he had learned conservation. It showed in him and in his carefully maintained clothes, out of style but serviceable. That way, against all odds, he survived.

"Too bad," Sid Berns said. "I was hoping to lay a bet." He glanced around, making sure no one was listening. "Carpentier don't belong in the ring with Dempsey. That's why they had him train in secrecy, so the newspaper guys wouldn't spot it."

Meister almost laughed. The statement had been made with such confidence that one might have suspected this was Dempsey himself talking, not some little Jewish hustler from the lower East Side. "I sort of doubt that."

"Hey," Sid Berns continued, glancing around again. "I got this straight from someone who was there! Tex Rickard was in to see Dempsey. 'Listen, Jack,' he says, 'the best people in the world are here today and this is just the beginning. Don't knock down the show. Don't kill the son of a bitch!' "

Meister was going to protest. The idea of Berns having such a connection was ludicrous. But the youth's manner wasn't easily challenged. He was either an accomplished liar or he did have inside information. There could be no in between.

"Well, we'll soon see," said Meister, turning his attention to the prefight activity in the ring. Dempsey and Carpentier would be coming out of their dressing rooms any minute now. He made it sound casual when he asked his question. "Incidentally, what happened to John?"

"He wasn't up to it," Sid Berns replied. "He told me to tell you he was sorry, but he had to get out of town for a while, straighten himself out. You know he had it pretty bad for my sister?"

Meister nodded. "Yes, he told me."

"Well, there's no chance of them getting married. She's Jewish." Sid Berns turned, pulling his nose, as if he somehow found that funny. "As a matter of fact we all are, the whole family."

Meister wasn't amused. "And—?"

"That's it, Orthodox Jewish. My old man would never give his permission. He'd rather die first. So, Nadine finally had to tell John no. The whole thing was really killing my father, and my mother too." Sid Berns looked away. "John? Well, he just couldn't take no for an answer, I guess."

Meister considered. He couldn't see why John Crain hadn't confided in him, but the rest of it was understandable. He, of all people, ought to know about the misery of a hopeless love. "When's he coming back?"

Sid Berns shrugged. "I dunno."

"Did he say anything else?"

"He said he'd be in touch."

"And that's all?"

"That's all."

Meister got out his cigarettes again. Like hell, he thought, unable to accept that, but he had no real basis for challenging it. What was he going to say? That John Crain was too good a friend to walk out on him?

The fight was about to begin. Carpentier was moving toward the ring, and the band, almost drowned out by the cheering crowd, had struck up "La Marseillaise."

"I'll give you odds!" Sid Berns shouted.

Meister looked at him. Did the boy really think he'd bet against Dempsey?

"Five to one," Sid Berns said, using his fingers to show Meister the odds. "My fifty against your ten."

Meister laughed. That was ridiculous. The last he'd heard, it was an even bet, the popular sentiment still for Carpentier.

"Well?" Sid Berns shouted, his bright eyes taunting, laughing at Meister's indecision.

Now Dempsey was coming out. The roar of the crowd was a murmur compared to the welcome given to Carpentier. There was a loud scattering of boos.

Meister got out his wallet. "You've got a bet."

Sid Berns snatched the ten. "I'll hold it."

The two fighters were in the ring now. The roar of the crowd filled the arena again and further conversation was suspended.

Meister sat silently watching while Jack Dempsey, never in trouble, took three and a half rounds—which was three more than he needed—to methodically destroy Georges Carpentier.

When it was over, Meister had no reason to doubt Sid Berns' claim that promoter Tex Rickard had asked Dempsey to carry Carpentier. He also accepted the explanation Sid Berns had given him for John Crain's mysterious behavior and sudden departure from New York.

Late that night, falling into bed, Greg Meister made up his mind about another thing, too. He decided to stay in New York. If Sid Berns could survive, so could he. If John Crain had to run away, he didn't.

He was a man and he had to stand on his own two feet. He would work hard and he would save his money and he would keep out of trouble.

Soon he was asleep, dreaming. A beautiful woman suddenly appeared out of the darkness. There was a glow about her, an incandescent quality.

"Hello, Greg Meister," she said, smiling in recognition....

CHAPTER 7

Nelson and Sandra Crain saw the Dempsey-Carpentier fight two days later, on the Fourth of July, at a glittering Washington party hosted by Ned McLean, a minor member of what some newspapers were starting to call "the Ohio Gang."

McLean, the son of John R. McLean, owner of the *Cincinnati Enquirer* and the *Washington Post,* was by virtue of his father's largess a hopeless alcoholic who couldn't hold a job. Sometimes he couldn't even hold a drink because his hands shook so much. He was also very rich.

Ned and his wife Evalyn had spent $200,000 to finance their honeymoon abroad. On their second trip to Europe they had bought the cursed Hope Diamond.

The McLean house on I Street was a grand pile that made 14 Washington Square look common by comparison. It occupied half a block. The ballroom, decorated with Barberini tapestries, could accommodate several dining tables, each a hundred feet long. The soaring living room had ample space for a three-story Christmas tree.

Ned McLean also owned a little house on H Street which he had loaned, for the duration, to Harry M. Daugherty, attorney general of the United States. Daugherty lived there rent free. "The love nest," Daugherty called it, and there he met a procession of visitors that boggled the senses. All of them were looking for something, most of them willing to give something in return. Harry Sinclair, the oil man, came by often.

Curious about the arrangement, Nelson Crain had once asked Sinclair why Ned McLean had loaned the house to Daugherty. Sinclair explained that it was out of profound gratitude. Thanks to Daugherty, Ned McLean finally had a job. At a salary of one dollar a year, Ned was a special agent of the Department of Justice, with his own badge and secret code number.

"Do you think we might be able to work a better deal than that?" Crain had asked.

"Yes, I think so," Harry Sinclair had replied.

One thing led to another. There had been, initially, a meeting with Jess Smith, a strange salivaspraying dandy who lived with Daugherty at the house on H Street and who seemed to handle more money, all of it under the table, than the U.S. Treasury. There had been a meeting with Edwin W. Denby, secretary of the navy, and there had been a meeting with Albert Fall, secretary of the interior. There had been several meetings with Attorney General Daugherty.

Now, at Ned McLean's Fourth of July party, there was to be yet another meeting, with Warren Gamaliel Harding, the president of the United States.

Nelson Crain had an enormous amount riding on the meeting. Harry Sinclair was the key to the upcoming deal since his Mammoth Oil Company had the required legitimacy to swing it. But it had been Crain's idea. If it could be consummated, everybody involved stood to make a great deal of money. Especially Sinclair. Sinclair had suggested that Nelson Crain's reward include an equal partnership in new oil ventures. From a power base such as that, a man could acquire truly vast riches. He could start a dynasty.

For more than a decade three tracts of oil-bearing government land had been set aside for the future hypothetical needs of the U.S. Navy. They were insurance against a possible shortage in an emergency. Two of the tracts were in California. The third and most valuable was at Teapot Dome, Wyoming.

The oil in these tracts was in danger of being drawn off by neighboring wells. Gushers had opened up right on the threshold of one of the reserves in California. The previous year, Congress, worried about further losses, had given the secretary of the navy almost unlimited power to conserve the reserves as he saw fit.

There were two possible courses of action. Offset wells could be drilled along the edge of the reserves to neutralize the drainage, or the reserves could be leased to private operators, on condition that they store an equitable amount of oil for the future requirements of the national security.

Woodrow Wilson's secretary of the navy, Daniels, had preferred to have offset wells drilled. Harding's new navy secretary, Denby, had decided to stick by that decision.

Crain's idea had been simple. If Denby wouldn't make a deal, how about Albert Fall, secretary of the interior? Fall had come into office as the ally of big oil interests. What if he saw a chance to do them a favor? What if Harding were to sign an executive order transferring custody of the reserves from the secretary of the navy to the secretary of the interior?

Harry Sinclair had liked the idea; he had liked it very much. All the preliminary meetings had now taken place, earnest money being passed each step of the way to the saliva-spraying Jess Smith, and everybody else involved had liked the idea, too. It got Denby off the hook and kept his hands clean while still permitting him to remain one of the boys. It gave Fall what he wanted, a windfall, Harry Sinclair's joke.

Now only one question remained: Did Warren Harding like the idea?

Sandra Crain wasn't quite sure what to make of the party. It was a marvelous affair, of course. President Harding and Florence were there, and Secretary of State Charles Hughes and other top cabinet members, also several ambassadors and a crowd of senators and representatives.

Yet, mixed up with them was a strange group she couldn't quite classify. There was Howard Mannington. When asked what he did, he just smiled disarmingly and said his job was "to help" the attorney general. Gaston B. Means was a jolly fat man who was supposedly a seven-dollar-a-day special employee of the Bureau of Investigation. But he had arrived in a chauffeur-driven Cadillac. Jap Muma, another import from Ohio, had shown up with what had been promised as the highlight of the party—a film of the fight between Jack Dempsey and Georges Carpentier.

Sandra Crain didn't know who these men were. All she knew was that there were a lot of them, Mannington, Means and Jap Muma being only representative, and that they all seemed to come from Ohio. As a matter of fact, half the executive branch was apparently from Ohio. If they didn't hold an official job or weren't heading some bureau or department, they held an unofficial one that somehow seemed to pay even better.

Another thing that disturbed her was the flow of supposedly prohibited spirits. There were two bars operating and in the upstairs study were trays with bottles containing every imaginable brand of whiskey.

Much the same double standard prevailed at the White House, she had noticed. In the hinterlands, Harding might deal sternly with illicit drinking, de manding rigid enforcement of Prohibition, but at home he could guzzle with the best.

And cards? Again Sandra Crain didn't have to rely on rumor for that, having heard it directly from the lips of Florence Harding. Complaining about the difficulty of getting settled into Washington, Florence had said her husband played poker two, three nights a week.

"Bless us, who's minding the store?" Sandra Crain had asked, trying to make light of it.

"I'm not sure," Florence Harding had replied quite seriously.

Still, things did seem to be in control, and that was some solace, Sandra Crain thought. If she had no head for business, which she was the first to admit, she also couldn't make head or tail of government. It was simply beyond her comprehension. Why Harding had to import half of Ohio to run Washington, for instance, was something she would never understand. Somehow she didn't think she wanted to.

Sandra Crain put all that aside and concentrated on developing her friendship with Florence Harding. The Duchess, Warren Harding's name for his wife, fascinated her. Without actually realizing it at first, she had taken on the new First Lady as—there was no other way to put it—a project.

She knew nothing about business and government, but Sandra Crain did know the social graces. If she could assist there, why not?

Florence Harding could be said to be lady enough for the job that fate had thrust upon her. Her father, Amos Kling, had been the richest man in Marion, Ohio. On her mother's side she could trace her ancestry back to a distinguished family of French Huguenots, who had landed in America early in the seventeenth century.

Though not a beauty, she was attractive enough, with striking blue eyes and the frail, delicate body of a gentlewoman. She also didn't lack intelligence. On the contrary, she was clear-minded, purposeful, decisive.

Still, there were faults. But Sandra Crain believed that, through their growing friendship, she might be able to gently smooth some of them, producing a proper lady.

Tactfully approached, Florence Harding might accept some suggestions for a more elegant, less informal household. She might even be persuaded, since she could be strong-willed when so inclined, to sweep out some of the riffraff infesting it. The counsel of a trusted friend might clean up things at the White House and, in the process, straighten a few things around Washington, too. One never knew.

Ned McLean announced that the Dempsey-Carpentier spectacular was about to be shown. His guests moved to their seats in eager anticipation. The film was contraband of sorts. A dozen years before, when Jack Johnson, the great black heavyweight champion, beat Jim Jeffries, a law was passed prohibiting the transportation of fight films across state lines. The original intent was to prevent "the humiliating spectacle of a white man beaten by a Negro" from getting around.

Sandra Crain rejoined Florence Harding and found herself sitting between Florence and Attorney General Daugherty. Jap Muma, the projectionist, made several false starts. During the lull, Florence conducted a whispered conversation with Daugherty.

"Isn't it illegal for Ned to have this film?" she asked.

"No," Daugherty said. "It's only illegal to transport it across state lines. There's no law that prohibits showing it."

"But couldn't Jap Muma get in trouble for bringing it here?"

"I suppose so, but he's got friends in high places, so he'll only get a minimum fine."

"Is he going to exhibit it anyplace else?"

"He'd better. The way I've got it figured, the damned thing is worth a million dollars."

"Really?" said Florence. "Good for him."

After the film, during which she kept her eyes closed most of the time, Sandra Crain joined her husband, who had watched it with President Harding and Harry Sinclair.

The president was shaking hands with Nelson Crain. "I like your idea, Nelson," Harding was saying. "I like it very much." He put his hand on Harry Sinclair's shoulder, squeezing it affectionately. Then, with a smile, he moved away.

Sandra Crain thought that she had never seen her husband look happier. His face glowed with pleasure, as if he had just inherited heaven. Harry Sinclair looked just the opposite.

"Enjoy the film?" Nelson Crain asked her.

"Oh, yes," his wife lied, not wishing to spoil his mood.

She was pleased that her husband was getting along so well with the president. As for her project … well, that was going to take some time, she decided.

CHAPTER 8

By September, Greg Meister's resolve to stay in New York was weakening again, for he had been unable to find a friend to replace John Crain. His fellow messengers at the House of Morgan were an odd lot with whom he had nothing in common. Most were older, married and had children, caught up in a hand-to-mouth existence. They came to work exhausted and they hurried home that way. They moved millions of dollars around the financial center of the world, and they counted their pennies.

It was, Meister thought, no life for him, but he had been unable to find an alternative. He had no trade and he hadn't completed his education. Without a degree he was unskilled, best suited as a laborer. He had considered that; perhaps it could lead to a foreman's position. But initially it was too much of a step down.

John Crain's solution, whiskey running, held no appeal for him. Crain's story of fleeing an ambush in a hail of bullets was still vivid in his mind. If someone started shooting at him, he'd shoot back. He'd end up killing again. He didn't want that.

What kept him going was Sid Berns' example. If that little hustler could survive, so could he, damn it. But he also needed a friend, an old one, preferably, and he had begun a search for Hal Rosen.

Rosen, the concert pianist turned Bolshevik, thanks to losing three fingers to the Kaiser in the war, had to be somewhere in New York, probably Greenwich Village. The Village was a hotbed of radicals, spouting a revolution that was never going to come, trying to form a communist party that didn't have a hope in hell of any popular support.

Meister wished he had thought to ask John Crain where Hal Rosen lived. His name had only come up once, on Meister's first day back in New York, and Crain's answer had been very vague.

"Him? Oh, he's probably playing the harp by now. You don't need all your fingers for that." Then, as he had with a lot of things, Crain had changed the subject, preferring to put the past aside.

John Crain had put a lot aside. He hadn't kept up with Pop Fagan even though Pop's wife, Sadie, was a maid in his parents' home. He hadn't kept up with Hal Rosen despite all those drunken bull sessions in the hospital at Vendeuil-Caply. Nor, Meister thought, some of the bitterness returning, had Crain kept up with him. There hadn't been so much as a letter since his sudden departure from New York. No phone call, nothing.

Meister had all but written him off. He was looking for Hal Rosen, not word of John Crain, when he entered the Apollo Club, which had recently booked McKinney's Cotton Pickers. Pop Fagan might still be playing with them. He might know how to reach Hal. Even if he didn't, it would be a lift to see Pop.

Meister had to admit that he had been as derelict as John Crain in not keeping up with Pop Fagan. It wasn't prejudice that had kept him away. He liked Pop, genuinely so. It was a cultural gulf so vast that he didn't know how to bridge it. Pop Fagan was Harlem and whorehouse jazz. Meister was Wall Street, or trying to be.

The Apollo Club hit him with smells he remembered from old nights on the town with John Crain. Alcohol, tobacco, cannabis hung heavy. Meister moved to a rear table, signaling to a waitress and wishing, for a moment, that he was with Crain. They had shared some good times. The shit knew how to have fun.

McKinney's Cotton Pickers were playing. Meister maneuvered his chair for a better view of the stage and spotted Pop

Fagan. A moment later he wouldn't have had to see him to know he was there. No one, no one else in the world, played that kind of magic guitar.

Meister closed his eyes to listen. He was back again in the boiler room at Vendeuil-Caply. The music was at once fey and sad. Hearing it, feeling it, he was transported. Nothing could match the sound of the blues.

The waitress came with his whiskey. "You asleep, Mister?"

"No," Meister told her, shaken from his reverie. He got out his wallet and paid her. "Good times—here's to them."

The waitress smiled. "Good times," she repeated, then went to another table.

Meister took a sip of his drink. Of late he had done a lot of dreaming. If he willed it, a beautiful woman would suddenly appear in the darkness....

He blinked. The dream was suddenly reality. Tandy Crain was pushing through the crowd toward the dance floor.

Instinctively, Meister started to get up. He sat down again immediately, realizing that she was following a partner. The man was tall, lean, darkly handsome and moved with the grace of a professional dancer. As he reached the dance floor, he took Tandy's hand and whirled her around, lifting her, making her scream with laughter. The other dancers had to move aside to make room for them.

Meister stared in disbelief. Tandy was dressed in typical flapper fashion. Her dress was so scanty it could have been packed into her handbag. As her partner lifted her again, there was a flash of flesh-colored stockings, rolled below the knee.

"Goddamn," Meister muttered. He got up and moved closer to the dance floor, thinking that he must be mistaken, that it couldn't be her. But the closer range confirmed it. The girl was indeed Tandy and she was every inch the flapper, her eyelids beaded and her cheeks and lips piquantly rouged. She was also drunk.

Meister returned to his table in confusion. The Tandy he knew, the only Tandy he had ever seen, was a demure young woman, elegant, regal. This painted, drunken, wildly laughing flapper being whirled around the Apollo Club's dance floor was someone else entirely. This was not the glowing creature he had fallen helplessly in love with. This was a brazen hussy and he wasn't at all sure how he felt about her.

"Goddamn," he muttered. He thought about just getting up and leaving but couldn't make up his mind. He was shocked. The transformation was so radical, as if she were two different people. Was it possible she led some sort of double life?

The waitress came to collect his glass. "You want another?"

"Yes." Meister had made up his mind to stay, to find out about her one way or the other. If she was just a high-spirited girl, kicking up her heels in one night on the town, fine. If there was more to it than that....

Meister got out his cigarettes. He didn't want to put words to the other possibility. Already he could feel the hurt starting, the anger and the jealousy.

Tandy's tall, handsome partner, his hair slicked down like some dance hall Valentino, had the look of a gigolo. He was a man who would want payment—one way or the other.

Meister sat smoking and watching. He'd stay, and he'd find out.

The Apollo was closing. The lights had gone down. McKinney's Cotton Pickers were putting away their instruments. Only a dozen patrons, most of them drunk, remained in the club.

Meister, cold-sober, sat in the shadows, finishing a whiskey that he'd nursed for hours. The waitress had given up on him long ago. He'd drunk his cover and that was obviously all he wanted.

On the other side of the dance floor, Tandy, her partner and another couple were loudly discussing where they should go next. The two girls wanted to go to an after hours spot where there would still be dancing. The men were in favor of eating.

Meister wasn't sure if the four had come together. He had the impression that they might have, were forced to sit separately because of the crowd and joined up when a table for four became available.

Anyway, they all knew one another. The other girl's name was Sylvia. Her boyfriend's name was Phil. Meister hadn't been able to catch the name of Tandy's partner. Like Meister, he had remained sober, somewhat aloof from the party.

Suddenly, the discussion became an argument. Tandy's escort grabbed her by the wrist, pulling her roughly to her feet.

"You'll do as I say," he told her.

Tandy tried to twist away. "You're hurting me!" she cried.

"Then do as you're told."

"No!" she maintained. "I'm not going!"

"Bitch," he said. With a swift, practiced movement he struck her in the face with the back of his hand, then pushed her down into her chair. His dark eyes flashed with contempt. "I should have known, another prissy little bitch."

Meister didn't react until the blow was struck. The argument had flared so suddenly, the violence coming so unexpectedly, he'd been caught unawares. Now he was on his feet, scrambling across the saloon, knocking over chairs in his blind rush.

Someone shouted a warning. "Nick! Look out!"

Meister swung at Tandy's abuser just as he was turning, catching him high on the left temple, a glancing blow that only staggered him. He backed into a table but managed to stay on his feet.

"What the—" He felt his head. He seemed more surprised than angry. He turned to look at Tandy. "Do you know this idiot?"

She was holding her cheek, fighting back tears, her body shaking. She couldn't have answered him if she'd tried.

"It doesn't matter," Meister said. "I'm still going to kick your ass. General principles." He pulled off his coat and threw it aside. "You want to slap somebody around? Then try me, Valentino."

"The name is Nick," the man said. From nowhere a switch-blade appeared in his hand, clicking open as he lunged.

Meister dodged, but not quickly enough. The knife ripped into his shirt and along the side of his chest.

Lucky, Meister thought, churning out of range. If he hadn't dodged, he'd have been severely hurt, might even have caught the knife in his chest up to the hilt. He jerked a tablecloth off a table, twisting it around his left arm. He raised that as a shield.

Tandy screamed. There was a scramble to make room. Behind him Meister could hear the remaining people yelling. Furniture was tipped over and glasses smashed as they hit the floor.

Nick lunged again.

Meister was ready this time. He took the knife in the bundled tablecloth, twisting just at the moment it hit, catching the blade in several layers. At the same time he kicked out viciously, catching his assailant in the pit of the stomach.

Nick doubled up, dropping the knife, gasping for breath.

Meister rushed forward, grabbing him by the hair, lifting his head and holding it like a punching bag. His huge right fist cocked and then exploded into the contorted face. Nick fell back like a stone, blood spurting. He was unconscious before he hit the floor.

Meister turned, looking for Tandy. There was another screamed warning. Too late, he saw a chair coming at him. The hard edge of the chair seat caught him behind the left ear, sending a sharp, searing poker stabbing into his head. He reeled away, the pain unbearable, and then, mercifully, he felt nothing.

The light was faint. He walked toward it, conscious of being in a round, damp tunnel, the walls wet and smelling of soap. Suddenly there was a roar behind him, a rushing flood. Before he could move he was caught up in it, carried away. He was going to drown. His nose, throat and lungs filled with soapy water, choking him.

Pop! He was in a bubble, floating out over a forest. The tops of the trees were very sharp. The bubble floated down toward them, hitting one, then another. He sat transfixed. Surely the bubble would break?

Pop!

Meister woke up, fully conscious, aware of who he was, where he was and who he was with. He was on a bed in a hotel room and the black face peering anxiously into his own belonged to Pop Fagan.

"Hello," Meister said, smiling weakly. He raised a hand, touched the back of his ear, which was throbbing painfully. "What did you give me?"

"Morphine," Pop Fagan said, relief showing in his wide, unblinking eyes. "You want another shot?"

"No," Meister told him. "Once is enough. You're not going to believe this, but I just arrived here in a bubble pipe."

Pop Fagan shook his head. "You arrived here yesterday, and you're sure lucky you arrived in one piece. If you didn't have a skull like a rock, there'd be two parts to it now, the left and the right." He finally managed a dazzling white smile. "Oh, boy!"

Meister felt behind his ear again. He wasn't so sure about Pop Fagan's findings. He seemed to have several heads and they all hurt. His side was taped, he noticed, and felt as if the knife was stuck in it. "What about Tandy?"

"The lady you saved?"

"Did I?"

"She's okay. From what I hear, she didn't like being arrested none, but all she got was a warning. Her first time, apparently."

"Arrested?"

"You got the whole damn club arrested." Pop Fagan laughed, slapping his knee. "You and Nick? That was just the start! Pretty soon everybody who was in there was punching, a four-alarm brawl going, tearing the place apart, so we had to call the cops. Talk about a mess! We ain't even opening again until tomorrow."

Meister looked at him silently, his eyes asking the obvious question.

"How'd you get here? Oh, me and the Cotton Pickers, we just hauled your ass out of there. Wouldn't want you to have a police record, not with all your other sins."

Meister smiled. "Thanks."

"You're welcome. Now, you want something to eat?"

"To drink, maybe."

"Coming up."

Pop Fagan got a bottle of whiskey and filled a couple of tumblers. He came and sat on the side of the bed, passing a glass to Meister, keeping the other for himself. He raised his glass in a toast. "To the ladies."

"The ladies," said Meister.

By the time they had finished their drinks, Pop Fagan had given a full account of the Meister-launched riot that had dismantled the Apollo Club. Luckily, the management, busy with other problems, hadn't noticed the Cotton Pickers spirit him away. From all indications he was in the clear. He'd just better not go back to the club, that's all. And it also might be a good idea to stay away from Nick.

Meister didn't argue.

"Who was the lady?" Pop Fagan asked then.

"You mean, you don't know?"

Pop shook his head.

"Tandy Crain," Meister told him. "John's sister." Pop's face clouded. "You chasing her?"

"No." Meister was puzzled by Pop's worried look. "I just happened to be there." He sat up slowly, his side aching, his head throbbing. "Hell, I was looking for you, what do you think?"

Pop didn't answer. Meister heard a little warning bell go off somewhere in his throbbing head. Obviously, Pop didn't approve of him and Tandy. "What are you trying to tell me?"

There was still no answer.

"Okay," Meister said. "I want to hear it. What's wrong with her?"

"Ain't nothing wrong with that girl," Pop Fagan said finally. "Oh, she likes to kick up her heels, all right, and sometimes she drinks a bit too much, but I don't know nothing wrong about her." He paused, considering. "She's a right pretty girl. I seen her in a couple, three clubs, and that's the worst she gets, high-spirited." There was another pause. "A right pretty girl."

"Then—what?"

Pop took the empty glasses back to the dresser.

"Oh, I get it," Meister said. The truth struck him like a slap in the face. "There's something wrong with me."

Pop looked at him in the dresser mirror. "I didn't say that."

"Sure," Meister said. He swung off the bed, reaching for his coat as he did. He pulled the coat on, standing unsteadily.

"What I said…" Pop Fagan began, his sad face glistening. "What I think…" He shook his head, pushing the bottle away. "What I think is, it ain't gonna pay you, calling at Washington Square, Mr. Greg Meister. All you're gonna find is a lot of heartache there."

"It was nice seeing you again, Pop," Meister said, heading for the door. "Thanks for the drink."

He was blocks away, walking blindly, not caring where he was headed, when he remembered that he hadn't asked Pop about Hal Rosen.

CHAPTER 9

Tandy Crain had expected it to happen earlier, but it wasn't until two weeks later, a Sunday afternoon in October, that Greg Meister came calling at 14 Washington Square.

"Miss Tandy, there's a gentleman downstairs," Sadie Fagan announced breathlessly. "It's Mister Greg—Greg Meister!"

Tandy tried to appear calm. "Did you tell him that John was away?"

"He don't want to see your brother," Sadie said. "He wants to see *you*!"

"Oh, he just wants to ask about John, that's all," Tandy told her. "Father can handle it, or ask my mother."

"Miss Tandy," Sadie said, exasperated. "I know when a gentleman comes calling. Greg Meister is sitting downstairs with a box of chocolates and a fistful of posies, and he sure didn't bring 'em for your father!"

"Both?" Tandy laughed. She couldn't remember when anyone had brought her candy *and* flowers. Such niceties had been forgotten in the current rush for equality. Normally her gentlemen callers brought only gin, discreetly tucked away in a hip flask.

"What'll I tell him?" Sadie asked. She was so excited that she couldn't stand still.

"To wait."

"For what?"

"For me, of course, silly," Tandy answered. She had teased the girl enough. "Tell him I'll be down shortly, and ask him to wait."

Sadie's eyes widened. "You're going to see him?"

"I certainly am."

"Yes, ma'am!" Sadie exclaimed, almost saluting. She took a deep breath for the run back downstairs and was gone. The door closed on the rest of what she had to say. "If that ain't something!"

Tandy Crain sank into a chair. Well, she thought, suddenly apprehensive, now you've done it. You've got to see him—and then what?

Greg Meister was an enigma to her. He was unlike any man she had ever met before. The first time he had come to the house she was still a child, still at Barnard, and he was a soldier and supposedly worldly wise, but it was obvious that he had been smitten. She knew the signs well enough. She had seen them in a hundred others before him. He was unable to take his eyes off her and barely able to carry on a conversation. Like an overgrown puppy, all he could do was wag his tail and drool.

Which was to be expected of a boy, but a *man*? A man and a soldier, someone who'd been to the war and Paris, someone who chummed around with her brother John in Harlem, consorting with easy women, how could someone like that be such a hopeless case?

If he was interested in her, why hadn't he written? She had a whole trunkful of letters from other admirers. If he was serious, why did he wait years to come back?

Why didn't he say something?

When John had invited him home about a job recommendation, she had purposely presented herself at the library door, letting him know that she was going out, thinking that he'd have sense enough to catch up with her so they could talk in private.

Instead, he'd stood on the corner in plain sight of the house and anybody watching, gawking like a fool. And then he had rushed away, swinging aboard a tram before she could get his attention.

Then, nothing. No call, no word of interest expressed through John. Nothing until.... Tandy shivered, remembering. She had come upon him at night in the square. It was so dark she hadn't recognized him until the last moment, hadn't realized it was him until she had already passed by, and by then she had been too frightened to stop, more afraid of him than a stranger.

He had been waiting for her, obviously. Why else would he have been there? Yet, he hadn't spoken. He had just stared at her like he was dreaming.

She had kept on walking. If he wanted to talk to her, surely he would call out, say hello. But he had made no attempt to stop her. When she reached the house and turned back to look, he was gone, swallowed up in the night.

She had seen him several times after that. Coming home she could spot him from a distance, waiting. Stalking her, she thought. It wasn't natural; it wasn't a normal thing to do, and she went out of her way to avoid him.

She hadn't told John—he was acting just as strangely lately—and she hadn't told her parents. She knew her father, he would call the police. Anyway, it was summer, time to go to Wicklow, and she had gone there and forgotten about Greg Meister, pursued by other men whose intentions were quite clear. If they liked her, they said so. If they wanted something, they asked. Sometimes they demanded and wouldn't take no for an answer. She had been in her share of wrestling matches.

Still, they were *normal.* Greg Meister, hovering in the darkness like a moth waiting for her light, wasn't normal. Greg Meister was a bug. That's how she had come to think of him: Greg Meister, the Bug.

And then?

Tandy smiled, amused both by recollection of the incident and her own sudden, complete reversal of opinion. Greg Meister's appearance at the Apollo Club had had all the elements of a bad movie. The heroine in trouble, assaulted by a sinister villain and then, suddenly, out of nowhere, comes the hero!

God, it was ridiculous, she thought. Yet at the same time it was marvelous, fabulous, wonderful! No one had ever rushed to her defense before with such reckless abandon. In the circles she traveled in, it was normal to try to settle disagreements with discussion. If the arguments got as far as fisticuffs, coats were removed first and a proper arena selected. It was normal to step outside and it was normal to desist after inflicting a reasonable degree of punishment. It was normal to shake hands afterward.

But Greg Meister? Well, he wasn't normal, was he? A man of few words, and when he finally got around to doing something, watch out!

She shivered. The violence within him frightened her—and fascinated her. She didn't fully understand, thinking only that within the worldly man there must also be an innocent boy. The man had experienced many things. He had gone to war and he had fought bravely. He had slain the enemy and he had saved a comrade's life. The boy within had never truly experienced an overwhelming love.

Not, Tandy Crain thought, until now. The boy within the man, the boy who couldn't speak because he was so smitten, that boy was waiting downstairs with candy and flowers, and she had to go to him.

He wouldn't be her first love, but she wouldn't let him know that. He was unfathomable. He was special. She would keep him that way.

Greg Meister sat waiting in the hall. Pop Fagan had suggested that he wasn't good enough for the Crains of Washington Square. Now, a thousand agonies later, he was here to find out if Pop was right.

In his left hand was a box of Laura Secord chocolates. In his right was a bouquet of sunflowers. In his mind . . . a shambles. He had no idea where he had found the courage to knock on the door, nor the will, once admitted, not to run away. He had no idea of what he was going to say to her.

So far, he had not spoken, not even to Sadie. Seeing him, Sadie had understood immediately, had said, "I'll—uh—tell her," and had returned after an eternity to say, "You're supposed to wait."

Meister had been unable to convince himself that this was positive news, that he was waiting for Tandy and not a firing squad being hastily assembled by Nelson Crain. Sadie's behavior would not permit it. Every few minutes she would check on him from a distance, and her expression indicated surprise at finding him still alive.

For some reason the house had grown quieter, each sound, when it came, magnified beyond reason. A door closed somewhere—a shot. Heels on marble—the guillotine's drum.

Neither Nelson nor Sandra Crain had appeared. Tandy wouldn't, or couldn't, come. At best, Meister thought, they were all gathered in emergency session, conferring on how best to politely send him away. If he could have moved, he would have left, saving them the trouble.

More footsteps. Anxiously, he looked up. Tandy Crain stood on the stairs, the child-woman he had fallen in love with so long ago, radiant in her haunting beauty. Her blue-green eyes met his and he saw immediately, cursing himself for a fool, that the past six months of torture had been wasted.

He should have brought his gifts that first day.

"Hello," he said, standing. His big hands held out the chocolates and sunflowers. "I brought you these."

She came to him, her eyes dancing with pleasure. "Thank you."

"Well ..." he began, and stopped. He didn't know what else to say. Surely she knew his heart was pounding madly?

Tandy smelled her sunflowers. You, she was thinking, are certainly a man of few words, Greg Meister.

Sandra Crain found her husband in his study. Even on a Sunday, Nelson Crain was busy with his account books, totaling a wealth that now, almost without bidding, multiplied every day.

He smiled in greeting, pleased not only with his accounts, but with the way he had devised to get money—new, untraceable money—to fix the deal for the oil reserves at Teapot Dome.

Harry Sinclair had asked for a few hundred thousand dollars. Nelson Crain had worked out a plan that would provide millions. That, even in Harry Sinclair's league, was impressive overage.

The scheme was simple enough. It required the incorporation of the Continental Trading Company, Ltd., a new firm based in Canada, safe from any unduly inquisitive regulatory bodies in New York or Washington.

Continental Trading was going to act as middleman in an extremely large oil purchase, the B in A, B, C, and nothing was more simple than A, B, C.

"A" knew where it could buy oil for $1.50 a barrel. It wasn't going to buy it, however. Instead it was going to let "B" buy it. Then "A," acting on behalf of "C," was going to buy the oil from "B," paying $1.75 a barrel. The difference, twenty-five cents a barrel, was going to be pocketed by "A," unbeknownst to "C."

Those quarters were going to add up. Over the course of time they should amount to more than $8,000,000.

Sandra Crain did not bestow her customary kiss on her husband. "Greg Meister is downstairs," she said.

Nelson Crain didn't understand. "Meister?"

"John's friend. The boy from Nebraska? The one you recommended to Jack Morgan."

Oh, *him*, Nelson Crain thought, remembering now. Months had passed, and Meister's presence hadn't intruded again, except for a polite thank you note. His fears unrealized, Crain had dismissed him from his mind. "To see John?"

"No."

"Me?"

"No, he's called on Tandy."

"Goddamn." Nelson Crain normally didn't swear in front of his wife. He pushed back from his desk, determined to get done with it immediately. He'd send the brash farm boy away. Kick his ass if necessary.

Sandra Crain put her hand on his arm. "I wouldn't do that, Nelson."

"Why not?" he demanded. They had discussed Tandy's future at length. If they hadn't agreed on who she should marry, they had at least decided on who she shouldn't, certainly not a country bumpkin.

"You know what she's like."

Headstrong, Nelson Crain was thinking, and he felt like swearing again. But he could never bring himself to openly criticize his daughter. Tandy, unbelievably beautiful, a rare creature he could hardly believe was his daughter, occupied a very special place in his plans to build a new dynasty. She was to be the linchpin that held it all together. It was required, it was absolutely necessary, that she marry well. Exceedingly well.

"If you send him away and forbid them to see each other, that could make it worse," Sandra Crain counseled, her hand still on her husband's arm.

"No!" he exclaimed. "I want this thing nipped in the bud, before it gets started."

"It *has* started. You're a man and you've only seen *him* looking at *her*, Nelson. I've seen this differently, through Tandy's eyes. She *is* interested. She always has been."

Nelson Crain stared at her. He couldn't believe she was counseling patience. If they waited it out, hoped for the best, anything might happen. Whatever had started must be undone. It had to be destroyed—*now.* "What are you suggesting?"

"That there are other ways," Sandra Crain said, her voice betraying what she meant.

Nelson Crain looked into his wife's eyes. They were cold, as they so often were lately, ever since John, fearful for his life, had fled New York. Her son's plight weighed heavily on her. There was always the fear, a fear Nelson Crain shared, that one day the phone would ring with news of his death.

John was in Chicago, cut off from them completely and mixed up in something unsavory, no doubt. The few letters they had received contained just the barest details of what sounded like a depressing, hollow existence. There was never any return address, just the postmark. He had never once telephoned since he had gone away. They had, in a way, already accepted his loss, resigned themselves to it. Now all their hopes rested with Tandy. She had become an obsession with both of them. This last child, this last chance, they mustn't lose her—or it.

"Very well," Nelson Crain said. "Nothing said to Tandy. But Mr. Meister? He'll hear from me."

CHAPTER 10

Greg Meister went to work that Monday morning trailing clouds of glory in his wake. He was Julius Caesar, triumphant, returning to Rome. He was Napoleon at Austerlitz. He was Alexander the Great.

The brief hour he had spent with Tandy Crain had transported him to Valhalla. He was certain he would stay there forever and that she would someday sit by his side.

Beautiful, wonderful, radiant Tandy! She hadn't sent him away. Quite the opposite, she had welcomed him warmly. It was as if she had known he was coming and been impatient for his arrival. Best of all, she *liked* him!

Meister was certain of that. He had seen it in her eyes, heard it in her laughter, felt it in her touch.

"May I see you again?" he had asked tremulously.

"Yes," she had answered. "I would like that, Greg Meister. I would like that very much."

They had agreed to meet again Thursday night. If he could get tickets, they were going to a play, to see Helen Hayes in *Golden Days.*

Golden days, Meister thought, rejoicing. They were all going to be golden from now on, filled with sunflowers.

He was whistling as he joined the other messengers on the long wooden bench in the dispatch room in the basement of J.P. Morgan & Company.

Fisher, a pockmarked gnome perched behind a high counter, had already started assigning the morning's runs, playing favorites as always. The ass kissers got to go across the street to the Exchange. The nose thumbers got to go across town.

Meister fell into the broad middle category. He did what was required of him, never asking for the easy jobs nor volunteering for the hard ones. Now, however, that was going to change. Now, because it was important to him, he was going to try to be a little more helpful to Fisher.

In a few weeks, he was going to apply for a transfer, for a job upstairs as a teller, a position that had a future. To get it, even just to have a chance at it, he would need Fisher's recommendation.

"Battistoni!" Fisher bawled.

The little Italian, perpetually angry, glared at him, ready for battle.

Fisher swung a large cardboard box atop the counter. "You've drawn the Bronx."

"The Bronx!" Battistoni screamed, outraged.

Fisher checked the label. "That's right."

"Hey!" Battistoni looked around for support. "Last week, *twice* to Queens! *Three times* to Brooklyn!"

The other messengers just stared at him. This was ritual, part of the fabric of their lives.

"What's the matter with Garibaldi?" Battistoni demanded. "He's sick? I'll buy him medicine. He needs a map? I'll draw him one!"

"There's nothing wrong with Garibaldi," Fisher said. "Gorky? Where's Gorky? You get to wear handcuffs this morning. We're going to trust you with a run to the Chase."

Meister smiled. Trust? There were only two keys to the handcuffs attached to the steel box. Fisher had one of them and the other was kept at the Chase. If, during the journey, someone wanted to take that steel box, they'd have to cut off Gorky's wrist to get it.

"What's in it?" Battistoni was yelling, still quarreling about his assignment.

"Julius?" Fisher called, ignoring him. "Where's Julius? I need two for this next mission. How about Harmon? Julius and Harmon, the dray horses of the service, on the road again."

Meister's mind wandered. He was going to be a teller and, one day, he was going to be a bank manager. Hard work, night school, dedication, a bit of luck—hell, why not? He would put some money aside, a bit every payday, building a nest egg. When he saw the opportunity for a small investment... why not?

It was going to take time. It was going to take effort. But one day soon he was going to be somebody.

"Harris," Fisher was saying. "I want you back, boy. I want you back by noon." The door slammed on an empty echo chamber.

Meister looked around. He was alone on the bench. All the others had gone. Fisher was staring at him, the gnome eyes empty, distant. Meister frowned. He had never been left to the last before.

"You got a job for me?" he asked finally, his voice sounding strained.

Fisher shook his head. "No, you're fired, Meister."

"Fired?"

"That's right." Fisher pulled a brown envelope from his vest pocket and laid it on the counter. "Here's your pay."

Meister felt something twist inside him. He leaned back against the bench, suddenly drained of all his grand dreams, as empty as Fisher's blank expression. "Fired? What for?"

"I don't know."

"Oh, come on," Meister said dully, all the fight gone out of him. The envelope was on the counter. He was through, done. "What did I do wrong?"

"I wouldn't know about that," Fisher said. He shoved the envelope closer. "Come on, lad, take it and go, will you?"

Meister struggled to his feet, trying to make his mind work. What was Fisher saying, that it wasn't his idea? That the order had come from upstairs?

Fisher gave the envelope another shove. "It's a week's notice. You're lucky."

Lucky? Meister tried to laugh, but it wasn't in him. "Listen, tell me, where did this come from, huh? Whose idea?"

"I wouldn't know about that," Fisher said again. The envelope got a last nudge. "Good-bye, Meister."

The rest of the morning was like a bad dream. Everywhere he went, the door was shut to him, as if he were a leper. Lamont, the man who had hired him, who had sent him down to Fisher, refused to talk to him now. Word came out of his office via a secretary. There was nothing to discuss, she said.

Davison, Lamont's senior, the man Meister had gone to after talking to Jack Morgan, claimed not to remember him. That word was also delivered by a secretary. If a fired employee had a problem, it should be taken up at the proper level, she said. The proper level was Mr. Lamont.

The Morgan Library, last court of appeal, was an impregnable castle with the drawbridge up. Mr. J.P. Morgan did not see anyone without an appointment. That was a firm rule. No exceptions. How did one get an appointment? If one didn't know, one wasn't liable to get one.

Meister reeled away with that bit of wisdom. He had been fired, summarily dismissed, and the House of Morgan had no intention of telling him why.

Back at his room there was another envelope waiting for Meister. It was stuck to his door with a thumbtack and he knew what it was even before he tore it open. An eviction notice: *Mr. Meister, I am going to need your room for a cousin. Will you please arrange to leave by Saturday? Regretfully, Emma.*

Meister crumpled the note and went back downstairs, knocking loudly on his landlady's door, determined not to be brushed aside again. He had to rap several times, increasingly louder, before she appeared.

"Yes?" she said, peering at him fearfully from behind thick, owlish glasses. A liver-spotted hand clutched at the greasy blanket she wore as a robe.

Meister shoved the crumpled note at her. "What is this?" he demanded angrily.

She refused to take it. "What it says. You've got to go."

"Why me? I've been here longer than others. I wasn't the last to rent."

"Just go," she told him. The door slammed shut.

He knocked on it again. "Do you hear me? I demand to know why!"

"You're a bad man," was her muffled answer. "The police were here. They told me."

"Told you what?"

"You're a Bolshie!"

Bolshie? What kind of nonsense was that? "Don't be ridiculous. What police?"

"Go away! I don't want you in this house!"

"Emma!"

"Go away!"

His anger growing, Meister considered kicking the door in, and then he thought, no. If he hadn't been man enough to kick in J.P. Morgan's, he had to be gentleman enough to spare poor Emma Goldfarb's.

Still, it made his blood boil. First his job, lost for no reason, and now his room, the police onto him by mistake. What the hell was this, some goddamn conspiracy? The thought made him laugh. He didn't even know anybody who wanted to give him trouble, except for Nick, the guy he'd beat up at the Apollo, Tandy's escort.

Meister laughed again. That *was* funny. That bastard going to the House of Morgan, displaying his damages, demanding that Meister be let go? He wouldn't get past the front door—with or without his switchblade.

No, it wasn't Nick. If a complaint had led to his being fired, it had to have been made by someone influential, some important customer he had somehow offended. But who?

Meister shook his head and started back upstairs. Hell, he didn't even know anyone influential, except Nelson Crain, of course.

He stopped, frozen. Nelson Crain?

Jesus Christ, Meister thought. He sat down on the stairs, feeling the way he had when Fisher told him he was fired, suddenly drained and empty.

Nelson Crain?

No, he told himself. But he knew it was true, that it was Crain. Who else? Crain had gotten him the job with a phone call. He could take it away just as easily.

And the police? Private police, probably, Meister thought. If Nelson Crain wanted to tell him something, it all fit together. No job, no place to stay ... and coming up next, along with lunch money for the trip, a train ticket back to Nebraska?

"The bastard," Meister said softly, certain now that it was all Crain's doing. Heavy-handed, but subtle, too. Nothing said directly. No proof. Yet the message loud and clear: Good-bye.

Meister climbed the stairs to his room, thinking that he should have listened to Pop Fagan. The heartache had already begun. He had ventured where he didn't belong. He could hardly believe it. After all this time, finally he had gone to Tandy and, to his delight and surprise and joy, she had consented to see him. In the normal course his next step would have been to ask permission of Nelson Crain. He had planned to do that, had planned to follow all the formalities, as soon as he was certain of Tandy's feelings.

But now?

Meister shook his head. What was the use? He didn't like giving up without a fight, but with Nelson Crain dead set against him, what chance was there? Nelson Crain considered him so unacceptable as a suitor that he had declared it, even before the question was asked. He wouldn't allow it to be asked, wouldn't condescend to listen. He was so damn sure of his power that he just ran roughshod over everybody and everything in his way. That's how he had gotten to the top and that's how he stayed there. So damn sure!

Or was he?

Meister entered his room, closing the door and leaning against it. Might not just the opposite be true? he wondered. For the first time since he had been fired, he felt better, relieved. It always helped to know the enemy. If you knew the enemy, you knew his weakness. If you knew his weakness, you had a chance.

So what are you waiting for? Meister asked himself. He started packing, working quickly, eager to get it done and to get away. He was ready in ten minutes.

Then, leaving the lights on, yellow fragments stabbing through the holes in the blinds visible to any "Bolshevik hunters" who might be watching from the street below, he carried his bags downstairs and left the building by the rear entrance. He climbed over the back fence into the neighboring yard and exited on Ludlow Street.

Here, a block away, he was a passing stranger, of interest to no one. He hefted his bags, getting a firm grip on each, then set out at a swift, steady pace. There was no one to watch him go. Nobody followed him.

Two hours later Meister was in another world, Greenwich Village. He found a flophouse on Barrow Street, beds for a quarter a night, but it was clean enough. It also had lockers. He paid a week in advance and locked up his suitcases and went back out into the night.

It was eight o'clock now, the dinner hour past, and the sidewalks were crowded with people. Many of the shops and stores were still open. Peddlers of some sort were in every block. Gypsies, drunks, tie salesmen, cardsharps, chestnut venders, cats who ate from a spoon and told fortunes. The streets churned with life and absurdity.

Meister stopped to get his fortune told at the feline sideshow. There were three cats and three tins of cat food: fish, chicken and liver. For a nickel he was allowed to make a choice. He picked chicken.

The sideshow operator dipped a small silver spoon into the tin of chicken. He passed it in front of the waiting cats. Which preferred the chicken?

The black cat did, a drowsy, fixed tom. Lazily he got up, stepping onto a wooden pedal. From the box below a slip of paper emerged from a slot.

"Your fortune, sir," the sideshow operator said. He gave the cat the spoon. It held it between its paws, licking off the chicken.

Meister put the slip of paper unread into his pocket. He continued walking, looking for shops with "Help Wanted" signs. Two blocks down on King, just off Greenwich, he found exactly what he wanted. A used-book store. "Girl" the sign said, but he wasn't particular and he suspected that the owner wouldn't be, either.

He pushed in, a bell tinkling, announcing his arrival. "We're closed," a voice called.

Perfect, Meister thought. He went to the first shelf, selecting a dog-eared novel, *Castles Burning.* He took it back to the counter and waited.

The owner appeared a moment later. He was a short, heavy man, out of breath from putting on his coat, and he reminded Meister of Emma Goldfarb. He wore the same owlish glasses and had the same fearful look.

"You should stay open at night," Meister told him. "Look at them out there. You'd do more business now than during the day."

The man studied him, impatient, wary. "I can't," he said finally. "The wife's afraid at night. She doesn't like to be left alone."

"Then why are you looking for a girl?"

"Huh?"

"The job," Meister said. He turned to the novel's flyleaf, where the price was marked. Ten cents. He got two nickels out of his change purse, placed them on the counter. "You think a girl is going to work at night?"

"You think a man is going to work for what I can afford to pay?"

"I will," Meister said.

"You? A fellow your size? You should be pulling a wagon."

Meister shook his head. "War wound. I'm a veteran."

"Oh . . . ."

"It's all right. Better than pushing up poppies. What's the job pay?"

"Twenty cents." The man hesitated. "I don't know you."

"So? What can I steal?" Meister asked. "Take a chance, you can still have your girl if you want. I'll work the night shift." He looked around, peering into the shop's dark recesses, black holes where anybody could be waiting, ready to strangle him for an old copy of *True Story.* "We'll both take a chance."

"Twenty cents?"

Meister nodded. "I'm driven by desperation."

The man smiled. "A lousy chauffeur."

"You know that one too?" Meister said, smiling back. "I'll see you tomorrow. Six o'clock all right?" He paused at the door. "Oh, and once in a while I'll need a night off, okay? I've got a girl."

The man shrugged. He knew better than to quarrel with a bargain.

Meister went back to his flophouse. He had accomplished enough for one night. Tomorrow he'd look for a day job. He'd also pay a courtesy call on Nelson Crain, asking his permission to see Tandy. He'd call on the enemy, and he'd probe his weakness.

There had to be a reason why Nelson Crain had not simply taken him aside and quietly told him he wasn't an acceptable suitor. Meister had a hunch it was the same reason why Nelson Crain hadn't simply forbidden Tandy to see him.

If nothing else, Nelson Crain was a shrewd judge of character. He must have seen in Meister what he saw in his own daughter. However bewildered and hesitant he might appear on the surface, he, Greg Meister, was his own man, damn it. And Tandy Crain was her own woman.

There was no profit in openly opposing a courtship. If both he and Tandy wanted it, it would only stiffen their resolve, bring them together. That left Nelson Crain with two alternatives. One, ignore the romance, let it take its course, hope that nothing came of it. The other? Come from behind, smash it.

Nelson Crain had decided to come from behind. What he had done so far was just a warning. If it wasn't taken, then something else would happen, something even more severe. And if that hint wasn't taken....

It all depended, Meister felt. He had no way of knowing Nelson Crain's degree of opposition. If he simply didn't like the idea, he'd ease off soon enough, for there was no sense in forever alienating a possible son-in-law. But if he was firmly against the match and determined to stop it by any means, then there would never be any letup. Nelson Crain would be on a long, narrow road. There would be no detours, no turning back for him.

And neither would he, Meister thought. Nothing could ever change his mind about Tandy. All that had changed was his job and his address.

Just before he closed his eyes that night, giving way to sleep, he pulled the slip of paper from his pocket, reading his fortune: *A compromise with your ideals will bring you lasting happiness.*

Meister sighed. He never got one that fit the occasion.

CHAPTER 11

By November they were in love, wildly, hopelessly in love. Greg Meister always had been. Tandy Crain had drifted into it gently.

Valhalla was a shared residence now. They sat there side by side, staring into each other's eyes, holding hands, laughing at nothing, whispering nonsense. It was glorious and, thus far, uncomplicated. They lived for their moments together. Nothing was said of the future. Only the present mattered. The future, however bright and shining, could never match the brilliance of now. They both knew that, rejoiced in it.

Meister, who thought he had been in love before, who had once used that word to describe his feelings for Kathy Jenkins, realized now that the relationship had been nothing more than a childhood crush. It had been without substance and passion. It had been children at play.

What he felt for Tandy, what happened to him at the thought, sight and touch of her, engulfed not only his heart but his soul. She possessed him, she meant everything, she *was* everything. He was certain he would die without her.

Tandy, who had been quite certain she'd been in love before, who could name half a dozen men who'd swept her heart away, saw now that all that had been a farce, wishful thinking. She had been eager for awakening, to become truly and fully a woman, and not knowing any better, had accepted what was false. Even her first incredible love, even that had been false.

What was true was how she felt now about Greg Meister. The boy-man she had once given up as a hopeless case, the befuddled moth she had christened the Bug, the enigma of shy bookworm and antic hero—all had combined into the perfect, the only man for her.

Every man she had known before was nothing beside Greg Meister. Heirs to vast fortunes, scions of grand families, dashing young executives—even the first man to possess her—none was a match for Greg Meister's candle.

He was real. In him a special flame burned. It might flutter at the sight of her, it might gutter in the winds of adversity, but it never, ever went out. It was what showed him the way and it would burn eternally. It was his strength.

When that strength took hold of her, when Greg Meister held her in his arms, Tandy Crain felt that at last she was a woman, a real woman, truly in love. All she wanted or needed was to be his and his alone.

Without him life would be empty and meaningless, she was sure. With him it was a paradise she had never suspected. He was her all. If he ever left her, she would cease to exist.

Nelson and Sandra Crain viewed the growing relationship with increasing alarm. In all ways but one—his background and its lack of wealth—Greg Meister could not be faulted.

Since coming to New York, he had gained a confidence that had not been apparent before. He was earnest, polite, intelligent, even witty at times. He was neatly groomed, well dressed, hard working, ambitious. He claimed to be holding two jobs; he studied at night and he was saving his money. He adored their daughter and would do anything in his power for her.

All in all, the young man was near perfect... for someone else. For a shopgirl in the Bronx? The find of the century. For a waitress in Brooklyn? The universe on a platter. For Tandy Crain? Unspeakable disaster.

Sandra Crain was at a loss. The whole thing, she felt, was her fault. She had counseled her husband not to openly oppose the relationship. She had given this advice with the best of intentions, drawn from her well of experience. Her parents had opposed her marriage to Nelson Crain. They had been aghast. They had fought the relationship from the start, had done all in their power to stop it and had, in fact, probably brought it about.

Even now, thirty years later and with no regrets, Sandra Crain could look back and see how her parents, through their unreasoning opposition, had sealed the marriage. They made it inevitable by denying her their own love and understanding. They left her no place to go but into his arms.

Sandra Crain had not wanted to see that mistake repeated with Tandy. The girl was headstrong, given to moods, caprices. It was best to let her have her way. Deny her and she would have it just the same, her will was that firm. Of age, she refused direction, following her own course. One could only post signs along the way and hope. To try and bar a path was almost to ensure that it would be taken.

So far this loose reins approach, although worrisome and haphazard, had proved effective. Besides being headstrong, Tandy was intelligent enough to know when she was getting into deep water. Several seemingly serious romances with not-quite-right suitors had been concluded before any damage was done and without need of intervention. Her occasional late nights on the town, from which she returned smelling of gin, were nothing unusual. It was how the modern set kicked up its heels, the new decade's version of spin the bottle. Harmless enough for a girl with her head on straight.

But this business with Greg Meister?

Sandra Crain shuddered at the thought of what was upon them. It had happened so fast, it had been like lightning—explosive. Tandy and Greg Meister were in love and the romance *had* to be broken up. But ... how?

It was too late to say that they opposed it. She argued this with her husband almost nightly. If it had been dangerous to fault the match at first, it would be fatal now, knowing Tandy's feelings. There had to be some other way. But what?

Nelson Crain was furious. It had been a mistake, a stupid, ill-advised, dangerous mistake, not to have come down like a ton of bricks right at the beginning. He should have gone downstairs and kicked Greg Meister's ass across the square. He should have forbidden Tandy to ever see him again and put her on the next liner sailing for Europe.

Other ways? His wife wanted other ways? Don't get Tandy on her high horse and quietly put the skids under Meister? Ha! Greg Meister didn't respond to other ways. Beneath that bewildered exterior was a cool, calculating, brash son of a bitch. Nelson Crain still hadn't recovered from Meister's call at the house the day after he had been fired from J.P. Morgan & Company. Luck, Meister had called it, staring him right in the eye, and the loss of his room had been a happy coincidence. His new job was just a short walk from his new address. "The real reason I called, sir, is I would like your permission to see Tandy."

See her? God in heaven, the moment that man laid his eyes on her, I should have plucked them out, Nelson Crain thought. He hadn't given his permission. Flustered by Meister's sudden arrival, he had replied that he would first like to discuss it with his wife and daughter. He had discussed it with his wife, and another joint decision, another stupid, ill-advised one, had been reached.

Say nothing. Give no answer. In the meantime, as quickly as possible, find some other way.

Nelson Crain laughed bitterly as he thought about it. Some other way? Greg Meister had been seeing Tandy for a month. He called at the house constantly. Twice a week, sometimes three times. The silent treatment bothered him not a bit. He was practically a part of the goddamn family, and yet the best private detective in New York still didn't know where he worked or lived.

Tonight was going to be special. Greg Meister prepared for it as carefully as Mark Antony must have readied himself for Cleopatra. He spent the whole afternoon in careful, fastidious preparation. He had his hair cut and, for the first time in his life, his nails manicured. He had his suit pressed instead of doing it himself. He bought a new shirt to make sure it would be clean enough. He bathed for an hour and he shaved twice.

He whistled and hummed as he went about his tasks, happy with himself, happy with life, happy with everybody. Finally everything was going right, he thought. Everything he put his hand to was ripe for harvest.

Ernst Frankel's Used-Book Store, the black hole he had retreated to when fired from the House of Morgan, had turned out to be a cornucopia overflowing with all his needs. It provided far more than a part-time job. It was home, place of business, social center, school and hide-out. This transformation, termed by Frankel as an evolution, had taken place with the dizzying speed of a runaway mule.

There was a large, unused room in the back of the shop. Meister made a deal with Frankel. Nominal rent, taken out of his pay. He turned it into bright, comfortable living quarters. He had his own bathtub, jerry-rigged to a laundry drain, and he shared the toilet next door not with a mob, but with Frankel and the newly hired girl, Sara Brown.

The shop itself was a hangout for writers and students who needed all kinds of help: research, tutoring, typing, editing, copying. Meister bought a secondhand typewriter, a handful of pencils, a couple of reams of paper and he was in business, working with what he loved best. Books.

He found his social life in the writers, students and fellow book lovers who frequented the shop. Unlike the messengers at

J.P. Morgan & Company, here were people he could relate to, talk to, enjoy. Here were his own kind.

In the evenings, when Ernst Frankel and Sara were gone and it was his turn to be clerk, the shop became his school. He'd sit at the counter and study far into the night, pouring through manuals on business administration, office procedures, accounting, billing, banking, warehousing, shipping, and all the other myriad aspects of the world of commerce. The subject had held no interest for him in college. Now he soaked it up like a sponge. Bank manager? No, the goal was larger now and more readily attainable. He would be entrepreneur.

The used-book store was one of untold hundreds in the teeming city. For Meister it also served as a hiding place from anyone who might wish him harm. Calling at 14 Washington Square, he always arrived from a different direction. If he thought he was being followed, and sometimes he was certain of it, he took a convoluted combination of trolley, elevated and subway, going far out of his way to the lower East Side, dodging through back streets and alleys, twisting and turning until not even a bloodhound would know his path. No one had ever followed him all the way.

Meister was sure of that, just as he was sure of his love for Tandy and, on this special night, of her love for him. He had seen it grow. Like a blossom it had opened, ready to take him in.

Tonight....

"A surprise?"

"Yes."

"When can I see it?"

"Close your eyes."

Delightedly, Tandy closed her eyes, giving her hand to Meister, letting him lead her outside.

"Now?"

"Yes."

Tandy opened her eyes. Parked in front of 14 Washington Square was a badly dented Chevrolet Royal Mail roadster, a wooden box attached to its rear deck. In 1914, when it was brand new, it had sold for seven hundred fifty dollars. Now, if one was lucky, it might bring one hundred dollars.

Actually, Meister, in partnership with Ernst Frankel, had contracted to pay one hundred fifty dollars. He knew something about motors, and the four-cylinder, twenty-four horsepower valve-in-head engine ran like a top. Also, the isolated gas tank had been moved from the rear deck and replaced with a serviceable box. This made it a dual-purpose runabout, not just some ordinary car.

"That's—that's it?" Tandy said. She was too stunned to say anything more. What she saw was a hopeless rattletrap. "That's yours?"

"Mine," Meister confirmed, mistaking her reaction for amazed approval. Being amazed himself, he saw no reason why others shouldn't be. "Well, not yet," he added quickly. "I'm buying it on installment, so much a month, and it's only partly mine really. The man I work for, we're partners in it. He pays half."

"Partners?"

"Yes, it's the perfect arrangement. I've got transportation and he's got something for hauling."

Hauling, Tandy thought, and she burst into laughter. She suddenly had an image of the Royal Mail piled high with junk or, better still, horse manure.

"What's so funny?"

"You," Tandy said, quickly controlling herself at the sight of his hurt, bewildered look. She grabbed his arm. "Sometimes you get so serious. It's only a car, Greg. The way you brought me out here, I thought I was going to meet your parents or something."

Meister flushed.

"Oh, now, look what I've done," Tandy said, shaking her head. They had never discussed anything like that. Actually, he hadn't even asked her to go steady, let alone spoken about getting engaged.

Meister stared at her helplessly.

"Well," Tandy said finally. "Now you've got a car." She groped desperately for the right thing to say next. "Are we just going to stand here and admire it, or are you going to give me a ride?"

Meister nodded soberly, still unable to speak.

"I'll get my coat," Tandy said. "You get it started." She took another look at Meister's new pride and joy. If she was lucky, it wouldn't go.

"Right!" Meister replied, finally coming alive.

Tandy went back inside the house, selecting a warm wool coat, matching hat, scarf, gloves and fur-lined boots. Though it was early November, the weather had taken a definite turn toward winter and she was certain that the little roadster would be drafty as a barn.

The truth was, she didn't like cars, or at least she didn't like going out in them with men. She had suffered several miserable experiences in what some of her escorts considered bedrooms-on-wheels. Public transit was safer. No one was going to wrestle your clothes off on the trolley. If you had to drive somewhere, a taxi was just fine, thank you. The driver served as chaperone.

"Are you going out?"

Tandy looked up at her mother, who had suddenly appeared and stood looking down at her as she struggled to put her boots on. "Yes."

"Who with?"

"Greg," Tandy said, finally getting the second reluctant boot on. She stood up. "We won't be late. It's just for a ride."

"Greg," Sandra Crain repeated, and Tandy thought she detected a coolness. "You're seeing a lot of him, aren't you?"

"Yes," Tandy said. She was certain now. So far her mother had been neutral on the subject of Greg Meister, as if she was giving him a chance before making any judgment. That was all Greg needed, a chance. She had appreciated her neutrality. Or was it actually a truce?

"All right," her mother said. "But I'd like you home early. I think it's time—" She stopped, seemed to change her mind, offered her cheek for a kiss. "Good night."

Tandy kissed her and ran out of the door. Time for what? Hopefully not to start a war over Greg. That would spoil everything. It was perfect now. She loved Greg and Greg loved her and everything was perfect. Even the silly little roadster was perfect.

Tandy went to it joyously, suddenly realizing that she could enter this car without worry or fear. Greg Meister was the kindest, gentlest man she had ever known. He would never harm her.

The Royal Mail's test ride went on forever, taking them down Fifth Avenue to Central Park, across the Queensboro Bridge to Astoria and then, in a marvelous mix-up between driver and navigator, smack into St. Michael's Cemetery.

Meister was like a child who had discovered magic. Suddenly he had wings and could go anywhere. Tandy was like a mother watching her child make that discovery. Through him it became equally wondrous, exhilarating.

They were breathless with the adventure when at last they stopped.

"Like it?" Meister demanded, eyes shining.

"Love it!" Tandy told him.

"You know," Meister said, "when you opened your eyes, I thought you didn't like it."

"I didn't," Tandy said.

"You didn't?"

"No, I *hated* it."

"Liar!"

"No, honest," she said, "I thought it was the worst rattletrap I ever saw! I was embarrassed!"

"Liar!" Meister cried, helpless with mirth. "You loved it from the beginning. You thought it was the most wonderful—" He stopped, unable to speak, choked with laughter. She really must have hated it, he realized. A junk pile parked in front of 14 Washington Square. "Be honest. The most wonderful, the most fantastic magic carpet." He looked at her. "Well? Isn't it?"

Her eyes met his. "Yes . . . yes, it is."

There was a long moment of silence. Meister looked away. "The reason I bought this disaster—the reason I'm buying it, I should say—I wanted to take my girl for a ride. Back in Bellville, that's what they do, you know? There aren't any trolleys in Bellville." He paused, smiling. "You're lucky. Back in Bellville this would be a truck."

"Your girl?"

"Did I say that?" Meister asked, looking away again. "I meant to ask you first. Would you like to be?"

There was no answer.

Meister slowly turned to face her. Her eyes were shimmering, filled with tears. He thought she would never be more beautiful than she was at that moment, wanting to say yes so badly she couldn't speak.

"I'm glad," Meister said softly. "I love you, Tandy. I always have . . . from the first day."

Tandy's tears spilled over. "Will you . . . will you, please?"

He smiled at her. "What? Shut up?"

"Kiss me."

Meister took her into his arms. He had never kissed her before. Gently, tenderly, he put his lips to hers.

Tandy responded as if in a dream. It was, she thought, not only their first kiss, but also, in a way, her first. Everything that had happened to her before this moment meant nothing. *This* was the beginning—and it was also the end. There could never be anyone else.

They kissed, and there was no past, there was only now. Meister's arms pulled her closer, feeling her surrender to him and then demand that he take her. Their mouths, their bodies, their very souls became one.

There was no thought, no reason, no control. There was only the give-and-take of lovers. Meister eased her down on the seat, and all too soon they were joined. They moved together as one, each striving to give the other the greatest pleasure.

"Yes," she urged softly. "Please."

They pulled each other close, surrendering to wild, reckless lovemaking. And then they peaked together in timeless union. The heavens exploded and the universe reeled. The ecstasy was unbearable, and then two sweaty and exhausted beings looked at each other in breathless passion.

Tandy clutched at him desperately. "I love you, Greg Meister."

"And I love you, Tandy Crain."

CHAPTER 12

Nelson Crain was at a meeting in a suite at the Hotel Vanderbilt. His friend Harry Sinclair, head of the Sinclair Consolidated Oil Company, was presiding over the informal gathering. The others present were Harry M. Blackmer, of the Midwest Oil Company, James E. O'Neil, of the Prairie Oil Company, Colonel Robert W. Stewart, board chairman of Standard Oil Company of Indiana, and Colonel E.A. Humphreys, owner of the fabulously rich Mexia oil field.

Humphreys had just nodded his assent to the largest transaction ever proposed to him. He had agreed to sell 33,333,333 barrels of Mexia oil at $1.50 a barrel. It was a bargain price, yes, but it was also guaranteed to be paid whether the market went up or down, and that made it a good deal for him. In one fell swoop he assured himself of $50,000,000.

Now Humphreys looked at the circle of oil company executives who had called him to the Vanderbilt. "How do you want it split up?" he asked. "Who's to get what?"

"We thought we'd simplify it," Harry Sinclair told him. "One entity would buy it all, the Continental Trading Company."

Humphreys was puzzled. "Continental? I never heard of it."

"It was just incorporated," Harry Sinclair revealed. "For this purpose, as a matter of fact."

"I see," Humphreys said, wary now. "But I still don't know anything about it. Who guarantees the contract of sale?"

"I do," Sinclair told him.

"And I," O'Neil chimed in.

Humphreys stared into Harry Sinclair's bulging, froglike eyes. Sinclair was a legend in the oil business. He had started his career as a drugstore clerk, inheriting a small sum when his father, the drugstore's owner, died. He had used that small stake to invest in options in the new Kansas oil fields. He had bought his first oil well in 1905. By 1915, he had become one of the biggest operators in Kansas. Now, six years later, he was a mover and shaker, one of the richest oil men in the world.

"If your name's on it, Harry . . . ." Humphreys said.

Harry Sinclair smiled. "Then I guess we've got a deal."

Nelson Crain started breathing again. The deal—*his* deal, because he had devised it—involved $8,000,-000 under the table to be shared by Blackmer, O'Neil, Stewart and Sinclair.

Continental Trading had a ready market for the Mexia oil. Midwest Oil Company, Prairie Oil Company, the Standard Oil Company and the Sinclair Consolidated Oil Company were all ready to buy it at $1.75 a barrel. Blackmer, O'Neil, Stewart and Sinclair would see to that. After all, it was to their interest. Not to their stockholders, but to their own.

So simple, Nelson Crain thought, aware of Harry Sinclair's appreciative glance. Their own under-the-table partnership was also sealed. It was onward and upward now. Next stop, Teapot Dome. And after that . . . .

Nelson Crain stood up. One never knew. The way he felt, he was ready to take half the world.

A private detective was waiting downstairs in the hotel lobby. His name was Hanson and he looked like what he was, a professional bloodhound. He had sad, rheumy eyes, a huge nose with black nostrils and brown skin that hung in loose folds. "Rover," his colleagues called him. He didn't mind; he made more money than all of them.

Nelson Crain was annoyed to see him. There were more discreet places than the lobby of the Vanderbilt. He excused himself to Harry Sinclair, saying that he'd just be a minute, and went over to talk to Hanson.

"What the hell are you doing here?" he demanded.

Hanson's expression didn't change at the reprimand. He always looked the same—abused, downtrodden, sorrowful. "You said to let you know right away."

"Yes, yes," Nelson Crain admitted. Actually, the word he had used was "instantly." If Hanson ever got a line on Greg Meister, something that appeared increasingly doubtful with each passing day, Crain was to be informed of it instantly. "Well, what is it?"

"Finally, the kid made a mistake," Hanson said, the pleasure in his voice contradicting his sorrowful look.

Nelson Crain's pulse quickened. "What kind?"

"He bought a car," Hanson said. "A car can be followed." He passed over a folded slip of paper. "There's what you wanted. He lives where he works and he's been right under our noses all this time! A bookstore in Greenwich Village."

Nelson Crain's fist closed around the paper. "You're sure?"

"Positive."

"Thank you," Crain said, opening the note, glancing at the address. "I won't be needing your services any longer. Here's your final bill." He started away, then turned back, smiling for the first time. "Oh, and Hanson, there'll be a large bonus, very substantial." "Thank you."

"Not for your good work," Nelson Crain said. "For keeping your mouth shut. You don't know me and you never did this for me, you understand?"

"Of course."

"You'd better."

Harry Sinclair had been an interested distant observer of the brief exchange.

"What have you got going there?" he asked when Crain rejoined him. "Another deal?"

Nelson Crain nodded. "You could say that." But what was at stake, his dreams of a Crain dynasty, made what had just been concluded upstairs child's play.

Nelson Crain couldn't sleep that night. He paced the floor of his study, thinking of the long years of struggle that had brought him to his pedestal of wealth and power. Now, by one miscalculation, it could all come tumbling down.

It had come close to toppling once before. John, not Tandy, had been the catalyst then, John getting himself involved on the wrong side of a riot at the offices of the *New York Worker* when he went to the rescue of a wartime buddy, Hal Rosen. A disenchanted member of John's unit overseas, a surly private named Charles Corless, was also at the scene and tried blackmailing Nelson Crain, threatening to go to the press with the story and expose John as a "Red."

The threat came at a difficult time for Crain. In his rapid advance to wealth and power he had been an outspoken advocate of free enterprise and, on a number of occasions, had warned about the Red menace. He was such a champion of the capitalist system that he became a target for a Bolshevik bomb plot.

When Corless came calling, Nelson Crain was in the middle of a difficult strike at one of his textile mills. He also had important business deals pending with both John D. Rockefeller, Jr., and Henry Ford.

How was it going to look if the press revealed that his son consorted with a dirty little Bolshevik like Hal Rosen? What was Henry Ford going to say?

His back to the wall, he had sent John away to supervise the construction of Wicklow, threatening to cut off his funds if he didn't go. He also made arrangements for two thugs to beat Charles Corless to within an inch of the blackmailing bastard's life.

The beating was too severe. Corless died of his injuries and Nelson Crain became an accessory to murder. A great deal of money, far more than Corless had asked for, had been required to put the lid on. The only good to come of it was that Corless, dead, made a poor witness. Hal Rosen died, too, of injuries received in the riot.

John! What a fool his son was, Nelson Crain thought, pacing his study. Thanks to him, the boy had gotten out of that scrape with nary a scratch, and then the idiot had to blunder into another mess, killing a gangster and bringing the underworld's wrath down on his head. There was no way of fixing that. John could only run and hide.

Nelson Crain had profited from his mistake with Charles Corless. He should have paid him off. Quickly, quietly, no one the wiser, he should have paid the bastard off.

It would have worked then and it would work now. Only one question remained unanswered: How much did Greg Meister want?

Greg and Tandy were blissfully unaware. When they looked back, they would always remember it as the best of times, that December, the happiest passage of their lives, never to be duplicated.

They were in love, so deeply, so completely that nothing else mattered—and no one else, either. It was just the two of them. Fourteen Washington Square existed only as a place to meet. From there they escaped into their own world, a private paradise of their own making.

A ride in the shuddering Royal Mail was a journey to the stars. Lunch in a cheap café was a feast for the gods. Holding hands was to clasp heaven and to kiss was to taste of ambrosia.

To make love, to come together as man and woman, was ecstasy beyond description.

To share anything, a glance, a word, the merest touch, was to make the other rich with pleasure. Life was joy and gladness and laughter. Life was love shared by two alone. If that was selfish, so be it. The magic, they knew, could only come once. They also knew that it couldn't last forever. With time, like all things, it would erode, become flawed. Some portion might remain. Enough, hopefully, to sustain. But not the full, dazzling, once-in-a-lifetime magic of the perfect joining of a man and woman.

At the moment, it was that—perfect. And so they rejoiced and shut out all the others.

Tandy knew now that her parents were strongly opposed to Greg Meister's courtship. Though they had said nothing to her directly, there were all the signs of a growing storm, a deluge to come.

Greg's name was not spoken. When he called, they never greeted him, remaining out of sight until he was gone. There was never an invitation for him to stay for a moment longer than necessary. Her mother never once suggested tea. Her father never offered a drink.

Together, by obvious compact, her parents had decided to totally ignore Greg's existence, and the storm gathered. They held long, private talks from which they emerged ever more cold and distant, like generals with battle plans still not agreed upon.

Tandy viewed them through a euphoric haze. It didn't matter what they thought or did or planned to do. It was Greg, only Greg, who mattered. The magic was now and she would not permit any outside influence to mar it.

Greg Meister didn't give a damn about opposition from any quarter. If Nelson and Sandra Crain chose to ignore him, so be it. He made no attempt to seek their attention and no effort to change their opinion of him. He was what he was. In the end they would have to accept that.

If there was a gathering storm, a time when the Crains would come and openly state their opposition, that time would be met firmly. They would be told the simple truth. There was nothing they could do to end or alter the relationship. Nothing. No threat, no act, no mischief, no power play, nothing could destroy what he had found with Tandy. He would protect it with all his heart and will. If required, he would defend it with his life.

The stolen hours in the back of the bookstore were the best of all. They would drink wine and share a forbidden marijuana cigarette and laugh and tell lies and make love.

When it's perfect, lovers can mock—and they did.

"I used to keep pigeons," he would tell her.

"From what?" she would ask.

She would claim to know F. Scott Fitzgerald, and he would know his photographer brother, f. stop.

They would solemnly agree to trade away bad habits: If he would stop slurping at every delight, she would never again say, "That idea has possibilities."

If he spoke of peace, she would remind him that her father had made millions out of war. If she claimed wisdom, he would ask her what she was doing in his bed.

When they made love, it was rapture. There never was a time when it didn't end with the same words as the first time.

"I love you, Greg Meister."

"And I love you, Tandy Crain."

CHAPTER 13

The package sat around for several days at Ernst Frankel's bookstore. Meister thought it was a book being returned. Some of the poorer students, unable to buy a particular book, would ask to borrow it. Meister never had the heart to turn them down. He would loan a book out on two conditions. One, that it be returned promptly on the date promised. Two, that the borrower tell no one, so as not to prompt similar requests. The store was, after all, a business, not a public library.

Meister was doing well on the first condition. He hadn't lost a book yet. On the second he wasn't too sure. Requests for loans were increasing to the point where he got two, sometimes three a night. He was either going to have to stop the practice or charge a fee. The latter would require consultation with, and a decision by, Frankel. Meister wasn't too anxious to broach him with still another innovation. The Royal Mail purchase had pushed the man to the limit.

In truth, though, Ernst Frankel took even more pleasure in the little converted roadster than Meister did. Now when he went to a book auction or a competitor's close-out sale, he wasn't restricted to buying only what he could carry home on the trolley. He could buy whatever his purse allowed. The Royal Mail sometimes returned loaded to the gunnels like a treasure ship.

Sara Brown, the day clerk, finally couldn't stand the suspense any longer. "Greg Meister," she said, "if you don't open that package, I will."

Meister laughed. He picked it up, planning to toss it to her, but then he became aware of its weight. It was far heavier for its size than a book. He turned the package over and saw then that it had been hand-delivered, not mailed, that it was directed to him as *Private and Confidential* and that a receipt had been requested.

"Why didn't you tell me it was personal?" he asked.

"I did," Sara replied. "Several times."

"I guess I didn't hear."

"How could you, with your head in the clouds?" Meister looked at her. Sara was a nice girl, pretty, sweet, fun to be with. He liked her very much, but not in the way she wanted. She had a terrible crush on him and it showed. "Who signed for it?"

"I did."

"Oh." Meister hefted the package, intrigued now. It really was surprisingly heavy.

"Well, aren't you going to open it?"

"Yes, but not in front of you, Brownie. You see what it says here? Private!"

"Fiddlesticks."

Meister laughed, but he took the package to his room at the back and locked the door on her. She called after him petulantly, "See if I care!"

He put the package on his bed and tore off the wrapper. Beneath the first wrapping was another, securely taped. He had to get scissors to cut it open. When he did, he stared in disbelief. Inside was a large sum of money. There must be thousands and thousands of dollars there in used fives, tens and twenties, he speculated. It was a fortune!

"What the hell?"

Meister picked up the outer wrapper. No, it wasn't a mistake. It was addressed to him. But why?

In a daze, he checked through the inner wrappings, looking for some indication of the sender. There had to be ten, twenty thousand dollars here!

He lifted a pile of the stacked bills, thinking that he should count the money, and then he saw the envelope underneath. It was also addressed to him: *Greg Meister, Esq. Private and Confidential.*

Meister tore it open with a sinking feeling. The enclosed note was typewritten.

> Greg,
>
> I am appealing to you man-to-man on behalf of my family—my father, my mother and myself. We are strongly opposed to your interest in Tandy. You're not our kind and you're not welcome. If Tandy is interested, it is only because she is still a willful, immature, inexperienced child and easily swayed. I beg you not to take advantage of her. This has happened before and the men have been gentlemen and have taken their leave when asked. Since you are not a gentleman, since you renewed our acquaintance on false pretenses as a means of gaining access to Tandy and since I, like a fool, made it possible by inviting you to my home, I propose—as the responsible party—to buy you off. It's not much compared to the fortune you obviously hoped to have someday, but it's all I can afford from my trust at this time. Take it, because it's all you'll get. There will be no wedding.
>
> John

Meister sat stunned. Suddenly everything was clear. John Crain's mixed reaction to his return to New York. A warm welcome, and then—sudden wariness. His growing coldness in the ensuing months as Meister continued to inquire about Tandy and, finally, the complete break and John's disappearance—heartbroken, according to Sid Berns.

No, Meister thought, that was probably only half of it. John Crain may or may not have been heartbroken, but he must also have been under terrible family pressure, attacked as a careless fool who had welcomed a scheming fortune hunter into the Crain household. Was that the real reason why he had left New York, sent away after a terrible family row? Was that why this pile of money sat now on Meister's bed? First, to buy him off and, second, to buy John back into the family fold? God in heaven, was that the kind of poison spilled here?

Meister put his head in his hands. Surely not, but what else explained it? There was no doubt of Nelson Crain's opposition to Meister's interest in Tandy. Hadn't he tried to drive him out of town by getting him fired from J.P. Morgan & Company and getting him evicted from his apartment? Wasn't he now giving Meister the silent treatment, hoping, apparently, that he would eventually get discouraged and take the hint? Act like a "gentleman" and leave?

Sandra Crain clearly shared her husband's feelings. Initially warm and friendly, she had become reserved and cold, never appearing when he called on Tandy except by miscalculation, and then excusing herself with as few words as possible. She, too, saw him as an intruder and hoped he would quietly go away.

The family's opposition couldn't have been more clearly, though silently, stated. They would have screamed it from the rooftops except they were afraid of driving Tandy into his arms.

Meister closed his eyes. Tandy, darling Tandy… it was too late, she already was in his arms and he would never let her go. Somehow, some way, the Crains had to be made to understand. He had never wanted her money, he only wanted *her.* Money wasn't important to Tandy, either, or at least not a lot of it. She only cared to have enough.

He smiled, recalling what she had said when he had driven her home after that first incredible mating in the Royal Mail.

"Let me take you away from all this," he had said, laughing, staring up at the huge fortress that was 14 Washington Square.

"All right," she had replied, meaning it. "But first get yourself a proper car!"

Why couldn't her family understand? Didn't they realize that love was all important? Was Nelson Crain rich when he married Tandy's mother? No! So, why did Meister have to be rich? Why did they think that this dirty pile of money might be worth more to him than the woman he loved? How dare they think that?

Meister glowed at the small fortune sitting in the middle of his bed. He picked up the note, reading it through again, and suddenly it struck him that he could be wrong, that Nelson and Sandra Crain might know nothing about it. It was written on their behalf, but nowhere did it say that they were aware of it. The note and the money could be—no, *were*—John Crain's doing!

The shit! Meister thought, rage filling him. John Crain had meant something special to him. He had saved John Crain's life and he had accepted his offer of friendship and given his own friendship in return. In a sense, they had become like brothers, from different worlds, but brothers nevertheless.

Meister went to the front of the shop where he knew there was a small black satchel. Years before, someone had left it, and it had never been reclaimed. Ernst Frankel was too honest to dispose of it.

Meister claimed it now and took it back to his room. He packed the satchel with the money and stormed out of the shop. He was going to find John Crain and give him back the filthy bone he had thrown.

"What was it?" Sara Brown called after him.

"Too much to swallow!" Meister shouted back.

The search took him all day and finally led him almost back in his old neighborhood. Almost, but not quite. Above Delancey he had been on the fringe of the slums that made up the lower East Side's melting pot. Here, on Avenue B, he was in the middle of it, the filth and the squalor and the defeat and humiliation which went with it filling his senses wherever he turned.

Meister entered the door of the tenement and sat on the stairway in the front hall, the black satchel at his side. There was no light. He would see anyone entering before they saw him, framed in the doorway. He got out his cigarettes and lit one.

His anger was spent now, drained by the long, tiring day. It seemed to him that he had been all over New York. The docks, the garment district, back to the docks, the fish market, backstage on Broadway—and back to the docks again.

If Sid Berns was a survivor, one reason was because he moved around a lot, never staying anywhere long enough for someone to get a clear shot at him. There were a number of likely candidates. At Farley's, for instance, the mere mention of Sid Berns' name raised hackles a mile high. Joe Lombardo, the club manager, a surly thug with a murderous glint in his eye, had made no secret of his dislike.

"That little bastard?" he had said. "No, he doesn't work here anymore, and if you track him down, tell him I was asking about him, will you? Tell him Joe Lombardo was asking what size boots he wore. And tell him Scarface Al sends his regards."

From Farley's, the trail had led to the docks and to a similar, if less intense, reaction. Sid Berns had a reputation as a troublemaker. Young as he was, he was already fighting the system, trying to change it. He lived off of it. That was how he survived. But he didn't like it. A little Jewish grabber, he was also a Philadelphia lawyer, reform politician and union organizer, all rolled up into one controversial package.

Meister sighed and lit another cigarette. He could understand why Sid Berns wanted off Avenue B. What he couldn't understand was his apparent desire to take everybody else with him. Like Hal Rosen, Sid Berns was an idealist, a reformer. He was looking to change the world. He might amount to something when he grew up. *If* he grew up. There were a number of people who had other plans for him. Joe Lombardo, for one, and Scarfare Al—whoever the hell he was.

Meister shook his head. How could one little guy stir up such rage? And then a shadow loomed in the open doorway and he felt some of that rage himself. If Sid Berns hadn't been such a troublemaker, he would have been easy to find. Instead, it had taken Meister all day.

Berns stopped at the door, alert and wary.

"Hello, again," Meister said tiredly. He took a last drag on his cigarette and ground it out under his shoe.

Sid Berns ventured forward a few steps and peered into the gloom. "Oh. It's you."

"Yes." Meister stood, picking up the satchel. "Is there someplace we can talk?"

"Uh—" Berns hesitated. "What's wrong with here?"

Meister considered. It was as good a place as any, he decided, at least to start. He sat down again, the satchel between his feet. "You're a hard man to find, you know that?"

Sid Berns moved closer, standing at the bottom step, leaning against the wall. "Yeah, I was wondering about that. How *did* you find me?"

"Persistence."

"Oh."

"I started at Farley's," said Meister, watching for a reaction. He got out his cigarettes even though he didn't want another just yet.

"Farley's?"

"Yes." Meister thought he detected an edge of concern in the voice, but he couldn't be sure and it was too dark to note any change of expression. "They'd like to know your shoe size there, so they can fit you for cement overshoes, apparently."

"Really?"

Meister leaned forward, offering a cigarette. A nerve had been touched that time. Behind the bravado, Sid Berns worried for his safety—as well he should. "Is that why you're so hard to find?" Meister asked.

There was an attempt at defiance. "What business is that of yours?"

"Mind your mouth!" Meister shouted. Without warning, he was on his feet, his left forearm pressed against Sid Berns' throat, pinning him against the wall. The match that was meant to light the cigarette now flared in the youth's face. "Understand this. I know your reputation, and you're not going to screw around with me."

Sid Berns stared with bulging eyes, unable to speak. His windpipe was closed, almost breaking under the pressure, and a hard knee threatened to crush his groin.

"I want some information," Meister said. "The answer to one question, and if you lie to me, I'll kill you." He released the pressure and sat back down on the stairs. "You understand?"

Sid Berns nodded. He still couldn't speak. His neck felt as if it had been squeezed to a pulp.

"John Crain," Meister said, getting out two more cigarettes. He lit both, passing one to Berns. "How do I find him?"

Sid Berns took the cigarette, holding it at his side. It had almost burned down to his fingers before he could get the words out. "The last … I heard … Miami."

Meister, who had sat silent the whole time, a remorseless judge waiting in the shadows, kicked viciously at the satchel, knocking it down to the foot of the stairs.

Miami? He had hoped it would be closer. "Do you have an address?"

"No."

"Then how do you know he's in Miami?"

"He's written me a couple of times. No return address, just the postmark."

"Shit." Sid Berns had to be telling the truth, he decided. Defeated, he moved down the stairs, retrieving the satchel. He held it in front of him. "I don't suppose you'd know anything about this?"

Sid Berns put what was left of the cigarette to his lips. He managed one careful drag before he had to drop it. He looked at Meister, measuring him, hating him. "That's two questions."

Meister almost smiled. "You're a tough kid, aren't you, Sid?"

"I'll do."

I'm sure you will, Meister thought. He considered for a moment the possibility that Sid Berns knew more than he was admitting. On impulse he opened the satchel, moving into the fading light of the doorway, displaying the money.

Sid Berns stared, bug-eyed. "Holy shit!"

"If you ever hear from your buddy, tell him I said no deal." Meister snapped the satchel shut. "And tell him if he wants the money back, he's got to come and get it—*personally*."

Sid Berns sank down onto the stairs. His neck still felt sore, but all he could think of was the money. He had never seen so much money being carried around loose like that. It looked like a king's ransom, and the schmuck was dragging it around town in a satchel?

His mind reeled with questions. Why was Meister so angry? Why would John Crain send him so much money? And why would Meister want to give it back?

Painfully, Sid Berns reached into his pocket, removing a folded letter. He opened it carefully and spread it on his knees. He struck a match and held the flame close. He read the now familiar words for the tenth time in as many days.

Dear Sid,

Finally settled and is this ever the land of opportunity! The town's wide open and there's room for all! A fortune to be made in demon rum, or whatever else suits your fancy. If you ever get tired of New York, come help me, will you? We'll both get rich!

Regards, John Crain P.S.
Keep this under wraps, huh? I'm still on the lam.
P.P.S. I'm registered here as John Marshall.

Sid Berns lit another match and held it briefly at the top of the page. The address was there: The Bishop Hotel, Chicago, Illinois.

He blew the match out and sat in the darkness. Boy, what a schmuck he was. John Crain was rolling in the bucks and needed help making more, and he hadn't answered the letter because he didn't believe it. He had thought it was just big talk with nothing to back it up. He often talked big himself when his pockets were empty. Everybody lied when they were down. That's how they got back up.

Schmuck! The image of the open satchel, a fortune stuffed in it, wouldn't leave his mind. It had to be for a buy, he decided finally. John Crain must have sent the money to Meister to make a special booze purchase—rum from Nassau or maybe champagne from St. Pierre.

Since Meister wasn't connected, Crain must have sent him the money asking him to hold it, to be the go-between. In a rush deal Crain might have been pushed into that kind of arrangement. Being careful, he'd have just sent instructions and not his address. The address would come later, by separate letter, so if either got intercepted, the two couldn't be tied together. Did that make sense? Did that explain why Meister didn't know how to reach Crain?

Hell, it didn't matter. What mattered was that Meister wanted no part of the deal. He was on a self-righteous rampage. He'd ram that satchel down John Crain's throat if he could get his hands on him.

Sid Berns struggled to his feet. There was a lot of money to be made in bootleg liquor. The proper kind of deal could double what was in that satchel. He couldn't let Meister screw it up for Crain.

The telephone roused John Crain from a dead sleep. He turned on the bedside lamp, found his watch and stared at it in disbelief. One o'clock? He'd only been asleep for a half-hour.

The desk clerk apologized for ringing so late, but it was an emergency, a call from New York.

Oh, Christ, *no,* Crain thought, suddenly awake. He knew the call had to be from Sid Berns. Sid was the only one who had his address. Crain's first thought was that something had happened to Nadine.

Sid's voice crackled, barely audible across the miles. "John?"

"Yes."

"Can you talk in private?"

"Yes! What is it for God's sake?"

"Meister's screwing your deal!"

Crain frowned, baffled. "I beg your pardon?"

"He was at my place tonight with the money. He doesn't want to go through with the deal."

John Crain was at a total loss. "What deal?"

Sid Berns sounded just as perplexed. "How the hell should I know? Aren't you making a booze buy?"

"Wait a minute," said Crain. "Let me get this straight. Greg Meister came to your place with some money."

"A *lot* of money."

"A lot of money," Crain amended, a possible explanation already dawning on him. "And he said what, exactly?"

"That he'd kill me if I didn't tell him where you are."

Oh, boy, Crain thought, sure of it now. "Did you?"

"I told him you were in Miami, no address."

"Nice going," Crain said, beginning to relax. "He bought that, did he?"

"Yeah. He says if you want the money back, you've got to come and get it personally."

"Was he mad when he said that?"

"Yeah."

Crain had to struggle against laughter. "How mad?"

"Hey," Sid Berns complained, "what's so goddamn funny? That son of a bitch almost killed me. He's got a satchel full of money he wants to shove down your throat and you're laughing?"

"Sid," Crain said, barely able to speak now. "Sid, tell me something, will you? Is Meister seeing my sister?"

"How the hell should I know?"

"He is!" Crain said, laughing. "Oh God, he is!" He dropped the phone, howling with laughter, then bent down over the side of the bed to pick it up. "Don't you get it? He's seeing my sister!"

"Hilarious," Sid Berns said. "Ab-so-lute-ly hilarious."

"Sid, thanks for calling," Crain managed then. "You're a good friend. If Meister ever asks about me again, tell him I moved to Hong Kong, okay?"

"Fuck you," Sid Berns said. "I'm telling him you're at the Bishop Hotel in Chicago."

The line went dead.

Crain fumbled the phone receiver back. Now that, he thought, is funny. His father had to be one of the biggest fools in New York. Greg Meister couldn't be bought off, never, not for any amount of money.

And when Meister found out the truth—who the payoff attempt had really come from—there'd be a wedge driven between those two never to be removed. The alienation would be permanent.

Crain fell back on his pillow. Greg Meister . . . courting Tandy? Like his father, perhaps he had made a mistake about Greg, too. If Meister was going after Tandy, the man still had balls. No brains, perhaps, but balls.

He stared up at the ceiling. Maybe he should get in touch with Meister. In Chicago, Crain could use the stake his father had so fortuitously provided.

He grinned. Why not? Meister thought the money was his, didn't he? Hadn't he just sent word for him to come and collect it?

John Crain started to laugh again. It was the first time he'd had something to laugh about in months.

CHAPTER 14

Sir,

I will not be calling at your home again as I accept, finally, that I'm unwelcome. I will continue to see Tandy, if she wishes. You may tell John, if he ever comes out of hiding, that I hold something which I expect him to collect—along with a thrashing.

Respectfully,

Greg Meister

Nelson Crain read the letter in a helpless rage. Greg Meister was not going to be broken. There was no use trying anymore. Quiet persuasion, broad hints, overt action, the silent treatment, nothing made a dent in that farmer's thick hide. An offer of twenty thousand dollars to take his leave, and he responded with a smart-alecky note!

Furious, Nelson Crain tore the letter into pieces, as if doing so might damage the author, who was safe, Crain knew, because he had nothing worth threatening. For Meister, one job was like another, of no real consequence. Where or how he lived was of even less concern. He had no fortune to lose, no power base to be toppled, no reputation to ruin, no talent to be destroyed. His lack of all consequence made him invulnerable.

To get rid of the bastard, you'd have to kill him.

Nelson Crain had given thought to that. Not seriously, perhaps, but it had crossed his mind more than once. He had, after all, arranged a death once, if only by misadventure. He was capable of it again under the right circumstances.

What deterred him now was the fear that Tandy would suspect him if anything happened to Meister. If she did, he wouldn't just save her from an unsuitable marriage. He would lose her—lose her forever. That was unacceptable.

The only alternative, the one option left, was to take action against Tandy. Until now Nelson Crain had been unable to bring himself to that decision. In the long conferences with his distraught wife, he had always veered away from such a course.

Tandy, armored by her past record as a child not to be tampered with, presented as formidable a challenge as her impossible suitor. Nelson Crain had been through this before. To forbid her to see Meister would only bring derision. Reason, pleas, tears and threats would all be dismissed. Her mind made up, she would do as she pleased. Nothing, short of locking her up, would stop her.

Nelson Crain sorely wished the times permitted it. He truly would have considered having her forcibly sent away somewhere. Europe, under guard, in custody. She deserved that. Yet, knowing her, six months, a year, whatever the time of separation, would that dampen her ardor? Probably not. Knowing her, it would only serve to fuel it.

Then what was left? Compromise, Nelson Crain thought bitterly. Compromise. He pulled open his desk drawer and removed a small address book. He opened it at the M's and ran a finger down the page to the name he wanted. Lawrence Montrose. He picked up his phone and dialed the number.

"Hullo?" a man's voice answered after several rings.

"Montrose?"

"Yes?"

"It's Nelson Crain."

There was a long moment of silence. "Now what could you possibly want?"

"I want to talk to you. How about lunch—the Union Club?"

There was another long pause. "Well ... it at least ought to be interesting."

"It will be," Nelson Crain promised.

It was twelve hours later, past ten o'clock that night, before Nelson Crain returned home, the smell of whiskey on him. But he showed no other sign that he'd been drinking all day. He had a last scotch at the library bar. One for the road, the last mile, he thought. Then he braced himself and made his way upstairs.

His wife's bedroom door was ajar. He knocked, pushed the door open, hitting a wall switch as he did. The lamp near her bed came on. "Are you awake?" he asked.

Sandra Crain sat up, startled. She squinted at him. "Nelson?"

He closed the door behind him. "Yes. I want to talk to you."

She looked at her bedside clock, then back at him. "Have you been drinking?"

"Yes," he admitted. "But I can't get drunk, damn it. I've tried all day." He came and sat at the foot of her bed. "This thing with Tandy, it's out of hand."

Sandra Crain stared at him uncertainly. She had never seen him this way before. He smelled like a distillery, but he seemed determinedly sober. "Perhaps we should talk in the morning," she suggested.

"No," he said. "I want it settled *now.* There's some things you have to know, and then you can make up your mind, all right?"

"Nelson—"

"Listen," he barked. "First, there's no getting rid of Meister. I've tried everything, including buying him off. Twenty thousand dollars and he's not having any of it. He's in for the long pull, all or nothing." He leaned forward, eyes blazing. "And he can get it too! Is that what you want?"

"Nelson, *please.*" She turned away. "I think you should leave."

"I'm sorry," he soothed, calming his anger and reaching out to reassure her. "Just tell me one thing. You are opposed?"

"Of course. You know that."

"Inalterably opposed?"

"Yes!"

"Then I propose that we marry her off," Nelson Crain said. "I suggest we make a proper choice for her and get it done with." He plunged ahead. "What would you say to Lawrence Montrose?"

His wife didn't answer.

"Why not?" he queried. "She was quite taken with him once. The same goo-goo eyes and heart all aquiver we're suffering now, only worse."

"She was only sixteen!"

"And a woman," Nelson Crain insisted. "And a woman."

Sandra Crain turned to look at him. "What's that supposed to mean?"

"That her interest in Montrose was such that I had to buy him off."

She turned away. "I don't want to hear this."

"You will, though. It applies. Today, at my invitation, I lunched at the Union Club with Mr. Montrose, who hasn't changed a bit, incidentally. He's still the handsomest man in New York, and he's still broke and open to offers."

"I won't hear of it!"

"You won't?" He took her by the arm, forcing her to face him. "Why not? There's not a better family in the country than the Montroses. If some of them have fallen on hard times, that doesn't make them any the less, does it? It's the breeding that counts!"

"That's what you want?" she demanded. "Breeding?"

"Yes, and I'm willing to buy it, hear me? I talked to the man. His bachelor days are palling and he's ready to settle down, raise a family. All he needs is the right beauty and the right dowry and he'll do the rest." "The man is thirty-six years old!"

"Yes, and the other one is a farmer!"

Sandra Crain was silent for a moment. "Is that the choice?"

"Isn't it?" he asked her. "You argued patience and this is what we've come to."

"That's not fair!"

"I'm not trying to be fair. I'm saying there's only one man who can break up this thing with Meister. *The girl's first love.* Do you understand? Her first *love.* I bought him off, but she doesn't know that."

There was another long silence. "What if she's no longer interested?"

"Granted," Nelson Crain admitted. "But what if she is?"

His wife leaned back against her pillows. "I don't like forcing her into anything."

"We're not forcing anything. We can't, that's our problem. We're arranging."

"I don't like such arrangements."

"Then start liking farmers," Nelson Crain told her bluntly. "It's your choice. You decide."

She turned away. "You hate the boy, don't you?"

Nelson Crain didn't answer. Yes, he did. She knew that already and she knew why. Greg Meister was the same common dirt he had once been. The same common dirt. After a lifetime of trying to escape, he didn't want it thrown back into his face.

Lawrence Montrose came calling on a bright Tuesday morning the week of Christmas. He was a tall, handsome, distinguished-looking man, full of vigor and purpose. He drew admiring glances wherever he went. He had strong, classic features—the head of a Greek god, some said—and the commanding bearing of a conquering general. His eyes, a deep, startling blue, were all-knowing, and his ready smile could disarm the worst pirate. Women literally fell at his feet, yet this was his downfall.

Sadie's reaction upon opening the door to him was typical. Oh my, she thought, staring at him in utter fascination.

"Is Miss Tandy in?" Lawrence Montrose inquired, in the tone of one who already knows the answer. He handed her a card along with his hat and gloves. "Would you give her that, please? Tell her I'll be in the library."

Sadie looked at the card. Only his name was on it: Lawrence Montrose.

"Thank you," he told her, smiling. He removed his coat and glanced about the foyer with a proprietary air. Without waiting for permission, he crossed to the library, carrying his coat with him. He threw it casually over a chair as he entered. Without breaking stride he continued on, making his way to the hidden bar.

Sadie stared after him in helpless wonder. She had no idea who Lawrence Montrose was, but, she thought, he certainly knew who he was!

Montrose pushed the panel that swung the bar around. He selected a brandy, found himself a snifter and poured out a generous drink. He sipped at it appreciatively and then began a tour of the library. He moved with assurance and an easy grace. Anyone coming upon him suddenly and not knowing any better would think him the master of the house. Actually, he had been in the library just once before, and then only briefly—just in and out to steal a bottle.

Tandy's reaction to the card was similar to Sadie's reaction to the bearer at the door. For a long moment she stared at it, unable to speak.

"You know the gentleman?" Sadie asked.

Oh yes, Tandy thought, waiting for the shock to pass. She knew him well, but not as a gentleman. Lawrence Montrose had been the first man to possess her, the first man she had ever loved—or thought she loved. There had been a time, when he broke off the relationship, that she had been sure her heart would break.

"Yes," she said finally. "I know him." She fingered the card, her emotions mixed. Why? After all this time, why? She was both intrigued and apprehensive. It had taken her a long time to get over Lawrence Montrose. Actually, she had never really gotten him out of her system, not completely, not till now. Not till Greg Meister.

"Are you going to see him?"

Tandy tried to think. Should she? Of all the men before Greg, only Lawrence Montrose, because he had been the first, still had any hold on her. He had once been what she lived for. The times with him had been glorious, the times between unbearable. He had once occupied her every thought, as Greg did now. Because he had been the first, the memory of him would never be totally erased from her mind. There were special moments, special times that would always linger. A part of him would always be a part of her.

But to compare him to Greg? That was ridiculous! They were two different men, she told herself. Lawrence Montrose was a professional lover. It was his occupation. Greg Meister, unschooled, was a gifted, specially endowed master. With Greg it was an art.

"Are you going to see him?" Sadie asked again.

"Why not?" Tandy replied, letting the card fall from her fingers. There might be memories, but no threat, no danger. Her love for Greg Meister and the gift he had given her kept her safe from all others.

Nelson Crain knocked gently, then entered his wife's bedroom. "He's here," he said simply.

Sandra Crain was staring out the window into her garden. It was bare and dead, the way she felt. She didn't answer.

"It's best," he told her, knowing what she was thinking and trying to share something of what she felt.

"Is it?"

"Yes. Don't change your mind now."

Again, no answer.

Nelson Crain touched her shoulder, then moved to the other side of the bedroom, dropping heavily into a chair by the fireplace. The fire was almost out, just a few faint, ash-dusted embers showing. He thought of putting on another log, then changed his mind. Let *it* die, too, he decided.

This bright Tuesday morning was a day for death. Today was the day love would die. Downstairs a professional waited. In a bedroom across the hall an innocent prepared to go to him. When it was all over, all of them would have died a little. Not only Tandy and Greg, but his wife and himself, and perhaps even Lawrence Montrose.

Yet, it was best, Nelson Crain told himself. Greg Meister was not suitable. Not now, not ever. He had to be stopped. If that meant bringing back Lawrence Montrose, paying the scoundrel for a seduction he once gladly performed for free, then that was the price one paid to chart the course of history. Dynasties were not fashioned by chance. They were built by deliberate, knowing, premeditated acts of artful selection, always looking to the future.

Lawrence Montrose was stopgap, not the perfect choice for the present but, praise heaven, he filled the future. A rogue, he looked like a god. A pauper, he had the bloodline of kings. From his loins, from Tandy's womb would come true treasure! A new generation worthy of Nelson Crain's toil. That was what he wanted. That was what he would have.

Tandy would succumb. He was sure of that. What he hadn't told his wife and what he could never tell her was the true extent of the affair between Tandy and Lawrence Montrose. In fact, she had been the aggressor. Love letters proved it, so torrid that he still flushed at the memory of them.

Nelson Crain had come upon one accidentally, half-written, and knew there had to be others, possibly saved by Montrose. So he had arranged to get them back. He had paid a private investigator very handsomely for their theft and return. Then, in a quiet visit to Montrose, he had suggested that the man never see or write his daughter again—or else. He had flung money at him, five thousand dollars, the price of breaking it off, the price of buying back Tandy's explicit letters.

Oh, Tandy would succumb all right, he thought. She had before and she would again. Montrose was irresistible. He'd have her, and Greg Meister, the poor bastard, wouldn't know what hit him.

So what if they all died a little? Everybody died a little every day. They died so others could live, and only fools failed to choose who would follow.

When Tandy entered the library, Lawrence Montrose was on his second snifter of brandy, leafing through what he considered an appropriate book, Fitzgerald's *This Side of Paradise*. He glanced up, smiling. "Hello."

"Hello," Tandy said, her heart beating faster. She paused at the door, getting her breath, surprised to discover that he still had such an effect on her.

"This is—" She stopped, flustered, made a helpless gesture.

"An unexpected pleasure, I trust," Montrose said, still smiling. He put the book aside and rose to greet her. "I know it is for me."

Tandy held back uncertainly. Whatever she had intended to say, she couldn't remember. Her mind was blank except for one question: How could he still have that effect?

"I was passing by and I thought I'd drop in," Montrose told her. He lifted his snifter in a kind of toast. "I, uh, took the liberty."

Tandy finally found her voice. The words came out strained, not as she intended. She had hoped to sound jocular. "Yes, I see you remembered where the bar is."

Montrose laughed. "What did we steal that time? Champagne?"

"Whiskey," Tandy said. She sat down, feeling faint. She couldn't believe what was happening.

"Well, it should have been champagne," Montrose said easily. He finished his brandy and put the empty glass on the bar. "Can I get you something?"

Tandy shook her head. "No."

"I didn't mean to barge in," Montrose told her. "If you'd prefer, I could leave."

The question hung in the air like a ticking bomb. If it went off, it would solve everything … or nothing.

"No, that's all right," Tandy said finally. "I'm just a little surprised, that's all." She looked at him and managed a smile. "I think my father might be too." Montrose laughed again. "God, let's not worry about fathers, shall we? You're a woman now."

Tandy looked away, acutely aware of the searching, all-knowing eyes. "I was then."

"Yes," Montrose admitted. He hesitated, then moved closer, sitting in a chair across from her. "Yes, you were, you are … a very beautiful, very lovely woman."

"Am I?"

"Yes … beyond all my expectations."

Tandy felt a floodgate open somewhere. She should never have tried to face him. Suddenly the memories were too much, engulfing her. As a child, as a virgin, she had loved this man, had surrendered totally to him. Had he wanted, she would have married him. And now he was back.

"What are you doing here?" she demanded, suddenly angry.

"I told you, I was just passing by."

Tandy turned on him. "Passing by? How can you say that? You used me! You discarded me. And now you come passing by?"

"You're wrong," he told her. "You were never discarded. If anything, like a rare wine, you were saved, Tandy. Put away to come of age."

The anger flared anew in her. "To mature, ripen?"

"Be serious. I couldn't ask a minor to marry me. Your father would never have consented."

Tandy was almost screaming now. "Is that what you're here for? Make up your mind! Are you just passing by, or is there another purpose for this visit?"

Montrose stood and came to her, taking hold of her hands. "Why do you ask? You know there is. I wouldn't have come here without one. If I hurt you, I hurt myself just as deeply. In my own case the wound has never healed. I came here . . ." His grip tightened on her. "I would like to begin again, and I hope, in time, that you will do me the honor of becoming my wife."

Tandy turned away. "You're too late."

Montrose pulled her back toward him gently, making her look at him. "Is there another man?"

"Yes."

"Do you feel for him as you felt for me?"

"Yes."

"As much?"

"No, more, damn you, *more*!"

Montrose fixed her with his all-knowing gaze. "No, Tandy," he said softly. "You know that's not true. Compared to what we had—what we could have again—what you hold for him is nothing."

Tandy laughed. This was why she had decided to face him. It was only justice that he be the first to know. She laughed again, joyously, safe, protected. "I said you were too late. I'm carrying his child."

CHAPTER 15

Greg Meister put aside the manuscript he had been editing. He took off his glasses and set them down on his desk. He turned in his chair slowly, carefully, almost fearfully. He was a man in a dream, and he didn't want to wake up.

"I said," Tandy repeated, her face flushed, shimmering with happiness and the exertion of a headlong run all the way from Washington Square, "will you make an honest woman of me?"

Meister stared at her in disbelief. "You?"

"Yes, me," she told him. "I'm pregnant. I'm going to have a baby, and like it or not, you're going to be a father." She put her hands on her hips. "Now, what's your answer? Do you want a bastard or a son?"

Meister rose out of his chair, an awkward giant confronted by a dazzling butterfly. He wanted to hold it, but he didn't know how. To touch it might harm it. To let it escape was unthinkable.

His voice was an awed whisper. "When?"

"That first night!" Tandy said, embracing him. "It must have been. Hold me, will you, please? I've run all this way and I want you to hold me. I want you to hold *us*."

Meister cradled her in his arms, lifting her from the floor, holding her body against his, gently rocking his woman and the seed of the child within her. His tears fell hot against her face. He wanted to shout with joy, yet he was crying. He wanted to speak, yet he could not utter a word.

"Greg Meister, I love you," Tandy sobbed brokenly.

"And I love you, Tandy Crain," Meister finally managed.

Later, it was all a jumble. If they had ever been called upon to recount who said what, it is doubtful they would have gotten half of it right.

When did she find out?

"Yesterday. I was going to wait—a Christmas present—but I just couldn't!"

When would they marry?

"What's wrong with now?"

"Nothing. The sooner the better."

"I can't wait."

"Darling, believe me, neither can I!"

What would they tell her parents?

"Nothing. Not yet. They're going to have a fit, you know that."

"You mean, elope?"

"Have you a better idea?"

"A proper church wedding."

"I said, a better idea."

"I love you."

"I know."

Where would they live?

"Not here."

"I didn't mean here, I meant where?"

"God, I don't know, an apartment?"

"Not in New York."

"Why not?"

"You know why not. You've seen what he's like. He'll make our lives miserable. They both will."

"So—what?"

"So, I want an excuse."

"To go away?"

"Please!"

How would they live?

"I can get a job."

"In your condition?"

"Darling, it's not a condition, it's a pregnancy!"

"But you can't work. You've never worked."

"I can help you."

"What? Correct papers?"

"I can spell. I've been to Barnard, remember?"

"Oh, shit, we're in trouble, you know that?"

Later, if asked to recall what was decided, Meister would remember three things clearly. If it was a boy, he'd be named Alexander. If they had to run away, the best place was a big city, somewhere with job opportunities, and the best bet was Chicago. Tandy had suggested it, then insisted. If they were going to exist until he got a job, they were going to have to scrape together every penny they owned, put it in a joint purse and pray to God that it lasted.

What Tandy didn't tell him was that the day before, she had withdrawn five thousand dollars from her savings account. She did it without letting him know because she didn't think he'd accept the money. It was the nest egg that would save them if necessary. What she also didn't tell him was that John Crain was waiting for them in Chicago. John had telephoned, asking about Greg, and she had blurted out her joyous news. John, after he'd gotten over the shock, had said, hell, if you're going to elope, why not come to Chicago? John had requested that she keep it a secret.

What Meister didn't tell Tandy, and could never reveal, especially now, was that he had twenty thousand dollars of Crain money in a satchel under his bed. He had no idea what to do with it now except wait. With this turn of events, his anger had to be put aside. He couldn't hate her brother. He couldn't beat him up. What would it serve to reveal the depth of her family's opposition? How would that help their marriage?

No, he'd just wait, that's all. Eventually the matter would be settled, the money quietly returned. It would be John Crain's secret and he could live with it, the son of a bitch.

When next they met, for Tandy's sake, he'd try not to kick the shit out of him. For Tandy's sake, he resolved.

They left on Christmas Eve. Sandra Crain found the note. She took it in to her husband. Dry-eyed, she handed it to him in weary, heartbroken resignation.

"They've run away," she said dully. "Tandy's pregnant. They're getting married."

Nelson Crain looked at the note without really seeing the words. "I know. Montrose told me. That's"—he let the note drop—"that's why my little scheme didn't work, if it ever did have a chance."

His wife looked at him. "Why didn't you tell me?"

Nelson Crain shrugged. "I don't know. I thought she'd tell you, I suppose. I thought you'd rather hear it from her." He retrieved the note, tried to read it, then let it drop again. The words were still a blur. "I'm sorry. I didn't know it would come out this way."

"Neither did I." Sandra Crain sank into a chair. First John, now Tandy, she thought. They'd lost them both. "She told Montrose, but not us?"

Nelson Crain was staring at the note on the floor. "Why should she? We weren't talking to her." He sighed. "Maybe we should have talked to her."

"No," Sandra Crain said, sure of that. There would have been terrible scenes. Words said that could never be forgotten or forgiven. If the marriage was inevitable, then silence was better. Perhaps one day the silence might heal.

Nelson Crain didn't argue. He'd been defeated, not by Meister, not by Tandy, but by a child. An unborn child.

"She didn't even take her presents."

Nelson Crain looked at the Christmas tree standing tall and bright in a corner of the living room. Well, he thought tiredly, they'd just have to send them on. If they ever heard from them, they'd send them on. All except one.

With an effort, Nelson Crain rose and went to the tree. He removed a plain-wrapped package the size of a shoebox from the pile of presents underneath. The only decoration on it was a small name-tag.

He took it to the fireplace and threw it onto the flames.

"Nelson!" his wife cried out in alarm. She ran to the fireplace to retrieve the package, but she was too late. The flames had already engulfed it.

In the instant that was left, she read the name on the tag, Greg Meister, then the tag curled and blackened and was gone. The package burned fiercely.

She turned to face her husband questioningly.

"Love letters," Nelson Crain explained. "Tandy's ... written to Lawrence Montrose."

Sandra Crain's face crumbled. She couldn't believe, didn't want to accept, such bitterness. "You were going to give them to Greg?"

He nodded.

"Oh, God!" Sandra Crain looked into her husband's eyes. "God, do you hate him that much?"

"Yes," Nelson Crain admitted, "I hate him. Why shouldn't I? He stole my daughter, didn't he?" Then he saw the look on her face and tried to soften his statement. "I burned the damned things, what else do you want from me?"

"Forgiveness!"

Forgiveness? Never, Nelson Crain thought, turning away. He stood staring into the fire, watching the letters turn to ashes. He wondered if, like a phoenix, anything would ever rise from them.

CHICAGO

CHAPTER 16

In that year, 1922, Chicago was on its way to becoming the most lawless city in America, all because of the Great Experiment.

The Great Illusion, it was to be called later. Herbert Asbury, in his history of Prohibition, was to say of it: "The American people had expected to be greeted, when the great day came, by a covey of angels bearing gifts of peace, happiness, prosperity and salvation, which they had been assured would be theirs when the rum demon had been scotched. Instead they were met by a horde of bootleggers, moonshiners, rum-runners, hijackers, gangsters, racketeers, trigger men, venal judges, corrupt police, crooked politicians and speakeasy operators, all bearing the twin symbol of the Eighteenth Amendment—the Tommy gun and the poisoned cup."

Even before Prohibition went into effect in July, 1920, the first trigger had been pulled in Chicago.

In May, Big Jim Colosimo, ruler of vice and rackets in the notorious Levee District, was shot down in an early morning ambush in his showplace restaurant, the Four Deuces Café. The assassin: Frankie Yale, boss of Unione Siciliano, imported from New York to do the job for ten thousand dollars. The mastermind: Colosimo's aide, Johnny Torrio, sometimes called "Terrible John" or "The Fox." The rationale: Big Jim wasn't thinking big enough. He didn't see the millions to be reaped from the illegal liquor business.

Colosimo was given a gargantuan fifty-thousand-dollar funeral, the model for all of gangdom's Prohibition-era funerals, after which Torrio, on the surface a gentle, courtly man, seized control with an iron fist.

He summoned Chicago's warring gangland factions and proclaimed himself *Capo di Turri.* He made a deal with Dion O'Banion, Colosimo's chief rival, letting him keep what he already had, and divided the rest of the city into districts, each headed by a captain. Within these strict territorial limits the captains and their henchmen were to handle all beer and liquor shipments, deliveries and collections. None was to stray outside his district, under threat of violent retribution. There was to be no more hijacking of a rival's supplies.

In this new, more formal underworld, Dion O'Banion, whose lieutenants included Hymie "the Polack" Weiss and George "Bugs" Moran, got the Gold Coast and the slums north of the Loop—in effect, the whole North Side. Torrio's bodyguard, Scarface Al Brown—who would soon assume his real name, Alphonse Caponi, or Al Capone—was appointed chief enforcer and given command of the West Side.

By 1922 the Torrio syndicate was at the peak of its power. The Fox had accomplished what he had set out to do. He controlled almost all of the supply and distribution of illegal liquor and beer in Chicago. He was personally grossing $4,000,000 annually from liquor, $3,000,000 from gambling and $2,000,000 from prostitution. His take from the suburbs was another $4,000,000.

Mayor William Hale "Big Bill" Thompson was looking the other way. The police were on the syndicate's payroll. Chicago, as many people were fond of saying, was a wide-open town.

Greg Meister arrived in Chicago as he had arrived in New York, an innocent. If he had grand plans, he had no idea, except in the most general terms, of how he was going to put them into action. He had no conception of the incredible amounts of money being made in the illegal liquor business. And he hadn't the foggiest notion that John Crain would be waiting for him when he carried his new bride across the threshold of their room at the Bishop Hotel.

"Surprise!" Crain cried out gaily.

Meister almost dropped Tandy. He did let her go, just barely catching her before she hit the floor.

"What in the name of hell?" Meister was too surprised to be angry. He just stood staring in disbelief.

John Crain was on the bed, leaning against puffed up pillows, a glass of champagne in his hand. He raised it in welcome and a toast. "Congratulations—and best wishes too!"

Tandy struggled out of Meister's arms and ran to him. "Oh, John, am I glad to see you!" she cried, hugging him. "It's been so long!"

Her brother returned her embrace with his free arm, holding his champagne glass aloft with the other, keeping a careful eye on Meister, who was still staring dumfounded.

Tandy kissed her brother soundly, gave him another hug, then grabbed the champagne bottle, filling the other two glasses on the bedside table.

"I'll be goddamned," Meister said finally.

"We thought you would be." Tandy laughed, handing him one of the glasses. "But not struck dumb. Go on, kiss the man or something." She turned back to her brother. "What is it that brothers-in-law do, anyway?"

"Bury the hatchet," John Crain said, still keeping a wary eye on Meister. "Then shake hands."

Tandy looked from one to the other, suddenly aware of the tension in the room. John had asked her to help him arrange this surprise meeting and she had agreed, thinking it would be a joyous reunion for all of them. Instead, Greg had a strange expression on his face. He seemed to be struggling to control a growing anger.

"Hey," she said, confused. "Is there something I don't know about?"

"Yes," John Crain admitted, swinging off the bed. "And something your husband here doesn't know either." He looked at Meister. "You and I, we've got to have a private talk."

Meister nodded grimly, putting his glass of champagne down. "The sooner the better."

John Crain emptied his own glass and handed it to his sister. "Greg and I, we're going to get a real drink downstairs, okay? Half an hour—time to let you freshen up. Then we'll be back and we'll all go out to dinner. My treat."

"Sounds good to me," Tandy said, reassured by her brother's wink. She kissed him again. "God, it is good to see you, you know that?"

"Likewise," he told her. He looked at Meister. "You've got yourself a great lady, nincompoop."

Meister followed John Crain downstairs to the Bishop Hotel's lounge in a barely controlled rage. He wasn't quite so ready to bury the hatchet, unless it was in his brother-in-law's head. If Tandy hadn't been present, the two-faced bastard would have been decked on the spot. And unless there was an awfully good explanation coming up, coupled with an apology, he was still going to get decked, Tandy or no Tandy.

John Crain led the way to a secluded booth at the back of the dimly lit lounge. He signaled to the maître d', who had just seated another party, that they would be wanting only drinks, not dinner. Another signal passed and, a few moments later, a waiter appeared with two glasses, a bucket of ice and a bottle, barely disguised by its towel wrapping.

"Thanks, Willie," John Crain said with the familiarity of a long-term guest. Careful to keep the bottle wrapped in the towel, he opened it and poured two shots, straight. He pushed the ice aside. "Drink up first," he told Meister. "Then we talk."

Meister shook his head. He was so angry he hadn't spoken since leaving the room and he still didn't trust himself to. It was hard to keep his big hands clutching the sides of his pants and not John Crain's throat. The promise he had made to himself in New York, that he would put his anger aside when such a confrontation came, seemed about to be broken.

"All right," John Crain said, showing no offense. "First we talk, then we drink." He leaned back into the booth's soft padding, getting out his cigarettes, his eyes never leaving Meister's. "There are three things you should know. One, I didn't send you that money. Two, I have no objection to your having married my sister. Under the circumstances, I think it only right and proper that you did. Third—you fucking nincompoop, how are you going to support her?"

Meister blinked. The last was said with such sudden, angry emphasis that his own anger was momentarily forgotten. It took him a long moment to recover and to appreciate all that had been imparted in Crain's three sharply clipped statements.

"You didn't send the money?" he finally said, deciding he could best deal with them one at a time.

John Crain shook his head. "No, my father did." "But the note . . ."

"If there was a note—and I'm sure there was—he sent that too," John Crain said. "Signed with my name. It's just like the crafty bastard, can't you see that? What would hurt you most—a note from him or one from me?"

Meister met his steady gaze. "You, naturally."

"Apology accepted," John Crain said, lighting his cigarette. "Once again, congratulations. Now I'd appreciate it if you'd answer my question. How are you going to support Tandy?"

Meister shrugged, flustered now, still trying to adjust to the fact that Nelson Crain, and not John, had sent him the money. He had done John Crain a terrible disservice. He should have realized that duplicity was a possibility. "Get a job?" he suggested, finally answering the question.

"Boy," John Crain said, exasperated. "You and Tandy, you do make a pair, don't you? That was her answer." He leaned forward. "Listen, my friend, I don't like to poke my nose into other people's business, but you *are* my friend and she *is* my sister. If you think some ordinary job is the answer, you are both in big trouble. Tandy may say that now. 'I'll live anywhere with Greg,' was her happy announcement to me. But how long do you think that's going to last? Her whole life the girl's lived in a mansion, maids to pick up after her, and you're going to put her in some dismal apartment?"

Meister stared at him miserably. For a while, yes, he had to admit. He wasn't happy about it, but there wasn't any other choice. With a child coming they had had to get married immediately and all the things that he had planned to do alone they now had to do together. There was no other choice. "We'll manage."

"Will you?"

"Yes, damn it!" Meister said, suddenly angry again. "I love her and she loves me. Somehow we'll manage. I'll get a job."

"Two jobs," John Crain told him, interrupting. "Tandy tells me you had two jobs in the Village. Two shifts, night and day, which was very admirable of you, and I'm sure you'll be able to do the same thing here. Then, exhausted, you'll wend your way home to your dismal apartment where your expectant wife, who has never cooked a meal in her life, will be happily waiting with a boiled potato supper. Providing, which I doubt, that she knows how to boil water."

"Whoa," Meister said, gritting his teeth. "Just a minute, Mister Millionaire's son. If I misjudged you, I'm sorry, but I won't take this, understand? If this is why you're here—to offer congratulations and then tell me the marriage won't work—you're way off base. You'll see, I'm going to make it work. Whatever it takes, I'll make it work."

"You just said the magic words," John Crain told him, smiling. "Whatever it takes." He got the two glasses he had set aside and pushed one across the table. "Let's drink to that, shall we?"

Meister ignored the glass, getting out his own cigarettes, his big hands clumsy because of his seething anger. "You're an infuriating son of a bitch, you know that? You disappear on me—no proper explanation. You show up by surprise, offering needless commentary. And now you sit there smiling when you know I'm ready to shake your teeth loose."

John Crain was still smiling. "You can try if you like. But first, drink up." He pushed the glass closer. "Go ahead. One sip."

Meister took the drink. He needed it, he thought. God, how he needed it! With one gulp, he downed half of it.

"A sip, I told you," John Crain said, still smiling. "I want you to taste it. I want you to tell me what it is."

Meister stared at him. God, this was too much, this was really too much. All this, and now the son of a bitch wanted to play games?

"Can you do that?"

For answer, Meister grabbed the bottle, pulling the towel away. "Here, this is what it is, and if you're not out of my sight in one minute, you'll be able to taste glass too, because it'll be down your goddamn throat!"

John Crain took a sip of his own drink, holding the whiskey in his mouth, savoring it, swallowing it with reluctance. "It's Dunbar's Special."

The look on John Crain's face, oddly triumphant, forced Meister to turn the bottle around, to read the label. It was Dunbar's Special and there was no doubting its legitimacy, as the aftertaste confirmed. He'd been too angry to realize it, but he had just drunk, despite Prohibition, the world's best whiskey.

"Yes," John Crain said softly, "and I can get more, Mr. Meister. I happened to meet, by pure chance, a frightened gentleman down here from Toronto, a Mr. Himie Koshevoy, and he's got what sounds like a boatload. I could get plenty more—if I had the money to buy it."

Meister looked at him. He already knew the answer, but he asked the question anyway: "What are you suggesting?"

"A partnership," John Crain said. "I've got the connection, you've got the money."

Meister shook his head.

"I'm not suggesting that you keep the money," John Crain said quickly. "I'm suggesting that you use it once." He took back the bottle. "Once, that's all it would take. I guarantee, whatever you've got, you'll double it."

Meister again shook his head.

"Why not?" Crain asked. "Hell, my father is in no hurry for the money or else he would have asked for it back, wouldn't he?" He smiled at his joke. "Come on, use it, benefit by it, then send it back to him. Where's the harm in that?"

"It's not mine to use."

John Crain slammed the bottle down. "Oh, *come on!* Don't get righteous on me. How can you worry about that? After what the man did to you? After what he did to both of us?"

"Use your own money," Meister told him. He started to get up.

"I don't have any!" John Crain said, grabbing his arm. "I'm on the dole, spent as fast as it comes in. The last six checks, I haven't even collected them. I'm behind on my rent here, for God's sake. I owe them for a month."

A month? Meister let himself be pulled down. "You mean, you didn't just arrive?"

"No, I've been here since November. How do you think I made that kind of connection—overnight?"

Meister lit his cigarette. If only he could do two things, he thought, control his temper and not jump to conclusions. Angry, he had assumed a lot of things: that Sid Berns had told the truth and that John Crain really had been in Miami, that however Tandy had gotten in touch with John, he could, because he was Nelson Crain's son, come all the way from Miami to Chicago just to be able to yell surprise and give some brotherly advice.

"You seem to be in the same fix as me," Meister said.

"How's that?"

"Poor." For the first time he felt equal. Rank had been stripped away. John Crain was no longer his lieutenant, he was just his brother-in-law. For whatever reason, and however temporarily, his wealth had been stripped away, too. Like himself, John Crain was worried about paying his rent.

"For the moment," Crain admitted. "Eventually

I'll get things worked out with my father. Then ...."

"Never mind that," Meister said. He wondered why it had taken him so long to realize that *they were equal, damn it!* Take away the money and John Crain had to scramble, just like him. There was no difference, no difference at all. "How much do you need?" "Ten thousand, minimum," Crain said.

Meister laughed. "I mean, for the rent."

"Oh, I don't know. Fifty, sixty dollars. What difference does it make?" He leaned forward. "Greg, listen to me. We've *got* to make this deal."

Meister laughed again. What difference indeed? There wasn't any difference, and while he was letting simple facts sink in, he might as well accept another. The ten thousand dollars was Crain money. If he returned it to John Crain, his duty was done. He'd hand it over to him and advise Nelson Crain. If John didn't give it to his father, well, it could always be deducted from his dole, couldn't it?

"Greg," John Crain pleaded, "don't be a fool. Don't let this chance pass by."

"All right," Meister said, the decision already made. "I'll give you the money. If you want to roll it over before it gets back to your father, that's your business, chum. But I'm letting him know, understand?"

John Crain only heard the first part. "Done!" he cried, exultant. He extended his hand. "Partners?"

Meister hesitated. He hadn't meant that, but it was tempting, now that the money was committed. Crain money and, if a profit was to be made on it, why not partly Tandy's and not all John's? If this was the start they needed, the difference between a cold-water flat and a decent apartment, why not partners for Tandy's sake?

"You'll never regret it," John Crain said, his hand still extended.

Hesitantly, reluctantly, Meister clasped it. In his mind, he hoped he would never regret it. In his heart, he knew he would. One day he'd regret it, but there was no turning back now. He was on the long, narrow road and there were no detours, no turning back.

Later that night, in bed with Tandy, holding her after they had made love, Meister confessed that he was going to take a one-shot try at the bootlegging business with her brother.

"We need a proper stake," he explained, hoping she would understand. "I'm just going to do it this once."

She was silent for a long time, and Crain grew anxious. "Where are you going to get the money?" she asked finally.

"John's got it," he told her, the one lie he had to tell. "He's the financier. I'm the muscle."

She was again silent for a while. "If it will help, I've got five thousand dollars," she offered. "It's from my savings account. I was going to keep it as our nest egg."

"I don't need it," he said, hugging her tightly. He had expected her to object, and he had certainly not expected her to offer money. "John has enough."

"All right, but if you can use it, say so," she told him. "If you're going to get involved, I'd rather you got a share, not just get paid for your muscles." She snuggled against him. "Not that I've got any complaint about them."

He kissed the back of her neck. "We'll see," he said, not meaning it.

CHAPTER 17

Meister took control of the buy. It wasn't a carefully deliberated, mutual decision, but a swift, brash assumption of power at the outset of negotiations, a headlong rush into a vacuum left by John Crain.

The first meeting was in Schlogl's, the literary restaurant on Wells Street, far from the usual haunts of the city's criminal element. Meister came, at least in the eyes of Himie Koshevoy, as the "money man" who would make the transaction possible.

"You're the bucks, huh?" Koshevoy said nervously, bumping the table as he stood up in greeting.

"Yes," Meister told him when John Crain made no attempt to suggest otherwise.

"Good," Koshevoy said. "Then we can get this done." He sat down as abruptly as he had stood up. John Crain seemed forgotten. Himie's soft brown eyes were glued on Meister. "How much of the action do you want?"

Meister again waited for John to answer. It was, after all, his deal, and the amount had already been agreed upon between them. The price was $2.50 a bottle, which meant they could buy three hundred thirty cases, twelve bottles to the case, at a total cost of $9,900. If they were lucky, they could quickly turn it over, very little other expense involved, for five dollars a bottle. There was perhaps $8,000 profit to be made for a few days' work.

"How much have you got altogether?" Meister asked when Crain didn't answer.

Koshevoy hesitated. He was a small, fearful man trying to take advantage of family connections in Toronto. He would have been the first to admit that he was out of his element. "You mean, the whole shipment?"

Meister ignored John Crain's sharp kick under the table. He suddenly realized, aware of the fear exuding from Koshevoy, that here might be an opportunity to make a much larger deal than anticipated. Hell, he thought, if the man was as scared as he looked, they might be able to take it all. "Yes: Everything."

"There's a thousand cases," Koshevoy said finally.

Meister did some rapid arithmetic. "So, you're talking thirty thousand bucks?"

Koshevoy nodded. "Yes."

"I think I can handle that," Meister responded, ignoring John Crain, who had turned ashen. "It would require some cooperation, though."

Koshevoy was immediately suspicious. "What kind?"

"Spaced out deliveries."

"What's that mean?"

"It means I'll take five hundred cases now and the other five hundred in two weeks."

Koshevoy was still suspicious. "Why not take it all now?"

"Because I'm careful and you should be too," Meister said, staring Crain down. "It takes me time to move things. I don't want a thousand cases sitting in one place at one time. Too big a risk. If it got hijacked, then what?" He shrugged, as if that would be annoying, but not fatal. "Why take that chance?"

"I'm taking it," Koshevoy pointed out.

"You have to," Meister said easily, "and you've made it so far, haven't you? Now ask yourself this: What's safer, moving that whole batch at once or making two smaller, spaced out deliveries?" He waited for a moment. "Hell, you were going to sell it piecemeal anyway, weren't you?"

Koshevoy nodded. "Yes, but not over two weeks. I want to dump it all in the next couple days."

"Yes, I know," Meister said, looking at Crain. He was still grey-faced, afraid to speak. "He told me and I can appreciate your hurry. Still, if it was me, I'd settle for a clean two-step deal, spaced out deliveries, spaced out payments." He waited a moment. "You know what this business is like, that's why you're doing it piecemeal. You're afraid of making the wrong choice and losing it all. This way, working with me alone, you've got the best of both worlds. Piecemeal and the assurance that I'm not going to slit your throat. If I was going to do that, I'd ask for it all at once, wouldn't I?"

Koshevoy considered, his soft brown eyes still glaring at Meister. John Crain had ceased to exist. "Two weeks?"

Meister nodded. "Two weeks. A little patience, that's all, and it could save you an awful lot. I don't know what other deals you've got pending, but how comfortable are you with them? How safe do you feel?"

"I've got to make a phone call," said Koshevoy.

"There's no hurry," Meister assured him. "Make as many as you want."

John Crain waited until Koshevoy had scuttled away from the table. "Are you mad?" he demanded then. "You've screwed up the whole deal! We haven't even got money for the first buy!"

"Trust me," Meister said softly, glad that the money was Crain's main worry. It meant that he saw the chance for the rest of it working. "We've got fifteen thousand altogether."

"How?"

"Trust me," Meister repeated. "If we're going to take it all, we can't be piddling the first time out. I had to take half of it. Five hundred cases—uh, at thirty dollars a case, that is fifteen thousand, right?"

"Jesus Christ!" John Crain said.

Meister ignored him. "Okay, in a couple of weeks we should be able to sell half the load at sixty bucks a case. That gives us our fifteen thousand back. We take the money, buy the second five hundred cases and peddle them—plus the two hundred fifty cases still on hand—for whatever the market will bear. It's probably a lot more than sixty bucks a case, but even if that's all we can get, that's a profit—less expenses—of forty-five thousand. Right?"

"Jesus Christ," John Crain said again, more softly this time. "Just tell me one thing: We've *really* got fifteen thousand now?"

Meister nodded in answer. Koshevoy was returning to the table.

"Okay, then," John Crain muttered. "Take it and run."

Meister turned his head, waiting for Koshevoy. He felt exhilarated, exultant. I already have, John, he thought. I already have....

Koshevoy slipped back into his chair. His fearful look was gone and he seemed more relaxed, confident.

"You've got yourself a deal," he told Meister. "Now, how do you want to handle it?"

Tandy was waiting impatiently when they returned to the Bishop Hotel. For economy's sake they had moved, after the first night, into larger, shared quarters—a two-bedroom suite with a small kitchenette.

It had been her idea. Her honeymoon had been in New York and on the train ride to Chicago and she was anxious to get down to serious married life. Any saving that brought that day closer was worth the sacrifice. Besides, to her surprise, she enjoyed John's company. After the first flush of elopement and escape, she found herself missing her home and the luxuries she had always taken for granted. John was a link to—and a help in the transition away from—Washington Square.

"Well? Did you do it?" she demanded when he and Greg staggered in, happy but exhausted.

"Do what?" John wanted to know.

"Make a deal!"

John Crain looked at Meister.

"I told her," Meister explained. "No secrets in a marriage. But I didn't expect the wretch to go blabbing to the whole world," he teased.

"Oh, we're all family," Tandy said, not to be denied a part of the excitement. She kissed her husband and then sat on her brother's lap, putting her arms around his neck. "Aren't we?"

"No," John Crain told her. "You were found on the doorstep. We took you in out of the goodness of our hearts." He winked at Meister. "Now, what is it you want?"

"A piece of the action," she said.

"Huh?"

"A piece of the action," Tandy repeated. "Greg told me all about it. You're the financier, he's the muscle. Well, if you want my husband involved, he's not going to be just a hired hand, hear me?" She looked at Meister. "Seriously, I've thought it over. If you're going to be involved in something like this, you really ought to have a share, Greg. It's only fair."

Meister didn't say anything.

"I've got five thousand dollars," Tandy said, turning back to her brother. "I want to put that in the pot on Greg's behalf, okay?"

"If it's okay by Greg, it's okay by me," John Crain said, looking at Meister.

There was a long silence. Meister finally broke it. "Okay," he said. "The five thousand will be enough."

"Are you sure?" Tandy asked.

"Yes."

"Then it's done," she said. She scrambled off John's lap and ran into the bedroom. "No peeking! It's in a secret hiding place."

John Crain looked at Meister. "Why didn't you tell me it was her money?" he demanded.

"You didn't ask," Meister said.

Crain looked uncomfortable. "She should keep that kind of money in the bank."

Meister nodded. "I know, but I didn't even know she had it until last night."

"Oh."

"Yes, 'oh,'" Meister said.

There was silence. Neither of them had anything more to say.

"There's just one condition I want to make," Tandy said as she came back into the room, directing her words to her husband. "You know what you told me last night, that it's going to be a one-shot thing, just this once so you can get a proper stake?"

Meister nodded.

"Okay," Tandy said seriously, glancing at her brother. "John is our witness. The condition is this: You're going to do it just this one time, promise?" She held out the money to him. "We're going to have a baby and I don't want its father to be a bootlegger. I want the baby to be decent and upstanding, so you've got to promise."

Meister looked from one to the other. John Crain's face was expressionless, nothing showing whatsoever, not even interest. Tandy's was filled with concern, everything bared, waiting.

"I promise," Meister said, taking the money.

That night Meister had trouble falling asleep. He felt disgusted with himself. He had been married hardly more than a week, and already he had done something he had thought he'd never do. Ask for and take Crain money.

This would be the first and last time, he vowed. This once he would use them all—Nelson Crain, John, Tandy. He would have enough to be independent of them, which he had to be. Otherwise, no matter how hard he tried, the marriage would fail.

He couldn't live with himself if he had to keep coming to his wife for money. And could she live with him if he made promises he might not be able to keep?

The next day, as arranged, a large delivery truck drew up in front of Schlogl's, its motor steaming like a teakettle in the bitter cold. Himie Koshevoy was in the passenger's seat, and a younger, tougher version of himself—his brother, Sam—was at the wheel. Meister and John Crain were sitting at a streetside window in the café.

Within a matter of seconds, Meister and Himie Koshevoy had traded places and the truck was on its way again, headed around the block. It took just that long, a circling of the block, to complete the transaction.

Meister was certain, from a random sampling of the cases, that he had received a full count and that it was genuine Dunbar's Special. Himie Koshevoy had counted one hundred fifty crisp new hundred-dollar bills.

When the truck returned it was John Crain and Sam Koshevoy who traded places. The Koshevoys stayed at Schlogl's for lunch. Meister and John Crain took the load of Dunbar's Special to a garage they had rented four blocks away, on Orleans Street. They had the whiskey unloaded and locked up and the truck parked back at Schlogl's before the Koshevoys had finished eating.

Meister tapped lightly on the café window as he and John Crain sauntered by. Same thing, same time next week? Himie Koshevoy smiled. Agreed.

"We did it!" John Crain cried as they rounded the corner. "You goddamn nincompoop, we did it!"

Meister wasn't quite so sure. Only the first step had been completed. Now they had to move the whiskey, half of it, in two weeks. John Crain had a list of private clubs and better saloons and speaks where he was sure he could sell it for sixty dollars a case. Some had already been approached and had expressed interest. There were, however, many pitfalls along the way—as Himie Koshevoy knew and had now avoided. Interest didn't necessarily translate into ready cash. Every potential purchaser was also a potential thief. When the word started getting around that a couple of straights were peddling Dunbar's Special, the crime syndicate's heavies might try moving in, demanding a part of the action, or even all of it.

Still, if they were careful, they had a good shot at moving half the stuff in two weeks with no trouble. If they did, they'd have the money for the next buy. If they didn't....

Well, that was Himie Koshevoy's problem, Meister thought, already hardened to the realities. Himie would pull up in front of Schlogl's with five hundred cases of the world's best whiskey and there would be nobody waiting for him. Not even Himie had avoided all the pitfalls. There was no way of doing that, not in the bootleg business.

"Who do you want to try first?" John Crain asked. He looked at the list he had compiled. "What about this place—Murphy's—that flashy speak on Michigan Avenue? I bet we could move twenty cases there."

Meister shook his head. By asking the question, John Crain had acknowledged that Meister was still in charge, and Meister felt that the main consideration, much more important than a quick, large sale, was caution. If they could place the first batch of whiskey in long-established private clubs, places the gangster element didn't frequent, they had a better chance over the long haul. Sooner or later the syndicate was going to take notice. Meister preferred that it be later, after the second buy. After the second buy there would be profits to keep, and he was anxious to repay the money he'd borrowed from Tandy.

"I want to sell to the private men's clubs first," Meister said. "You can be the front. You've got the look for it." He looked down at the list. "What's the Everleigh Club?"

John Crain laughed. "The town's most famous whorehouse."

"Oh." Meister reddened. "Well, pick the right ones, will you?"

"You nincompoop," John Crain said, but he didn't challenge the decision.

It was a long, arduous task. The private men's clubs might be safe sales, but they were also difficult, time-consuming ones. John Crain found himself greeted by suspicion, and the initial contact never resulted in an immediate sale. Always he was asked to leave a sample bottle, to call back later. "I swear they're holding membership meetings," he complained, and sometimes three or four calls were necessary before everyone involved was satisfied that it really was Dunbar's Special. Once the decision to buy was made, however, there were some large purchases. The smallest of the transactions moved ten cases, and on the second Friday, getting down to the wire, the Terminal City Club, which had looked like a waste of time, suddenly decided to buy all that was left. In one afternoon they sold fifty cases for three thousand cash.

"We did it!" John Crain cried, driving away from the Terminal City Club. This time Meister shared his elation. The two weeks' work, difficult, perhaps, but nothing compared to two weeks on the farm, had netted them the necessary fifteen thousand dollars. They could make the second buy. After that, taking their time with sales, going after whatever the market was willing to pay, they stood to make maybe fifty, sixty thousand. It was a fortune. Even *half* was a fortune! And half would be his, Meister thought, barely able to keep from shouting.

"Hell, if we keep this up, we could be millionaires by year's end!" John Crain said. "You hear me, nincompoop? Millionaires!"

Meister laughed. Millionaires? No, not millionaires, he decided, happy enough with the small fortune that already was within his grasp. If he got that, he'd be more than satisfied, he told himself. This was strictly a one-shot deal, a way to make a quick stake. When he got it, he'd quit, just as he had promised

Tandy. He'd invest the money in some nice legal business and live happily ever after. It wasn't necessary to be a millionaire.

He kept telling himself that as they finished up for the day, depositing the Terminal City Club's three thousand in the bank and turning in the small delivery truck they had rented for the week. Be satisfied ... you don't have to be a millionaire.

CHAPTER 18

On the way home they stopped off for a drink at a high-class State Street speak called Preacher's, one of the few places they'd sold Dunbar's Special that wasn't a private club.

John Crain was in an ebullient, playful mood. For twenty dollars, four times what they'd sold it for, he bought back a bottle of Dunbar's Special, insisting that they stay and celebrate.

Meister wanted to stay, but he also felt guilty about Tandy being stuck alone at the Bishop Hotel. He hadn't gotten back until almost midnight all week. To do that to her again, needlessly, was unfair.

"Come on, don't be a stick-in-the-mud," John Crain complained, yanking the cork out of the bottle. Without benefit of glass, he took a long, healthy drink. "Do you realize what we've accomplished these past two weeks?"

Meister nodded. Nobody had to tell him. They'd made back their money and they still had half the first buy—two hundred fifty cases—sitting in the garage on Orleans Street.

"Then why aren't we celebrating?" John Crain demanded. He took another swig from the bottle. "God, that's good whiskey." He glanced around the speak, as if looking for better company. "The world's best—and we've got it!"

"Shush," Meister told him good-naturedly. If it wasn't for Tandy waiting, he thought, he would stay. His own plans called for a celebration when it was all over and done. Until then he wanted all his wits about him. But they hadn't run into trouble so far, and the chance of trouble lurking in Preacher's was remote.

"We've got it," John Crain repeated. "You and me, my friend." He pushed the bottle across the table. "Come on! One drink?"

"No," Meister replied, making up his mind. There was Tandy. He wouldn't feel good about her until he was back at the Bishop. "I'm going home. You be careful, hear?"

John Crain shook his head in disbelief. "You're leaving me?"

"For Tandy."

"Oh, yeah ... Tandy," John Crain said, as if he'd forgotten her existence. "Yeah, that's nice. You've got a girl." He looked around again. "My sister."

"Get your own girl," Meister told him, laughing. He gave him a farewell shove and left. John would be safe enough. All the man wanted to do was get drunk and find himself a girl. He'd done that before, plenty of times, and it hadn't hurt him yet.

Even with his good intentions, it was still after ten o'clock when Meister got back to the Bishop Hotel. Tandy was already asleep.

Three nights in a row? Not goddamn likely, Meister thought, making a production out of getting undressed and leaving the bathroom door ajar while he took his shower.

"Was that a hint?" Tandy asked sleepily when he joined her in bed.

"What?"

"All that noise, does that mean you've missed me?"

"Yes," Meister said. Gently he took hold of her, turning her around to face him. "Very much, if you want the truth, very, very much."

She laughed and snuggled against him. "You smell good."

"You too," he told her, amazed at how she always did. She was like a flower with magical properties. She would, he was sure, always be beautiful. And when he came to her she would always smell sweet.

"John back too? I didn't hear him."

"No, he's having a party."

"Just the two of us then?"

"Yes."

"We can make all the noise we want?"

"We can wake up the dead."

"Good!"

Meister laughed, holding her close.

"Just a minute," she said. "I want to know what's going on first. How come you're home early for a change and John is having a party?"

"I'll tell you later."

"No, I'll fall asleep later."

Meister laughed again. That was true, his beautiful flower wilted when he took her. Happily exhausted, she would fall asleep almost immediately, drained of everything except contentment.

"We got our money back and can make the second buy," he told her.

"The whole fifteen thousand?"

"Uh-huh."

"Good," she said. "I was hoping that was it." She pushed closer to him, taking the initiative now, kissing his chest. "It's scary here alone, waiting, wondering . . . ."

He tipped her face up to look at her. "I know and

I'm sorry. But it won't be much longer, just the one more buy."

"Are you going to make it?"

He hesitated. Something in her eyes had betrayed her. She wasn't asking a question, she was making a request. "That was the idea," he said carefully.

"I see." This time it was her voice that betrayed her. She didn't want him to.

Damn, if he quit now, running scared, selling off the remaining two hundred fifty cases as quickly as possible, averaging sixty dollars a case, all they'd make on the deal was fifteen thousand. His share would be $7,500. Was it enough?

For some reason, not anymore, he realized ruefully. A week and a half ago it had been a fortune he hardly dared imagine. Now, with it almost in hand, but with so much more to be made, it seemed a piddling sum.

The trouble, if it could be called that, was that the second buy was where the real money could be made. He had only lately come to realize it. Once made, there wouldn't be any rush to sell, because there would no longer be any deadline to meet. They could sit on the booze as long as they wanted, seeking out a select market, demanding and getting a premium price. Why let it go for only sixty bucks a case? Why not seventy? Why not more? Just because Himie Koshevoy was afraid, anxious to dump it before he lost it, didn't mean they had to run scared, too. Not anymore.

Meister couldn't put the almost staggering amounts out of his mind. At seventy dollars a case, seven hundred fifty cases would bring in $52,500. At eighty a case, sixty-thousand. Now his share of the profits wasn't $7,500 but four times that. Make the last buy, sell it slowly and carefully at a premium price, and he stood to pocket more than thirty thousand.

"You're going to make it, aren't you?" Tandy asked.

"Let me think about it," Meister answered, and he wondered if his voice had betrayed him.

John Crain, at this moment, was entering the Four Deuces Café, a highly recommended whorehouse on Wabash Avenue in Chicago's red-light district. Here, his taxi driver had told him, he would not be disappointed, provided he could make it to the fourth floor. There was a saloon on the first floor and gambling traps on the second and third. The girls-for-hire, some of the best in the city, held sway at the top.

"No problem," John Crain had told him, and he meant it. He had drunk all he could hold and gambling had never interested him. He preferred, when it was available, a sure thing.

He went into the bar not for a drink but in hope of spotting a few celebrities while he rested for the assault on the stairs. The driver had told him he might bump into anybody in the late hours. Caruso had frequented the saloon, and Flo Ziegfeld. So did George M. Cohan and Gentleman Jim Corbett. The place was still fashionable despite the violent death two years before of its original owner, Big Jim Colosimo.

When the bartender approached him, John Crain waved him away, indicating that he'd soon be going upstairs. "I just want to watch for a while, if you don't mind," he said, eyeing the crowd. Despite the late hour, the place was filled. Dinner was still being served and the smell of rich red wine and spicy Italian dishes pervaded.

The bartender, a roughhouse Irishman who seemed strangely out of his element, looked him over carefully, eyeing the bulging overcoat pocket that held the half-consumed bottle of Dunbar's Special.

"Normally, we wouldn't," he said, "but we don't like our customers to bring in their own stuff."

John Crain had forgotten all about the bottle. "Huh?"

"If you're just going to watch, why don't you let me hold that, pal?" the bartender suggested. With surprising agility he leaned far over the bar, whisking the bottle away before Crain had time to react.

"Hey, what have we got here?" The bartender stared at the label.

"That?" John Crain reached for the bottle too late. "Just some private stock, that's all. Give it back, will you?"

"Dunbar's Special?" the bartender said in wonder, backing well out of reach. He removed the cork and sniffed it. "Is it for real?"

Crain made another ineffective grab. "Come on! Give it back!"

"In a minute," the bartender told him. Without asking permission he got a glass and poured out a small sampling, which he committed to his mouth and swirled several times. His eyes gleamed as he swallowed. "Mother of mercy, it *is*!"

"Give it back!"

"In a minute," the bartender repeated. He examined the label in a better light, as if seeking to refute his taste buds, then, unable to resist, he poured himself another drink, a full shot this time. "I haven't seen Dunbar's Special in years. Where'd you get it?"

John Crain watched helplessly from the other side of the bar. "I told you, private stock."

"No kidding," the bartender said. He took a sip of the drink he had poured, swallowed reverently. "How much have you got?"

John Crain tried to think. The last thing on his mind was making a sale. All he wanted to do, the fates willing, was go upstairs, find himself the prettiest girl and go to sleep in her arms. "Some," he said at last, the only answer that seemed safe.

"Would you like to sell it?"

"Not really," John Crain said, which was the truth. He was certain of it now. All he wanted to do was go upstairs.

"It might fetch you a good price."

Crain waved that away. It was no doubt possible, but later, much later. He would return. "Listen," he said, trying not to slur. "I don't want to talk business right now... maybe next week. In the meantime, you just keep the bottle, okay?"

"No," the bartender said. "You stay put, pal." He yelled down the bar. "Artie! Get on the blower to the boss, will ya? Tell him I got a live one."

"Now listen—" Crain started to protest.

"Stay put!"

Crain waited without further argument. In his condition, brain numbed, reflexes slowed, the bartender would have him by the scruff of the neck before he got halfway to the door. The best thing he could do was—what? Lie, he decided. Otherwise this was going to take forever. If they started talking deal, he'd never get upstairs, and that was all he wanted to do, get upstairs. So he'd lie. He'd tell them—what?

While Crain was trying to decide, a stocky, swarthy, baby-faced hoodlum materialized from somewhere in the back of the Four Deuces Café. He moved behind the bar as if he owned it and took custody of the bottle the bartender was holding out to him like an offering.

"Look at this, will you, Al?" the bartender said. "Dunbar's Special, the real thing!"

John Crain froze, suddenly sober. As the hoodlum turned to face him, a scar, what looked like a knife wound, came into view, running from his left ear to his lip. Scarface Al Brown, Crain thought, unable to move. Instinctively he knew that this was the gun-for-hire who had threatened to kill him for shooting Tony Capullo.

"Dunbar's Special," the gangster said, talking to the bartender but looking at Crain. Though baby-faced and pudgy from too rich a diet, he radiated a cruel, ruthless power. He had dark, probing black eyes, a flat nose and thick lips, and his round head was set on a bull neck. "What's so special about it?"

"It's the best whiskey in the world."

"You don't say?" The hoodlum looked surprised. "I never heard of it before." For an instant he seemed about to hand the bottle back to the bartender, but then his dark eyes left Crain, moving out over the busy tables in the saloon. "Some of these swells out there, I suppose they'd recognize it, huh?"

The bartender nodded solemnly. "Yeah, and pay top price for it."

The next question was for Crain. "Where did you get it?"

"He says private stock."

"I'm asking *him*," the hoodlum said, dismissing the bartender. "You got customers waiting. Get back to your job."

Behind him, Crain could hear people talking in awed whispers, as if they might be in the presence of Caruso, but the name they were using was Al Capone. Again, Crain knew instinctively the moment the name registered in his whiskey-numbed brain, that Scarface Al Brown and Al Capone were one and the same.

He stared in fear and disbelief. Al Capone, a young hoodlum barely in his mid-twenties, was already a legend in Chicago. Johnny Torrio, boss of the crime syndicate, had hired him as a bodyguard after the murder of Big Jim Colosimo. In two swift years Capone had risen to the position of enforcer. It was his job to see that the city's gangsters stayed in their own territory. If they strayed, it was his job—with Torrio's blessing—to exact violent retribution.

The question was asked again: "Where did you get it?"

"Preacher's," Crain replied. It was the only answer he could think of. That, at least, was the truth. If he lied, if he started weaving a tangled web, he'd get caught in it. He'd get caught and he'd be killed.

"How much did you pay for it?"

"Twenty dollars."

Capone's dark eyes hardened. "That's a lot of money for a bottle of whiskey."

"Yes," Crain admitted, barely able to speak. "But it's the best."

"Uh, hang around for a moment, will ya?" Capone requested. He put the bottle aside and moved down the bar to the telephone. Glancing once at Crain, he dialed a number, not having to look it up. "Harry?" he said when his call was answered. "Al Capone. Listen, what I'm hearing around town, you're stocking a new brand, Dunbar's Special." There was a long pause, during which his expression slowly changed, his scowl giving way to a knowing smile. "Harry, you don't have to apologize. I understand. If the world's best booze suddenly starts floating around, you want to cut yourself some, naturally. It's no big deal." He was about to hang up, then asked one more question. "By the way, how much you charging a bottle? . . . Twenty smackers, huh? Okay, thanks. I'll be talking to you, Harry."

John Crain had stood frozen the whole time. He couldn't move without permission, and he wasn't certain that he was going to get it.

"Yeah, that checks out," Capone said after returning. He picked up the bottle of Dunbar's Special and passed it back to Crain. "Just don't drink it here, okay?"

John Crain silently accepted the bottle.

"Where you from?"

"New York," Crain told him, unable to lie, sure he'd get caught if he did.

"Yeah, I thought so," Capone said, dark eyes making a second, more leisurely appraisal. "I'm from there myself. Five Points." He smiled. "I guess you wouldn't get up that way?"

"No," Crain admitted. "It's, uh, kind of off my beat."

"It ain't as tough as it sounds," said Capone, still smiling. "I was back for a visit last year. . . ." He paused, a shadow suddenly falling across his face. His whole mood changed; the memory had triggered something inside him. When he spoke again his voice was full of menace, though he was trying to be friendly. "Listen, don't be a stranger, Mr. Special. Now that I've met you, I'll be looking for you."

John Crain nodded good-bye. He put the bottle back in his overcoat pocket, turned and made a slow and careful exit from the Four Deuces Café. All the while he was expecting a knife in his back, a bullet in his head. Did Capone know? he wondered. Did he suspect? What had Capone meant, "I'll be looking for you"?

Meister was shaken from a deep sleep. "No, not yet," he muttered, thinking it was morning. "Just give me another couple minutes. . . ." He pulled away, rolling over.

John Crain pulled him back roughly. "Greg!" he whispered urgently, shaking him. "Wake up, damn you, wake up!"

Meister opened his eyes, aware of the smell of whiskey first and then, looming out of the darkness, John Crain's anxious face.

"What's wrong?"

"Everything," Crain told him. "Get up, I've got to talk to you." He moved away from the bed, headed for the door, not waiting for an answer. "And don't wake *her* up!"

Meister glanced over at Tandy. She was on the far side of the bed, her face buried in a pillow, the only movement her light, rhythmic breathing. She hadn't been disturbed.

"All right," he said, still only half awake himself. "Give me a minute." He found his robe at the bottom of the bed, pulling it on as he got up, trying to read the time on his watch.

John Crain was sprawled on the living room sofa, still wearing his overcoat, melting snow making dirty puddles around his overshoes. The bottle of Dunbar's Special, only a quarter full now, was on the coffee table in front of him. There was an empty glass beside it.

"Don't you think you've had enough of that?" Meister asked, indicating the bottle.

"I've got to get out of here," Crain said, as if he hadn't heard. "I'm leaving tomorrow. First thing. Just send me my cut, the half that's coming to me so far, and I'll be out of the deal. The rest is all yours."

Meister took possession of the bottle and glass, surprised to find the latter dry, unused. "If you like," he said carefully. He had never seen Crain in such a state. He looked like some animal run to ground, too tired to go any farther, waiting for the inevitable. His hands shook when he lit a cigarette. "Don't you think you should tell me what this is all about?"

"I—" Crain looked at him with feverish eyes. "Pour me a shot of that, will you?" He held out his shaking hands. "I don't seem to be able to manage."

Meister poured the drink and set it down on the coffee table. Then, deciding he needed one himself, he went into the small kitchenette to get another glass.

Crain had finished his drink by the time Meister returned. "This," he said, chuckling at his condition, "is the first time I've ever been scared, do you know that? Even in the war"—now his laughter rang out—"they had rules!"

Meister sat down across from him. "What are you talking about? What happened?"

John Crain blurted it out. "Al Capone... I met him tonight. He's the guy I've been running from. Al Capone, for God's sake!"

Meister frowned. None of it made sense. He knew the name and who Capone was, the Torrio syndicate's enforcer, but that was all. John Crain had briefly explained the syndicate's organizational setup when they first set out on their bootlegging venture, information he had picked up during his two months in Chicago. At the time he had demonstrated no fear of Capone, so why should he be afraid of him now? Meister wondered.

"Oh, God," said John Crain, not knowing where to start. "What I didn't tell you before... well... was the reason I had to leave New York. I killed a man there. Tony Capullo, my boss at Farley's."

"Killed him?" Meister said softly. He leaned back, closing his eyes, a sickening feeling filling the pit of his stomach. "Oh, Christ!"

"I had to do it," Crain continued. "He was going to kill Sid Berns. He had a gun on him and it was my fault and—" He stopped, out of breath, unable to explain it all at once. "I'd better start at the beginning. Maybe then you'll understand."

Meister nodded, opening his eyes, seeing a stranger sitting across from him. It had to be a stranger, he thought. A friend would have told him already, a long time ago, when he first arrived back in New York.

"It started with Hal Rosen," Crain said, getting another cigarette. "Remember him?" When he lit the cigarette his hands were steadier, as if he was already finding relief in confession. "I ran across him by chance. He was getting the shit beat out of him in an anti-Bolshevik riot at the *New York Worker.* I managed to get him out of it and into a taxi. He wanted to go home, not to a hospital, so I took him back to this place, this crummy tenement on the lower East Side. That's how I met Nadine and Sid. They lived in the same building."

Meister nodded. He'd been there, bracing Sid. "Okay," Crain said. "Well, all of a sudden I fell in love with Nadine. She was just a kid, so I didn't do anything about it, and then the next summer Sid came up to Wicklow to tell me Hal Rosen was dead. He came all the way just to deliver Hal's deathbed message: 'Thanks for trying.'"

"Hal Rosen is dead?" Meister asked. It was the first time he had interrupted. He wondered why *that,* of all things, should have been kept a secret.

"Yeah," Crain confirmed. "His kidneys were damaged and there was nothing that could save him." He paused, remembering, then picked up the narrative again, eager to get it all told. "Anyway, when I got back to New York, I looked up Tony Capullo. He'd offered me a job once—this was when I was still in the army—and now he was running Farley's."

Meister nodded again. He'd been there, in Harlem, celebrating the Armistice, when John had met Capullo.

"So I got the job," said Crain. "And who should turn up again but Sid, like a bad penny. He was assigned as my helper for a whiskey run out of Canada—I told you this part, right?—and he was wounded coming back. I took him home and there's Nadine, all grown up, and I'm in love *again.*" He paused, remembering, his eyes clouding. "I started seeing her and her parents started going crazy. They're Orthodox Jews and I'm a goy, you know? Then…" He wiped at his eyes. "Where the hell am I?"

"In love."

"Yeah, and Capullo asks me to make another run and I tell him to stuff it, because suddenly I want to live forever. I quit him and I get a job at the stock exchange, and the same day some Bolshie blows Wall Street apart. So that's my out—I've been killed in the explosion. I tell Sid to tell Capullo. I'm not coming back because I'm dead."

"And he bought it?"

"Yeah. Only, later, Capullo spots me somewhere and he's mad at Sid, because he's the one who lied to him. He's so mad he's going to kill him, and that's when I show up."

"Why?"

John Crain didn't answer.

Meister looked at him. "Why?" he repeated.

"This is the hard part," Crain said finally, putting his head in his hands. "I found out Nadine was sleeping with her boss, the owner of the cosmetics company where she worked, Rupert Tilden. She was his mistress. Sid had known about it all the time, but he hadn't told me. He thought we'd have to break up anyway, on account of me being a goy. So what do I do? I blame Sid. I can't blame Nadine—I'm too much in love, you know?—so I get drunk and I blame Sid and I go looking for him at Farley's."

"With a gun?"

"The Luger," Crain informed him, shaking his head. "I don't even know why I took it. I was getting dressed and it was sitting there in the drawer and ... I don't know, I just took it, that's all." He looked up. "What can I tell you? I was drunk."

"How does Capone figure into it?"

Crain shrugged helplessly. "He was a friend of Capullo's. When it happened, he was still in New York, or at least back there on a visit, and he was still using an alias—Scarface Al Brown. I got the word that he was after me, a gun-for-hire with three murders to his credit, and how the hell do you protect yourself against that?" There was another helpless shrug. "Hell, until tonight I didn't even know what he looked like!" "Or who he really was."

"Yeah," John Crain said, the hunted animal look returning. "Would you believe it? I'm running away from Al Capone and I run to this town! Torrio and Capone, they *own* Chicago."

Meister decided it was time he had a drink of Dunbar's Special. "You said you met him tonight. He obviously didn't recognize you."

"No," Crain admitted, pushing up from the sofa, "but I got him interested in me. I had that bottle and he wanted to know where I got it and I said Preacher's. The son of a bitch called and checked before he let me go." Crain came around the coffee table and stood over Meister. "He called me 'Mr. Special.' He *knows* me. 'I'll be looking for you,' that's what he said. If he ever puts two and two together, I'm dead, Greg. I'm dead!"

Meister couldn't argue with that logic. For all he knew, John Crain could have been followed back to the hotel. But the hoodlum tracking him, or some other hoodlum down the line somewhere, waiting to put in an appearance, could be an import from New York familiar with Farley's and acquainted with the circumstances of Tony Capullo's death. Both Torrio and Capone had started their careers in New York. Who knew how many others were here? It only took one to point the finger.

"Yeah, I guess you've got to go, John," Meister said, taking a sip of his drink. "The sooner the better. And I understand, okay? I really do." He twirled the glass in his hand, thinking that the Dunbar's was as advertised, the world's best whiskey. "How come you never told me all this before?"

"I didn't think you'd want to hear it," Crain answered. "That first day—that place in Times Square? The main thing you wanted to talk about was how much you hated killing. You said it gave you nightmares. So what was I supposed to do, tell you that I had just killed somebody? That I needed your help to kill a hood who was after me?"

Yes, Meister thought, taking another sip of his drink. John Crain was supposed to have done that. Friends, true friends, could tell and ask each other anything, because that's what friendship was about. It was meant to be tested. You could never be certain you had it until it was tried and found not wanting. "How come you never told me about Hal Rosen?"

"I don't know," Crain said. "He was too much a part of it, I guess. He started the whole chain of events." He picked up the bottle of Dunbar's Special. "Does it matter?"

"Yes, it matters," Meister said. He finished his drink and stood up, handing the empty glass to Crain. "Hal Rosen was a friend." He turned and headed back toward the bedroom. "If I don't see you before you leave tomorrow, good-bye."

CHAPTER 19

With John Crain gone, Meister felt terribly alone, abandoned, betrayed. He had no quarrel with Crain's hurried departure. All things considered, only a fool would have stayed. But the rest of it was beyond any understanding or acceptance. If John Crain had confided in him, told him the whole truth from the start, things would have turned out differently. Together they could have handled Al Capone, one way or the other.

A year ago Capone had been just another hoodlum. His sudden demise, should that have proved necessary, would have caused barely a ripple. Today, Capone was the number two man in what, from all indications, was the best organized and most powerful crime syndicate in the United States. To go up against Capone now was suicide. Touch him and a dozen killers would be after you, probably more. John Crain's decision to run rather than fight meant he now had to run forever.

Greg Meister hated killing. He still suffered nightmares. All the same, if justified, he would take gun in hand again. If the only way to ensure John Crain's safety was to kill Al Capone, then, yes, he would do it, damn it! Al Capone was an animal. He killed for money and the sheer joy of killing. He deserved to die. If someone put a bullet in his brain, they would be doing the world a favor. Even now there was still that justification.

Justification, yes, Meister mused, but rationale? No, not now. There was no sense to it at all now. If he killed Capone, he not only ensured his own death but probably John Crain's, too. Maybe even Tandy's. The Torrio syndicate wouldn't rest until it had fully avenged its enforcer's death. The only way it held on to power was by that kind of ruthless retaliation against any attack or threat.

It was too late. A year ago Capone was a mere soldier. Today he was a general and there was a whole army to be faced. John Crain had no other choice. He had missed his chance and now all he could do was run.

Alone, abandoned, betrayed, Meister felt all these things as he went ahead with his decision to make the last buy of Dunbar's Special. As far as he was concerned, there was no true friendship between himself and John Crain. If he had benefited from someone whom he now angrily labeled merely an acquaintance, so had Crain.

John Crain, starting with nothing but a connection, had made $3,750 in less than two weeks. He was $3,750 richer than he would have been if Meister had not provided the seed money, whatever its source. So they had simply used each other, and if Meister chose to go one alone, staying because he didn't have to run, then why shouldn't he profit?

If it was convoluted logic, he had to live with it. He was, sooner than expected, on that long narrow road, and it seemed impossible to get off or turn back. He was driven. There was no stopping.

If he hadn't made up his mind when Tandy asked him to stop, he had now, with John Crain gone. With Crain out of the picture, any chances he took where his own. So were any profits to be made.

Meister couldn't resist such a temptation. Because he planned to hold on to the whiskey longer, possibly not try to move it for several months, his expenses might run a little higher, but not by much. He stood to clear, all for himself, as much as sixty thousand. He simply couldn't pass it up.

In one fell swoop he would be independent. He'd never again have need to go hat in hand to anybody. He'd have enough, more than enough, to support Tandy properly.

It was all there, waiting. A good home, fine furnishings, a decent car, the better things in life. Not just for Tandy, but for the child that was coming, too.

How could he resist?

Himie Koshevoy and his brother Sam, driving the same truck as before, showed up on schedule at Schlogl's. This time Meister stopped Himie at the restaurant entrance. "I've got the money on me," he told him, patting his coat pocket. "I'll give it to you in the truck, okay?"

Himie stared at him uncertainly. "Where's your partner?"

"He couldn't make it," Meister said, taking out the packet. He opened it to show a thick wad of new hundred-dollar bills. "Don't worry, it's all here. I'll give it to you in the truck."

Koshevoy nodded and led the way back, opening the truck's passenger door for Meister, indicating that he should get in first.

"What's wrong?" Sam wanted to know.

"Nothing," Meister told him, climbing over the seat and through the canvas into the rear of the truck. He waited until Himie was in and the door closed. "Just drive, will you?"

Sam looked at Himie, who nodded tightly, saying nothing. The truck moved away.

Meister made a quick count to make sure that he had five hundred cases. Then, choosing one at random, he ripped it open. There were twelve bottles. He again made a random choice, selecting a bottle, breaking the seal and removing the cork, taking a small, sampling sip. It was genuine. There was no mistaking the taste of Dunbar's Special.

Himie Koshevoy was standing beside him. "Can I make my count now?"

"Sure," said Meister. He handed over the packet of money and picked another case at random, going through the same process as before, breaking the seal on one of the bottles and taking a sip.

"You're being extra careful this time," Himie said, busy counting his money. It was an observation, not a complaint.

Meister nodded, picking two more cases at random, breaking two more seals.

"You satisfied?" The question came from Sam, glancing back through the parted canvas.

Meister nodded again.

Himie Koshevoy had gone through a similar process, making an initial count, then closely examining several bills chosen at random. "I am," he said, putting the last bill back in the packet. "Now, how do you want to do this?"

Meister bent down, parting the canvas farther, looking out the windshield. They were on their fourth turn, headed back for Schlogl's. "What's wrong with the usual? You boys have lunch and I'll bc back in an hour or so."

"Suits me," Himie said. He held up the packet, indicating that he wanted to put it in his overcoat pocket.

"Okay?"

Meister did it for him, stuffing it in and giving it a pat. "It's been nice doing business with you, Mr. Koshevoy. If you ever get another load, let me know."

"You got it," Himie assured him. "How do I get in touch with you?"

"I'll let you know," Meister said. "What say we get together in a couple of weeks?" He smiled, feeling good, all the tension gone. Nothing was going to happen in the middle of the day on a busy street. "Schlogl's okay? I still haven't eaten at the goddamn place."

"Suits me."

Meister let himself relax. He liked Himie. For an ugly little fellow—five-foot-nothing and all nose—he nevertheless had a certain elfin charm. John Crain, teasing Himie, had asked him once how much he'd charge to haunt a house. Himie, after thinking it over, had wanted to know how many rooms.

The truck stopped in front of Schlogl's. Himie got out, exiting via the passenger door, and Sam slid across into the passenger seat, letting Meister replace him behind the wheel. It was then that Meister felt the sharp jab of a gun in his ribs.

"Drive, sucker," Sam said harshly, the gun digging deeper. "Drive—or I'll blow your fucking heart apart!"

Himie jumped up on the running board. "Sam! Are you crazy? What are you doing?"

"Taking it all," Sam told him, the gun digging still deeper. "It's perfect! All we gotta do is dump him!"

Himie pulled ineffectually at his brother. "Jesus," he told Meister. "I swear, I've got nothing to do with this. I swear!"

"It's okay," Meister said. "Your goddamn brother isn't going to do anything. If he kills me in this crowd he'll never get away, and I'm not going anywhere."

Sam rammed the gun as hard as he could. "I said, *drive!*"

"Fuck you," Meister said, wincing. "You've got two choices: Pull the trigger and get yourself arrested, or put the gun in my pocket and say you're sorry."

"Like hell!"

"I mean it," Meister said, smiling at a woman who was gingerly venturing out in front of the truck, preparing to jaywalk. She was one of a dozen people in plain view and the street was clogged with traffic, slick with ice. It had to be the dumbest place in town to attempt a hijacking. "Put the gun in my pocket."

"Do what he says," urged Himie.

Sam shook his head. "I'll kill you," he told Meister.

Meister kept smiling at passers-by. "Only if you want to fry, kid. Only if you want to fry."

Himie was in the cab now. He squeezed into the passenger seat alongside his brother. "Sam … please … do what he says!"

Sam looked out at the busy street, the truth slowly dawning on him. If he wanted the load, he had to kill Meister here and now. But if he killed him, he'd never get away.

He swore softly and let the gun sag. Meister guided Sam's hand into his coat pocket. The gun was left there and their hands emerged together, Meister's fingers entwined with Sam's.

Meister, still smiling, honked the horn, drowning out Sam's scream as he twisted back the youth's fingers, breaking them. With the same move Meister pushed him down to the floor of the cab, jammed a foot against his throat.

"Get out," he told Himie, still smiling.

Himie fumbled for the door. "Don't kill him," he begged.

"Get out!"

Himie looked down in horror at his brother. "Please! He's just a kid! I don't know what got into him!"

"Get out!"

Himie scrambled out of the cab. Meister reached after him, pulling the door shut, taking his foot off Sam's throat. Sam started to rise, gulping for breath, trying to escape. Meister punched him in the face as hard as he could. The youth's head snapped back and he crumpled to the floor, unconscious.

Meister started the truck. He gave two toots on the horn, a friendly good-bye to Himie, then he carefully eased out into the traffic, still smiling. Himie stood like a stone on the curb. Anyone watching would have thought nothing amiss.

Later, on a deserted side street, Meister hauled Sam out of the truck and propped him against a building. He took note of the location and called the police, telling them there was a drunk that needed picking up. Then he headed the truck for the garage on Orleans Street.

Himie had said he didn't know what had gotten into the kid. Meister shook his head sadly. Greed, it was as simple as that. Greed, and it could happen to anybody ... including himself.

Tandy was weeping bitterly when Meister returned that night to the Bishop Hotel. The sight of him brought on fresh tears. She put her hands to her face and went rushing blindly into the bedroom.

"Oh, go away, please!" she cried, flinging herself across the bed. "Leave me alone!"

Meister kicked off his galoshes and followed her in helpless bewilderment. Despite her objections to his making the second buy, she had been bright and cheerful, her usual self, when he had left that morning. He couldn't imagine what could have made her so wretched in his absence.

"What's wrong?" he asked, standing in the bedroom doorway. He didn't want to go to her, afraid of making her feel worse.

"Nothing you can help!" she cried, pushing her face deeper into her pillow. "Just go away, will you? Just go away and leave me alone!"

"Why?"

"Because I don't want you to see me this way!" Neither do I, Meister thought. He had come home filled with good news, the ugly incident with Sam pushed aside and all but forgotten. The five hundred cases of Dunbar's Special were safely stored in the garage on Orleans Street. Himie Koshevoy's truck had been left, without incident, at its usual drop-off point—down the block from Schlogl's. Meister would soon be returning her five-thousand-dollar nest egg, and his own bank account would be bulging too.

"Come on. Don't tell me that," he said gently. "I want to see you however you are." He removed his overcoat and came to her, patting her back soothingly. "We're supposed to share, remember?"

"I don't care!"

"I do," he said firmly. A moment later his arms were wrapped around her, holding her tightly, refusing to let her go. "Cry if you must, but don't tell me to leave. I love you too much."

This only brought more tears. Meister, not knowing what else to do, simply held her in his arms, waiting for her to cry herself out. He comforted her as best he could and took his own comfort from the fact that she really didn't want him to leave. She needed him.

"It's this place," she said finally, sobbing brokenly. "I hate it." The admission made, she tried to pull away, burying her face in her pillow again. "Oh, Greg, I've tried to put up with it, but it's a hotel—not a home—and it's so lonely!"

Meister had wondered if that wasn't part of it. "With John gone?"

"You're *both* gone," she sobbed. "All day—and what am I supposed to do? I can't fix this place up, it's not ours."

Meister held her tighter. The loneliness he could understand, although he did wish she would go out more. As for the hotel suite, he didn't see why it needed to be fixed up. "Is this the girl who was happy in a small room in back of a bookstore?" he asked teasingly.

"That was different and you know it," she said. "You were there then. You can't compare—" She stopped, lost, crying.

"Can't compare a love nest and a hotel suite?" he offered.

"And a home!" she sobbed. Desperately, she turned to him, burying her tear-stained face in his chest. "Oh, Greg, I'm sorry. I've tried, really tried, but I'm so unhappy here!"

Meister stroked her hair, thinking that John Crain had been right about one thing. Tandy, no matter how brave her talk, wasn't cut out for a cold-water flat. If this hotel had broken her spirit in such a short time, a cheap apartment would send her fleeing in horror back to 14 Washington Square.

"I called home," she said, as if in confirmation that her thoughts were already there. "I had an excuse—to say John was on his way back—and father was so awful." She stopped, choking on the words, her body racked with sobs. "He—he said he didn't care about John. He said as—as far as he was concerned, he didn't have a—a son anymore. That he didn't have a *daughter*, either! He called you a scoundrel. He said you were a thief!"

A thief? Meister stroked her hair. "What did he mean by that?" he asked cautiously.

"How should I know?" she sobbed. "You stole me, I suppose. Damn him! How can he be so cruel?"

Meister kept stroking her hair. A thief, was he? Earlier he had had the defense of semantics. John Crain was holding the ten thousand dollars that belonged to his father, John Crain was using it. Now, however, with John gone, Greg Meister was using it, and no amount of word twisting could spare him from that fact. He was keeping and using Nelson Crain's money.

But did that make him a thief?

No, Meister decided. He hadn't stolen the money, he'd just kept it longer than necessary. The worst that made him was a scoundrel. He accepted that label and found, to his surprise, that it didn't bother him all that much. The "loan" was secured by Dunbar's Special and could be paid off immediately, if necessary. Sell a few hundred cases of the whiskey at a bargain price and Nelson Crain could have his money by the end of the week.

Tandy was weeping uncontrollably. "I'm sorry… I've tried… I've really tried to be brave."

"Hush," Meister said softly, trying to soothe her. "Hush." That was it. He'd pay the old bastard off and that would be the end of it. They could start afresh. They had enough to keep them going until he felt secure enough about selling the rest of the Dunbar's Special.

"I hate it here," Tandy sobbed.

"Hush, it's only temporary."

"Months? You call that temporary?"

Meister held her tightly, wishing he could offer her something more, an immediate move to a fine home, but there was no way for him to do that. He would be taking enough of a chance selling just ten thousand dollars' worth of Dunbar's Special. With Al Capone's interest perked, he risked losing it all. That would be stupid as well as tragic.

The proper strategy was to let the whiskey sit for a few months. It was safe in the garage and, like money in the bank, grew in value the longer it remained there. He was sole owner of seven hundred fifty cases of the world's best whiskey. So, why take risks? It was sacrifice that was needed now. He wasn't asking that much, really. Wait, girl, you'll get your home. You'll get. it all—if you'll just wait....

Tandy was still crying. Meister held her, rocked her gently. It wasn't her fault, he thought. It was her goddamn father who had touched her off. He wouldn't let them alone. What was he trying to do now?

Nothing, Meister suddenly realized. Nelson Crain had no real power over them or, at least, not over Meister. He could do as he damn well pleased! For instance... if he decided to keep the "loan" a few months longer, who or what was to stop him? His conscience? Hell, it suffered well enough. If it had to suffer a little longer, wasn't that better than holding an unhappy wife in his arms? Wasn't that better than taking a stupid risk to raise ten thousand for a man who had so much money he probably couldn't even count it?

Meister swore. God, what a fool he was sometimes! Here he was, worrying about Nelson Crain when his real concern should have been with Tandy and the child she was carrying. If he had any sense he would get them a fine home immediately, and he would take no risks whatsoever with the whiskey.

The cache of liquor was their whole future. He knew he could sell it for as high as eighty dollars a case. He'd paid thirty a case and he could get eighty. The arithmetic had run through his head a thousand times: seven hundred fifty, times eighty, equaled sixty thousand dollars.

"Listen, Tandy," he said softly, "this is important. Listen to me, please. If we bought a house now, how much do you think we'd have to put down?"

Tandy's voice was muffled against his chest. "What kind of house?"

"A fine house."

"We can't afford that, you know it!"

"No, I don't know it," Meister answered, suddenly laughing. "I don't know it at all and neither do you." He pulled her gently up to face him. "But we're going to find out. You've got a five thousand dollar nest egg. I'll soon pay that back to you and more. I think that's a good down payment on a fine house. I don't know, but we're going to find out!"

Tandy stared at him with tear-swollen eyes. "Are you serious?"

"Yes," Meister said, laughing joyously now. "And do you know something else? I love you! More than anything in this world, I love you, Tandy Crain!"

CHAPTER 20

It took them three months, until it was the middle of April and spring was in the air, before they found the house they wanted and could afford. But it was worth all the time and effort.

In Cicero, near Morton College on Central Avenue, patiently waiting for them to discover it, was a two-story brick Greek revival house that stole their hearts on sight.

It was a simple, solid block of a house, grand and trim and neat all at the same time. The service wing, kitchen and porch were hidden discreetly at the back.

Meister saw it as a real man's house. The roof pediment and cornice and the door with its surrounding ornamentation were the only deliberately decorative features, unless one counted the shutters. The rest was a serviceable, if striking, brick box.

Tandy thought it delicate, entranced by the white doorway which had a pair of Ionic columns on either side—a low relief architrave on top—and an elliptical arch with a sunburst fanlight, all enclosed within a brick arch complete with keystone. She also loved the windows, multipaned, long and narrow, set flush under fretted lintels.

Either of them would have bought the house with out even inspecting the inside. Yet there again, to their mutual delight, was exactly what they both wanted.

Meister was no student of architecture, but he knew what he liked. The foursquare exterior, with its formal door and window placement, gave the inside of the house an order and space he appreciated. It was disciplined, everything in its proper place.

There weren't a bunch of Victorian wings, bays and projections wandering off in every direction. There was, simply, the formal hall, the stairs leading directly from it and, in four linked rectangles, the library, parlor, dining room and kitchen. Upstairs there were four bedrooms, each with a bath, plus the small servants' quarters above the kitchen. Meister was immediately at home in the house and thought he would never want anything else.

Tandy, used to luxury, saw quality, which she appreciated even more. The house had been solidly built and close attention had been paid to the smallest detail. There were marvelous special touches at almost every turn. The stairway, though narrow, was almost noble in character, its balusters miniatures of the Ionic columns at the door. At the landing the columns were repeated, giving the second floor an imposing, delicately crafted entrance of its own.

The rooms were all high-ceilinged, the dining room half-vaulted, giving the impression of a small banquet hall. All the walls, even those on the second floor, were paneled rather than papered, all done in natural English pine. There was no plaster anywhere, not even on the ceiling, which was covered with pressed tin. The woodwork, though simple, was scrupulously carved. The fireplace mantels were exquisite masterpieces, the subtle reeding still another repetition of the Ionic columns. Italian tile combined with brick for the fireboxes.

The floors were all gleaming oak except for the quarry tile in the kitchen. This, a place apart, was almost Colonial in character and had its own stairway to the quarters above. With its huge cast-iron stove and the brick ovens built into the chimney, it was very much a place of labor, not repose. The mistress of the house, if she was wise and could afford the luxury of hiring help, would venture here only to direct operations.

They made their inspection in a kind of awed silence.

"Do you like it?" Meister asked finally when they returned to the hall.

"Like it?" Tandy turned, looking around for the agent, who had made himself scarce. "Greg, I love it! I adore it! I *must* have it! If we can buy this house, I swear I'll never ask for another thing. Never." She moved closer, hugging him tightly, looking up into his eyes. "And I promise to be always very, very good."

"Gee, I don't know," he responded. "We haven't even looked at the basement. Suppose it's settling or something? I noticed a crack—"

"Greg!"

Meister laughed. "Yes, my love, we'll buy it." He would do so no matter how onerous the terms. He had never seen her happier. This house was going to bring back the magic of their love. He would pay any price, even if it meant going public and selling off more of the Dunbar's Special. So far, over the three-month period of their search for a house, he had quictly sold a hundred cases to private parties, averaging seventy-five dollars a case.

Tandy hugged him again. "Oh, Greg, thank you!" she cried. Then, catching herself, she stepped back, looking up into his face. "Darling, you do like it, don't you? It's not just for me?"

"I like it very much," Meister assured her. "Now, let's see if we can find the agent. If you don't mind, I'll conduct the negotiations. If he sees that glint in your eye—well, if I were him, I'd ask the moon."

"Oh, God, I don't dare go near him," Tandy admitted. "You do it. I'll just keep looking around."

Meister nodded. That would be best. He set off in search of the agent. The asking price of the house was high, $36,000, which was probably why it was still on the market. The advertisement also said that the owner wanted a substantial down payment. Meister just hoped that five thousand would be enough.

The agent was in the kitchen. A thin, dour Scot by the name of McIntyre, he was trying, unsuccessfully, to keep warm in front of an unlit fireplace. "It's the idea," he explained, rubbing his hands above nonexistent flames in the first indication that there might be some humor in him. "And before you say a word, the price is firm."

"Yes, I saw that in the ad," said Meister. "I also saw that a substantial down payment is required." He paused. "How substantial?"

McIntyre didn't bother looking at him. "You tell me."

"Five thousand dollars," Meister said, deciding to take the plunge. "And I'd like to buy it on an agreement for sale, four percent interest, all due and payable in five years with no penalty for prepayment." He paused, trying to think if he'd forgotten anything. "Monthly payments of three hundred and fifty."

McIntyre kept staring into the nonexistent fire. "What do you do?"

"I'm an importer."

"You ought to be a real estate agent," McIntyre said. "I can speak for the owner. What you have just offered, young man, is the lowest he'll accept in all categories. I'd call that brilliant."

Meister didn't say anything. He'd call it luck.

Driving back to town, the deal concluded, Tandy couldn't stop talking. They could move into the house on the first of May and, as she pointed out, they didn't have a stick of furniture.

There, Meister thought, when the name Chippendale came up—hard on the heels of Sheraton and Hepplewhite—went all his new fortune, and more.

"I know what you're thinking," Tandy said, seeing his look. "But I will be patient. I have been so far, haven't I? Whatever I buy will be an investment, not just a purchase, all right? And, first things first"—she looked at him adoringly—"tomorrow I go shopping for a bed."

Meister blushed. God, he did have a woman, didn't he? He concentrated on the problem of how to keep her happy. As claimed, she had been patient. Once the decision to buy a house was made, there hadn't been another complaint out of her about hotel living, as long as the search had taken. The promise had been enough to sustain her.

And, Meister had to admit, it had taken them so long because of the condition he had imposed, that they get out of Chicago into the suburbs. That left only a few choices, considering the type of neighborhood and house they were seeking, but nevertheless, they had thoroughly investigated them all.

Now, finally, they had it, a jewel of a house set amidst stately mansions in what had been Meister's first choice: Cicero. It was a quiet, prosperous village completely apart from the city, untainted by its gangsterism. Yet in less than an hour's drive, Meister could be at State and Madison, the world's busiest corner, the center of the Loop, the heart of Chicago.

They had it—they had it all! Now, how to keep it? How to keep Tandy and, yes, himself, happy.

Meister already knew the answer, or at least part of it. The time had come to go public again with the Dunbar's Special. The private market, wealthy men willing to buy one or two cases for their own use, couldn't sustain him now. It worked only on referrals and the sales were slow, if safe. But how to move the whiskey quickly and stay out of trouble in the process, that Meister still hadn't figured out, and he had to soon.

The past three months had been more expensive than he had anticipated. The hotel, the rental of a car, too many meals out during their house-hunting expeditions—all had severely drained his bank account. With the check written for the down payment on the house, he had less than a thousand left in the bank.

There was no putting it off any longer. Tomorrow, while Tandy went shopping for a bed, he'd have to start selling again, ready or not. There was a price to pay for everything—including happiness.

"... and then, if you don't mind, I'd like to choose your desk for the library," Tandy was saying, still talking a mile a minute. "I saw this perfect golden oak roll-top the other day, really divine. You'll be choosing all the books, won't you? That's your department." She smiled at him. "Darling, these are just plans. I do promise to be patient... Greg, are you listening to me?"

Meister pulled the little rented roadster over to the side of the road.

"Yes," he told her, shutting off the engine. "I've been listening to every word and do you know what?"

She stared at him uncertainly.

"I'd rather be making love to you." Meister pulled her close and kissed her passionately.

She struggled free, breathless. "Not here, Greg!"

"Why not?" he demanded. "We did it once before, didn't we? Isn't that how we got into all this trouble?"

Now it was her turn to blush. "You fool."

"If it was dark, you would, wouldn't you," he said, pulling her back into his arms. He again kissed her deeply. "Wouldn't you?"

"Yes," she whispered.

"God, woman, you make me happy."

She returned his kiss, gently, lingeringly. "You make me happy too."

Nelson Crain, sitting in the basement card room of Attorney General Harry Daugherty's house on H Street in Washington that night, was feeling just as happy as his daughter and her husband. That morning, at a secret meeting which he and Harry Sinclair had attended, Interior Secretary Albert Fall had leased the Navy's Teapot Dome Reserve to Sinclair's Mammoth Oil Company.

It was the perfect deal, better than anything he'd find in the cards, Crain thought, impossible to fault. The lease was fair to the government. No undue profits would accrue to Mammoth Oil. Large profits, perhaps, even vast profits, but not *undue* profits. And there was sufficient excuse for the absence of competitive bidding and publicity in the fact that it was a military arrangement.

The perfect deal, and all it had cost was a mere $260,000 in Liberty Bonds, to be paid to Albert Fall in installments. A small investment for millions of dollars in profits that could never be called "undue." Oil companies were supposed to make millions. It was their reward for taking risks.

Sandra Crain, visiting at the White House with Florence Harding, could find no reason to share her husband's happiness. He had only hinted at the reason for their trip to Washington. "It's to help with a windfall!" was all he said. Yet she had reason to doubt the morality involved.

The more she visited with Florence Harding, the more she saw of the White House and Washington, the more Sandra Crain feared for the country, which seemed to be lacking any sense of propriety.

Florence was unhappy with the president. It was apparent in her every reference to him—to his neglect of her and his inattention to the day-to-day operation of the government. The way Florence told it, Harding cared more about drinking and playing cards with his old Ohio cronies than he did about running the government of the United States. And yet she still wasn't telling all. There was some terrible hurt she was holding back.

Sandra Crain's own observations only made Florence's complaints seem all the more valid. Apart from a few key choices—Calvin Coolidge for vice president, Charles Hughes for secretary of state, Mellon in Treasury and Hoover in Commerce—Harding was demonstrating almost no discrimination in the choice of his friends and advisers.

Florence's brother had just been named superintendent of prisons. Florence herself was the first to admit he was totally unqualified. D.R. Crissinger, a lawyer back home in Marion, Ohio, whose executive banking experience had been limited to a few months as president of a local bank, had been selected as comptroller of the currency. The family doctor, Charlie Sawyer, who had been retained as Harding's personal physician, was now being called—for absolutely no good reason—a brigadier general. He'd also been deputized to study the possible coordination of the government's health agencies.

Like Attorney General Daugherty and Jess Smith and Ned McLean and Howard Mannington and all the other cronies Sandra Crain had met on her last visit, these people were ill-suited for their jobs and positions of trust. President Harding was treating important offices like sugarplums and passing them out like an overly benevolent father.

If Florence's complaints and Sandra Crain's own eyes were to be believed, every lobbyist, fixer and purchaser of privilege in Ohio had descended on Washington. Those who hadn't been given positions of influence and power were assuming them.

Surely the president knew that, inevitably, such men would use their positions to their own advantage? Yes, they might be old friends and acquaintances, political pals and allies of yesteryear, but did he have to reward them all? And was he keeping a reasonable watch on what they were up to in this suddenly free-wheeling atmosphere?

They might be his friends, but where were they taking him?

CHAPTER 21

Sooner or later, of course, it had to happen, but Meister was caught totally unawares when it did. He was leaving the Regency Club, one of the most exclusive private clubs in Chicago, after concluding the successful sale of twenty cases of whiskey when a Packard limousine pulled up in front. Instead of the to-be-expected business tycoon headed for a leisurely, expensive lunch, a swarthy young hoodlum got out of the car, right hand jammed menacingly into his coat pocket.

"Get in," he told Meister, holding the rear door open. Inside, sliding back to make room, was another young hoodlum who was not quite so concerned about appearances. He had his gun out of his pocket and pointed at Meister's stomach.

Here? On LaSalle Street? This was Meister's initial reaction. Having successfully foiled Sam Koshevoy's hijack attempt by the simple strategy of pointing out the crowded, public conditions, Meister had lulled himself into thinking that the next attempt—if one was ever made—would be in some half-deserted slum district where nobody gave a good goddamn. But in broad daylight in the financial district in front of one of the best private clubs in town?

"Now!" the first hoodlum said, giving Meister a shove.

Meister got in, sliding into the middle of the seat, making room for the man to follow. There was no other choice. Unlike Sam Koshevoy, either of these two hoodlums would gladly, happily pull a trigger, no matter who was watching. The larger the crowd the better, probably.

The door slammed shut and the Packard pulled away at high speed, heading north toward the Loop. Meister's own car, a rented Ford, which he had parked in the next block, was passed without anyone paying any attention to it. The driver of the Packard, who was wearing a chauffeur's cap, the only thing that suggested that he belonged in a limousine, was interested only in the traffic. The hoodlum who had been waiting in the back seat had put his gun away and was now interested in his fingernails. The hoodlum who had worked the sidewalk seemed to have fallen asleep.

"May I ask where we're going?" Meister requested.

"No," was the answer and he wasn't sure who gave it, possibly all three.

Shit, Meister thought, becoming worried now. He'd have been happier if they had stopped to steal the whiskey he had stashed in the trunk of his Ford. To pass that up meant they weren't after small potatoes. Somebody obviously wanted it all, and from the look of his escort it was the Torrio syndicate.

"Mind if I smoke?"

This time there was no answer.

"They're in my shirt pocket," Meister said, pointing. "May I?"

Again there was no answer.

Meister gingerly reached into his pocket and removed the pack of cigarettes. Then, just as gingerly, he got his lighter from his trouser pocket, careful not to make any sudden moves. He hadn't been searched and his escort had no guarantee that he was unarmed.

Maybe they'd like him to try something. Then they'd have an excuse to kill him. He lit his cigarette and inhaled deeply, savoring the rich-tasting smoke, wondering if it might be his last. He had only one defense against the syndicate and he was by no means sure that it was going to work....

Johnny Torrio's office was in his home, a three-story mansion on Riverside Drive within sight of the Navy Pier. It stood alone on a large piece of property in an area that had otherwise given way to luxury apartment buildings. A brick fortress, it was almost Federal in character, boasting a Palladian window, decorative lintels, classical dormers and twin chimneys with parapets and roof balustrade. Meister's own little jewel in Cicero looked mean compared to this shuttered castle looming starkly behind still-bare elms.

Though already May, it was a late spring, and a bone-chilling wind was blowing off Lake Michigan. Meister was still shivering from it when, after passing several checkpoints, all of which required a search, he was led into the second-story room that looked out on the lake from the Palladian window.

"So, you're Mr. Special, huh?" Torrio asked, getting up from behind an elegant parlor table with a white marble top that apparently served as his desk. There was a lamp on it and several ledger books, one neat stack of papers and the obligatory ashtray.

"Yes," Meister admitted.

"Or one of them," Torrio said, moving around the table. He indicated that Meister should make himself comfortable and chose a stiff-backed chair for himself. "Whatever happened to your partner, the blond dude who couldn't hold his liquor?"

Meister sat down, too, thankful that he'd been brought here without Tandy. The room was furnished with Renaissance revival pieces that she would have given anything to possess. Two of them—a center table and a dressing chest—she might have killed for.

"Him?" Meister said, as if he had trouble remembering. "Oh, he left town months ago."

Torrio smiled. "Couldn't stand the heat?"

"Couldn't stand the winter," Meister replied. He got out his cigarettes, not bothering to ask permission this time, having been searched so often on the way up.

"Yes, it does get windy, doesn't it?" Torrio noted, easily falling into what could have been taken as idle conversation. "When did he leave? January?"

Meister nodded, lighting his cigarette. It was easy to see why Torrio was called "The Fox." The man was small and quick. His eyes, little black ball bearings, were crafty as an animal's.

"I thought we'd lost you," said Torrio, counting on his slender fingers. "January, February, March, April—four months and not another sale." He got out his own cigarettes, selecting an oval Turkish blend from a gold, platinum-inlaid case. "After a while, I figured you'd simply run out of the stuff, but what you're selling now, it's from the same batch. So you must have just laid low after the blond ran into Al at the Four Deuces?"

Meister didn't answer. It wasn't necessary. Torrio had all the answers he needed.

"Smart," Torrio continued. "And getting rid of your buddy, that was smart too. And the way you've been selling, slowly, carefully, only to the private clubs? That's intelligent. And the way you can lose a tail so I can't get a line on your cache, that's pure genius." The room filled with the acrid aroma of his cigarette. "Now, do you want to hear what's dumb?"

Meister almost had to laugh. "No."

"You guys never do," Torrio said sadly. "What the fuck does it take? There's a hundred broken heads out there, more graves than I want to count, and still you guys keep coming?"

"Greed," Meister told him, remembering Sam.

"Sure," Torrio said, sounding plaintive now. "But can't you be greedy someplace else? Detroit, Cleveland, Philadelphia? How about Washington? They invented the word there." He shook his head. "No, you gotta fuck with me in Chicago?"

"Only by accident," Meister said, deciding he'd better explain—and fast. "Purely by accident. My buddy met this Jewish fellow from Toronto. He had a thousand cases of Dunbar's Special on a trawler sitting out in the middle of the lake and he was scared shitless of taking it to you or O'Banion. He'd read too many newspaper stories and he was afraid you'd rip him off, cut his throat, dump him in the river. He wasn't going to negotiate with the syndicate, not on your life." Meister looked at Torrio, taking a last drag on his cigarette, killing it between his fingers. "But... the first non-Italian with an honest face?"

Torrio didn't say anything.

"Believe me," Meister said. "I wasn't muscling in. If I hadn't bought that load, it would have moved on. You never had a chance at it, no way. You've got the wrong rep."

"But you haven't?"

"Precisely," Meister answered, beginning to relax. "There's two things you can do with me. Kill me or use me. If you kill me, you're going to make yourself maybe forty thousand bucks at the most, which is about all I've got left, give or take a few cases, of Dunbar's Special. If you use me, the sky's the limit."

The crafty ball bearing eyes suddenly gleamed with interest.

"Why not?" Meister demanded. "Al Capone? Bronfman would shit if he ever showed up in Toronto. But me? Bronfman will talk to me and he'll be willing to deal too. I can package the kind of crème de la crème booze shipments you've been missing out on. I can give you the top of the line."

"It's a small part of the market."

"Yes, but it's the top."

Torrio didn't say anything and Meister remained silent, too. Everything that had to be said had been said. If Torrio didn't understand the importance of appointment to "his majesty," or the equivalent thereof in Chicago, all was lost. If he did, Meister had a job and, more important, a few more years of life.

"What kind of a cut are you talking about?" Torrio asked at last.

"The usual," Meister said, having no idea what that might be.

"Okay," Torrio told him. "I take twenty percent off the top—that's gross, not net. You buy in your name and you sell in mine.

You show me your books quarterly. If I catch you cheating—if I even *think* you're cheating—you're dead." He got up and returned to his table desk. "Deal?"

"Deal," Meister agreed. He stood, pausing to examine the center table, which was the most beautiful piece of furniture he had ever seen. It was made of walnut and various imported woods and had a scrolled apron and pendent tassels. The circular top was inlaid with an elaborate multicolored marquetry design representing a musical trophy.

"You interested in antiques?" Torrio asked.

Meister shook his head.

"Your wife, then," Torrio concluded. He pushed a button, a signal that his visitor was ready to depart. "Incidentally, when do you think my cut should start?"

"It already has," said Meister, giving away eight thousand. He turned to look at Torrio. "Smart?"

"A genius." Torrio nodded approvingly. He opened a ledger, the meeting over, a problem solved, another addition made to his sprawling crime empire.

Meister walked to the Loop and caught the El, then took a trolley back to his car. The Ford was where he had parked it and had not been tampered with. The trunk, untouched, still contained four cases of Dunbar's Special.

Having trailed him and knowing, or at least suspecting, that there was a load of liquor in the car, Torrio's troops had to be a thoroughly disciplined group. A month's salary for at least a couple of them was here, and it would have been simple to come back and rip him off. Yet, they hadn't, and that said something for The Fox. He truly ruled with an iron fist. It wouldn't be wise to cross him.

Meister was glad that he had offered Torrio a twenty percent cut on the Dunbar's Special still stored in the garage on Orleans

Street. For all he knew, Torrio, despite his disclaimer, was well aware of the cache's location. The claim that his men couldn't keep a tail long enough to find it could have been a test of a new associate's loyalty. In a twisted way it made sense, Meister thought, because if he could be tailed to the Regency Club, then he could be tailed to Orleans Street.

On a hunch, Meister drove back downtown to the garage rather than heading home. He had devised a simple method of determining if the garage had been opened in his absence. Every time he locked up, he put a thin wire seal, easily snapped, at the top of the door. Would it be broken now?

It was.

Jesus Christ, Meister thought. For a moment he was sure the garage would be empty, that Torrio, not content with a twenty percent cut, had taken it all. But if that was so, what was the sense of the meeting? Torrio wasn't the type to waste time. Unless, which was another possibility, he enjoyed a good joke before he buried a competitor.

Meister unlocked the garage door, not knowing what to expect. If the whiskey was there, he still had his deal. If it was gone, he was, too.

The whiskey was there. The remaining five hundred cases, just as he had left them, except for one that had been opened and the contents of a bottle sampled. There was also a note: *Happy selling, kid,* it said. There was no signature.

Meister began to breathe again. He got out his cigarettes and sat down on one of the cases, wondering when the note had been left—before or after his meeting with Torrio.

Before, probably, he decided. Torrio knew that the exclusive men's clubs were the best market for Dunbar's Special. He also knew that his hoodlums, who all looked like they belonged in police line-ups, would have little success selling there, so why disturb a good thing?

Did it matter who sold what as long as Torrio got his off the top? Was this piddling cache worth stealing when—as Meister himself had said—the sky was the limit?

He lit his cigarette, feeling numb. He hadn't sold himself to Torrio, quite the opposite. Torrio had already bought him, lock, stock and barrel, before he ever walked through the door. Without asking, Torrio had made him a part of the syndicate, knowing he couldn't refuse.

Well, he really was on that long, narrow road, Meister thought. No exits—and no turning back.

Tandy was engrossed in the positioning of a gilded oval mirror when Meister returned to the house in Cicero.

"Hello," she said, accepting a kiss on the cheek and then returning immediately to the mirror. "Do you like this? It was a steal—twenty dollars."

"I love it," Meister told her, even though he thought a chair would have been a more appropriate purchase. It had been two weeks since they had moved in and they were still sitting on crates. Tandy, true to her word, was being patient in her selection of furniture. In fact, she was being downright slow. Nothing would be acquired unless it was exactly what she wanted and at the price she wanted to pay. Their long search for the right house had proved the wisdom of persistence. She would not be rushed. "What's for dinner?" Meister asked.

"Nothing yet," she admitted. "I just got in myself." She stood back, admiring her handiwork. The mirror, hung on the right wall of the hall between the front door and the stairway, only magnified the bareness of all it reflected. "It needs something more, perhaps candle holders on each side. What do you think?"

"I think I'm hungry."

"You," she said, fiddling with the mirror, trying to get it exactly straight, "are always hungry. Seriously, what do you think?"

Meister came and stood behind her. In the convex glass her image was distorted, but she was still the most beautiful woman he had ever known. It still amazed him to realize that she was his wife. Her backward method of furnishing the house, the fact that she hardly ever fed him properly, didn't know the meaning of a square meal, did not disturb him greatly. He loved her quite blind to any flaws. There was, in truth, little to fault, except her pampered upbringing. "I think you're beautiful."

"The mirror, silly."

"It's beautiful too, because you're in it."

Tandy stuck out her tongue, so close to the convex glass it was grossly magnified. Meister, not to be outdone, moved closer to stick out his own tongue. "To you too!" Tandy said, thumbs in her ears.

Soon they were both mugging, pulling and twisting their features, making silly faces, two clowns in a fun-house mirror. Then, laughing so hard they couldn't stand, they collapsed in a heap on the floor.

"There's a bed somewhere," Meister said, taking her into his arms.

"I'd rather do it here," she told him.

Later, in the bed, Tandy asleep beside him, Meister decided that he wouldn't tell her that he had been forced to join the Torrio crime syndicate. He had meant to; if a marriage was going to stand, it had to be built on a foundation of truth, he believed. Yet now he felt that the knowledge would upset her.

What was to be gained from telling her, except to make her unhappy? It wasn't as if anything could be altered. He'd had no choice but to join. It was done and there was no turning back. The only real alternative, which he refused to consider, was to leave everything and run. The house, the rest of the liquor cache, the prospects for more—and for more money.

Maybe someday running would be a way out, but certainly not now. There was too much money to be made. In the past three weeks, averaging eighty dollars a case, he had made twelve thousand, selling one hundred fifty cases of Dunbar's Special. The remaining cases, even after Torrio's cut, would bring him another thirty-two thousand. He was on his way to becoming a rich man. He couldn't stop now, he told himself.

That was the simple truth. Torrio wouldn't let him stop.

And why tell Tandy that? Why frighten her?

CHAPTER 22

Tandy had never been happier. Greg was the perfect husband, loving, attentive, considerate. The sexual side of their marriage was an impossible dream come true. When he made love to her she was lost to pure ecstasy.

Her new home was equally perfect. Their Greek revival treasure house, she called it, finding new pleasures at every turn. It had been built with special, loving care, and that was how she wanted to furnish it, choosing only those pieces that matched its perfection, carefully husbanding her resources. The search for treasures to fill the treasure house took up almost all of her time and she was glad of it. It was her contribution, one she knew how to make and was good at. If she couldn't cook or sew, if she had never done housework, she at least had good taste, a heritage from her mother.

When she was finished, the whole house would be perfect, inside and out. The perfect house for the perfect marriage. Though there was no rush to make it so, there was a timetable. The baby was due early in August, three more months. She wanted it done by then.

Only three more months. If it was possible for her to be happier, she would be then. There would be a child to complete their circle of love. God, make it a perfect child, she prayed. It had to be. The perfect child to match everything else that was so wonderful in their lives. And they would all live happily ever after.

Fairy tale? No, Tandy thought; it would and could happen. If there was a cloud in all this, it was that in order to afford all this perfection, Greg had had to make his start in the illegal liquor business. But that didn't mean he had to stay in it forever. It was just a way of making a stake. Once he had enough, he would go into some other type of business. He had promised her that and she intended to see that he kept his promise.

He had to, and she knew exactly when to remind him of it. When the baby was born, when she gave him that perfect gift, the child who would complete their circle of love.

Meister sold the last of the Dunbar's Special at the end of June. The Terminal City Club, one of his first and biggest customers, bought the last ten cases, willingly paying almost twice what it had originally, and eager to have more as soon as it was available.

"You're always welcome here," Grant MacPherson, the club president, told Meister sincerely, vigorously shaking his hand. "An honest man with a good product. When it comes to buying whiskey, do you have any idea how rare a combination that is today?"

Yes, the secret of his success. Meister thought. There was no shortage of rotgut whiskey in Chicago. A legion of whiskey-makers infested the slums. The tenements ran with alcohol. For hundreds of miles around there was another legion of moonshiners, professional and amateur alike, spewing out still more bad booze, a supply that always exceeded the demand.

But quality liquor? That was in short supply. It shouldn't have been, for there was a lot of good rye whiskey being legally distilled in Canada. And with a border almost four thousand miles long, not even an army could properly police it. But no one could be sure he was getting what he paid for when he took a supposedly Canadian rye whiskey in hand. Too many bootleggers had elected to peddle inferior homemade brands under Canadian labels and make a killing on the price. There was no guarantee you were really drinking Louis Hunter or Four Aces. You could just as easily be drinking rotgut.

As for good scotch, none was made in Canada, scotch being the centuries-old preserve of the British Isles. What little was starting to trickle in was staying on the East Coast. There freighters were lying outside the limit, selling most of the top brands—Haig & Haig Pinch, Dewar's White Label, Black & White, Ballantine's and J & B—for ten dollars a case. The Coast Guard's supposed blockade was a sieve. Runners were getting through all the time. But New York, a sponge, was soaking most of the liquor up. It was a rare runner who couldn't find a market east of Chicago, where the Torrio syndicate—at least so far—wasn't all that interested.

For people like Grant MacPherson, the quality they wanted was hard, if not impossible, to come by. They were men who knew their whiskey and who preferred scotch, not rye. The Dunbar's Special was nectar for the gods compared to what was usually offered, and its rarity made it all the more valuable. Dunbar's Special was not bottled in large quantity or produced at a hurried rate. Age, that's what made its quality and reputation. No miracle could quicken that aging process. In the whole world, for example, there was at that moment only so much twelve-year-old Dunbar's Special. The richest man on earth could snap his fingers forever without changing that fact. A new supply wouldn't be ready until next year. Time decreed it.

Nor. of course, could you fake it. Rve could be faked. There was some fairly good imitation Louis Hunter making the rounds in Chicago. Good gin was even easier. A three-gallon can of Belgian Hol and some juniper berries, and if you were drunk enough you'd think it was Gordon's.

But Dunbar's Special? To the discerning taste, faking it was impossible. The same was true of Something Special, a top-quality aged scotch. It was, in fact, not worth the effort, with so many millions to be made peddling inferior stuff.

Yet a select market—the Regency Market, Meister called it—did exist and so far no one was exploiting it. Meister had proved that with how easily he had moved the last five hundred cases of Dunbar's Special.

In a city glutted with whiskey, working on his own, he had sold out in just a few weeks at a premium price. His overall profit on the entire deal came to more than thirty thousand.

Meister could barely believe the figures he had drawn up. From an initial investment of fifteen thousand dollars—ten thousand from Nelson Crain and five from Tandy—Meister figured he could realize a total profit of thirty thousand dollars! And that thirty was just for him.

Meister shook his head. How was it possible?

It had been, admittedly, an unusual situation. Anxious to cut and run, Himie Koshevoy had sold out cheap. Nelson Crain was not going to be paid interest or profit for his unwitting participation, and Tandy had provided her share without any thought of compensation. A similar set of circumstances would not arise again.

Still, it showed what could be accomplished, even in a glutted market, if you had the right product. That was the secret: the right product.

Meister leaned back on the crate that still served as his chair, lighting a cigarette. He smoked it thought fully. The Dunbar's Special was gone. How was he going to get the right product again?

The Dunbar's buy had been strictly chance and John Crain's doing, not Meister's. Crain had made the lucky connection with Himie Koshevoy before Meister had even appeared on the scene. And Himie, after the hijacking incident with his brother Sam, had not kept the appointment two weeks later at Schlogl's but taken his money and disappeared.

So, another source was needed and soon. If it were only him, Meister thought, he could afford to wait. But he had an associate now, Johnny Torrio, and when The Fox said he would take twenty percent, he didn't mean of nothing. There had already been a telephone call to that effect. It's that time of year, time for a quarterly look at the books, and what have you got going next, kid?

Meister sighed, suddenly deflated, sorry now that he had been so quick to tell Torrio that he could make an easy connection with the Bronfmans in Canada. Hell, he didn't even know them, he didn't know if they had any Dunbar's Special and he certainly had no reason to believe that, if they did, they would rather sell it to him than to their regular customers.

All of which meant starting from scratch... without doing anything to annoy Johnny Torrio.

Meister locked his personal statement away and picked up the ledger he had started on the day he had gone into partnership with Torrio. It covered the sale of the last five hundred cases of whiskey and told when they were sold, to whom they were sold and for how much. The eight thousand due Torrio was in a neat packet stuck in the ledger. The money, plus the honest, detailed accounting, ought to buy him some time, Meister hoped. He stuffed the ledger into a briefcase and quietly left the house, wondering who had been the smartest back at the crossroads, he or Himie Koshevoy. Himie had made very little money on the deal. On the other side of the ledger, he was still his own man and, on this bright June morning, didn't have to go see Johnny Torrio.

Tandy watched from her bedroom window as Meister drove off in the rented Ford. He hadn't said good-bye, so he must have thought she was still asleep. Of late, the baby only two months away, she had taken to staying in bed most of the morning.

A colored woman, Miranda, had been hired as a combination cook and housekeeper, so there was no need for Tandy to rise early. She got all the rest she needed and spent the afternoons hunting furniture. Slowly but surely the house was being furnished. The job would be completed in a few more weeks. Then, the last month before the child came, she planned to go into what would amount to confinement. She would take no chances with this baby.

Most of the major pieces had been purchased. Last week she'd had Greg's roll-top desk delivered, tied with a bright red ribbon. She smiled, remembering his reaction, delighted with the desk but astounded that a chair hadn't come with it. "Backwards," he had said, kissing her. "What little paperwork I have I could do in my lap, but first I need a chair!"

A swivel chair, that was one of the things still to be bought. She couldn't leave her husband sitting on a crate. Their child was coming—she could feel it kicking, wanting out—and when it was born, its father was going to be a businessman, not a bootlegger. He'd made that promise. He had to keep it.

Johnny Torrio was sitting behind his elegant parlor table. He rose, dismissing a huge, powerfully built black, as he welcomed Meister to his office.

"Mr. Special, how are you?" Torrio greeted, as if the visit were unexpected. "Come in, come in." The ball bearing eyes flicked briefly to the hulking black. "Jack was just leaving. Jack Williams, meet Greg Meister. Hello, good-bye."

Williams, who was sweating profusely, beads of wetness sticking to his forehead like raindrops, didn't bother to even look at Meister. He just kept on going, moving like a wayward tank, so tall he had to stoop to get out the door.

"Black Jack runs the street whores in the Loop," Torrio imparted, as if that explained the big man's hurried departure. "He's down almost five percent in the second quarter, and with spring in the air . . . ." Smiling, indicating a chair, Torrio returned to the other side of the table. "He thinks he may have made a mistake in his books. He's going to check."

Meister nodded and passed over the ledger and the money packet. Torrio didn't bother to open the packet. Instead, he wrote the amount on the outside, and below that a code number: MB 16/2/22.

Meister, trying to decipher it, decided he was one of at least sixteen people with a last name beginning with M who was in the booze business with Torrio. Another, much fatter, packet on the table—apparently left by Jack Williams—bore the code WG3/2/22. The figure above it was $26,250. Meister did some quick arithmetic of his own. That meant Jack Williams was taking $131,250 quarterly, or $525,000 annually, from just street whores in the Loop. "That's a lot of whores," Meister exclaimed, whistling softly.

"Yeah," said Torrio. "When you consider we've just got the pros." He closed Meister's ledger, pushing it back to him. "Think of all the amateurs." Then he smiled. "Not that they stay amateurs all that long."

"No, I guess not," Meister said, thinking of Jack Williams making the rounds. He'd be a hard man to say no to.

"And how about you?"

"Me?"

"Yes." Torrio smiled. "When are you turning pro?" He indicated the ledger. "That's all very nice, but it's amateur night, isn't it? One brand, five hundred cases. You've just whetted their appetites."

"I'll be bringing in some more," Meister said, reaching for the ledger.

"Dunbar's Special?"

"Maybe. I'm still negotiating. The price has gone up, now that they realize what it can be retailed for."

Torrio frowned. "You still haven't got a deal?" "The good ones take time. We're talking crème de la crème, remember?"

"Sure, but—when?"

Meister returned the ledger to his briefcase. "I'm going to be taking a quick trip. Toronto, Montreal, probably back via New York. I'll be gone a week, maybe ten days. Then you'll know."

"Is the wife going?" Torrio asked casually.

Meister shook his head. "No, she's—"

"Too far along?" Torrio finished the sentence.

Meister, closing his briefcase, didn't look up. The son of a bitch, he thought angrily. Now Torrio had been sending his hoodlums around checking on Tandy.

"If you're worried about leaving her alone, I can have someone keep an eye on the place," Torrio offered. "Nothing elaborate, just a drive by once in a while."

Meister looked up, staring directly into the ball bearings. "No, that won't be necessary. You just keep an eye on me."

Torrio shrugged, smiling easily. "Whatever," he consented, standing up. He pushed the button that would bring in his next caller. "Incidentally, that's a nice house you've got, Meister."

Meister nodded tightly. He was still angry.

"You've got it all, kid," Torrio told him. "Beautiful wife, elegant home, pleasant town... I've always liked Cicero. A nice place." He paused, looking at the door. "Yeah, you've got it all. Make sure you keep it, huh?"

Meister stared at him. Hey, he didn't need any threats. He was going to say so, but it was too late. Several men had entered the office. They weren't the usual hoodlums, but more mature, conservatively dressed. They looked like businessmen, Meister decided, but then he changed his mind. Politicians? They all had that good-old-boy look about them.

"Come in, gentlemen," Torrio was saying. "Mr. Meister was just leaving." He was looking at the newcomers as he spoke. "Mr. Meister, meet some friends of mine. Hello, good-bye."

Meister nodded politely and left. By the time he reached his car, he was certain that at least one of the men was a politician. He had finally placed him, recognizing him from pictures in the paper. The heavyset, florid-faced man, the one smoking the cigar, had been Mayor William Hale "Big Bill" Thompson.

Jesus Christ, Meister thought, remembering John Crain's fear-filled statement that Torrio, backed by Capone, owned Chicago. Maybe Torrio did. While he was thinking about it, did Torrio own him, too?

CHAPTER 23

On a hunch, Meister decided that he ought to try New York first, not Toronto or Montreal. New York, in a sense, was home territory. He knew his way around there. Canada was completely foreign. He knew nothing about it except the one name Himie Koshevoy had mentioned, that of the major distillers, the Bronfmans. Besides, given a choice, he'd rather ship interstate than cross the border.

Tandy was another reason Meister chose to try New York first. It made it less of a lie saying he was going there, being able to show her the train ticket. He was leaving her, hopefully briefly, at a bad time, toward the end of her pregnancy. A business trip to Canada would make her immediately suspicious. New York she could more readily accept.

The story that he made up, that Sid Berns had stumbled upon an excellent business opportunity—the distributorship for a new car company, Lancer Motors—made a lot more sense with a New York backdrop. And Sid Berns was someone she knew, if only by name. This was a friend telling of an opportunity not to be missed, not some stranger trying to sell him a bill of goods.

He lied because he had to lie. There was no way he could keep his promise to her and get out of the bootleg liquor business, and he felt the truth would be too much for her right now. Later, after the baby was born, would be soon enough to tell her.

Meister also clung to the hope that some miracle would happen and he would never have to tell her. The bootleg business was explosive. The whole power structure could change overnight and anything could happen. By the time he returned, Torrio could be dead, cut down like Big Jim Colosimo. Someone else would be the kingpin and Meister might be forgotten in the shuffle, might be left alone to go his own quiet way.

It could happen and it was another reason, however improbable, for putting off the inevitable. Someday he would have to tell her, but not now.

"You'll be careful?" she said, driving him to the train station.

"Me?" He laughed. "You're the one who's got to be careful. I want you to give up furniture expeditions while I'm gone. Put your feet up and keep them there. Let Miranda do the work. That's her job."

"I promise," she replied, but there was still one thing she had to get: his swivel chair. She wanted it at his desk when he returned. "And remember *your* promise—you're out of the bootleg business, right?"

"Right."

They parted that way, telling lies to each other, but for the best of all possible reasons—because they were in love. They didn't want to worry or hurt each other.

Meister knew she was lying. He knew the truth from Miranda. That afternoon, right after lunch, the two of them planned to hit all the antique stores on State Street. He knew and understood and didn't mind. Miranda would take good care of Tandy. If she got too tired, she'd be whisked home. The housekeeper had more control over his wife now than he ever could, having successfully produced six children of her own.

And did Tandy know that he was lying? Meister wondered. She had accepted the announcement of his trip with an unusual degree of equanimity. For a moment he tried to tell himself that she knew the truth, but then he realized what he was trying to do. He was trying to tell the ultimate lie. He was trying to lie to himself.

"I love you, Greg Meister," Tandy said, kissing him good-bye.

"And I love you," he told her, wishing he didn't have to lie, and wishing that she knew and understood. Someday there would be a reckoning. There were times when he wondered if, when it came, their love would be strong enough to survive it.

Sid Berns came rushing through the door of the tenement building. He started up the stairs before he realized that his way was blocked. He stopped abruptly, staring into the darkness, waiting for his eyes to adjust.

"Miami, huh?" Meister said softly.

Sid Berns froze. He recognized the voice. Unconsciously his hand went to his throat, which had almost been snapped on his last encounter here with Meister.

"No hard feelings," Meister said quickly. "I appreciate a man who is loyal to his friends. As it happened, I managed to locate John anyway." He got out his cigarettes and offered the pack. "He and I did a bit of business in Chicago. He—uh—didn't happen to mention that, did he?"

Sid Berns cautiously took a cigarette. "Yeah. I've seen him a couple, three times since he's been back. He said you made a quick killing bootlegging." When the match flared there was no fear in his eyes, only undisguised curiosity. "You married his sister, huh?"

Meister nodded, lighting Sid's cigarette first, then his own. Purposely he dropped the still-burning match on the step where, briefly, the flame revealed a black satchel sitting between his feet.

Sid Berns stared at it, his mouth suddenly dry. The last time he had seen that satchel, it had been filled with money.

"Open it."

Berns looked at Meister.

Meister struck another match, holding it close to the satchel. "Open it."

Sid Berns did. As before, it was filled with money, but not with fives and tens this time. From what he could see in the flickering light, they were all crisp new hundred-dollar bills.

Meister shook out the match and closed the satchel.

Sid Berns couldn't keep the awe out of his voice. "How much you got in there?"

"Enough," Meister told him, settling back against the stairs. "You remember the first time we met? The Dempsey-Carpentier fight?"

Sid Berns nodded.

"You impressed me then," Meister said. "A kid who got around and who heard a lot. If you'd only had the money to take advantage of the information, you could have made a fortune on that fight, right?"

Sid Berns nodded again. "Ain't that always the way?" He puffed on his cigarette. "That first big stake, how do you make it? Until you do it's just nickels and dimes." His gaze moved to the satchel that he really couldn't see in the darkness. "But that's not your problem anymore, huh?"

"Different problem," Meister admitted. He reached into his pocket, taking out a folded piece of paper, passing it to Sid. "You still work the docks?"

"Yeah—at the moment."

"I'm willing to take anything on that list," Meister said. "Buy it, steal it, it doesn't matter, just so long as the price is right."

Sid Berns unfolded the sheet of paper. Meister struck another match so he could read it. There were seven brands of scotch listed: Dunbar's Special, Something Special, Haig & Haig Pinch, Dewar's White Label, Black & White, Ballantine's and J & B. There were also two Irish whiskeys, John Jameson's and Old Bushmill's. At the bottom there was another line: Any rare wine. Any vintage quality champagne.

"Lots of luck," Sid Berns said when the match died. "You know who's the king of booze now in New York? Lucky Luciano."

"He says he is," Meister said, stuffing his matchbook in Sid Berns' shirt pocket. "But he hasn't got it all organized yet. He's two years behind where Torrio is in Chicago. There are still a lot of warring factions... which means there are still a lot of holes."

Sid Berns snorted. "You know so much, how come you're talking to me?"

"I know there are holes," said Meister, putting out his cigarette. "And when there are holes, things can slip through." He kicked at the satchel between his feet. "You're still looking for your first big stake? It's in there—if you can get me a load of anything on that list."

Sid Berns laughed now. "You know what you're asking? For me to get myself killed."

"Bullshit," Meister said. "You're not thinking." He got himself another cigarette. "The world is full of brave men who lose their nerve at the moment of truth. That's what happened in Chicago. This brave little Jew, Himie Koshevoy, arrived in town with a thousand cases of Dunbar's Special, and suddenly he realized he had to deal with Johnny Torrio. So what does he do? He shits his pants. He *gives* the stuff away."

Sid Berns' voice had an edge to it. "Because he was a Jew?"

"No. You're missing the point. He didn't want to deal with Torrio, and in all New York there's got to be somebody who doesn't want to deal with Lucky Luciano. Comprehend?"

Sid Berns was silent for a long moment. "What's in it for me?"

"If I buy it, ten percent off the top. If I have to steal it, we negotiate."

"If I get involved, it's going to be a buy," Sid told him. "How much are you thinking of spending?"

"Thirty thousand dollars."

There was another long silence. "That's how much is in that bag?"

Meister nodded.

Sid Berns leaned against the stairwell. "You're just carrying it around?"

"Who do you think it would be safer with?" Meister asked, smiling. He took hold of the satchel and stood up. "You've got four days to make yourself three thousand bucks. Call me if you get lucky."

"How do I reach you?"

"There's a phone number in the matchbook." "What matchbook?"

"The one I put in your pocket."

Sid patted his shirt. "Oh, yeah."

"To help light your way." Meister pushed past him and was gone.

That night Meister had dinner with John Crain, more to bring him firsthand news of Tandy than out of any personal feelings of his own, which were at best ambivalent. He doubted if things would ever be the same between them again. Too much damage had been done.

Crain, for his part, made every effort to be friendly, and it was not an unpleasant evening. Finally unburdened of his secrets, he was much more open, willingly telling all about himself. With Capone in Chicago, he felt reasonably safe in New York, had in fact come out of hiding and returned to his old job at the stock exchange. He was still living at 14 Washington Square.

"What I guess I'm saying, a man can't run forever," he said, ending his account of what had happened to him since their parting in Chicago. "There comes a time when he has to take a stand."

Meister nodded solemnly. He could have told him that a year and a half ago if he'd been asked.

"And what about you?"

"Me?" Meister paused, then said, "It's like I told you, I did very well by our venture but now I'm in so deep I can't get out."

"And you haven't told Tandy?"

"No."

"Don't," John Crain advised. "If you can get away with it, keep her in the dark—the longer the better."

Meister laughed hopelessly. "How?"

"Two businesses," John Crain suggested. "One—your front—legit. The other your bootleg stuff."

"Sure. And how do I find the time for both?"

"Hire someone, nincompoop. You're in the bucks, aren't you?"

Meister looked at John Crain. It had been a while since he'd been called a nincompoop, and it no longer applied, he thought.

"Sorry," John Crain said quickly. "Listen. My father doesn't tell my mother everything. If she knew all the details of how he made his fortune ... well, they wouldn't be married, that's for sure. I think that's why she claims to have no head for business. She doesn't want to know."

"Maybe you're right," Meister decided, accepting the apology. It had been apparent in John Crain's hurried response and the tone of his voice. It had been settled without need for discussion. He'd no longer be called a nincompoop. "I sometimes feel that way about Tandy, that she's trying to tell me that what she doesn't know won't hurt her. And then I tell myself it's wishful thinking."

John Crain shrugged. "I just know what I'd do if I were you. Start another business as a front. Keep her in the dark. What she wants is a home and the good life. What she doesn't need are all your troubles and woes."

"That's a Crain trait, is it?"

"What?"

"Nothing," Meister said. "Speaking of family, does the old man still hate me?"

"With a passion."

"Even with his ten thousand back?"

"I think that made it worse. He can't call you a thief anymore."

"Just a scoundrel?"

"Yes. He's limited now."

"Well, it's better than nincompoop," Meister said, unable to resist.

Crain laughed. "You can never leave well enough alone, can you?"

"A Meister trait." Meister got out his cigarettes and changed the subject again. "Do you think Sid will be able to come up with something? I'd sure as hell hate to go cold to Toronto."

"What did you say you gave him? Four days?" Meister nodded.

"My last advice of the evening," John Crain said, leaning across the table, flicking his lighter. "Wait."

The telephone call came on the fourth day.

"I think we've got it," Sid Berns said.

Meister let out a sigh of relief. "You sure know how to cut things close."

"These things take time," Sid Berns laughed, unable to keep the excitement out of his voice.

Yeah, Meister thought. He could remember saying much the same thing to Johnny Torrio. The good ones take time. "What is it?"

"Something Special!"

Meister heard the excitement in his own voice. "You're talking brand name, I trust?"

"Uh-huh."

"Good." Meister could hardly believe he could be that lucky. In his ratings, after Dunbar's Special came Something Special. Then, too, he liked the idea of keeping the name that Torrio had bestowed on him: Mr. Special. "As a matter of fact, excellent. How many cases are we talking about?"

"Ten thousand."

"You mean, bottles."

"No, cases. Ten thousand. All or nothing."

"Are you crazy? I can't buy ten thousand cases!" For a moment Meister almost hung up, but Sid's excitement, the eagerness he transmitted, stopped him. "What's the angle?"

"They're willing to sell on installment, the same kind of deal you put together in Chicago."

"Oh? How much a case?"

"Five dollars."

"Five?" It had to be worth at least twice that.

"You heard me."

Meister whistled. The price was right. As a matter of fact it was too good to be true. "You're talking about somebody who wants to sell a hundred thousand dollars' worth of booze for fifty thousand," he said.

"I know."

"And you're saying he's willing to do it on the installment plan?"

"Yeah."

Meister shook his head. That didn't make sense. "Okay, Sidney, what have you still got to tell me?"

"Well, the truth is, we've got to help steal it."

Meister almost dropped the phone. "*Steal* it?"

"Yeah."

Jesus Christ, Meister thought, stunned. Ten thousand cases of scotch and he was suggesting they steal it? "I thought you'd only get involved in a buy," he said at last, because he didn't know what else to say. Nobody could steal ten thousand cases of scotch, not even Lucky Luciano.

"I think we'd better have a talk," Sid Berns said.

The meeting was at Turner's, a small speak on Carlisle, just off Trinity. It handled a Wall Street clientele, mostly young brokers, and if anyone from the docks came there it would be by the sheerest accident. Or, as in this case, by design.

Meister showed up late and reluctant. He had talked bravely of being willing to steal, if necessary, but to actually do it was something else. He also didn't know how to handle such a large amount of whiskey. He had no way to move it, no place to store it, no system for distributing it.

He wanted to remain a small operator working alone. This deal, supposing it was possible, would put him in the big league. He didn't want it, it was too dangerous, but the excitement in Sid's voice, imparting the idea that it was somehow feasible, had drawn him to the meeting.

Sid called from a booth in the rear. "Greg! Over here!"

Meister nodded and pushed his way through the crowd. The stock market had closed a half-hour before and the place was rapidly filling up. The boys had a couple hours of heavy drinking to do before joining the rush for Grand Central. Prohibition, what a laugh!

In the booth with Sid were two older men, one a fat, red-faced, civil servant type and the other a lean, hard-looking longshoreman. Sid handled the introductions, waiting for Meister to get seated, identifying the men with him only by first names. The civil servant type was Bill; the longshoreman was Tom.

Meister thought Sid might have been a little more original in the choice of aliases, if that's what they were. He also noticed that Sid had called him by his real name. Not that it mattered. He didn't know what the game was, but these two were too old—too poor and too old—to be talking about hundred-thousand-dollar heists.

"You want something to drink?" Sid asked.

Meister looked at the beer bottle in front of the man called Tom. The label identified it as Cincinnati Cream. "You can get that here?" he asked, surprised. Despite its name, the beer was imported from Canada, and Meister had been under the impression that it was only distributed to the Chicago market.

"Occasionally," the man called Tom said. "It depends on my mood." Then, prompted by Meister's baffled look, he offered an explanation of sorts. "My kid brother owns this joint. Sometimes I slip him a case or two."

"Tom works on the docks," Sid said, explaining the rest of it and confirming Meister's guess that the man was a longshoreman. Tom not only had the build, he had the look, too. The man had been at too many show-ups where there were twenty jobs for eighty men and had gone home disappointed too many times. He'd drop his mother if he thought she'd make salvage.

"I'll have that," Meister said. He noticed Sid wasn't drinking and that Bill, the civil servant type, was satisfied with spiked coffee. A fine lot to be discussing Something Special. "Well, where do we start?"

Bill elected himself spokesman. "The boy," he said, making a fluttering motion toward Sid, "tells us you're interested in buying some whiskey, is that correct?"

Meister nodded.

"We've got some," Bill said. "Or," he continued, making a quick correction, "we know how to get some." He paused, sipping his coffee. "The boy told you, did he? Ten thousand cases... Something Special?"

Meister nodded again.

"It really is special," Bill said, lowering his voice. "To my knowledge, the only British Isles to New York shipment to get caught in this kind of shuffle. When it left there it was legal. When it arrived here it was illegal. It got confiscated and they've been arguing about it for years. Now—and this is bureaucratic brilliance come to full flower—it's supposed to be poured down the sewer. Ten thousand cases, all unpacked, ready to be trucked out, and it's destined for the fucking sewer."

Meister was becoming interested. "Oh? How do you know that?"

"I'm the guy who's supposed to pour it."

The rest came from Sid. "Bill is in customs."

"In a position of trust," Bill quickly added. "I'm high enough up to swing this on my own. Nobody else in the department involved." He leaned forward, lowering his voice, as if justifying a lax system were more confidential business than any plan to take advantage of it. "The way they figure, you can only be dishonest once. Besides, two can be tempted as easily as one. Then there's the real reason—it's all covered by insurance and it's the property owner, not the government, who's paying the premium."

"Even on whiskey that's headed for a sewer?"

"An exception, but then this whole thing is exceptional."

Meister accepted his Cincinnati Cream, which, he noticed, was served by a smiling waiter, just like it said on the label. He thought that the deal was becoming more interesting all the time. Hell, it might even work. "Tell me more."

"I'm one of those fancy-free fellows," Bill said, sipping his coffee. "My wife's dead and there aren't any kids. When my retirement comes up—and it's due next year—I'm liable to go just about anywhere. The Canary Islands, for instance, or maybe Rio de Janeiro." He smiled for the first time. "Anyway, someplace where it's warm."

"And you might be considering an early retirement?" Meister suggested, sampling his beer, savoring the taste-the-hops bite.

Bill patted his jacket pocket. "The passport is right here."

Meister looked at Tom.

"Me?" The tough old longshoreman laughed. "Someplace where there's girls."

"You're already retired?"

"Semi. There's not much work for us old sots. You know what they say, youth must be served."

Meister took another drink of his beer, deciding he'd be on safer ground talking business rather than philosophy. "You've got to move it all at once and I've got to pay on installment. How do you figure this is going to work?"

"The kid says you've got thirty thousand," Bill said, again making a fluttering motion. "That'll do as a down payment and to cover expenses. We'll take twenty-five thousand now and the other twenty-five as you can manage it, but all due by the end of the year, more or less." He smiled again. "The kid says you're not the type to welsh—a new wife and a kid on the way."

Meister sat drinking his beer. The idea of Bill coming back from the Canary Islands to do him harm was amusing. Tom, on the other hand, might leave his girls long enough if properly provoked.

"Why don't you peddle the stuff here?" Meister wanted to know.

"To the Unione Siciliano?" Bill made a snorting sound. "If they knew about it, they'd take it and I'd have my early retirement, all right." He jabbed a thumb over his shoulder. "In St. Theresa's, six feet down."

"New York's not the place to sell it anyway," Sid said. "If that much Something Special suddenly turned up here, the cops would know it was the customs stuff. They might get sticky with some of the speaks for selling booze stolen from the government."

Meister glanced at Sid, worldly beyond his years and hustling for his cut. "I could run into the same problem in Chicago."

"Sure, but not as likely," said Sid. "Besides, ain't you got the fix in there?"

"An associate has," Meister told Bill, noticing the older man's sudden worried look. "He just takes a cut of my action." He sipped his beer, his eyes on Bill. "Whatever deal we put together is just between you and me, nobody else."

Bill was still wary. "Tom is in this. He gets ten percent."

"I'm talking about my end," said Meister. "I work alone." Then, noticing Sid's expression, he added, "With expenses all along the way, of course."

"Then we've got a deal?" This was from Tom.

It sure sounded like it, Meister thought, wondering why he wasn't feeling more elated. For some reason the adrenal glands weren't pumping. Quite the opposite. He felt tired, almost weary. He told himself it was too big, that's why, too heavy a burden to shoulder. Yet how could he turn it down?

"Let me hear the mechanics first," he said, finishing his beer. He looked at Bill. "I take it you've got the key to the warehouse?"

Bill nodded, his pale, washed-out eyes moving to Tom. "Yeah, and Tom's got a good crew lined up so there'd be no trouble getting the stuff all loaded in one night. All you've got to do is have the trucks and drivers there."

"How many trucks?"

"Ten."

"Ten?"

"It's a lot of whiskey."

Yes, and a lot of trucks. Meister told himself again that he was in way over his head. Ten trucks, ten drivers, ten swampers—he'd never keep all that under control. He'd be hijacked before he got off Manhattan. "How long before it has to be moved?"

"By August first," Bill said. "Actually a couple days before. That's the day I'm supposed to spill it." He glanced at Tom. "We're not anxious to wait that long, though. It's too tight."

Meister didn't answer. He was trying to think of some other way to move the whiskey. With a month to work with there was time, for example, to repack it… perhaps even crate it. "What kind of access do you have?"

"I told you, I've got the key."

"No guards?"

"No, but if you're thinking about moving it during the day, forget it. There's too much activity in the neighborhood. Everybody knows it's a customs shed."

"Neighborhood? You mean, the stuff's not on the docks?"

"No, it's been off the docks a couple of years. If it had been left there, it would have been long gone, huh?" Bill glanced at

Tom, then back at Meister. "It's in a bonded government warehouse in an industrial area. I've got the key 'cause I'm so high in the service. Hell, you can't imagine the pension they're going to pay me—sixty dollars a month." There was a hint of impatience in his voice now. "Listen, are you interested or not?"

"Maybe," said Meister. "You really got me interested when you said it was off the docks, but you also got me worried. What's that do to rail lines?"

"What do you mean?"

"Where's the nearest?"

"Railway?"

"Yes."

"There's a spur track right behind the shed," Bill said slowly. "But if you think the New York Western is going to move your whiskey for you, you're mistaken."

"Then let's not ask them," Meister said, the weary feeling suddenly gone. With a spur that close, there was a way. And it was easy! "We'll ask them to move some heavy machinery instead."

"Machinery?"

"Golf balls, if you like that better," Meister said. "What I'm saying is, whatever you want to call it, crate it and freight it."

Bill looked stunned. "Where?"

"To me."

"But that way it can be traced."

"Not if I move fast enough on my end," Meister told him. "What if it got shipped to a similar kind of shed in—oh, for example—Gary, Indiana? Spur at the back and truck door at the front. In and out in a day, right?"

Bill nodded.

"So, now what have the police got?"

There was no answer.

"Two empty buildings," Meister told them. "And with any kind of luck you're sunning yourself in the Canary Islands and I'm getting rich in Chicago." He turned to Tom. "He said you have a good crew. Put them to work on the crates. We'll build them right in the shed." He turned back to Bill. "A couple truck-loads of lumber going in, that's not too much activity for you?"

Bill shook his head. "No, I'm not worried about stuff going into the place, just taking it out. Loading onto a train?" He shrugged, still looking a little stunned. "Nobody is going to ask questions about stuff coming in."

"How about a little hammering and sawing?"

"No, that's normal. We could be putting up partitions."

"Listen," Meister said, laughing, "are you interested or not?"

Tom finally spoke up. "How do we get paid?"

"Along the way. Five thousand now—that's earnest money. Five thousand when it's aboard the train. Fifteen thousand when it arrives safely at the other end."

"How do we know we'll get it then?"

"Because you'll be standing there when it arrives."

Tom looked at Bill; his expression suggested that he'd prefer a full down payment.

"I'm not risking more than ten until that whiskey is in my full possession," Meister said flatly. "I want you to have as much at stake as me. The crates built properly, for example. I don't want them falling apart on me. I also don't want some jackasses waiting at the other end."

Bill frowned. "We're trusting you. What about all the other payments?"

"Yes, and if they're not made, you know where to find me," Meister said. "I'm established. But you two? When that train moves out, you're going to be will-o'-the-wisps." He pushed back slightly, an indication that, if necessary, he was ready to withdraw. "It's the only way I'll do it. Take it or leave it."

Bill considered for a long moment, not looking at Tom, making up his own mind. "And when do you propose to make the other payments?"

"In two stages by the end of the year. You'll get half on October thirty-first and the rest on December thirty-first. Cashier's checks. Mailed anywhere in the world."

Bill was smiling now. "Swiss bank?"

"If you like," Meister concurred. He rubbed his eyes, weary again. It was too big, he thought, far, far too big. But it was the only game in town.

As he had every night, Meister phoned Tandy in Cicero, reporting on his progress, telling her more lies. The Lancer Motors distributorship had fallen through, but now he was onto something bigger, better, much more profitable.

"Oh, Greg, why don't you just come home?" she asked. "I miss you so. There'll be plenty of time later to get into business. We've got enough money for a while."

"We've also got plenty of bills," he told her, taking the offensive. "Listen, I'm sorry, but now that I'm here, I want to get something accomplished, okay? This new thing looks marvelous."

"What is it?"

"You'll see. I want it to be a surprise."

"Greg..."

"No," Meister maintained, remembering John Crain's advice to keep her in the dark. "If it doesn't pan out, you'll just be disappointed. You like surprises, don't you?"

There was no answer.

"Listen," Meister told her, his voice softer. "Who's the business head in the family, me or thee?"

"When did you start using thee?"

"When I discovered I was missing you," he said. "Which was the first day. I want to get home just as badly as you want me there, understand? It's just..." He stopped, becoming too entangled, not knowing where the lies stopped and the truth started. "I've got to see this through. I'll be home when it's done. You've got to accept that."

"And if it doesn't work out?"

"Then I'll be on the next train home," he lied again. If it didn't work out, he'd be on the next train to Canada.

There was another silence. Finally she said, "You'll call me every night?"

"Yes," he said. Another lie.

He hung up, wondering how he was going to cover himself for that last one. The way he had things planned, he wasn't going to be able to call for a week or more, probably ten days.

His hand reached for the shotgun he had purchased after leaving the meeting at Turner's. That was, of course, supposing that the plan worked. If it didn't. . . .

Don't think about that, he told himself, the gun's metal cold to his touch, sending a chill through him. Don't even think about that.

CHAPTER 24

Despite Meister's apprehensions, everything went smooth as silk. At eight o'clock Monday morning, a normal time for a shift to start, two rented trucks backed into the loading ramps in front of Customs Shed Number 14, a windowless, red-brick former icehouse on South Street above the East River.

Meister, accompanied by Bill Hamilton—they were on a full-name basis now—was in the first truck. Hamilton's partner Tom Haley, Sid Berns and a carefully chosen crew of four close-mouthed longshoremen were in the other.

Bill Hamilton, wearing the uniform of a customs inspector, unlocked the shed and opened the loading ramp doors. The rest of them, all dressed as carpenters, unloaded the trucks of pallets, pre-cut lumber, tools, nails, six mattresses and, in several large boxes, enough canned food and drink for more than a week.

It was all done very routinely.

Bill Hamilton then locked everyone but himself and Sid Berns in the shed. Hamilton returned to his normal duties. Sid Berns, making two trips, took the trucks back to the rental agency, exchanging the last one for a car, which he rented for two weeks. Then, with papers drawn up by Bill Hamilton, he went to the freight offices of the New York & Western Railway to confirm prior arrangements for a freight car.

Inside the shed the four longshoremen, working under Tom Haley's direction, set about building wooden crates big enough to hold forty-eight cases of liquor. The special pallets and the pre-cut lumber made the crate assembly relatively simple. The pallets served as a ready-made base. The liquor was loaded on them—twelve cases, four levels high—and the crate was built around the stack. Working in pairs, the men managed to build an average of one crate an hour. The day's total output, after a twelve-hour shift, was twenty-four.

They did this for eight and a half days, producing, at the end of the marathon session, two hundred ten fully loaded crates. No one left the building during this entire period. They ate the canned goods that had been brought in, slept on the mattresses. They washed up as best they could using the sink in the shed's lavatory. In the evenings they played poker for amusement, a nickel limit. Beer was the only alcohol allowed and they were restricted to four bottles each.

Neither Meister nor Tom Haley did any physical labor. Instead they took turns standing guard, armed with Meister's sawed-off shotgun. The shotgun was ostensibly to guard against intruders, but there was an unspoken understanding that it would be used against anyone who tried to leave before the work was done.

The job was completed on schedule by noon the following Tuesday. The rest of that day was spent cleaning up the shed and moving the crates to the railway spur loading doors at the back end. Two additional crates were assembled, one to hold an odd lot of thirty-two cases and the other to hold the tools, mattresses and other evidence of their stay. The same shipping labels and stencils were applied to all two hundred ten crates. They were being shipped to Bethel Industries, 362 Union Street, Evanston, Illinois. The contents were identified as typewriters. The crates were marked FRAGILE and THIS SIDE UP.

Still, no one was allowed to leave. They again spent the night, sleeping on the mattresses, the only things left to be packed.

The next morning, Wednesday, eight o'clock sharp, Bill Hamilton and Sid Berns arrived in the rented car. Bill opened the shed's rear doors. Sid gave Meister the black satchel. Everything was ready now. The mattresses and a few other odds and ends had been stuffed into the last crate. It was closed up and put with the others for shipment.

Two hours later, which was two hours behind schedule, a New York & Western freight car was shunted behind the shed and unhooked from its engine. The brakeman opened the car's door and left the padlock with Bill Hamilton. He then ran to catch up with the engine.

Under Bill Hamilton's direction, the freight car was loaded, an all-day job. It was almost dusk by the time the last crate was trundled aboard. Then the freight car was padlocked and the shed doors closed.

Again no one was allowed to leave. They sat waiting in the empty shed, playing cards—the only things that hadn't been crated—and they listened for the sound of the engine's return.

It came at ten o'clock that night. Meister, sitting with the shotgun in his lap, the black satchel a kind of pillow between him and the wall, could visualize all that was happening from the sounds outside the shed's doors. Two freight cars banging together. The connection made on the second try. The pin being dropped by the brakeman. The whiskey being pulled away. Hot steam blowing, the train's wheels screeching. And then, finally, silence.

Meister opened the satchel. He took out four envelopes, passing one to each of the longshoremen, who immediately ripped them apart, greedily counting the money. For nine days' work—"With room and board, don't forget," Tom Haley told them, smiling—they had each been paid five hundred dollars. Most of that was for the risk they had taken, although Bill Hamilton had been prepared to say, if anything had gone wrong, that they had believed they were working for customs.

Hamilton unlocked the shed. One by one the four slipped off into the night, on their own now.

Meister watched them go with a mixture of relief and concern. He was glad the work had been completed without incident and that they were finally gone. Yet each of them represented a danger. It took just one to get drunk and talk too much, or turn government informer in the hope of some reward, or—worse still—tip off the Unione Siciliano. "The hazards of joining the criminal world," Bill Hamilton said, reading Meister's mind. "Let's go, shall we?"

He locked up and the four of them went out to the rented car. Sid Berns drove, Tom Haley sat up front with him and Meister and Bill Hamilton sat in the rear, Hamilton counting his five grand, which had also come in the satchel. He gave five hundred, ten percent, to Tom Haley, who had also collected ten percent of the initial five thousand payment.

Meister's mind was elsewhere. The criminal world...he really had joined it, hadn't he? Until now he had skirted around that truth, having learned—during his continuing negotiations with Bill Hamilton—a little more of the history of the wayward Something Special.

After all the arguing and delay, the exporter had been willing to take his whiskey back, but the storage fees, plus transatlantic shipping costs, didn't make that practical and customs had refused to negotiate on the storage fees. Rather than accept half, which the exporter had offered, customs wanted all or nothing, applying its regular rules to an irregular situation. Unlike other confiscated goods, the whiskey couldn't be auctioned off to cover storage costs, so negotiation would have been the sensible solution. Yet customs, in its wisdom, was actually intent on spending more money—the cost of dumping—rather than bending the rules.

Under the circumstances, Meister had tried to tell himself, he wasn't so much stealing from the government as he was doing it a favor, saving it from its own stupidity. It wasn't an argument that would stand up in court, but it served, for a time, to salve his conscience.

Now Bill Hamilton's joking comment shattered that shaky perspective. There was no use trying to fool himself any longer. He truly had joined the criminal world—and with a vengeance. He hadn't stolen anything in his life before, not so much as a nickel, and suddenly he was the mastermind of a hundred-thousand-dollar heist.

Meister wasn't sure how or why it had happened to him. He'd changed, that's all, abruptly and completely. From being an honest man he'd become dishonest. He had used money that wasn't his to buy and sell bootleg liquor and he had lied to his wife. And now this. If he was caught, it would be enough to put him behind bars for a long time. The fact that the whiskey had been headed for dumping was no defense for court or conscience. The truth of the matter was that he had become a criminal.

How? Why? He knew why. Prohibition was a stupid law, flouted at every turn, unenforceable. Half the people in the country openly ignored it. John Barrymore, interviewed in Europe, asked what he thought of Prohibition, had provided the classic answer: "I try not to think of it at all."

When you had a law that half the country ridiculed, it was easy after a while to simply not regard it as a law. It was easy to regard it as a piece of stupidity. Especially if in so doing, you stood to make a good deal of money without causing any harm to anyone. If you were lucky.

Why? He knew why. He was about to become a very rich man.

Sid was dropped off first, then Tom Haley at his home on the lower East Side, in a tenement very much like the one Sid lived in. Finally Bill Hamilton was dropped off at an apartment near the main customhouse in downtown Manhattan.

Bill Hamilton's farewell was final. He and Meister wouldn't be seeing each other again unless there was a problem about future payments. Their arrangement was for Hamilton to remain at his job until the last possible moment before pulling a disappearing act. Meister didn't want customs getting suspicious and checking the sheds under Hamilton's management until the whiskey was clear of its freight destination.

Tom Haley's good-bye was only for the moment. With Hamilton keeping up appearances at customs, Haley would be the one on hand when the whiskey arrived in Evanston, waiting to collect the additional fifteen thousand due. He was to be picked up the next evening. The plan was for Meister, Sid Berns and Tom Haley to go to Evanston together to await the whiskey shipment.

Meister wished it were going to be the other way around and that Bill Hamilton and not Tom Haley would be waiting in Evanston. Hamilton could be handled with ease. Tom Haley, despite his age, was as tough as nails. He was going to be difficult when he discovered himself waiting for a shipment that was never going to arrive....

The next morning, Meister telephoned several real estate brokers in Joliet, Illinois, finally locating one with the kind of listing he wanted, a duplicate of the rental he'd already arranged in Evanston. It was an empty warehouse with an operating railroad spur at the rear and a truck dock in front. He gave a false name and agreed to pay two months' rent in advance, promising to have a cashier's check in the mail that day.

That accomplished, Meister called several brokers in Berwyn, a suburb immediately adjacent to Cicero, and again rented a duplicate warehouse with a rail spur in the rear and a truck dock in front. He gave another false name, again agreeing to pay two months' rent in advance and to mail the check immediately.

Next, he called a half dozen trucking firms in the Chicago area, using his real name now, to try to make arrangements for the short-term rental of a fleet of trucks. He always found something wrong with the arrangements. Either the rate was too high or the available dates didn't suit him.

Then, with waybills in hand, Meister went to the freight offices of the New York & Western to change the destination of the "typewriter" shipment already on its way west, requesting that "for business reasons" the change be kept confidential. Instead of Bethel Industries, 362 Union Street, Evanston, the shipment was to be rerouted to PSL Financial Corporation, 1214 Larkin Street, Joliet. And instead of regular freight, it was to go express, switching trains at Philadelphia. This would put it in Joliet two days ahead of its originally scheduled arrival in Evanston.

A dirty trick, and Tom Haley was going to be boiling when he found out, but then that was the nature of the bootlegging business, Meister thought. You never knew what was waiting around the next corner, and if you did, you sure as hell didn't tell a ten-percenter.

Ten-percenters couldn't be trusted. They didn't have enough to lose—and they had too much to gain.

In Evanston, they checked into a small hotel—the Forsythe—taking three adjoining rooms. They were early, the freight wasn't due for three more days, but Meister had insisted on that much leeway. The warehouse had been rented sight unseen. If it wasn't suitable, he said, he wanted ample time to make other arrangements.

Due to his specific instructions to the broker, it was entirely suitable, the last building on a dead-end industrial street. The other buildings in the block all had some reason to be serviced by heavy trucks. A couple more trucks working the street would not cause undue attention.

"So what do we do now?" Tom Haley complained. "Sit around playing cards again?" Then he swore, suddenly realizing there were only three of them present. "Shit, we haven't even got enough for a hand!"

"I don't know about you, gentlemen, but I've got an expectant wife in Chicago, so I think I'll take a run down to see her,"

Meister said. He looked at Tom Haley. "Unless you've got some objection?"

"I sure as hell do!" Haley flared. "The arrangement was that we wait together. I want that money here!"

"I'm not taking the money," Meister said calmly. "It's in the bank here, you know that."

"Sure—in your name."

"Would it make you feel better if I put it in your name?"

"Mine?"

"Well, yours and Sid's," Meister said. "We'll take my name off the account and make you two cosigners. That's more protection than you've got now. It means we've *got* to pay you, because we can never get the money out of the bank without your signature."

Tom Haley thought it over. "That does tie it up, doesn't it?"

"Like a drum," Meister assured him. "And you can put the money into any bank you want. That way you'll know there's no fix."

"Now wait a minute," Sid Berns said, genuinely alarmed. "I don't want to be put in the middle. What if there's a problem?"

"Sid, get off my back, will you?" Meister requested. "I've got a pregnant wife and this is nothing. If you've got a problem, call me."

Tom Haley looked at Sid Berns. There could be no doubt that the proposed arrangement was entirely new to Sid and that he really wasn't happy with it. Meister pictured the wheels turning inside Tom Haley's head. How could he fault the arrangement? It tied up the money, providing a guarantee he didn't have now, and it left him, should push come to shove, with only Sid Berns to contend with.

"Well, all right, I suppose," he said finally. He was still looking at Sid Berns, who was still looking miserable. "My name on the account, Sid here as cosigner ... and I pick the bank?"

"Any bank in town," Meister nodded. "It doesn't matter to me. A bank is a bank."

Instead of going home to Cicero, Meister rented a large truck and drove to Berwyn, making certain that his warehouse there was suitable. Satisfied, he kept on going—passing within a few miles of home and Tandy—continuing on to Joliet, thirty miles to the south. Here again he satisfied himself that the warehouse was suitable.

He then telephoned New York & Western and confirmed that his freight car would be in Joliet on schedule the next day, a Tuesday. He asked if it could be unloaded immediately by a railroad crew if he paid extra, and he was assured that it could. With that assurance he went to the freight office of the Erie Line, a small local railroad serving Cook County mainly, and made arrangements to have a freight car at the Joliet warehouse early Wednesday to take on a large shipment going out that same day to Berwyn. He also made arrangements for a railroad crew to handle all the work, the loading and unloading, at either end.

When all this was done, Meister, still driving the truck, made a number of trips to and from the Joliet warehouse, giving the impression that he was taking on loads. He did so for two days, all during the time that the whiskey was being unloaded into the warehouse by New York & Western and almost immediately removed by the Erie Line crew.

He stopped only to eat and call Tandy, assuring her that he would be home soon now and asking her to tell anyone who called that he had just stepped out and would be back shortly. He also called Tom Haley at the Forsythe Hotel in Evanston, assuring him that he was just a few hours away and requesting that he be sure to call if the shipment arrived ahead of schedule.

When the Erie Line freight car was taken away, Meister broke a bottle of scotch on the warehouse truck dock out front, leaving a few shards of glass but no label. He then hurriedly drove home to Cicero to await the phone call that would be coming the next morning from Sid Berns.

The call came after a loving reunion with Tandy. She was still asleep when the phone rang. He rushed downstairs to take the call in private.

"Yes," Meister spoke into the receiver, knowing it would be Sid.

"I don't know what you're trying to pull," said Sid Berns, sounding both angry and fearful. "But the whiskey didn't come and there are four guys here with guns in my ears telling me it ain't gonna come. Tom Haley just phoned New York & Western. They claim it was rerouted to Joliet, but they won't say where. Confidential."

"Four guys? You mean our longshoremen carpenters?"

"I mean our longshoremen pissed off carpenters." "Funny they should show up."

"Funny you should leave."

"Who else was going to protect our investment?" Meister asked. "Sidney, this isn't a problem. You don't know where the booze is and they know you don't. You're worth fifteen thousand dollars to them and they know you are. Go to the bank with Tom Haley, cosign the money over to him and then stay there, understand? *Stay* in the bank."

"For how long?"

"Until the cops come and take you away."

"Are you serious?"

"Yes, and I'm also serious about bailing you out tomorrow. Unless you do something stupid, the charge will be loitering."

"Okay," Sid Berns agreed, sounding relieved. "But we've got a lot of things to talk about, Mr. Meister, like for example, why the fuck didn't you tell me?" "Because you're a ten-percenter, Sidney," Meister told him. "It's nothing personal. See you tomorrow." He reached over to kill the connection.

Instead of returning to bed, Meister remained downstairs in the library, swirling around in his new swivel chair. Sidney was safe and so was the whiskey. It wouldn't take Tom Haley and his boys too long to locate the warehouse in Joliet, but they would assume the whiskey had been moved by truck because that was the normal thing to do. Besides, all the evidence pointed that way—all the calls he'd made to trucking firms asking about rentals, the truck going back and forth, the spilled scotch and broken glass on the truck loading dock. If they happened to discover that the load was put on another freight, they would arrive in Berwyn too late.

Tomorrow, one last time, with the help of Sid Berns, the whiskey was going to be moved again. Then no one would be able to track it. Only the two of them would know its location, he and Sid Berns.

Meister spun his new chair around to his new desk. He got a pad and pencil and did some rough arithmetic to figure his probable profit after percentages and expenses were paid. At twenty dollars a case, Meister stood to make a total profit of $84,000, just for himself.

Meister decided he liked that, he liked it very much indeed. Sid Berns was no longer a ten-percenter and he, Meister, if he could keep this up, was someday going to be a millionaire!

CHAPTER 25

The baby was born on the sixth of August, a boy they named, as previously agreed, Alexander. Meister thought the child looked exactly like him. He was too long and too thin, another scarecrow, and he looked stunned and bewildered, as if he'd just been hit across the face, not the bottom. Tandy also thought the boy looked like her husband, but for different reasons. She thought he was the best-looking thing—apart from Meister, of course—that she had ever held in her arms. Love, especially a mother's love, can be blind.

Alexander and his mother were taken home from the hospital in grand style, driven in a new Royal Mail. This was Meister's gift to Tandy to mark the occasion. Mother and child were delivered to the care and custody of Miranda. The moment they crossed the threshold, she was in charge, completely so. It is doubtful if even firing her would have changed that.

Not that Meister was inclined to argue. Miranda, mother of six, knew more about children than anyone else he had ever encountered. "I've spilled more than you'll ever know," was the way she put it, a maxim she applied to everything. "I don't want you in the nursery except on a visit. Hear?"

With that, Miranda headed up the stairs, one arm around Tandy, the other holding Alexander.

Meister was left to retire to his library and consider his good fortune. The mother was doing well. As a matter of fact, she was radiant. His son was strong and healthy and might possibly possess some intelligence to offset his appearance. He, Meister, was master of all he beheld, with the exception of Miranda. The future had never looked brighter.

Irresistibly drawn to his accounts—this was a day for totaling assets—he sat at his desk and opened his ledgers. In one month, July, he had sold five hundred cases of Something Special, each for twenty dollars a case, for a total of ten thousand dollars. If he could keep up that pace over the next five months, and he thought he could, it would mean another fifty thousand. By the end of the year he'd have his initial investment and projected expenses covered.

That amount, the entire sixty thousand, was going into a special reserve fund to cover his risk and to make certain there'd be enough money to pay the installments owed Bill Hamilton. If he should somehow lose the whiskey cache, and the possibility always existed, he wanted that debt paid. Tom Haley, the ten-percenter, might have been a double-crossing son of a bitch, but there was no evidence that Bill Hamilton, basking in the sun in the Canary Islands—if that's where he was—had had anything to do with the hijack attempt. So it was an honest debt and had to be paid. The best way of guaranteeing payment was to set the money aside.

Starting in January, though, it was going to be all profit, just a matter of slicing up the pie, with the biggest slice going to him. If he kept the sales at five hundred cases a month, he'd be taking in ten thousand a month through February, 1924. Of that, two thousand went to Torrio, two thousand to Sid Berns and the rest—six thousand—went to him.

It was neat and clean and everybody had agreed to it, especially Sid. Torrio, too, after some argument. The Fox had wanted to start getting his cut right away, but he had finally agreed to Meister's demand that the first priority be the reserve fund for Bill Hamilton.

"In this business, the worst thing you can do is welsh, right?" Meister had said, and Torrio had laughed, saying no, welshing was far down the line—after getting convicted for murder and certainly after bungling a hijack. The story was all around Chicago how five longshoremen from New York had visited empty warehouses in Evanston, Joliet and Berwyn, before accepting defeat at the hands of the wily Mr. Special. Torrio loved it.

"I've been dining out on that for a week," he told Meister, impressed not only by his associate's caution but also his resourcefulness. "Okay, why quarrel with success? Do it your way, kid."

Meister sat totaling up his assets. His once bulging bank account was down to less than eight thousand. Besides the initial outlay for the Something Special, the freight and warehouse charges had been horrendous and there had been a lot of little things associated with the buy, like train tickets and hotel bills and car and truck rentals. He'd be getting it all back, of course. It was his portion of the reserve fund. But it wouldn't be available to him until the first of the year.

That meant he had to live for five months on eight thousand dollars a month, and he had a lot of expenses. Tandy's furniture bills were stacked up a mile high. She'd gone through her own five thousand nest egg. There was the mortgage on the house, and the utilities and insurance and taxes on top of that. The grocery bills and Miranda's salary and now the hospital bills and…

Meister stopped, aghast. What was he saying? That he might not be able to live on sixteen hundred a month? Laughing, he pushed his ledgers away, thinking of the thirty cents an hour he'd been making just a year ago at J.P. Morgan & Company and how far he had come in such a brief time.

He was Mr. Special. He was sitting on a hundred thousand dollars' worth of excellent scotch. Johnny Torrio, the only man who could do him harm, liked and trusted him. He had almost eight thousand in the bank and as of January would start to draw, free and clear, a monthly income of six thousand dollars.

Mr. Special? Mr. Lucky, Meister thought, especially considering all the help he'd received along the way, first from John Crain and then from Sid Berns. Still, none of it would have happened if he hadn't put his hand to it, so some credit belonged to him, too. He was the catalyst, the man who made it happen. Modesty was all well and good, but give the devil his due.

Miranda suddenly appeared at the door to the library. "All right," she told him. "You can go up now."

"Thank you," Meister smiled. "You do give me credit for some of that?"

"Oh, I suppose you played a minor role," she grudgingly admitted. "But from my experience, 'played' is the word. So don't start getting uppity with me, Mr. Meister." She looked at the wall clock. "Five minutes and that's all. They both need some sleep."

Meister visited with his new son first. It was the first time he'd been alone with him and that somehow made it different, special. He didn't change his mind. Alexander was another Meister scarecrow with no sign of Tandy's contribution except in the dark hair and the eyes. But being alone with him at last gave Meister a sense of real possession.

My son, he thought, picking the baby up without Tandy or a hovering nurse or a know-it-all housekeeper expecting him to drop the child. My son! He held the baby close, surprised to find it so small and fragile but knowing that soon enough—how swiftly the years would slip by!—the boy would be a man.

It had happened to Tommy, hadn't it? He could remember when his kid brother was this size, a baseball for a head, the rest of him a collection of sticks. And now?

Meister suddenly realized that he didn't know *what* his brother looked like now. Had he filled out, become more like their father, or was he still like him, a scarecrow? He hadn't seen his brother in over a year and a half.

Suddenly, holding his son, part of his flesh and blood, a feeling of guilt swept over him. He had other flesh and blood and he had forgotten them for far too long. The last letter he had written had been months before. The last card he'd sent was at Easter. That wasn't right, he decided. He tried to picture his own father, holding him this way when he had been a baby and probably thinking the same thoughts. How swiftly the years would slip by... and how soon the boy would become a man.

Meister gave his new son a last gentle hug and then returned the child to its crib. He'd have to keep up, he thought, with this boy and with his brother and sister, his father and mother. They were all part of a cycle that was not supposed to be broken.

Tonight he'd write his parents, tell them the news. They'd had their first grandchild and, even if he didn't look like much, he could well be intelligent and he appeared to be normal.

"Alexander, you're good news," he told the baby. A new bond, he thought, and maybe the child would serve to stop the drift, bring his family back to him. They had been close once, almost as close as he now felt to his son. Perhaps, if he made the effort, they could be close again. His new life was good, but he didn't want to abandon the old one entirely. It was still a part of him and that was why, alone for the first time with his first child, he had thought of his brother Tommy.

Tandy was propped up in her bed, still looking tired and drawn but also radiantly beautiful.

"Well?" She asked the question she had asked a dozen times already. "What do you think of him?"

"I think he's the best-looking boy in the world," he told her, because he knew that's what she wanted to hear.

"And?"

"He's going to be a fine-looking man."

"And?"

"Thank you."

"You're welcome, darling." Her eyes filled with tears. She held her arms out, asking him to come to her. "You're very, very welcome."

Meister went to the side of the bed and embraced her. For several minutes they simply held each other, not speaking.

"I did do okay, huh?" she asked finally.

"Yes," he assured her once again. He grinned. "As a matter of fact, with what you had to work with, you performed a miracle."

They both laughed then, hugging each other more tightly, still in love and the baby making the marriage all the more wonderful.

Miranda's army-sergeant bawl came up the stairs. "Your five minutes are up!"

Tandy held him tighter still. "Don't pay attention to her."

"Are you kidding?" Meister said in mock horror. "Orders are orders."

"I want to talk to you," she insisted.

"Later. After you've had some sleep. It's your nap time." He kissed her and let her go. "We'll talk tonight. After dinner. Okay?"

"Promise?"

"Yes."

Meister kissed her again and left the bedroom, wondering what she wanted to talk about. But in his heart he knew the answer. She wanted to talk about the promise he'd made and hadn't kept.

Tandy closed her eyes, letting sleep take her. Her life, she thought, was perfect. Husband, child, home—it was all perfect. She didn't want to do anything to spoil it, but she had to know.

Greg had said he was trying to get established in some kind of legitimate business. That had been the purpose of his trip to New York. Yet he had returned to tell her that everything had fallen through and that he would just have to keep on looking. She wanted to believe that, but all the evidence suggested otherwise. Greg, worried about the future before, no longer seemed to give it a thought. He still had found no business opportunity that interested him. She had even suggested several herself. The newspapers were full of ads—businessmen looking for partners, inventions to be invested in, new products to sell. But Greg always replied that there was plenty of time. From being in a hurry he had become too patient, even disinterested.

What worried her most was that, just before going to the hospital, she had come across his bankbook. There had been staggering withdrawals, one for thirty thousand dollars just before he left for New York.

What could this mean? she wondered. The money could have been a transfer of funds involving the proposed Lancer Motors distributorship. For all she knew, it was safely in another bank account. Her father had dozens of accounts. Greg, who had spent so much time studying business administration while working at Ernst Frankel's bookstore, might be following the same practice for some good reason. Different accounts paid different interest rates, she knew that much.

But she didn't know what had happened to the thirty thousand and she had to ask, no matter how much the answer might disturb her perfect world. If it was in another account and she could be shown that, fine. If it wasn't....

She brought up the subject over an after-dinner drink in the library. Her first night home from the hospital, a celebration was in order and Miranda had decided she would permit that, but just one drink.

Meister made it a stiff one, a double shot from one of the bottles of Dunbar's Special he had kept for himself, and he made himself one.

"Ice?"

"Yes, and ginger ale."

Women, Meister thought, but he ruined the drink anyway, taking the glass to her and raising his own whiskey in a toast. "To the boy."

"To Alexander," she said.

"To Alexander the greatest."

"You really think so?"

He laughed. "God, woman, how many times do I have to tell you that? Yes!"

She took a small sip of her drink and patted the cushion beside her, indicating that he should sit next to her on the sofa. "A woman likes to be reassured."

But Meister sat down instead on the ottoman across from her. Here it comes, he thought, and he wanted to be able to look her directly in the eye.

"I'm not a snoop," she told him, looking away. "I know we've discussed this before and that we both have our responsibilities. I'm to take care of the house, you're to take care of business and we're not supposed to interfere, especially me." She hesitated, then plunge ahead. "Still, you made me a promise. I want to know if it's been kept."

Meister waited for her to look at him. "Am I or am I not in the bootlegging business?"

She nodded solemnly. "Yes or no?"

"No."

"All right. I accept that. But one last question." Again she hesitated, then rushed ahead. "Before I went to the hospital, I happened to find one of your bankbooks. You'd left it on your desk. There was a large withdrawal... thirty thousand dollars."

Meister was looking directly at her. "And the question?"

"Where is it now?"

"In another bank account."

"Can you prove that?"

"Yes."

Tandy was near tears. "Greg, I'm sorry, but I don't want you to just say you can. I want you to do it. I want you to prove it."

Meister put his drink down. He got up and went to his desk and unlocked the drawer where he kept his accounts and ledgers. He took out a bankbook which showed an initial deposit of five hundred dollars and then, starting a week later, a long list of additional deposits of varying amounts. They totaled $32,846.

He handed the book to her. "Does this satisfy you?"

Tandy stared at it, not quite comprehending what he was showing her. Obviously it wasn't a simple transfer of funds from one account to another, and there was more than thirty thousand.

"I've been playing the market," Meister claimed, taking the bankbook back before she had a chance to study it further. The initial five-hundred-dollar deposit was real enough, but the rest was false. "I spread it out—a couple dozen stocks—and I sold as soon as anything went up a point. I did pretty well." He glanced briefly at the book before closing it. "Almost ten percent on my money in a month. Not bad."

Tandy's tears started to spill over. "I'm sorry I asked."

"That's all right," Meister said. "I understand." He took the bankbook back to his desk and locked it up. "There's one thing I'd appreciate, though."

Tandy had her handkerchief out and was dabbing at her eyes. "What?"

Meister returned and sat down on the ottoman, picked up his drink. He took a large swallow, holding it in his mouth, savoring the very special whiskey—the world's best—that had made him his fortune, or at least the start of it. He savored it, then let it go. It went down warm and good.

"Don't ask again," Meister demanded. "Don't ever ask again."

CHAPTER 26

The lie made everything perfect again and kept it that way. Her doubts erased, Tandy turned her thoughts to the care of her new baby and the running of her household, tasks that, even with Miranda's ample help, filled her day. She had no time for mean suspicions.

If Greg said he was out of the bootlegging business, that was good enough for her. Her one regret was that she had asked him for proof. It was the only time she had ever experienced his anger directed toward her and it hadn't been pleasant. He wasn't her Greg then. He was a cold, ruthless stranger. The incident, though brief, was seared into her mind. If she was ever to question him again, she would make sure she had good reason to do so, she vowed. Suspicions would not be enough. She wouldn't permit herself to have them. Like her mother, she would keep out of her husband's business affairs... unless, of course, he asked for help.

Greg, however, didn't seem to need any help, and she was proud of him for that. Given his chance, he had taken full advantage of it. He was providing her with a home and a standard of living that, when they started out, she'd had no hope of their ever attaining. The most she had expected was a very gradual rise in comfort and security to a modest upper middle-class existence.

Yet in less than a year she truly had everything she could desire in material possessions. A marvelous home, fine furnishings, a new car of her own and a generous allowance for clothes. There was no stinting on the household budget and she had enough help in Miranda. What more could a new bride ask for?

Nothing, Tandy thought, especially when she was desperately in love with her husband and a new son who was the image of him. Nothing, and she shouldn't, wouldn't, question her good fortune. Greg was special, one in a million, and she would let him go his way. Like her own father, he came from humble beginnings. That accounted for the drive in him, the drive that was now missing in her brother. John had had it all on a platter. Greg, who had started with nothing, would make something of his life, as he had already demonstrated in spectacular fashion.

It was unfortunate that it began with an illegal liquor purchase. Still, many a prominent fortune had had a similar questionable beginning. The important thing was that Greg had kept his promise, she thought. He was out of bootlegging and into the stock market and again looking into business opportunities. He was a go-getter, her husband, and she was a very lucky woman. She had it all.

Meister, for his part, felt like he was living in a glass world. One false step and it would shatter.

Sid Berns had not wanted to stay in Chicago. Once the liquor had been safely moved to its final hiding place—a former casket factory in Berwyn—he'd been anxious to return to New York. His parents needed him.

Regretfully, Meister let him go. He had not tried to recruit someone to take Sid's place, because that would mean trusting a stranger with a hundred-thousand-dollar secret. His only alternative was to work alone, making all the sales, deliveries and collections himself. It wasn't difficult. He had regular customers now and they usually took the same amount each month, so all it amounted to, actually, was making the rounds.

Still, his deliveries took him all over the city, into almost every part of it, and Johnny Torrio's protection did not extend to Tandy. Meister lived in mortal fear of bumping into his wife some day on one of her frequent outings with Miranda. She'd have the baby in her arms and he'd have a case of liquor in his . . . and the glass world would shatter.

It was an untenable situation. He was making a small fortune, yet he had to be his own delivery boy. That gave him neither the time nor the opportunity to establish a second, legitimate business.

John Crain's advice—"Hire someone, nincompoop!"—didn't apply. The someone, whoever he was, would take one look at the cache in the old casket factory and his first thought would be how to steal it.

Meister knew that from bitter experience. There was so much easy money to make that it made instant thieves of honest men. Sam Koshevoy, Tom Haley and, yes, Greg Meister. He, too, had become a thief. He didn't expect any less of some kid answering an ad for a delivery boy. Nor would it help him to become a minor Torrio and create several levels of hoodlums, all watching each other, excessive salaries buying their questionable loyalty and the threat of violent retribution hopefully ensuring it. That route made him a true gangster, no better than Torrio or Capone, and in order to keep control, sooner or later there'd come a time when he'd have to order someone killed as an example to the others. That would take him from associate membership to full enlistment in the Torrio crime syndicate. Then he'd never get out. Then his glass world would be even more fragile.

The answer? Meister didn't know, but he'd have to find one soon. Tandy believed and trusted in him. She lived in what she called a perfect world, one he had created for her. In fact, however, her world was flawed, as fragile as his own. If she ever learned the truth, both their worlds would be shattered.

In Washington another world was also in danger of being shattered. Sandra Crain, in a state of shock, sat listening to an ugly outpouring from the president's wife, Florence Harding.

The Duchess had taken Sandra Crain into her private apartment in the White House and tearfully disclosed that Warren Harding was having an affair with a girl from Marion, Ohio, named Nan Britton.

Sandra Crain had suggested that this might just be a rumor, but Florence Harding had insisted it was true, that she had known about it for years and that the affair had started in the girl's childhood.

"Her childhood?" Sandra Crain exclaimed.

"Yes, her early teens," Florence Harding responded. "She was a greatly overdeveloped child and wore extremely short dresses—above the knees. It was not considered quite decent. She did everything on earth she could to attract Warren's attention." She turned away, hiding her face. "Believe me, it has been going on for years."

Sandra Crain was too alarmed to try to comfort her. Warren Harding's mismanagement of the federal government was bad enough. But this new disclosure was appalling. What if it became public knowledge?

"Who else is aware of this?"

"I don't know," Florence Harding admitted. "I just know that many public men—many great men—have had their careers utterly ruined and the lives of all their loved ones, too, by such indiscretions. They've had to forfeit everything that was dear to them because of an act of weakness."

Sandra Crain could not argue that. This was something that might very well force the president from the White House if the newspapers should get hold of it. People might overlook the cronies from Ohio with their hands in the till, but for the president to be consorting with another woman?

"I don't know what to advise you," she confessed.

"There's more," Florence Harding cried, breaking down and sobbing. "There's a child!"

Sandra Crain was almost too stunned to speak. "A child?"

"Yes, a girl. She was born four years ago."

"Oh, God! And the president is the father?"

"Nan Britton claims he is!"

Sandra Crain grasped at that straw. "But... there's no proof?"

Florence Harding looked at her with tear-filled eyes. "How can I disprove it?"

"I—I don't know," Sandra Crain answered, wishing that the Duchess had chosen someone else to confide in. She had had no experience with anything so sordid. The fact that it involved the president of the United States, the one man in the country who should be above such a thing, was staggering. Warren Gamaliel Harding, the father of a bastard child?

Florence Harding buried her face in her hands. Sobs shook her frail body.

"We've got to disprove it," Sandra Crain heard herself saying. Unbidden, a terrible burden had been put upon her and she had to shoulder it. It wasn't just the honor of the man that was at stake, it was the country's honor. "We *must* disprove it."

"How?"

Sandra Crain tried to think. "A private investigator? If you could hire one, he might find evidence that some other man, not your husband, is the child's father."

"A detective?" Florence Harding shook her head. "How can I do that? I can't call one into the White House, Warren would hear about it. And I'm under escort wherever I go."

Then it would have to be a government investigator, Sandra Crain decided. Someone with access to the White House who would be sensitive to the need, if it was at all possible, to protect the Nation's honor. That was really what was at stake: the Nation's honor.

"How about Gaston Means?" she suggested, remembering the jolly fat man she had met at the home of Ned McLean, at the party where they had shown the contraband film of the

Dempsey-Carpentier fight. Gaston Means was a special employee of the Bureau of Investigation.

"Gaston?"

"You do know him?"

Florence Harding nodded. "Oh, yes. He works with Jess Smith."

"Would he treat this matter with the utmost confidence?"

"I think so."

Sandra Crain felt relief sweep through her. "Then that's our answer!"

CHAPTER 27

Greg Meister found his answer one bitterly cold December afternoon in Clancey's, a speakeasy on South Water Street, the center of Chicago's produce houses. The owner, Gang Clancey, an effervescent Irishman, had persuaded Meister to stay awhile, there being no sense, as he put it, in freezing one's ass off.

One drink of Something Special had led to another and then another. The warmer Meister got inside, the less he felt like venturing out into the cold, where the rapidly falling temperature, if the mercury gauge outside the frosted window could be believed, had hit twelve below zero.

Besides, Gang Clancey, a man of endless and uproarious anecdotes, was a favorite of all his customers. A jolly, ribald, top-of-the-morning host, Clancey ran the best speak in town as far as Meister was concerned. He sold only the best whiskey, he gave fair measure and he kept a firm hand on proceedings.

You could have all the good time you wanted. That, in fact, was almost guaranteed. But if you got drunk or rowdy or started looking for trouble, out on your ass you went—posthaste. Gang Clancey saw personally to that. For all his good humor, there was also a dark side to him, and he served ably as his own bouncer. He didn't need any hoodlums to do his dirty work. If he had a problem, he handled it himself.

Meister liked to think that the two of them had a lot in common. One-man operations, doing things their own way and staying as clear as possible of the syndicate. Like himself, Gang Clancey paid tribute to Torrio—he had to if he wanted to stay in operation—but he drew a line. He refused to serve any of the syndicate's rotgut. In Clancey's you got a good drink and you got fair measure. Always.

It was, in fact, Johnny Torrio who had put Meister onto Clancey's. Normally, Meister wouldn't have thought he'd find anyone in the produce district interested in buying Something Special. He hadn't bothered to canvass the speaks there. But in October, when he was reviewing Meister's third-quarter sales, Torrio noticed that Clancey's wasn't on the list and demanded to know why.

"For Christ's sake, you're the only one who can keep the stubborn bastard in business," Torrio had complained. "He'll only sell the genuine article and it's getting harder to come by. His stock is down to nothing and still he won't budge."

Meister had hurried to the rescue, four cases of Something Special in the back of his new Packard, and he had found a soul mate in Gang Clancey. They'd hit it off right away and been good friends ever since.

The rescue, however, was only temporary, because Gang Clancey was about to lose his saloon to the Chicago Plan Commission. The commission, after years of dispute, argument and lawsuits, had finally won the right to move the produce merchants to a new locale. South Water, a teeming, fantastically disorganized street, would be replaced by a sweeping, double-decker drive. Come spring, Clancey's would no longer exist, becoming a hole for a caisson for one of six hundred concrete pillars that would carry what was to be called Wacker Drive.

Meister had counseled Clancey to move to another location, but the Irishman had neither the money nor the heart for it. A marvelous host, he was a lousy businessman. He made ends meet and that was all. His bank account was precariously close to overdrawn.

The main fault, Meister soon saw, was that the man was too generous. He paid, at twenty bucks a case, $1.67 a bottle for Something Special, and got twenty-five out of it—actually less, allowing for spillage. He charged only a quarter a drink. The best he could turn on a bottle—fair measure—was about $4.50.

Meister didn't have any other place on his list, except some of the ultraexclusive, ultrarich private clubs, where they let Something Special go for less than fifty cents a shot. After Dunbar's, it was the best whiskey in town. You expected to pay a premium price for it.

"Fair's fair," was all Gang Clancey would say, applying similarly modest markups to his other wares. If his customers were richer for it, he certainly wasn't.

As for moving to a new location, Gang Clancey felt, perhaps with justification, that there could be only one original Clancey's. The name and the reputation he could move, but not the place. It had its own special style and atmosphere, one of the city's earliest saloons, founded by Clancey's paternal grandfather, a stalwart named Gassy Jack. In truth, Clancey's was a landmark and it was going to be a tragedy to see it go, but try telling that to the Chicago Plan Commission. It was coming down, like everything else in the way, and to try to re-create it elsewhere would not only be too expensive but blasphemy.

"No," Gang Clancey would say to Meister, the day of reckoning coming ever closer. "It wouldn't be the same, so why the hell try? Let it die in peace, will you? And me too." Then, eyes twinkling, he'd quickly change the subject, knocking Meister off his stool with a dirty story.

This cold December afternoon, though, fortified with too much Something Special, Meister wasn't taking no for an answer. It occurred to him that, not only would he be losing his favorite speak, he'd also be losing his favorite bartender. Gang Clancey wasn't inclined to work in someone else's speak, where he'd have to short-serve, water down, pour rotgut. He refused, he said. He'd rather push a broom.

"You can't do this to me," Meister lamented, ordering one last drink for the road. There were just the two of them in the place now, a couple of produce-house owners having gone home to a belated supper. The after-dinner clientele, if they were coming at all this bitter night, had not started to show yet. "Where will I find warmth when it is cold? Where will I find light when it is dark? Where will I find laughter when the black dog is upon me?"

"Your own place," Gang Clancey told him. "Your own home sweet home." He poured Meister a final shot of Something Special, too generous a shot, as usual. "Here's to you, lad."

Meister had only heard the first part. His own place?

"Cheers," Gang Clancey said, lifting his glass, waiting for acknowledgment.

Meister was a million miles away. His own place? And then he thought: Why not? And then: Why not with Clancey?

"Are you with me?" Gang Clancey raised an eyebrow quizzically.

Goddamn, Meister thought. What a great idea! He'd start his own place—a private club in Cicero—and he'd install Gang Clancey behind the bar, pouring overly generous shots of only the best whiskey, because that's the kind of place it was going to be. He already had the name for it—Something Special!

"Are you with *me*, that's the question," Meister replied, wondering why he hadn't thought of it before. His own club was the perfect front for someone in his circumstances. It gave Tandy the legitimacy she required of him, provided an explanation for his income and fit, hand-in-glove, with his present occupation. It was the reason why Big Jim Colosimo—and now Torrio after him—had the Four Deuces Café.

"Doing what?" Gang Clancey wanted to know. He still had his glass raised, waiting for it to be clinked. He never took a drop without that ritual.

Meister lifted his own glass, touching the Irishman's. "How would you like to start a business with me?"

Gang Clancey's question remained the same. "Doing what?"

"Operating a club in Cicero."

Gang Clancey looked at him. "You mean, a high-class place catering to the swells?"

Meister nodded. "Something Special." He took a sip of his drink. "That's the name, incidentally. What do you think?"

"Of what?"

"The idea."

"I don't know," Gang Clancey said slowly. "If you want the truth, I never spent that much time in Cicero. What's the competition like?"

"Who gives a shit?" Meister demanded. "If we open a club, it's going to be the best, isn't it?" He took another sip of his drink. "Well? Isn't it?"

"True," Gang Clancey admitted. He thought for a moment. "Something Special, huh?"

"You know it," Meister told him. "The very best. Top of the line."

They looked at each other for a long moment Then, wordlessly, they reached across the bar, shaking hands on the deal.

They were partners. The details? They'd work them out later.

Meister told Tandy the week before Christmas. By that time he had found the ideal location—an old brownstone on the north side of Cicero, on Burden Lane, a couple of blocks west of Grand. Though the building needed some renovations, it was in a busy, quality commercial district, the street lined with attractive business and professional offices and smart, exclusive shops. There were a few small restaurants in the area and also a small hotel, but none of them served liquor. There wasn't a saloon or speak within miles.

It was, Meister thought, a golden opportunity. So far the syndicate hadn't moved into Cicero. If he could get a strong foothold, serving quality food and liquor to a high-class clientele, the village could become his private preserve. He'd pay the usual tribute to Torrio, twenty percent off the top, to keep the syndicate happy.

As for the local police, they were looking the other way at the few small, independent speaks that had sprung up, so they certainly weren't going to bother a properly managed private club. Meister already had that assurance, if off the record, from the police department's vice squad chief, Captain Joe De Marco. "Keep it class, and you'll get nothing but cooperation from us," De Marco had told him. "What we don't want here is the syndicate and its hoodlums."

Translated, that meant the village council knew what was going on in Chicago and that, sooner or later, the booming bootleg liquor business was going to spread to Cicero. Meanwhile, they were trying to be picky about what came in. Compared to some they'd given the rush to, Meister looked like a godsend. There were no guarantees, though. The village council could change its mind tomorrow and clamp down the lid tight.

"You could end up as a supper club, period," was the way De Marco had put it, but Meister was willing to take that chance. Frankly, he didn't think it would ever come to that. The good residents of Cicero liked a drink just as much as their counterparts in Chicago. If he gave the village a class operation, it would be more than happy to have him in its midst. That's what he was going to provide, class all the way... something special.

Tandy was doubtful at first. "Doesn't that get you involved again in bootleg liquor?" she asked.

"Yes," Meister admitted, "but only in a small way—and who isn't? Your father's Union Club, in New York, you think it doesn't serve liquor to its members?"

She had no answer for that.

"Well, it does, of course," said Meister. "So does every exclusive men's club in Chicago. So do many of the fine hotels and restaurants. Prohibition isn't working, it's scoffed at almost every place you go, so please don't expect me to be the only club operator in the country paying attention to it."

"That's what you want to be, a club operator?" "Owner, actually. Gang Clancey, he's going to operate it. I'm just going to sit in my office, feet up, counting all my money." He took hold of her hands. "Come on. Smile, will you? I thought you'd be happy. How long have you been nagging me to get into some business?"

"I don't nag."

"Okay, how long have you been showing me ads for business opportunities?"

"You call that nagging?"

"You call that a smile?"

Finally, she did smile. He gathered her in his arms and embraced her. "I've already got the name for the place," he whispered. "It describes you to a T."

"The lady of the house?"

"No. Something Special."

"Oh, go open your damn club, Greg Meister," she surrendered, lifting her head from his shoulder and gazing into his eyes. "You know you're going to anyway."

Meister smiled. That was true, but he was glad to have her approval. What was really nice about it was that he hadn't had to tell her one lie.

CHAPTER 28

It was their second-best Christmas. John Crain came to visit, making it a kind of family reunion, and he brought a whole trunkful of presents from 14 Washington Square, most of them for Alexander, but also a few for Tandy and even one for Meister—a handsome cashmere sweater.

Tandy was overjoyed when she saw it. Tears filled her eyes and she took the sweater from him, holding it out in admiration.

Meister didn't understand.

"My mother knit it for you," John Crain explained. "I'm not saying you're accepted yet, but at least your existence is acknowledged."

Tandy showed him the label inside the collar. *By Sandra Crain,* it read.

"See?" Tandy said, sniffing back the tears. "I knew it as soon as I saw it. She made one for both of us—for me and John, when we were kids." She looked at her brother. "When did we get them?"

"I don't know about you, but I got mine on my sixteenth birthday," John Crain remembered. "When she thought I wasn't going to grow anymore, but I proved her wrong."

"I think I was twelve. I refused to wait," Tandy said. "I know I've still got it somewhere." In the middle of opening everything, she excused herself and ran upstairs.

Meister looked at his sweater with surprised glee. "How many has your mother made?"

"As far as I know, that's number three," John Crain answered, laughing. "Despite her original enthusiasm, she soon lost interest. Father kept pointing out that he owns several knitting mills."

Gang Clancey, a part of the day's proceedings—dressed as Santa Claus for the doubtful benefit of Alexander, who'd burst into tears at the sight of him—saw Meister's look. "Why don't you put it on?" he suggested quietly.

Meister did, removing a favorite cardigan—a gift from his mother many Christmases ago—slipping on the pullover that was a new Christmas gift, a very special one, from Tandy's mother.

It was a good fit. "She knows a scarecrow," Meister said, examining himself in the mirror above the library fireplace.

Tandy returned, breathless, a match for his sweater draped over her shoulders, the sleeves loosely knotted across her chest. She had received hers as a child and now she was a woman and would never be able to wear it again.

Still, she's kept it, Meister thought, blinking back tears of his own.

"Maybe I should have brought mine?" John Crain said lightly.

Neither Meister nor Tandy were listening. They went to each other, silently embracing. They didn't have to say anything. Sandra Crain had knitted three sweaters, one of them for Meister. That said it all, didn't it?

"Merry Christmas, everybody!" Miranda shouted, and Alexander started crying again. John Crain decided he could use a drink of Something Special, and Gang Clancey, playing Santa Claus, knew that of all the presents under the tree, he'd already handed out the best.

CHAPTER 29

During the first few months of the new year, Meister worked harder than he ever had in his life. Gang Clancey still had his own saloon to operate—the wake wouldn't be held until May—so Meister had to oversee most of the renovation of the old brownstone that was to be their new club and at the same time keep up with his regular deliveries of Something Special.

Meister didn't mind. Having a free hand made the club all the more his, and he had some very definite ideas on how he wanted it to look. On his delivery rounds he'd been into every exclusive men's club in Chicago, if only via the side door, and had developed an appreciation of understated elegance.

He brought that to the renovation procedure, changing only what was necessary in the once grand old building, but he was willing to go down to the bare walls and floors and start over where necessary. He wanted it right, every inch of it, and he also knew *what* was right.

Ben Johnston, the contractor he'd hired, was delighted to be working for someone who didn't want to cut corners. He had quickly decided to put just as much effort into the place as Meister. All of Cicero's swells would be passing through its portals when it was finished. One of the first questions they'd be asking was who the contractor on the job was.

The answer would be on a brass plaque at the entrance: *Hay House, a pioneer Cicero residence erected 1860. Renovated 1923, Ben Johnston, General Contractor.*

The plaque had been Meister's idea. Johnston had gone to him asking if he might, when the club opened, discreetly pass out his business card. "Hell, no," Meister had told him, but he would put up a plaque. He knew what was right.

With that kind of recognition, Ben Johnston was certain that he was going to get all the work he could handle. Feeling he had just as much at stake as Meister and possibly more, he, too, was giving it his all.

Meister and Johnston would meet early every morning to discuss and plan the day's work. Every night on his way home, Meister would stop by to inspect what had been done. Johnston would often be waiting for him. If ever he wanted a satisfied customer, it was Meister.

The brownstone was four stories high. The first floor, a half basement, had originally been the servants' quarters and later a small restaurant. It had a side entrance off a picturesque cobblestone alley that ran between the house and the adjacent building. This, too, had been a private residence at one time, but was now offices, housing mostly attorneys and accountants.

The second floor of Meister's brownstone, five feet above street level, was reached by a wide, ornately carved granite stairway, and the double doors were also set in an ornate granite border. This had been the main floor of the house, with a parlor, living room and dining room, the latter served by a basement kitchen. Its last use had been as a clothing store. Prior to that it had been an antique shop.

The third floor, originally bedrooms, had been recently turned into offices, and the top floor, not much more than a loft, had only been used for storage. Indifferent, absentee ownership had led to the building's decline. It had been vacant except for one tenant—a tailor in the basement—when Meister had come upon it, large "For Lease" signs in the windows on either side of the ornate stairway.

That stairway was what had first caught his attention. Meister liked grand entrances. They gave the impression that you were really going somewhere, he thought, and the rest of the place, though run-down, fitted nicely with the stairway. The windows were set in carved granite borders and the theme was continued in the roof's elaborate granite facade. Three gargoyles, fierce lion heads, jutted out from it—one in the center and one at each corner.

Inside, the place was nowhere near so grand, not anymore, but it did have great possibilities. The rooms were enormous, the ceilings high and the basic structure sound. No major structural changes were necessary. The biggest jobs involved putting in a proper fireplace on the main floor and widening the staircase to the floor above. Beyond that, the work was essentially cosmetic, though extensive. The place needed new paneling and new flooring and all new fixtures.

Essentially, Meister was returning the house to its original state, altered only to serve his purposes. The basement would again house the kitchen, pantry and storage. The main floor would be half restaurant, half lounge. On the next floor would be several small, intimate dining rooms for private parties. On the top floor, now a loft, would be a card room and, off in the back, Meister's office.

"No girls?" Tandy had teased on her first inspection tour. Meister had claimed to be sorely tempted—being the owner, wouldn't he get a special rate?—but the truth, he told her, was that he liked cards better than girls.

Tandy said she doubted that. One thing led to another and, since no one else was about, Meister spread his coat on the floor of the loft and took his wife into his arms in a totally spontaneous and uninhibited union.

As they lay there together, it was like their first time together in the old Royal Mail. There was no thought, no reasoning, no control. They simply united in abandon, wild yet gentle. Like the first time, the ecstasy was almost unbearable, and they fell apart exhausted.

"You're going to have to carry me home," Tandy said when she could finally speak. "Oh, God, Greg, I love you!"

He was still gasping for breath. "And I love... and adore... you!"

For a long time, they remained there, Tandy on the coat, Meister on the floor beside her. If they were uncomfortable, they didn't know it. Nothing had ever been quite so good between them before.

"Are you thinking what I'm thinking?" Tandy asked.

"What's that?"

"That this was the best?"

"Yes," he admitted, smiling.

She sighed, contentment filling her. "How is it possible?"

"I don't know," Meister said. "Maybe because we're happier. We're getting the things we want—the baby for both of us, the kind of house you wanted. And now this business for me." He reached out to hold her hand. "We're finally putting it all together, aren't we?"

"You mean, if you feel good about other things, making love is better?"

"All the wisdom of the world, right here in this loft."

"I don't know about *that*," Tandy said, pulling him closer to her, making room on the coat. "But all the *love* is. If you can do it again, I'll give you a quarter."

"How about a medal?" Meister asked. "I was denied one in the war. Did I ever tell you that?"

"Several times. But when have you been denied lately?"

"You mean, I'm going to get a medal?"

She took hold of him and pulled him against her. "Well," she murmured, "it certainly *feels* like it."

CHAPTER 30

Meister's Something Special liquor deliveries, though an onerous task, were down to a science now, an established, unvarying schedule. He called once a month on each customer, delivering a month's supply of whiskey, taking the next month's order at the same time, keeping to the five-hundred-case limit he had originally established.

By the end of December, right on schedule, he had taken in sixty thousand dollars. Since January, still charging twenty dollars a case, he had been clearing ten thousand a month, pocketing six thousand of it for himself and putting two grand aside for Johnny Torrio and mailing the other two to Sid Berns, care of a post office box in New York. Now, on the first of April, time for his quarterly accounting to Johnny Torrio, Meister felt reasonably secure for the first time since he'd entered the bootlegging business.

He no longer had a bankbook showing fake accounting. The reserve fund book he could show to Tandy any time. The money—$35,000—was really there, every cent of it.

The original eight thousand he'd put into renovating the brownstone was a solid investment even if he never got his club open. Under the terms of his lease, he had the building for ten years, renewable for two additional ten-year periods, all at a low, fixed rate as compensation for the renovating.

If worst came to worst, he could simply sublease the building for a restaurant and offices, making, he estimated, a twenty percent annual return on his money. He was turning an eyesore into one of the finest buildings in the village of Cicero. He'd be able to demand—and get—premium rents. He didn't want that, of course. He wanted much, much more. But he still had that protection.

He was being careful to design the club so that it could serve equally well as an elegant restaurant. The foyer was being enlarged and, if necessary, could be readily partitioned. One part could serve as the restaurant entrance and the other could open onto the stairs leading to the upper floors.

I've covered everything, Meister thought as he headed for Johnny Torrio's mansion on Riverside Drive that April morning. If it all fell apart right now—if his whiskey cache was looted and he was somehow stymied in his plans for the club—he still had, altogether, over forty thousand in the bank, plus a very leasable building nearing completion.

If he never did another lick of work for years, he'd still be on easy street, and that gave him a good, solid feeling. That gave a man the security and confidence he needed to reach out, which was what he was now going to do.

The idea had been kicking around in his head ever since he had first talked to Cicero's vice squad chief, De Marco, who had given him the conditional go-ahead for the club, warning him that there was no guarantee.

Meister hadn't met many high-ranking police officers, but everything he read, heard and saw indicated that most of them had to be on the take. It was the only way Chicago could stay such a wide-open town.

De Marco was an exception. He seemed as straight and honest a cop as one could hope for. He didn't want a piece of the action. All he wanted, apparently, was a nice, clean town, and he was realistic in the way he went about the job of getting it that way. He knew the art of compromise.

To keep the syndicate out, De Marco was willing to let people like Meister in. In a way, it was another version of the Himie

Koshevoy story. Himie had preferred Meister to Torrio. So, on a different level, did De Marco. The vice cop's ready acceptance of him as the far lesser of two evils had convinced Meister that he was thinking too small. Why just open a club in Cicero? Why not go for broke and handle the illegal liquor business for the entire village? If he did that, he could concentrate his operations in one place, not have to go running all over Chicago. His chances of getting dragged deeper into the syndicate's maw would be lessened. He'd have his own territory and the pressure to build sales elsewhere would be off his back. And with De Marco running a clean shop, his only price a clean town in return, Meister could stay clean himself. He wouldn't have to get involved in bribes and payoffs. He wouldn't have to import hoodlums to push people around.

If he couldn't get out of the bootlegging business, he'd at least have a nice, neat operation—all in one place, the club as his front. He'd at least be able to keep it, and the town, clean.

Meister was sure De Marco would go for the idea. The vice chief was very impressed with the renovations on the brownstone. Like Meister, he was convinced the club was going to be an asset to Cicero. De Marco had even hinted that he'd like to see Meister doing more. "I wish everybody showed the same class," he had said. "If you were the mob, I wouldn't have any worries, would I?"

That was practically an invitation and there was no good reason why he shouldn't accept it, Meister decided. If, while still giving Torrio his twenty percent cut, he could keep the syndicate out of Cicero, he would be doing everybody a favor, including himself.

Cicero was crème de la crème and it ought to stay that way. It would if he could have it as his private domain. The one person who could give it to him was Johnny Torrio. Today, Meister was going to ask for it. The worst Torrio could do, he hoped, was say no.

Johnny Torrio, as usual, was sitting behind the marble table that served as his desk, the top of it clear except for a few ledgers and one stack of papers.

This time he didn't stand up in greeting when Meister entered. That formality had been gradually dropped. Now Meister was just another one of the boys.

"Put your ass to rest, Mr. Meister," Torrio said, by way of salutation, pointing to the chair he himself had occupied upon their first meeting. "The word I get, you've been running it off."

Meister first placed his ledger and the packet of money he owed on the table. He wondered where Torrio had heard that and why it should have been important enough to be passed on to him, let alone mentioned now.

"Spies, they are everywhere," Meister said, pretending to check to see if he had any ass left. Then he sat down, not feeling as secure or confident as when he had entered. He purposely hadn't mentioned his plans for the club on his last visit, early in January. It would have been too easy then for Torrio to have opposed it. Now, the club close to becoming a reality, it was too late to deny permission, not that Torrio had any basis for doing so. More clubs in operation meant more money for Torrio. Besides, Cicero was outside the syndicate's declared territory.

Torrio made a quick, impatient check of the ledger, and then, not asking confirmation, wrote six thousand—the sum he was owed—on the money packet. He added the code and date and set his pen aside.

"Five hundred cases a month," he said, the ball bearing eyes fixing on Meister. "You could be moving more."

"Not much," Meister told him. "I figure I've got the market just nicely undersupplied. Keep 'em hungry, that's my motto." He smiled, getting out his cigarettes. "Or should that be thirsty?"

Torrio wasn't amused. He stared at Meister, his slender fingers drumming softly on the marble tabletop. "What the fuck are you up to, Meister?" he suddenly demanded.

Meister lit his cigarette. It was the first time he had seen Torrio angry. Now he realized why this small, rather ordinary-looking man could command an army of cold-blooded hoodlums. There was an awful fury burning in his eyes. The ball bearings were molten lava.

"Would you like to be a little more specific?"

"That club you think you're opening!" Torrio screamed. "Who the fuck gave you permission to do that?"

"Was somebody supposed to?" Meister asked, hoping he looked as calm as he had managed to keep his voice. Inside, his gut was twisting.

The scream got louder. *"Me!"*

"Hey, that's the first I heard," Meister told him. Deliberately, he stood up, retrieving his ledger book, trying to display it as evidence. "The only deal we ever made was this one. Anything else I figure is my business."

"Not when you work for me!"

"I don't work for you."

Torrio looked at Meister, the anger gone as suddenly as it had appeared, a puzzled, almost baffled, expression replacing it.

Meister sat down again. "I don't, Johnny," he said seriously. "All we've got is one deal."

"I don't know about you, kid," Torrio said, shaking his head. "You're either awful dumb or awful fucking smart. Either way, you got balls, I'll give you that much. Balls." He searched Meister's face. "You don't know, do you?"

Meister was suddenly at a loss. "Know what?"

"Jesus Christ," Torrio said. He pushed a button, a signal to the outer room. The office door opened immediately and one of the young hoodlum guards looked in expectantly.

"Yeah?" the young thug said.

"Is Jacoby still around?" Torrio asked.

"I think so."

"Then tell him to get his ass up here," Torrio ordered. He waited for the door to close, then added by way of explanation, "My director of planning, Jacoby."

Meister was still at a loss. "I didn't know you had one."

"I don't," Torrio said affably. "But he likes to think he is, so go along with the gag, okay?" He pushed himself up from his desk. "Think you can handle that?"

"Sure," Meister told him, unable to believe the transformation he had just witnessed. A minute ago, Torrio had been ready to kill him. Now he was acting as if they'd always been the best of friends, sharing a confidence about one of his lieutenants. It was as if the screaming session had never happened.

Torrio moved over to another table, unrolling a large map, holding the edges down with ornamental brass paperweights cast in the images of fornicating animals.

"When are you thinking of opening this club of yours, kid?" he asked. The question was friendly, casual.

"I'm not sure," said Meister. "I was hoping for the Fourth of July, but I think we're too far behind schedule. Now it looks like maybe August or September."

"July, huh?" Torrio seemed to be making a point of that.

"Yes."

Torrio got his map spread out to his satisfaction. "Come over here."

Meister rose and joined him. What Torrio had unrolled was a map of Greater Chicago, including outlying cities such as Evanston, Joliet and Gary, Indiana. Chicago was marked off in numbered squares. Someone, using colored pencils, had shaded in the various suburbs, giving each one a different color. They weren't numbered. Not yet.

"What do you think we've got here?"

The conflict of colors reminded Meister of a map of the world, which was really what he was looking at. Johnny Torrio's world, all neatly divided up into principalities, some of them already taken, others marked for invasion.

"Plans?" Meister guessed.

"Intentions," Torrio corrected softly. "Dever is really trying to put the lid on here. He's already had me busted once in that raid on Sieben's Brewery. I gotta start branching out."

Meister nodded sympathetically. Chicago's reform mayor, William Dever, was leaning pretty hard on the syndicate. Torrio's recent arrest in the brewery—along with Dion O'Banion, who ruled the North Side—was a real sore point with him. The raid had come right after Torrio had purchased O'Banion's interest in Sieben's.

There was a knock on the door and a tall, thin, scholarly-looking man entered. He had a bird's bright eyes and half-frame reading glasses perched at the end of a long aquiline nose. His collar was unbuttoned and his tie was hanging loose. He mismatched suit looked like he'd slept in it.

Meister remembered university professors cast from the same mold. This must be Jacoby, the so-called director of planning. Perhaps he had an ivory tower somewhere in the mansion where Torrio allowed him to play with colored pencils.

"Come here a minute, will you, Paul?" Torrio requested. "I was just showing this gentleman our map. I thought you might like to interpret it for him."

Jacoby appeared surprised and a bit flustered by the request. It was as if, quite unexpectedly, he had been ordered to divulge state secrets to a stranger. He wasn't quite sure how much, or how little, he should tell.

"It's okay, Paul," Torrio said. The rest was directed to Meister, but for Jacoby's benefit: "Paul heads up planning for me. He prepared the map."

Jacoby joined them at the table, adjusting his half-frame glasses, sizing up Meister. He smelled very strongly of peppermint—a pungent cover, Meister suspected, for liquor on his breath. At closer quarters he had the look of an alcoholic, his body not so much thin as it was wasted.

"It's really quite simple," Jacoby said, addressing himself to Torrio. "The colored squares indicate the areas we will be expanding into over the next—" He hesitated, obviously searching for the right, ambiguous word. "The next while."

Torrio had to prompt him. "Yes, and when do we plan to start?"

"July."

"Correct. And where do we plan to start?"

"Cicero."

"Thank you, Paul," Torrio said, looking at Meister. Now Jacoby was really flustered. "That's ... all?"

"Yes. Thank you."

Jacoby gave a little shrug. He adjusted his glasses, took a last look at the map and, without further comment, turned and left the office.

Torrio was still looking at Meister. "You understand what you've done, kid? You've jumped the gun on me. You're one of my boys, and you've got yourself a head start in the first new territory I've staked out for expansion!"

Meister started to protest. "I'm not one of your—"

"Hey," Torrio said, holding up a hand. "That's accepted. You're right, you're not one of the boys. What we've got is the one deal and that's all." Again his face took on that puzzled, almost baffled, look. "Who *else* do you think knows that?"

Meister considered the question for a moment, the light finally dawning. "Nobody?"

"Jesus Christ," Torrio said, laughing now. "You really are just off the farm, aren't you, kid? It takes awhile for things to sink in. That's right—*nobody.*"

Meister had nothing to say. He felt like a fool.

"I'll let you in on a little secret," Torrio told him. "I run the biggest and most profitable crime syndicate in the country. I hold it together all kinds of ways. Connections, payoffs, threats, busted heads, a ride once in a while. Whatever it takes, I'm willing to do it. Understand? I can't stay on top if I'm not tougher than the next guy. *All* the next guys." He paused, not looking tough now, but very plain and ordinary. "But you know what really holds the whole thing together? Appearances, that's the glue, kid. Appearances... and assumptions."

Meister couldn't argue with that. On one visit he had made such an assumption himself, deciding, purely on appearances, that Mayor William Hale Thompson, later ousted by Dever, was in Torrio's pocket. He still believed that assumption was valid, but he could understand why the guards in the antechamber, the guards downstairs and at the gate, plus any number of assorted hoods in Torrio's syndicate, might make the same assumption—based on appearances—that he, Greg Meister, was one of the boys. It might be bad for morale, especially at the higher levels, if someone should assume—based on appearances—that he was getting a break denied them in Cicero.

"You hear what I'm saying?"

"Loud and clear," Meister answered. "What can I tell you? I guess I got out of line."

"Way out," Torrio said, but the anger was gone now. "So let's not have it happen again, huh? It makes for..." He twirled a slim hand, trying to think of a suitable term. "Misunderstandings. Bad feelings. You know?"

"Yes, and I'm sorry."

"You're sorry." Torrio smiled, shaking his head. "Well, maybe you will be. You're clear with me. Go ahead and finish your little club. But if you'd taken the trouble to ask, I could have told you, before you signed the lease, that I was giving Cicero to Al."

Meister looked at him, surprised. "Capone?"

"The one and only," Torrio confirmed. "He's leading the charge. I want it done right—an example set, you know? Everybody gets in line... or else."

"I hear he's tough," Meister said, feeling the fool and feeling sorry for De Marco. He looked at the map and the red-shaded square that was Cicero. It was too late to ask for it now. He'd never had a chance any way. His ambition had outgrown his good sense. No one started at the top in the Torrio syndicate. Favors were granted to tried and proven lieutenants. Halfhearted associates standing on the sidelines got nothing.

As if to prove that, Torrio lifted one of the brass paperweights, letting a corner of the map roll up. Cicero, in that instant, disappeared. "Yeah, Al's a tough boy," he said, talking more to himself than Meister. "Well, good luck, kid."

Meister's gaze moved to the paperweight, a casting of two bears fornicating. He felt like the one on the bottom. Al Capone, huh?

CHAPTER 31

Meister waited for the wake at the saloon before he told the bad news to Gang Clancey. The final closing of the doors at Clancey's was an excuse for Meister, the produce district and, it seemed, half the city, to get feeling good. Meister wanted to be feeling good and he wanted Gang Clancey feeling good, too, when he brought up the name Al Capone.

Gang Clancey didn't like the Torrio syndicate. For him one of the main attractions of opening a club in Cicero was the chance to be free of it. Now, instead of being free, they were not only going to have to contend with the syndicate, they were going to have to do so in the person of its chief enforcer.

Meister wasn't even sure if Gang Clancey would stay in the deal when he heard. He might, with justification, back out, for this changed the whole complexion of it. And if Gang Clancey backed out, Meister wasn't sure that he wanted to stay in either. Something Special wouldn't be anything like he imagined it unless the effervescent Irishman was around as cohost. The club had to have more than class. It also had to have life and an honest hand at the helm.

As far as Meister was concerned, Gang Clancey was the only man for the job. He hadn't even thought about someone to replace him. If Clancey backed out, he'd run the club himself, Meister thought, or scrap the whole idea and sublease.

The latter plan held a lot of appeal. Ever since Torrio had told him he was sending Capone into Cicero, dashing his hopes for a small, private domain of his own, Meister had lost much of his enthusiasm for the club.

Capone was unpredictable. There was no telling what he had planned for Cicero. He might, God forbid, try to turn it into another Chicago, with the village administration bought and paid for, all the cops on the payroll and the place wide-open as hell.

Could an elegant private club survive in that kind of atmosphere? Or would it get tarred by Capone's heavy-handed brush? The man didn't use a velvet glove; he preferred a meat hook.

So Meister waited until he was feeling good. Awfully good. And then he took Gang Clancey aside. Today, in the merry month of May, they were laying Clancey's Saloon to rest. If need be, they could also lay Something Special to rest. Two wakes for the price of one. Meister's Lutheran thrift was showing.

"You haven't drunk with me yet," Meister told Gang Clancey, taking out the bottle of Dunbar's Special he had brought along to mark the occasion. "The time is now... while I'm still standing."

Gang Clancey eyed the bottle label with keen appreciation. "Oooh, where you been hiding that, lad?"

"Up my sleeve," said Meister. He poured a tumblerful for Clancey and another for himself. This would be his last drink and then he was going home—possibly in an ambulance—to his beloved Tandy. "Well, what are we toasting? Past or future?"

"With you, the future," Gang Clancey said fondly. "Here's to that new club of ours and all the good times we're going to have there. Here's to you and me—here's to Something Special!"

Meister raised his glass. Gang Clancey's rousing toast had rekindled the dream and his enthusiasm for it. Suddenly, Al Capone didn't seem to be quite such a threat. "Yes, here's to that!"

They took hearty swallows and set the tumblers back down on the bar.

"There's one thing I've got to tell you, though," Meister said, thinking it had to be now or never. "I got this straight from

Johnny Torrio. The syndicate is moving into the suburbs, starting with Cicero. It's going to be run by Al Capone."

Gang Clancey was still savoring the Dunbar's Special. "God, that's good whiskey, lad! How could you have that up your sleeve and me drinking swill?" The next question came almost as an afterthought: "When?"

"July."

"Well," Gang Clancey said thoughtfully, "we won't be beating 'em by much, will we? It'll take them six months, maybe a year. They'll have it all sewed up by then and everybody dancing to their tune." He took another, smaller sip of the Dunbar's Special. "Too bad. I'd have preferred more time to get properly settled. Still, it's enough, and it was bound to happen sooner or later."

Meister only nodded. He hadn't expected such a calm, resigned acceptance of the syndicate's plans.

"There's no escaping them," Gang Clancey explained. "If you want to sell whiskey, sooner or later the bastards are going to be there, hands out for their cut." He paused, suddenly frowning. "You're not thinking of backing out, are you?"

Meister quickly shook his head. "No."

"Good. For a moment you had me worried, lad." He took another careful sip of his drink, which he had obviously decided to conserve. "You know how seldom I give advice? How many times have I told you this? A man's got to take a stand somewhere. Cicero is probably as good a place as any."

"Yes." Meister nodded, trying to think where he'd heard that advice last and then remembering. It was from John Crain. "That's true."

"That what's got you down?"

"Nothing," Meister answered. "I just wish ..." He looked at Clancey, thinking that of all people he had to tell *him* the truth. "I wish it were somebody else than Capone."

"Oh, fuck Capone. He's going to have his hands full between playing enforcer and directing expansion too. If we don't give him any trouble, he won't give us any. The cut, that's all that's important. If we pay it, no problem." The frown returned. "There's no bad blood between you and Capone?"

Meister had to think before he answered. In a way there was, through his relationship to John Crain. Yet he personally had had nothing to do with Tony Capullo's death. Capone could hardly connect him with that or blame him for it. "No," he decided.

"Then stop your damn worrying." Gang Clancey ordered. He raised his glass, waiting for it to be clinked. "Here's one more toast—to the devil you know!"

"To Al Capone," Meister said, committed.

CHAPTER 32

Nelson and Sandra Crain had intended to spend the entire summer at Wicklow, but in July an invitation came to join the last leg of what President Warren Harding was calling a "Voyage of Understanding."

The president and his wife, along with a large entourage of aides, friends, newspaper reporters and Secret Service men, had departed June 20 on the trip, which was to take them through the Middle West and far West and on up into Alaska. The invitation asked the Crains to join the presidential party in Tacoma for the thousand-mile Alaska voyage.

Nelson Crain was reluctant to accept it. Of late, Warren Harding had been giving patronage-dispensers short shrift, and Crain had been unable to arrange another deal like the Teapot Dome oil lease he had put together for Harry Sinclair.

Harding, it appeared, was looking forward to next year's election and trying to rise above his old friends and cronies, aspiring, belatedly, to statesmanship. Newspapers reported that all across the country he'd been talking mostly about the need for a world court. There were also reports that he'd sworn off drinking.

To Nelson Crain, the trip sounded very much like a bore. "If he's dropping his old friends, I don't want to be helping him gather a new constituency," he grumbled.

Sandra Crain, on the other hand, was very anxious to accept the invitation, because she knew it was really meant for her, that it had been sent at the request of Florence Harding.

Ever since Florence had confided in her, revealing that Warren Harding had a mistress and that he might have fathered an illegitimate child, the two women had kept in close touch. Florence, at Sandra Crain's suggestion, had assigned Gaston Means to investigate, to see if it was possible that some other man was the child's father. The reports of Gaston's probings—which thus far had proved nothing either way—had been the topic of many a telephone conversation.

Now, with an election campaign due next year and so much at stake if the matter ever got into the newspapers, Sandra Crain very much wanted a long visit with the Duchess. The Alaska cruise would provide the perfect opportunity for them to talk.

"I'd love to go," she told her husband, and because he could deny her nothing within reason, they had closed Wicklow in the middle of the summer and headed for Tacoma.

Initially, as Nelson Crain had predicted, the voyage was a bore. Harding had worn himself out on the train trip across the country. He'd insisted on getting out at every whistle stop for a speech and was physically exhausted when he boarded the ship for Alaska.

The Crains saw almost nothing of the Hardings. All the president wanted to do was play bridge—every day, from breakfast to midnight—and because he seemed so tired and ill, Florence Harding stayed near him most of the time.

Left to their own devices, Nelson and Sandra Crain had to try to make friends elsewhere, but the presidential party, after a month on the road, had already formed into closed groups. The Crains always seemed to be the odd couple at whatever activity they attended.

Nelson Crain was ready to charter a plane and fly home by the time the ship was halfway up the Alaskan coast. He'd had more than his fill of shuffleboard and movies and group singing and Navy band concerts.

Sandra Crain was quite willing to go with him as the ship reached its northernmost destination and turned to make its way back south. Thus far she'd had two very brief meetings with Florence Harding, and on both occasions others had been within earshot. She'd had no opportunity whatsoever to discuss what was uppermost in her mind.

"We will get together," Florence had promised, holding her hand tightly, but nothing had come of it. The Duchess—and she was acting like one now, Sandra Crain thought—was too preoccupied with her husband's failing health.

Then, shortly after the ship had turned around, a seaplane landed alongside and a packet was sent aboard. There were immediate rumors that a long, coded message had been given to the president. He had retreated to his stateroom to hold a hurried conference with Secretary of Commerce Herbert Hoover.

Later that day, Florence Harding, greatly agitated, came to Sandra Crain, asking if they could talk in private. "I must confide in someone," she said. "You're my only true friend, the only one I really trust aboard this whole ship. Please help me."

Nelson Crain excused himself and left the two women to their private discussion.

"It's not—?" Sandra Crain began, certain that there'd been some public disclosure of the president's relationship with Nan Britton.

"No, it's some other scandal," Florence Harding told her. "And it's left him completely devastated. It couldn't have come at a worse time, he's so ill."

"What kind of scandal?"

"I don't know," Florence Harding said. "He won't tell me much. But it seems to have something to do with Jess Smith and some cases in the Department of Justice. It may be that Harry Daugherty is also involved."

"Is that why the president met with Mr. Hoover?"

"Yes. He wanted to ask his advice. 'If you knew of a great scandal in our administration… would you, for the good of the country and the party, expose it publicly or would you bury it?'"

"What did Mr. Hoover say?"

"'Publish it.' He said Warren would at least get credit for integrity."

"And?"

"Warren said it might be politically dangerous. He destroyed the report. He burned it."

Sandra Crain was suddenly filled with shame. Warren Harding, she thought, was not an honorable man in any sense of the word. He did not deserve to be president. Whether or not he had fathered an illegitimate child was a moot point now. He was guilty of something even more despicable. Against the good of the country—and those were his own words—hc was burying some great scandal.

"I feel so helpless," Florence Harding said. "Promise to stay on until we're back in Washington. I need someone I can trust… someone I can confide in. Please!"

"I promise," Sandra Crain said, but she was only doing so out of friendship. She had no intention of trying to save the Harding administration. It didn't deserve to be saved.

Nelson Crain also wanted no more of Harding, certain that the president was star-crossed, doomed. The ship had struck a destroyer amidships as it came, through heavy fog, into Puget Sound. Harding's comment, as relayed by Florence, had been, "I hope the boat sinks."

Later, after going ashore to address a crowd of sixty thousand at Seattle Stadium, Harding had fallen seriously ill, his ailment diagnosed as acute indigestion from eating tainted crab meat. The night before, wandering about restlessly, Harding had found Reddy Baldinger, a reporter who had been one of his newsboys on the *Marion Star.* Baldinger was alone in the ship's dining room, eating a mess of crabs he had bought for himself. Harding had joined him—he wanted to talk about the old days—and had shared the crabs.

"God has abandoned him, don't you see that?" Nelson Crain suggested, urging to his wife that they immediately return to New York.

Sandra Crain was inclined to agree, but she had made a promise, so they compromised. Nelson Crain returned home alone. His wife continued on with the presidential party as it boarded a train for San Francisco.

They arrived there on a Sunday, checking into the Palace Hotel. By Monday the president had taken a turn for the worse. His temperature rose to 102 and his pulse to 120. He was rapidly developing bronchial pneumonia.

Once again Florence Harding seemed to forget all about Sandra Crain, intent only on her husband, who was being treated by several doctors, including a heart specialist. On Tuesday he seemed better. By Wednesday he was sitting up in bed, taking solid food and reading the newspapers. His temperature was normal and his pulse rate had dropped below 100.

On Thursday, August 2, Florence Harding finally visited Sandra Crain, telling her that they ought to be able to head for home Sunday. "He's so tired, so tired," she said. "But he thinks he's out of the woods."

"I hope so," Sandra Crain answered. "I've been praying for you." She consciously made that distinction, that it was for her friend, not the president, that she prayed. She could not wish such a man well.

"Can I see you later?" Florence Harding asked. "Yes, of course."

"Tonight? After dinner?"

"Yes. I'll wait up for you."

As she waited that evening, Sandra Crain wondered if she was being too hard on Warren Harding. He was, after all, not alone in his misdeeds, and it did seem—until that secret report had arrived—that he was trying to chart a new and more honest course.

It was his friends who had betrayed him, she thought. Attorney General Harry Daugherty, for example. He was so afraid of a sick man's ire that he hadn't even visited the president. In San Francisco all week on government business, he'd been hiding out at the St. Francis, though there was a room available for him at the Palace.

Florence Harding had mentioned that the secret report seemed to have something to do with Jess Smith and Daugherty. Earlier that year, Jess Smith, who had lived with Daugherty in the Washington house loaned by Ned McLean, had committed suicide, shooting himself in the head. The newspapers had quoted Daugherty at the time as saying that Jess Smith had destroyed all of his—Daugherty's—house accounts and personal correspondence. Jess Smith's papers had been destroyed, too.

There were so many who could be at fault, Sandra Crain decided. Daugherty, if he was indeed involved, was just the tip of the iceberg, that was certain. There would be many, many more below.

There was a knock at the door. Sandra Crain hurried to open it. Florence Harding was standing outside, looking terribly stricken, barely able to stand.

"Oh, no!" Sandra Crain cried.

"He is dead," Florence Harding confirmed. "He is dead." Like a woman in a trance, she held up a copy of the *Saturday Evening Post*. It was open to an article about Harding titled, "A Calm View of a Calm Man." She let the magazine fall from her fingers. "I had just read him this—he wanted me to read it all to him—and then I returned to my room. When the nurse went in to give him his medication, his head dropped and he died. He is dead!"

Sandra Crain bent to retrieve the magazine. Irresistibly drawn to the last words Harding ever heard, she saw that it was a favorable article, suggesting that he had been following a good, steady course.

Yes, that was what he would have wanted to hear, she thought. She tried to think of something to comfort Florence Harding. "His friends betrayed him," she said finally. It was the only sincere comment she could make.

"Perhaps," Florence Harding said, taking back the magazine. "But don't be too quick to condemn. Before this is all over, you may find that your husband was one of those friends."

CHAPTER 33

Something Special opened in October, three months behind schedule but worth the extra time it had taken to make it what its name implied—the finest private club in Cicero.

Even Meister was a little awed by what he had wrought. Though relatively small and intimate, it was indeed as elegant as any of the private clubs in Chicago. He had been in them all, peddling his whiskey, and if you weren't concerned with the size of the club, then his creation didn't take second place to any other.

The restaurant and adjoining lounge were both finished with rich oak paneling. The floors were also a gleaming oak. All the fixtures, from lamp standards to overhead fans, were solid brass. The bar and the mirror behind it, taken intact from Clancey's Saloon, were an antique treasure.

Upstairs, the private dining rooms, each decorated and furnished in a different period, would have done credit to any mansion. The card room on the top floor, with garish floral wallpaper that was a close match to the kind in Sim's Café in Bellville, was a proper, no-nonsense gambling den.

The place was perfect except for Meister's office. This was still bare studs, the money having run out before he could finish it. He'd spent forty thousand dollars, twice what he had originally intended, but it had been money well spent. The value was there and he had an elegant showplace.

Opening night was by invitation only, engraved cards having been sent to a select group of business and professional men and, of course, everyone who rated as society.

Meister hoped that two hundred of those invited would show up, or roughly half. Gang Clancey, growing more and more pessimistic as the day drew closer, scaled it down to fifty at best, convinced that they had a disaster on their hands. He didn't believe in engraved invitations. He preferred large signs in both windows, screaming OPEN FOR BUSINESS.

As it happened, more than four hundred showed up, not all of them invited, and many of those who *were* invited brought along friends or extra couples.

Meister didn't realize it, but over the course of that summer, everybody who was anybody had developed an interest in Something Special. It was, after all, Cicero's first new private club since the advent of Prohibition. That alone made it a curiosity. What made it a four-star attraction was the daring lack of official sanction.

Everybody who was anybody knew the fix wasn't in yet in Cicero. Al Capone had been trying all summer to put it in and had gotten nowhere. Now someone else, who was apparently not connected with the syndicate, was opening up in grand style without asking anybody's leave. All he was asking, apparently, was to be accepted on his merits, and he was willing to risk being closed down the night he opened for the chance.

Who could pass up an invitation that promised either a new era or a police raid?

No one, apparently. The rush started the moment the doors opened, at six. There'd been a line down the stairs and onto the sidewalk. By ten o'clock, when the party was supposed to be over, it would have taken a fire to get anybody to leave.

Gang Clancey, working the bar with two other bartenders, could hardly keep the drinks flowing fast enough. Miranda, in charge of the kitchen, had been forced to send out twice for more hors d'oeuvres, and McKinney's Cotton Pickers, especially imported for the evening, were in danger of being signed up for the season. The dance floor was packed with society types kicking up a storm.

Meister moved through the happy bedlam like a man in a dream. It was going to work. It really and truly was going to work! He had a roaring success on his hands.

Even Tandy, who had been concerned about the club linking her husband to the bootlegging business, had come around completely and was proud and delighted.

"You've done it, Mr. Meister," she whispered in his ear at the start of the evening. "You've really gone and done it!"

Then she'd gotten into the spirit of the thing, first out on the dance floor, twirling around with old Douglas McCormack, one of the town's social elite. She was having as a good a time as anybody. Maybe better.

It looked as if the party might run into the wee hours and Meister decided to let it go on. It was a great crowd and there were no problems at all. If some of them wanted to linger, why not? The small cost, a few more cases of liquor and some overtime, would be well worth it. Nobody liked to get kicked out when they were having fun.

Meister had gotten Gang Clancey's agreement to stay open and was crossing over to the band to get McKinney's okay when he noticed De Marco, the police department's vice chief. He was sitting in a corner by himself, trying, rather unsuccessfully, to blend into the woodwork.

"Hello," Meister greeted softly, mouthing the word rather than actually saying it. He was surprised to see De Marco. Some of his men had been in earlier, taking a quick, casual look around. They'd asked if it was a private party and had left when assured that it was. Meister had assumed that would be the only show of the law for the first night.

"Nice party," De Marco remarked.

Meister looked around, wondering if De Marco expected him to sit down, then decided that he should stay only briefly. He signaled to Pop Fagan to keep the music going for a while longer and changed course. De Marco set the rules in their delicate situation. He'd leave things up to him.

"Have you got time to sit down?" De Marco asked.

"Sure," Meister told him, noticing that he was drinking coffee. "You want something stronger?"

De Marco smiled. "No thanks. Not while I'm on duty."

Meister motioned to a waitress. He'd have coffee, too, he decided. After all, as Johnny Torrio said, appearances were the glue that held it together. Appearances and assumptions.

"The boys told me the place was really jumping," De Marco said. "I thought I'd drop in and see for myself." He took a sip of his coffee. "Incidentally, how come I didn't get an invitation?"

"I wasn't sure about the protocol," Meister replied, "and I figured you'd drop by when it pleased you. Besides, it saved me a stamp." He took a deep breath, thinking that everybody must be staring at them by now and wondering what was going to happen. "There are no problems, I trust?"

De Marco looked past Meister's shoulder, surveying the crowded lounge, the dance floor beyond. "You don't seem to be having any. Half the swells in town are here, and I don't see nobody in a hurry to go home."

Meister tried not to sound too enthusiastic. "That's because I'm picking up the tab. Wait till I start charging, then we'll see." His gaze met De Marco's, waiting to be contradicted. "Everybody likes a free party, but will they be back?"

"Oh, they'll be back," De Marco said. "Don't look so worried. I'm not planning on closing down the place. Listen, these people love it. They're just the same as anybody else. They like a good time once in a while, and why drive all the way to Chicago when they've got one of the best clubs around right here in Cicero?"

Relief flooded Meister. "No complaints?"

"Not from me," De Marco assured him. "Nor, so far, from any of the brass. It's like I told you, they know they've got to loosen up, but they don't want to make any deals." He paused as Meister's coffee was delivered. "You heard what they told Capone?"

Meister shook his head. He really hadn't kept abreast of the syndicate's move. All summer long he'd been wearing blinders, all his attention focused on the club. He'd hear the news, good or bad, soon enough, he figured. He had his third-quarter report to make to Johnny Torrio.

"They told Capone to get fucked," De Marco said. "The mayor, the council, the chief—the whole brass band. They all told him to get fucked."

Meister stared at him in disbelief. How did a small village administration expect to stand up to the most powerful crime syndicate in the country? "You're kidding!"

"No, dead serious."

"Jesus." Meister shook his head. He still couldn't believe it. "So, now what?"

De Marco shrugged. "Who knows? Either you're a long time without competition or you get the syndicate for Christmas. What I hear is, Capone is thinking of running his own slate in November."

"The village elections?"

"Yeah. Neat, huh? If he can't buy them after they're in office, he'll buy them before they get into office."

"You think he can?" Meister inquired, wishing now that he'd had the time to keep in closer touch. "Buy the whole election, I mean? Hell, that's only a month away, isn't it?"

De Marco shrugged again. "Money talks, isn't that what they say? If he spends enough, I guess he might swing it." He looked at his watch and took a last quick sip of his coffee. "Well, I've got to run, my friend. You're not the only party in town, you know. Just the best." He got his hat and coat and slid out from behind the table. "Congratulations. The place really looks fabulous."

Meister stood up with him. "Thanks."

De Marco pulled on his coat, then set his fedora at a suitably rakish angle, all business now, the social visit over. He looked over the crowd as if he were making a count.

Meister stood next to him uncertainly. A number of heads had turned their way.

"I've never asked you for favors, have I?" De Marco asked.

No, Meister thought, and he wondered what was coming now, half the people in the club suddenly watching. He'd been so certain that De Marco was that rarity around Chicago, an honest cop, but by the sound of this, he'd been wrong.

"I'm asking one now," De Marco said softly, moving away. "Vote Republican."

Afterward, the last few stragglers sent on their way, they had their own private party, just the two of them, Meister and Tandy.

Miranda had left at midnight to relieve Alexander's baby sitter. Pop Fagan, though he'd wanted to stay for a longer visit, had pulled out at two a.m. with the rest of McKinney's Cotton Pickers. They were headed for their next night's date, in Terra Haute. Gang Clancey, exhausted by his eight-hour shift of non-stop bartending, had called it a night a short time later, taking his two helpers with him and telling the cleaning crew to finish up in the morning.

Meister locked the door on all of them and went back to the bar to join Tandy. She was perched on one of the leather stools, wife of the proprietor, trying to look important.

"Is that the last of them?" she asked, slightly drunk.

"Yes," he assured her, getting out a bottle he had saved, one of the last of the Dunbar's Special. It was what had launched him—lanuched them, he thought—and it was only fitting that, together, they break open the very best. From now on, as long as his cache lasted, the bar's whiskey was going to be Something Special, the club's name and trademark.

"No sweepers?"

"Nobody."

"You're positive?"

"Yes, for God's sake. Why?"

"I want you to kiss me," Tandy told him, turning precariously on her stool. "And, as I recall, things can get out of hand here, Mr. Meister."

Meister laughed, the comment triggering a vivid recollection of their session on the card room floor, the best it had ever been between them—before or since. It had been real magic on that morning. He leaned across the bar and pecked her on the cheek.

"That's a kiss?"

"Be patient, woman," he requested. He got the bottle open and set two shot glasses on the bar. "First, a toast."

Tandy looked doubtful about having more to drink. "I don't know. If you want to take advantage of me, you already can."

Meister grinned. "I do and I will, but first a toast, huh?" He filled her glass and put it in front of her, then filled the other for himself. "You can just take a sip, okay?"

She nodded and carefully picked up her glass. "Listen, what did Pop Fagan mean ... that he'd been wrong about us?"

"Us?"

"Yes, when he was leaving. I heard him talking to you and that's what he said. 'I sure was wrong 'bout you and your lady.' "

"Oh," Meister said. He downed his whiskey, wondering if he should tell her the truth and deciding that he should ... whenever possible. "You remember that night at the Apollo Club?"

"When you kicked the hell out of Nick?"

"Yeah. Well, Pop took me home after that, and I don't know where he got the idea—maybe I was talking in my sleep?—but he got the idea I might be interested in you."

"He did, huh?"

"Yeah ... and he told me I wasn't good enough for you."

"Oh, no!" Tandy cried in genuine distress, tears coming to her eyes. She put her glass down, spilling half of the whiskey. "That's not true!"

"What's not?"

"Both! He didn't say it—and it's not true, darling. It's not true!"

"You're right," Meister decided. "I am, all things considered, a pretty good catch." He opened the bottle again and refilled her glass, then his. "Industrious, faithful—" He hesitated. What the hell, he thought, and said, "Truthful." He got his glass. "You ready for this toast?"

Tandy raised her glass, her hand trembling. "You know what really makes me sad? John not being here."

"John?"

"My brother."

Oh, him, Meister thought, wondering how John Crain had suddenly come into the picture. They were talking about what a nice guy *he* was, not John Crain. Still, give the devil his due. Like this bottle of Dunbar's Special, John Crain had been instrumental in launching him—launching them—on the path to success. "Yes, I'm sorry too. He ought to have been here."

"Do you think Father had anything to do with it?"

"Yes, of course."

"You do?" Tandy exclaimed. "You really think Father stopped him from coming?"

Meister had to back up. That wasn't what he'd been thinking about. He'd meant to give credit to Nelson Crain for launching them on the path to success. The original ten thousand dollars, that's what did it. That's *all* that did it. No ten thousand, no club. "I meant, he might have."

"He did," Tandy decided. "He's such a shit."

Meister downed his shot of whiskey. "No, it's your brother who's the shit," he said, amazed at his wife's language and at himself defending Nelson Crain. "Your father's a—a vastly misunderstood man."

"*My* father?"

"I don't want to argue," Meister told her. He took her glass and filled it again, then filled his own. "What I want to know is, are you ready for this fucking toast?"

Tandy looked at him, aghast. "I beg your pardon?"

"Oh, boy," Meister said, turning red. He'd tried not to use such language in front of her and he couldn't understand what was wrong with him... unless he was drunk, but he didn't remember getting drunk. It must have snuck up on him awfully fast. "Am I drunk?"

"I don't know why not," Tandy said, laughing now. "I am!"

"I can't even remember what I was going to toast."

For some reason, Tandy found that hysterical. "Docs it matter?"

"Yes," Meister complained. "It's ritual." He searched his suddenly fuzzy head for the lost toast. What was it—to her, to them, the club? To Prohibition, which had made it all possible?

"I know a better ritual," Tandy confided. "If you can just get me upstairs."

"The card room?"

"God, what a memory," she teased, slipping carefully off the stool. "Good God, what a man!" She waited for him to come around and get her. "That Pop Fagan, he's full of shit You're the best damn man... you know that?"

Later, Tandy asleep in his arms, Meister finally remembered what he had wanted to toast. He had the club, that was certain. But he once again had a chance, depending on the outcome of next month's election, of eventually taking all of Cicero.

He had wanted to toast democracy.

CHAPTER 34

The way things turned out, it would have been a waste of good whiskey, just as Johnny Torrio predicted. When Meister made his quarterly accounting, the subject of the election came up. Specifically, what came up was Al Capone's hastily assembled "reform" slate.

"You think you can take it, huh?" Meister had asked, handing over his six thousand in tribute, which was now Torrio's standard quarterly cut. The Something Special whiskey sales were being held at a firm five hundred cases a month.

"Buy it," Torrio had corrected him, holding up the packet of money. "This'll buy anything, kid. Wait and see."

Meister had returned home to watch it happen. Capone's hand-picked candidates, bought and paid for, flooded the papers with full-page advertisements, all financed by the syndicate's ample purse. They promised government for the people, not the elite, progress versus stagnation, jobs versus unemployment and, unbelievably, honesty instead of corruption.

The Republican incumbents, no angels themselves, perhaps, but at least not syndicate yes men, responded too late to the onslaught. They were overwhelmed before they knew what hit them.

Capone used every trick in the trade to guarantee a victory. The ballot boxes were stuffed, the dead voted and hoodlums patrolled the polling booths handing out five-dollar bills to converts, giving the fisheye to the Republican faithful.

Cicero awoke the next morning in the iron grip of the Torrio syndicate, the strangle hold even stronger than the one it had on Chicago. Joseph Klenha, the new mayor, was at Capone's beck and call. So was most of the village council. The town was now Capone's, to do with as he pleased.

De Marco could only shake his head in helpless bewilderment. He, too, didn't know what had hit him when he came up to the bar that afternoon at the Something Special.

"Give me a defeat drink," he told Gang Clancey, taking his badge off and putting in on the bar. "A double."

Gang Clancey stared at the badge. "You quitting?"

"No," De Marco said, managing a wry smile. "Just off duty." He turned to greet Meister, who had come up from the kitchen, surprised to find De Marco there. It was barely four o'clock and they had just opened. "That's my orders... from the Emperor himself."

Meister looked at the badge and then at De Marco. "Capone is giving you orders? Directly?"

"That's right," De Marco told him. "The son of a bitch was so sure of winning he gave them to me last night. He had me over to the Hawthorne Hotel—this is before the polls are even closed, you understand?—and he tells me I'm off duty."

Meister was stunned. "Fired?"

"Naw, just off duty," De Marco said, taking his drink from Gang Clancey. "From now on, if I see a vice law being broken, I'm to look the other way. Prostitution, gambling, drugs..." He raised his glass. "This stuff? It's none of my business anymore. I'm off duty."

Meister still couldn't believe it. Capone was putting himself completely above the law. How the hell could he expect to get away with that?

"Here he can do it," De Marco told him, guessing what Meister was thinking. "You have the doubtful privilege of residing in a town that has just been bought by the syndicate, lock, stock and barrel. Every public office of any consequence has a dummy syndicate candidate in it, including, I just found out, the city attorney's office." He took hold of Meister, shaking him. "Wake up, will you? You're living in a syndicate barony. When Capone says jump, you jump!"

Meister removed De Marco's hand. "Easy."

"Aw, I'm sorry," De Marco said. "It's just so—" He took out his frustration on the bar, slamming it with his fist. "It's just so goddamn unbelievable. They bought the town, the whole fucking town!"

Meister slid onto the stool next to him. That realization, the fact that the syndicate had taken it all, was finally starting to sink in. If what De Marco was saying was true—and Meister had no reason to doubt him—Capone's intention was to make Cicero the mother lode of suburban gold mines, an empire unto itself. This was Capone's big opportunity to show Torrio how to really milk a territory, and what better choice than Cicero? The bucks were here and it was virgin money, waiting to be raped. That was why Meister had chosen Cicero for his own club. If allowed to operate, it couldn't loose. It was a guaranteed money machine.

Capone saw the same thing, but on a much larger scale. One club? He'd have a dozen running soon enough. Booze and a friendly card game? Hell, give him enough time, he'd have a whorehouse on every corner, a casino in every block.

"I'd quit if I thought it would make any difference," De Marco said bitterly. "But how would that help? There's five guys waiting to take my place, all willing to look the other way, only more so. They wouldn't see an old lady get run over by a car. Eyesight difficulty? They'd be legally blind—the only legal thing about 'em." He downed his drink in one gulp. "Give me another, will you? The same."

Meister waited for Gang Clancey to refill De Marco's glass, then indicated that he would like the same. A good strong double, and after that, maybe another.

I outsmarted myself, Meister thought. He'd picked the best possible location for his club, never stopping to think that if it was best for him, it was best for the syndicate, too. Even when Torrio himself told him that the syndicate would be moving in, he had imagined it would be in only a small, careful way, skimming off the top, not taking it all. He had had all of Greater Chicago to choose from, and like a goddamn nincompoop, he had picked what was destined to be the heart of the syndicate's operations in the suburbs: Cicero.

"Fuck Al Capone, huh?" Meister said, taking his drink from Gang Clancey.

Gang Clancey poured one for himself. "I guess I was a little hasty," he admitted, referring to the conversation they had had when Meister broke the news to him about the syndicate move into Cicero.

Yeah, Meister thought, but he wasn't blaming Clancey. It had been his idea. His alone. Right from the start.

"You quitting?" Gang Clancey asked, the same question he'd put to De Marco.

Meister clinked his glass against Clancey's. "No. A man's got to take a stand somewhere, remember?"

CHAPTER 35

Al Capone didn't stand still. Overnight, Cicero became the most wide-open town in the 932 square miles of corruption known as Cook County. Even Chicago had to take a back seat.

Capone opened the syndicate's flagship casino, the Ship, in Cicero. A wide assortment of other enterprises—more casinos, saloons, speaks, whorehouses—soon sprang up. At the same time Capone led the syndicate's advance into other suburbs, buying the police and the politicians in Chicago Heights, Burham, Calumet City and other outlying areas, putting the lock on most of Cook County.

With Cicero captured so boldly, the rest quickly fell into line, almost eager to be under the syndicate's benevolent aegis. The "ice," the payoffs to the cops and the politicos, was generous and regular. The local criminal element was placed under a discipline it understood. Play it cool ... or else.

Tandy was alarmed by the change in Cicero. The pleasant, peaceful village was suddenly jumping—a kind of Harlem for white folks—and she didn't like it. She wished all the drinking and gambling and vice had been kept in Chicago, where it belonged. She couldn't help thinking, since he had opened the first club, that the change was partly her husband's fault.

Meister's intense interest in the Something Special's operation, his almost slavish dedication to every aspect of the enterprise, was also disturbing her. Tandy had the feeling that she had become secondary in Greg's life, that the club was more important to him than she was. He spent almost all of his time there.

When he did come home, he was tired, irritable. He barely talked to her. He paid little attention to Alexander.

If this was what success meant, she didn't want it. Even her father, who worked long hours and often wasn't a conscientious husband, found time for her mother. He made a point of setting aside the time for them to be together.

But Greg? With the club such an obsession with him, it was catch as catch can and putting a real strain on their marriage. It was nowhere near as happy as it had been.

What had happened?

"A minor crisis," Meister told her when she at last made an issue of his neglect of her and Alexander. "There's so much competition in town, I've really got to keep the club the very best, or I'm going to lose my customers. I was lucky to get a jump on things, but I can't stay ahead unless I keep running."

"But when can you stop?" Tandy asked.

"I can't," he answered. "Not right now. There's no way. It's the nature of the business."

"Then why don't you get into some other business?"

Meister laughed. "Be reasonable. What else could possibly be so rewarding?"

"Financially it is, yes," Tandy admitted. "But I don't like what it's doing to you. I don't like what it's doing to us."

"To us?"

"We're drifting apart."

Meister took her into his arms. "No, we're not. That's your imagination."

"We are!" Tandy insisted. "You hardly talk to me anymore. And do you have any idea when we last made love?"

Meister hugged her. "If that's what's bothering you, I can fix it now."

"It's everything," Tandy told him, pulling out of his embrace. "Can't we get away somewhere? Just the two of us? A real vacation together?"

"Sure," Meister said. "That would be nice." He hesitated, looking away. "But not just yet, huh?"

"When?"

"Soon."

Tandy wasn't satisfied. When this crisis was over, there'd be another. She had the terrible feeling that she was losing her husband. He was in the wrong business—and he was getting in deeper and deeper. She was afraid it would never stop. Would there be any end to it? she wondered. Or would he just be dragged deeper and deeper . . . until he was gone?

CHAPTER 36

Al Capone let Meister and the Something Special go their own way until spring the next year. It wasn't until April that a Capone emissary, Rags Ragulia, a slim, effeminate dandy, came calling as a syndicate liquor salesman.

Rags. The nickname came from his love of fine clothes. He would have been a joke to one and all if not for his syndicate connection. Whatever the season, he dressed like a fop, his trademark a tailored pinstripe suit with a small white carnation in the lapel. He always carried grey chamois gloves, and at the least suggestion of inclement weather, he put on a chesterfield with a velvet collar and added spats—grey chamois to match the gloves—to the ensemble.

He posed no physical threat whatsoever. Frail to the point of being dainty, he seemed to dwell on his lack of masculinity, indulging in an aftershave lotion one could only buy at a perfume counter. His most remarkable feature was eyes so sad that he could easily have hired out as a professional mourner.

Gang Clancey sent Rags right along to Meister. "I can't handle this," Clancey confessed. "I'm sorry, but if we're going to avoid a syndicate war, you're going to have to keep him out of my sight."

Meister laughed and took Rags upstairs to his unfinished office, where he knew the little dandy, sitting on a crate amid bare studs, would be most uncomfortable. He, too, didn't want Rags around any longer than necessary. The man was an offense to other men.

"What brings you around anyway, Rags?" Meister asked on the way up, even though he knew perfectly well. Rags made his living selling syndicate booze, and the club hadn't purchased a drop of it since Capone had taken over Cicero.

"Social call," Rags replied, out of breath after one flight of stairs. "And I was hoping we might transact a little business too." He stopped to inspect the private dining rooms on the second floor. "A very nice place you've got here. Elegant."

"We like it," Meister said, going on ahead. He was already seated at his desk when Rags at last made it up to the office, his heavy breathing sounding like a death rattle.

"*Whoosh,*" he said, patting his forehead with a silk handkerchief. "You're up a ways, aren't you?" He looked around, desperate for a place to sit, distressed to see that there was only a crate.

"Park it." Meister indicated the crate.

Rags reluctantly sat, looking around the office, more distress showing in his sad, mournful eyes. He patted his forehead some more and returned the silk handkerchief to the breast pocket of his pinstripe suit.

"Social call, huh?"

"Well, business, actually," Rags admitted, managing a faint smile. "I should have been around earlier, but you know what it's like opening up new territory. Busy, busy."

Bullshit, Meister thought, but he said nothing. Under normal circumstances, Rags' first call would have been at the Something Special, because it was the biggest, most successful club in Cicero. What had kept him away so far was Meister's deal with Johnny Torrio. The syndicate got twenty percent off the top of the operation and stayed out of the rest of it.

"Anyway, I'm here now," Rags said. He made a production out of locating a gold pen and a slim leather notebook. "I was hoping you might see your way to placing an order. We have some very nice—"

"No," Meister cut him off. "I won't be needing anything today, thank you. Nor, as a matter of fact, in the foreseeable future."

Rags' pinched expression became even more pained. "Perhaps I should rephrase that. *Mr. Capone* would like to see you place an order."

"I'm sorry," Meister told him, pushing away from his desk. "The answer is still no. If that's the business you came here to discuss, you're wasting your time and mine. The Something Special's reputation is built on serving top-quality, genuine-brand liquor. There's no place in our bar for syndicate stuff. Capone knows that. You know that. So what are you doing here?"

Rags hesitated.

"Following orders?" Meister was starting to feel sorry for the little dandy.

"Yes," Rags said, flushing slightly. "But then, doesn't everybody?"

Meister didn't reply. Within the syndicate, yes, he thought, but he wasn't in the syndicate. He had his own deal, damn it, and he wasn't following orders—or placing one, either. What could he do with syndicate rotgut except pour it down the drain?

"It's, uh, a matter of appearances," Rags said, trying again. "Surely you must appreciate our position? If you don't buy from us, that gets the other club owners thinking, Why should they? After a while it can cause difficulties." He managed a faint smile. "We should all do our best to avoid difficulties, wouldn't you say so?"

"The answer is still no," Meister said firmly.

Rags blinked. He obviously hadn't expected a refusal after this explanation. He put away his gold pencil and leather notebook and rose gingerly from the crate that had been serving as his chair. "Well—I'll—I'll tell Mr. Capone."

Yeah, Meister thought, no doubt. But he wasn't going to change his mind. Once Capone got his foot in the door, there'd be no letup. Two cases—a token buy—would soon become four, then six, then eight. They'd keep the pressure on until it was all syndicate booze and then the whole idea of the club would be down the drain. The Something Special would be just another joint peddling rotgut. Meister wasn't going to let that happen.

"When you tell him, tell him why, will you?" Meister requested, getting up. "I'm also a great believer in appearances. I wouldn't want it to appear that I was being difficult without good reason. The Something Special *is* special. It is not only to my advantage, but to Mr. Capone's to keep it that way. You might ask him to drop in and see for himself."

Rags looked a little shaken by that suggestion. "Mr. Capone?"

"Is welcome to drop in anytime."

"I'll—uh—tell him that."

Meister escorted Rags downstairs and out the door, then returned to the bar for a conference with Gang Clancey.

"Well, sooner or later it was bound to happen and it just did," Meister told him. "They want us to start buying syndicate liquor. Token purchases—for appearance's sake."

Gang Clancey was drying glasses. He held one up to the light, examining it for spots. "What did you tell him?"

"No."

"And what did he say?"

"He'll tell Capone."

Gang Clancey set the glass aside, a strange expression crossing his face, as if something wasn't quite right. His eyes narrowed and his nose wrinkled up. Meister stared at him. This had all been settled between them long before—that they were going to take a stand—and now was no time to back down. Rags was out the door, running with Meister's message to Capone, translated as: Get stuffed.

"Will you get away from me?" Gang Clancey demanded. "Do you know what you smell like? A precious little flower, all perfumed!"

Meister sniffed himself. "I do?"

"Go wash," Gang Clancey ordered. "Take a bath. Burn your clothes." He moved down the bar, backing off in mock horror, one hand raised in alarm, the other holding his nose. "Mario! Quick! The disinfectant!"

"Fuck you," Meister said, laughing at him. But it really wasn't funny.

Al Capone wasn't going to like getting no for an answer....

At home, Meister pretended that all was well even though Tandy, by simply reading the newspapers, was getting a continuing update on the syndicate's ever-increasing strangle hold on Cicero.

There could be no doubt in the public's mind that Al Capone was the town's real ruler. A gossip columnist had gleefully reported that Capone had lost his temper over some trifling matter and knocked down Mayor Joseph Klenha on the steps of City Hall. This while the police stood amiably by.

Meister thought that Tandy might have made more of it, except that the newspapers were also full of reports of larger scandals, the legacy left by Warren Harding. Occasionally there appeared, to Tandy's utter dismay, the name of Nelson Crain.

Crain was somehow linked to what appeared to be one of the major scandals of the Harding administration, the granting of government oil leases without competitive bidding to some of the Nation's largest oil companies. Harry Daugherty, the attorney general, and Edwin Denby, the secretary of the navy, had already been forced to resign because of it.

There were reports of criminal charges pending against Harry F. Sinclair, owner of the Mammoth Oil Company, which had received one of the oil leases—at Teapot Dome, Wyoming. Nelson Crain was being mentioned as Sinclair's possible partner in the deal and in other ventures under investigation by a special council appointed by President Calvin Coolidge.

With her father in the national limelight, linked to Harry Sinclair in what appeared to be a multi-million-dollar swindle, Tandy could hardly fault her husband for a comparatively minor involvement in the illegal liquor business.

And, in point of fact, it *was* minor, Meister thought. The Something Special booze haul in New York had been his one big escapade. Since the opening of his club, he had made only much smaller buys, all from small operators who, like Himie Koshevoy, didn't want to get involved with the syndicate.

He had the name and reputation of Mr. Special, the man who wanted only the best and was willing to pay for it. He had become that, a specialist, making only careful, selective purchases. He took his pick of rare wines and vintage champagnes. Perhaps two or three times a month he would buy a truckload of the better scotches—Haig & Haig Pinch, Dewar's, Black & White, Ballantine's and J & B—plus Gordon's Gin.

He stockpiled what he needed for his own use and laid off the rest to the private men's clubs that had been his original best customers. He gave Torrio his cut—even on the liquor he kept for himself—and The Fox seemed happy enough with the arrangement.

With its expansion into the suburbs, the syndicate was making so much money that Meister had become a very minor cog in the wheel—or so he thought. Personally he was making a fortune, but it was small potatoes compared to what the syndicate was scooping up for Torrio. He had become so small that he should have dropped from sight. It really didn't make sense for Capone to start pushing him around.

And, Meister thought, maybe he wouldn't. Maybe it was just Rags Ragulia trying for a few extra bucks. Surely Al Capone had better things to do than worry about Greg Meister.

CHAPTER 37

Meister couldn't have been more wrong. On a slow Tuesday afternoon in July, shortly after the doors opened at four o'clock, Al Capone showed up unexpectedly at the Something Special, a retinue of hoodlums in tow.

Gang Clancey, getting the bar set up, whistled softly as they trooped in. They looked very much like a private army. Despite the heat they were all dressed the same, wearing wide-lapeled dark suits and dress shirts with ties. White straw boaters were the only concession to the fact that it was the middle of summer.

"Hey, rube," Gang Clancey muttered to himself. He was all alone, the first in.

Capone took off his boater, looking around appreciatively. "So this is it, huh?"

His retinue—six in all—did the same, the boaters coming off almost in unison.

"Welcome, gentlemen," Gang Clancey greeted. "You're, uh…"

"Al Capone." Capone winked at Gang Clancey, as if to indicate that he meant no harm. Then he began a leisurely inspection of the club, moving about with a proprietary air. He acted like a man who had just bought the place, or intended to at the first opportunity. "Is the boss in?"

Gang Clancey had been following Capone's movements with growing apprehension, wink or no wink. "Meister?"

Capone turned to look at him. "Is that his name?"

"Yes."

"Then that's who I mean. Is he in?"

"No," Gang Clancey said, looking at his watch. "He—uh—doesn't come in at any regular time. Maybe five, five-thirty?"

Capone pulled a chair out and sat down. His boys took up positions elsewhere, one in the foyer, another at the entrance to the kitchen, the others in a kind of wide circle that protected Capone from all sides.

"I'll wait," he said, getting out a cigar. "But I don't want to wait that long. *Capice?*"

Gang Clancey picked up the phone to call Meister. He sure did understand. When Meister arrived ten minutes later, they were all in the same positions, Capone sitting in the middle of the lounge smoking his cigar, his hoodlums spread around him in a circle, straw boaters in hand. Gang Clancey was standing behind the bar, sweating.

Poor Clancey, Meister thought, surveying the scene. He at least had had time to prepare himself during the drive over from his home. Having the bunch of them drop in out of the blue, full of unstated menace, had to be unnerving.

"You're the—uh—proprietor, huh?" Al Capone said.

Meister nodded. "Yeah. Meister."

"Meister," Capone repeated slowly, as if he'd never get it right. He removed his straw hat from the chair next to him, indicating that he'd like Meister to join him. "Meister," he said again.

Meister started across the lounge, looking at Clancey. "You poured the boys a drink?"

"The boys don't drink," Capone said. "Me? I've been waiting for you." He lifted a French cuff, glancing at an expensive gold watch. A large diamond ring, the stone so big it was almost distasteful, flashed with the movement. "Thanks for being so prompt."

Meister slid into the chair that had been indicated. Capone hadn't offered to shake hands, so he didn't, either. He simply sat down, ready to get on with the business.

"What would you like?"

Capone spent a moment considering. "I understand you stock the world's best whiskey."

Meister called over to Gang Clancey. "Break out a bottle of the Dunbar's, will you?"

Capone said nothing more. He sat smoking his cigar, waiting for the drink, studying Meister.

Meister stared back just long enough to show that it didn't bother him. Then, an excuse to keep busy, he got out his cigarettes, borrowed an extra ashtray from a nearby table and lit up with all the calm and assurance that he could muster. Inside, his stomach was a small, hard knot.

It was his first close contact with the syndicate's chief enforcer and he was finding it decidedly unpleasant. Quite apart from his apprehension about having to argue with a killer, he had the feeling, strangely intense, that he was sitting with a pig. The expensive clothes, the impeccable grooming, the gold watch, the diamond ring—none of that could alter the impression he got of a moody, unpredictable, dangerous swine.

Gang Clancey came over with a silver tray. There was a bottle of Dunbar's on it, still unopened, a bowl of ice, some distilled water and soda, and two gleaming, spotless glasses.

Meister nodded his thanks and opened the bottle of whiskey. He poured double shots in each glass, then looked at Capone.

"How do you drink it?" Capone asked him.

"As is."

"Then that's fine by me."

Meister passed him a glass, raising his own in a half toast but saying nothing. He didn't wait for Capone to drink before he took a sip himself. He held the whiskey in his mouth, savoring it, then, very slowly, swallowed it.

Capone had taken careful note of the process with his probing black eyes. Now he drank in the same fashion. A small sip fully savored and slowly swallowed. "That's the berries, isn't it?" he said then, licking his thick lips.

Meister nodded.

Capone took hold of the bottle with renewed interest, reading most of what was on the label before he returned the bottle reluctantly to the table. "How much do you charge a shot?"

"We don't," Meister said, which was the truth. "There are just a few bottles left in stock, so we don't sell it anymore." He produced a smile that really wasn't in him. "It's for special occasions—special guests."

Capone gave no indication that he had been paid a compliment, sincere or otherwise. "It's not your bar whiskey?"

Meister almost laughed. Dunbar's Special? "No, our bar whiskey is Something Special. That's where we get the club's name."

"Oh," Capone said. He took another sip of his drink. "I thought it was this stuff."

Meister couldn't believe it. Capone really was a pig. The chief enforcer for the king of bootleggers, and he didn't even know his whiskey!

"You'll pardon the unexpected visit?" Capone said, obviously not caring whether Meister did or not. "The boys and me, we were taking a drive—it's such a nice day, isn't it?—and I remembered Rags saying he'd run into some trouble with you." Now the black eyes fixed on Meister. "You don't want to buy our booze?"

"No."

"Why not?"

"Because we can't sell it."

"Oh, yeah? Who says?"

"Me."

Capone put his drink aside, exchanging it for his cigar. "Maybe Rags was right. He thought you were—how should I say it—determined to be difficult?"

"Not true," Meister told him. "I'm just being realistic. The club's reputation is built on high-quality name brands. I switch now and what happens to my customers? They take a walk—and who is that going to help? You? Johnny?" He got another cigarette, taking his time lighting it. "You guys have got twenty percent of this place, every month, off the top."

"So?"

"So why fuck up the operation?" Meister demanded, barely containing his anger. "I've built it up, now you're trying to tear it down. What kind of sense does that make? We're all going to lose, because it's your business too."

Capone considered for a moment. "Rags didn't explain the big picture to you?"

Meister laughed. "You mean, if we don't fall in line, then maybe some of the other clubs won't? That's nonsense. You've got 'em all scared shitless."

"Then how come you're not?"

Meister looked into those probing black eyes. The question was so unexpected that he didn't have a ready answer. He *was* afraid, but he certainly wasn't going to admit it. He had a deal with Torrio, but he wasn't going to brandish it. That, maybe, was the ace up his sleeve, and he didn't want to play it in the wrong hand.

"You see what I mean?" Capone said softly. "The system don't work unless everybody's scared." He took a last quick drink of his whiskey and pushed up from the table. "Next week, Rags is gonna be around again. If I was you, I'd make a buy—for your health's sake. *Capice?*"

"That's really stupid," Meister said angrily. "Can't you understand? If you fuck with this club, you screw yourself!"

Al Capone turned back to face him. If he was angry, it didn't show. He just seemed thoughtful. After a moment he knocked the ashes from his cigar, purposely letting them fall into Meister's glass of Dunbar's Special.

"What did you say your name was?"

"Meister."

"Meister," Al Capone said, moving away. "I'm gonna have to remember that."

Gang Clancey waited until they had all left. Then, ashen-faced, he came over with two fresh glasses, falling into the chair that had been vacated by Capone.

"Jesus Christ, lad," he said, pouring two new drinks with a shaking hand. "Do you think all of that was wise?"

Meister shrugged helplessly. How would he know? But if not wise, it was the truth, damn it. The club business would go to hell if they started selling rotgut whiskey. People could buy that at a hundred other places in Cicero. The moment they stocked it, they'd stop being something special. They might as well take down the sign, close up.

"What would you have done?"

"About half as much as you did, and I'd be a proud man," Gang Clancey said earnestly. He raised his glass, clinking it against Meister's. "I'm also proud to be associated with you." He took a long, healthy pull, not bothering to savor it, just getting some whiskey in his belly. "What worries me, how long do you think that's gonna be?"

CHAPTER 38

The next morning, before anyone else was up, Meister was out of the house, headed for Chicago and Johnny Torrio's mansion on Lakeshore Drive.

He had to get this settled, one way or the other. If, for the sake of appearances—everybody in line, or else—the syndicate really wanted to ruin his business, there wasn't much he could do about it. He wasn't so foolish as to think he could.

Still, he'd made a deal with Torrio and he wanted to hear from Torrio, The Fox himself, that the deal didn't stand anymore. If it didn't, okay, he'd fold to Capone, and he'd make the best he could of the resultant disaster. He'd hold on and he'd sell the club as quickly as he could, then he'd get the hell out of Cicero. Being associated with crooks and murderers was one thing. With fools, another.

The guard at the gate tried to turn him away. It was only eight o'clock, and on a normal day Torrio didn't start seeing callers until ten. He kept late hours and he liked to sleep in.

"Is there somebody you could ask if he's awake?" Meister demanded.

The guard considered. "Yeah, the housekeeper, but that don't get you in."

Meister took a fifty-dollar bill out of his wallet and passed it to the guard. "That's for asking the housekeeper if he's awake. If he is awake, there's another fifty if she tells him I'm here and that I'd like to see him."

The guard took the money. "What did you say your name was?"

"Meister." For someone who supposedly was causing the syndicate so much trouble, he wished somebody—anybody—would remember his name. He parked his Packard and waited while the guard went into the gate house to make a telephone call.

A few minutes later the guard returned, his palm outstretched. "You owe me fifty. She told him you're here and that you'd like to see him."

Meister handed the money over. "Okay, frisk me and open up, huh?"

The guard smiled. "How do you know Johnny said yes?"

Meister grabbed the guard by the crotch, which was part of the frisk procedure, only the other way around, and squeezed very, very hard. "How much is it going to cost me to find out?"

"Nothing," the guard said, his eyes bulging.

"Then what did he say?"

"He—uh—said go on up."

"Thank you."

Meister released his grip. The guard backed off and opened the gate. He didn't bother making a search, which would be repeated twice anyway, once at the door and again inside the mansion.

"The name is Meister," he said, starting the long walk up the driveway. "Try to remember that, huh?"

Johnny Torrio met with Meister in his kitchen. He was still in his bathrobe and he hadn't shaved yet. He was drinking a cup of coffee and watching a Filipino houseboy make his breakfast.

"Lotso' peppers," he instructed, turning at the sound of Meister's approach. "Put in lotso' peppers." The rest was for Meister. "What you doing here this time of the morning?"

Meister shrugged. He didn't know. It could have waited, he supposed, but the stupidity of the whole situation was like a plague upon him. He knew he'd have no peace until Torrio made a ruling one way or the other.

"Oh, good, you don't know," Torrio said. He found a cigarette he had left burning on the edge of a tile counter-top and returned to his supervision of breakfast. "This is Manuel Guerrero," he added, introducing the houseboy. "Manuel is new. We're teaching him to cook."

The boy beamed. "Lotso' peppers."

"Lotso' peppers," Torrio agreed. He glanced back at Meister. "You eaten yet?"

Meister shook his head. "No."

"You had coffee?"

"No."

"Oh, good," Torrio said again. "What makes me think this sounds like trouble?" He got a cup out of the cupboard and pointed to the coffeepot bubbling on the stove. "Help yourself."

Meister took the cup and filled it with steaming black coffee.

"More lotso' peppers," Torrio told Manuel. He got three eggs and set them alongside the three that were already waiting on the sideboard next to the stove. Again, the rest was for Meister. "You like omelets?"

"Sure."

"Good. That's what you're getting." Torrio watched while Manuel added another handful of chopped green peppers to the mixture he was stir-frying in a huge cast-iron pan. "What's on your mind, kid?"

"I want to know if we've still got a deal. Yes or no?"

Torrio turned, frowning. He wasn't used to blunt questions, nor being spoken to in that tone of voice. "You want to back up?"

Meister shook his head. "Just tell me. Yes or no?"

Torrio stubbed out his cigarette. "If you've got a problem with the deal, tell me what it is." He tightened the belt on his bathrobe and led the way to a breakfast booth on the other side of the large kitchen. "Come here."

Meister followed with his coffee.

"Now," Torrio said, easing into the booth, "what the fuck is wrong, huh?" He kept his voice low, glancing significantly at Manuel. "And don't tell the world."

"Capone was over to my club yesterday."

"So?"

Meister sat down, aware that he had to get this said quickly and simply. Torrio was staring at him impatiently, not at all pleased with the way he had been challenged.

"Capone wants me to start buying syndicate booze for the club."

Torrio's expression changed. "What do you mean, 'start'? You mean, you're not buying now?"

"No," said Meister. "I never have. That was our deal. You'd take twenty percent off the top and leave me alone to operate the club my way."

"Yeah, but—"

"My way is with *my* booze," Meister maintained. "It's like I told Capone. If I start selling my customers rotgut whiskey, I'm going to lose them. They're used to the best and that's why I've got them as regulars. I can't suddenly switch on them."

Torrio waved his hand impatiently. "Yeah, yeah. Now I remember. The crème de la crème." He considered for a moment. "How much does Al want you to buy?"

"That's not the point," Meister said. "I can't use any of it. One case or twenty, I don't want it, I can't use it. Why push the shit off on me?"

"Hey, you gotta understand Al's position, kid," Torrio answered. "Cicero is his personal turf. He can't let nobody tell him no. What's that gonna look like?" He reached out and gripped Meister's chin, making him look him in the face. "You remember me telling you something? The importance of keeping up appearances?"

"Yes, and I've got appearances to keep up too," Meister complained. "The club's whole reputation is built on quality. It's like I told Al, if he fucks with the club, he screws himself."

"You said *that* to Al?"

"It's the truth."

"Kid," Torrio said, his attitude changing. It was as if he had suddenly become a concerned father. "We gotta get this settled. I don't want you messing with Al. That's just—" He stopped, deciding the next would be better left unsaid. "I know your situation. You can't sell our poison to your own customers, but why don't you make a minimum buy and then lay it off to some other club?"

Meister almost laughed. "In whose territory? The way you've got the lock on, I'd have to truck it out of state."

"Yeah," Torrio admitted. "Still. . . ." He leaned back in the booth, concern showing in his face. "We gotta figure some way of making Al look good. I appreciate your problem, but if Al don't look good, I don't look good."

"Shit." Meister was ready to give up. "If it's just appearances, why don't you have Rags Ragulia come in once a week, take a phony order, and whenever I've got a load of my good stuff coming in, Rags can ask a couple of Al's boys to stand around and watch us unload. They'll look like they're riding shotgun on a syndicate delivery and everybody's happy."

"Okay."

"What?"

"I said, okay," Torrio repeated, pushing out of the booth. "That solves it, right?"

Meister looked at him uncertainly. "Yeah . . . I guess so."

"Let's eat." Torrio headed back toward the stove. Halfway there, he stopped, turning around. "Oh, and about Al—what you told him? Don't worry about it. I'll talk to him and get it smoothed over."

"Thanks," Meister said, meaning it.

Torrio smiled. "Hey, you're all right, kid. You're smart and you're honest and you got some balls. I like that." He put his hand out. "I'm gonna make you a promise. You keep your nose clean and, as long as I'm running the syndicate, you also keep your ass, okay?"

Meister reached out to shake hands. "That sounds fair to me."

"It is," Torrio assured him. "And it don't happen all that often." He was laughing as he returned to the supervision of Manuel. "That's the way. Lotso' peppers. Manuel, today I'm giving favors. How'd you like to be Italian? I'm serious—listen to me, ya bum—I got more going here than the Pope. You want to be Italian? Just tell me… yes or no?"

Meister couldn't keep it a secret. He felt like cheering. Ever since the club opened—even before that—Al Capone had been like a sword over his head, ready to drop without warning. Now that sword had been taken away, and he had to tell someone. Returning home, the natural one to tell was Tandy.

Even though it was after ten a.m., she was still in bed, half asleep. He quickly undressed and got into bed with her. He pulled her to him, cupping a hand around one of her breasts, kissing the nape of her neck.

"Hey," she grumbled, "where have you been? You smell like onions."

"And peppers," Meister told her. "Lotso' peppers. I was over to see Johnny Torrio."

"This early? Whatever for?"

"Business," Meister said, feeling her stiffen at the word. "But not what you think. I'm not getting in any deeper, quite the opposite." He hugged her tight. "I made a deal with him. I don't ever have to buy syndicate booze. Not ever."

Tandy frowned. "Hasn't it always been that way?"

"Yes, but you know what it's like. People can start pushing, trying to change things—you know?"

"Capone?"

"One of Torrio's hired hands," Meister said, wanting to tell her the good news, not the bad. "Just a salesman." He made her look at him. "Anyway, I talked to Torrio and it's all settled. The syndicate is going to stay out of my operation. No ifs, ands or buts. I've got a free hand to run things my way, period."

Tandy made no reply, still frowning.

"Hey! What more do you want? I just got a personal guarantee from the big man himself. From now on, no worries, understand? He's going to protect me." He again made her look at him. "Is there something wrong with that?"

"Yes," she said at last.

"What?"

"That you're in the kind of business where you need protection."

"Oh, come on, will you?" Meister let her go. He looked away, disappointed. "I come home, busting with good news—" He turned down the covers, starting to get up. "Women."

"Where are you going?"

"I don't know. To brush my teeth, I guess. My loving wife tells me I've got onion breath."

"Well, okay," Tandy said, smiling now. "Brush them. But be sure to come back. I haven't told you *my* good news."

Meister looked at her. Something in her voice indicated that whatever it was was very special.

"You're not . . . ?"

"Brush your teeth."

Meister went into the bathroom, his mind in a whirl. That would explain a lot of things, he thought. She had been sleeping in, complaining about being tired, and she had been moody again of late—little spells of depression coming and going like the wind.

"Are you pregnant?" he shouted from the bathroom.

Tandy laughed. "A girl can't keep anything secret around this place."

Meister returned to the bedroom.

Tandy had her arms extended, the frown gone, happy tears filling her eyes. "Are you glad?"

Oh, God, yes, Meister thought. He was glad about a lot of things. And with another child on the way, he was especially glad to have his family protected.

CHAPTER 39

After that it seemed as if nothing could go wrong. During the next few months, Meister went about in a kind of happy daze, all his dreams coming true, nothing to complicate them.

Al Capone stayed clear of the club. Only Rags Ragulia called, coming in once a week, making a show of taking an order that wasn't going to be delivered. Then, when a truck-load of Meister's own brand was delivered, a couple of syndicate hoodlums would be standing by, pretending to be connected with the shipment.

It was all show, but it did keep up appearances, satisfying the syndicate's needs. Just as important, it freed Meister's hand to run the most elegant operation in Cicero.

Before, he'd been holding back somewhat, fearful that he might lose it all. Now, with Torrio's guarantee that there would be no interference, he could afford to invest more money and effort. He upgraded the dining room, buying better linens, china, crystal and silver. He also improved the kitchen and brought in a new chef, Alberto, who had an excellent reputation, having worked at several of the most prestigious private clubs in Chicago.

Within weeks of these changes the gross was up substantially. When Meister next visited Torrio, making his quarterly report early in October, he was able to prove the wisdom of being left to his own devices.

"Hey, I never had any doubts, kid," Torrio told him, clapping him on the back. "It was just a matter of figuring out a way."

Meister had returned to the club walking on air. He had it all, he thought: wife, family, home, a successful business, a marvelous partner, the protection of Johnny Torrio.

What could possibly go wrong?

Everything.

In November, Dion O'Banion, who had been given the North Side as his preserve when Torrio sliced up Chicago, was killed in an ambush in his flower shop on North State Street, across from Holy Name Cathedral.

Mike Merlo, first president of the Unione Siciliano, had died two days before. Orders for elaborate floral tributes had poured in from members of the underworld. Torrio had selected a ten-thousand-dollar display. Capone had picked out an eight-thousand-dollar item.

O'Banion was alone in the front of the shop, fussing with one of the displays, when three men came in to pick up an order phoned in the previous night. O'Banion limped toward them. Evidently he knew them. He extended his right hand in greeting.

The man in the center of the group took O'Banion's hand and held it tightly. The other two men drew revolvers and pumped six slugs into O'Banion's head and torso at extreme close range. Dion O'Banion slumped to the floor, dead before he landed. The trio fled in an undertaker's limousine that had been waiting at the curb.

In all the rumors and talk that reached Meister at the Something Special, it seemed most likely that the killing had been ordered by the Terrible Gennas, the six Sicilian brothers who presided over the tenement liquor-makers on Chicago's West Side.

O'Banion had been feuding for more than a year with the Terrible Gennas. He claimed that they were selling their corn-sugar alcohol in his bailiwick at three dollars a gallon, undercutting him by more than half. The Gennas, in turn, claimed that he was hijacking their liquor.

O'Banion had also insisted that Angelo Genna pay off—*or else*—thirty thousand in IOUs he'd spread around the syndicate's gambling casino, the Ship, in Cicero. Capone, nominal boss of the Ship, had wanted to write off Angelo's losses as trifling, but O'Banion had stoutly maintained that a man should pay his debts. Advised that the Gennas were excitable and might get violent, O'Banion had been quoted as saying, "Aw, to hell with them Sicilians."

That, Meister thought, was not a good way to talk about the Terrible Gennas. The finger of guilt certainly did seem to point at them. They were the type ready to kill at the smallest personal slight.

But Meister knew that Johnny Torrio also had had a beef with O'Banion. Money, not personal pride, was involved in his case. O'Banion, talking vaguely about possible retirement, had persuaded Torrio to buy out his $500,000 interest in the giant Sieben Brewery. Then Chicago's reform mayor, William Dever, had ordered a police drive on illegal beer operations. Both O'Banion and Torrio had been arrested in a raid on Sieben's, and Torrio could never shake the nagging suspicion that O'Banion had known the crackdown was coming before he sold his piece of the Sieben action. O'Banion had a lot of connections.

So, who really had ordered O'Banion bumped off—the Terrible Gennas or Johnny Torrio? Meister hoped that it wasn't Torrio. After O'Banion's gaudy funeral, Louis Alterie, one of his toughs, had publicly challenged the assassins to come forward and fight a pistol duel with him. Alterie had boldly declared that he would meet the enemy any time—including high noon—at State and Madison Streets, the world's busiest corner, the center of the Loop.

It was possible that blood was going to flow again. And it could be the blood of Meister's benefactor and protector, Johnny Torrio.

"What do you think?" Meister asked Gang Clancey, returning to the club after O'Banion's funeral. "Does it stop, or do they keep on killing?"

"If you ask me," Gang Clancey said, staring straight ahead, "those guys are too fond of funerals to stop now."

It wasn't what Meister wanted to hear, but it was probably the truth. O'Banion's sendoff had supposedly cost a hundred thousand dollars. He'd lain in state in a ten-thousand-dollar bronze casket with solid gold candlesticks and silver angels at either end. Some forty thousand people had filed past the bier in three days and the funeral itself had drawn another twenty thousand. His lieutenants had wept real tears at his graveside.

Meister swore softly. He wondered who'd be crying next... and for whom?

It was Sandra Crain. She was crying for a lot of people, including herself. The Duchess, now living on Doc Sawyer's farm in Marion, Ohio, had summoned her one last time... for a deathbed visit.

Sandra Crain went with a heavy heart. She feared that Florence Harding's last words to her might cast some dark shadow on her own husband's reputation. The day Harding died, Florence had hinted as much, and then the investigations had started, one of them linking Nelson Crain to Harry Sinclair in the slowly unraveling Teapot Dome scandal.

What if there were more such revelations?

Harry Daugherty was doing his best to keep the lid on everything. He had refused to turn over his files to a Senate investigating committee. The committee had asked for documents on a number of issues—bootlegging, oil deals, the distribution of fight films, failure to prosecute large corporations on monopoly cases. But Daugherty had held firm. He claimed that the senators pushing the probe had close links with the Soviet Union. It was a matter of national security, and that's why they couldn't see his files, he said. It had cost him his job as attorney general. President Coolidge had demanded his resignation.

Florence Harding also seemed to have done everything possible to cover up any scandal. Upon her return to the White House, she had spent several weeks burning the president's papers, according to newspaper reports.

But had it been enough?

To her dismay, Sandra Crain no longer wanted the great scandal, whatever it might be, cleansed by public revelation. If her husband was involved, even if only on the fringe, that changed the whole complexion of it.

National honor? No, she wasn't worried about it anymore. It was personal honor that concerned her and she approached Florence Harding's deathbed with mixed emotions. If the Duchess had some final secret to confide, Sandra Crain wanted her ears to hear it, not someone else's. Yet, in truth, she would have preferred to hear nothing. In a way—and the admission almost made her ill—she was glad that Florence Harding was dying. She wanted the woman's tongue silenced.

Doc Sawyer, Harding's personal physician, had died the month before of a heart attack. Now Florence was dying of an old, recurring kidney ailment.

Sandra Crain found her in low spirits, thin and terribly yellowish-pale, as if ready to slip away any moment.

"Thank you for coming," Florence Harding said weakly, a wasted hand beckoning. "This is very kind of you. I realize it was a long trip." She tried to smile, but could not move her stiff features. "You ... you've always been a good friend."

Sandra Crain nodded solemnly. "I've tried to be."

"That's why I wanted you to come," Florence Harding continued, her voice very faint. "I have something important to tell you." The wasted hand beckoned again. "Come closer."

Sandra Crain did so fearfully. She didn't want to hear. Whatever it was, she wanted it buried. Buried with Warren Harding.

"It was the scandal that killed my husband," Florence Harding whispered. "I know that. He couldn't live to face it. And it's killing me too. It is all too much to have to live in the shadow of disgrace." She paused to get her breath. "One loses one's will."

"Don't tire yourself," Sandra Crain cautioned.

But the dying woman went on. "I must tell you this. I did my best. I burned all the papers I could find … from his desk … his wall safe … all his files … the contents of a safe-deposit box. At first I tried to sort them out, destroy whatever might hurt his reputation, save historical documents that would put him in a good light." Again her breathing became labored. "It … was … too much."

Sandra Crain clutched at her. "What are you saying? That there is something left?"

Florence Harding shook her head. "No … nothing … I gave up trying to save anything. I … tossed boxes onto the fire without … looking to see what was in them."

"Then there's nothing to worry about?"

Again Florence Harding shook her head. "I … can't promise that. There must be many more papers and letters … documents … all over Washington." She fell back. "No … I can't promise."

Sandra Crain stared at her. Was this why she had been asked here? To hear that?

"It is your task," Florence Harding said. "It is you who … must protect your husband. You who must save him from himself. Do you remember what I told you? Many great men have had their careers ruined … the lives of their loved ones wrecked … by indiscretions."

Sandra Crain turned away. "I don't want to hear this."

"Your husband's business dealings," Florence Harding persisted, her voice rising. "Some of them … have not been honorable … ." She reached out to tug at Sandra Crain's sleeve. "Listen to me … you have a responsibility. You cannot make the same mistake I did. You cannot stand aside and … let him take whatever path he wants. If he continues … your lives could be wrecked."

Sandra Crain pulled free. Florence Harding was proposing the impossible. She had never interfered in Nelson Crain's business affairs, and in over thirty years of marriage, he had operated with a completely free hand, telling her almost nothing.

"It's … your duty."

No, Sandra Crain thought. How could it be?

"Promise me that … you will save yourself. Don't let him bring you to this … end."

Sandra Crain stared at her helplessly, remaining silent, making no promise. It was so ironic. She had had such grand plans once. In the beginning, she was going to help the Duchess to be a real lady and, in the process, perhaps help clear up the mess in Washington. The truth—the ironic truth—was that she could not even clean up the situation in her own household.

"Promise?"

Sandra Crain didn't answer. It was thirty years too late to ask such a thing of her.

Nelson Crain would continue to go his own way and reap whatever harvest awaited him. If he survived this scandal, if he went on to others, if he lost or won his battles—all that would be his own doing. How could she do anything? She had no head for business.

She started to cry.

CHAPTER 40

What Greg Meister feared most took place in late January. There was an attack on Johnny Torrio. The Fox had been out shopping with his wife. Instead of returning to the mansion on Lakeshore Drive, they had gone to a hideaway apartment Torrio kept on Clyde Avenue.

Torrio parked his car in the street and his wife went on ahead to unlock the door while he gathered up their packages. He had started for the apartment when two hoodlums ran at him from across the street and opened fire.

Torrio went down with five garlic-tipped bullets in his abdomen, chest, arm and jaw. He was still alive. He was a lot tougher than he looked. But his reign was over. The Fox knew when to quit.

Meister watched with a kind of morbid fascination as the syndicate's mantle of power was slowly but surely transferred from Johnny Torrio to Al Capone.

After Torrio was discharged from Jackson Park Hospital, he went directly to the Lake County Jail to begin serving the nine-month term he'd drawn when caught in the raid on the Sieben Brewery.

Torrio didn't have to go, because the appeal process wasn't over, but he obviously preferred the security of the county's bed and board to his own Lakeshore Drive fortress. He also didn't have to relinquish control of the syndicate since he could have given his orders from jail as readily as from anywhere else. But apparently he'd had enough.

For a while, Rags Ragulia, now Meister's main link to the syndicate, continued to refer to Torrio as the Boss. He would also preface remarks with "Johnny says..." More and more, however, the talk was of Al Capone, and it soon became evident that Capone, not Torrio, was making the syndicate's policy decisions.

Rags made it official in February.

Meister came into the club with a box of expensive cigars under his arm, Tandy having just given birth to her baby, another boy.

"Mother and child doing well!" Meister announced happily, passing out the cigars to everyone in the place, including the waitresses.

"It's a boy—Frederick," he told Gang Clancey. "A Crain, not a Meister. A butterball, not a scarecrow. Now we've each got one. Pretty good, huh?"

Gang Clancey dug into the dwindling supply of Dunbar's Special. "Private stock time!"

Meister sensed that the Irishman's enthusiasm was somewhat forced. He looked around the lounge, checking to see if he'd missed something coming in, and spotted Rags. The little dandy and his cologne remained one of Gang Clancey's pet peeves. But hell, that was no reason to spoil a new father's celebration, damn it.

"What's the matter?" Meister demanded, annoyed. "Is our perfumed chum getting you down?"

Gang Clancey lit his cigar. "Yeah, and he'll be real happy to tell you why."

Oh, no, Meister thought. His high spirits van ished, gone as quickly as the flame of Gang Clancey's match. He didn't have to ask. He knew. "Pour me that drink, will you?"

Gang Clancey opened the bottle and poured two shots. They clinked glasses, nothing said. Then Meister got a cigar out of the box, wishing he'd gone straight home from the hospital instead of stopping off at the club. It had sure been a short-lived celebration. He walked across the lounge, the cigar in one hand and his drink in the other.

"Did I hear say it was a boy?" Rags inquired, moving a derby and umbrella to make room for Meister in the other chair at his table.

"Yes," Meister acknowledged. He tossed the cigar into the middle of the table and sat down with his drink. "His name's Frederick and he's a butterball."

Rags raised his glass of Vichy water. "Well, here's to Frederick."

"Yeah."

"Did Clancey tell you?" Rags asked then, unable to wait any longer.

Meister shook his head. "No, he thought he'd leave that pleasure to you."

"Capone has it all," Rags said gleefully. "Johnny gave him the word yesterday. He had him over to the pokey and that's what he told him. 'It's all yours, Al,' he says. 'Me, I'm quittin'. It's Europe for me.'"

Meister took a careful sip of his drink. Europe, huh? It was one hell of a gift to Capone. Bill Dever, the reform mayor, claimed the syndicate was grossing $70,000,000 a year from bootleg liquor, gambling and prostitution. Now it was all Al Capone's?

Bullshit, Meister decided. It was all bullshit. It had to be! Nobody gave away that kind of money. Torrio was just pretending to hand it all over to Capone. That way Al could wield unchallenged power until Torrio finished his term in Lake County Jail.

It was appearances that were all-important! How many times had Torrio told him that?

"Things are going to be different," Rags said, smirking.

Maybe, Meister thought, feeling better. Maybe... and then maybe not. He wasn't going to panic. He'd wait and see.

CHAPTER 41

The wait brought increasing tension and, in the end, more bloodshed.

Hymie Weiss, who had succeeded O'Banion as ruler of the North Side, had reputedly drawn up a long list of people to be killed to avenge O'Banion's death.

Torrio was supposed to be on it, and so were Al Capone and all six of the Terrible Gennas. Rumors were rampant, and if but one in a hundred was true, a full-scale gang war was liable to break out at any moment.

Al Capone, in turn, was supposedly drawing up his own hit list. Many of the O'Banion gang were said to be on it—Weiss, "Bugs" Moran, Louis Alterie, Vincent Drucci. It was also said that Capone was going to import Frankie Yale as his hit man.

In the crossfire of rumors, Meister got word that he, too, was on Capone's list. It came from Morton Schriver, who, like Himie Koshevoy, had a family connection in Toronto. He was also Meister's main supplier of Gordon's Gin.

Schriver asked if he could talk to Meister privately, in his office. Meister agreed, thinking it was something about a liquor buy, but once the office door was closed, he could see that more than that was involved. The gin runner suddenly started to tremble like a leaf.

"I could get myself killed for this," Schriver said, the words barely audible. "But you're a good guy, you always treated me fair."

Meister got out the bottle of whiskey he kept in his desk. "Take it easy, Morton. You want a drink?"

Schriver shook his head. “No, I just want to tell you this and then cut out.” He lowered his voice even more. “I heard this in Toronto, that Al Capone wants you dead.”

Meister tried to laugh it off. “Me? That’s ridiculous. Besides, what the hell do they know about Al Capone in Toronto?”

“Plenty,” Schriver said. “There’s bootleggers running back and forth all the time, you know? And when they get up there—well, at that distance, they talk more, understand?”

Meister did. His apprehension grew. “Okay, what are they saying?”

“That there’s always been bad blood between you and Capone. It’s supposed to go way back. You got a brother-in-law? Somebody named Crain?”

Oh, God, Meister thought. Was Tony Capullo going to come back to haunt him? “Yes, what of it?”

“That’s it,” Schriver said. “The buzz is that Capone wants you dead for something this guy Crain did in New York.”

“You haven’t heard anything else?”

“Yeah. That you and Capone had a run-in once, but I heard that here. This Crain thing is strictly out of Toronto.”

“Who’s saying it?”

“A couple guys who work between here and Toronto. They wouldn’t say where they picked it up.”

“Do you know them?”

“Just their first names. A guy named Alfie and a guy they call Quarts.”

“They here now?”

“No.”

“Okay,” Meister said. “I appreciate your telling me. Don’t worry, nobody’ll know you mentioned it.” He pushed up from his desk, taking Schriver’s hand, shaking it firmly. “You’re a good friend to have. Thanks again.”

Schriver seemed more relaxed now. He had stopped trembling. “If I hear anything else, I’ll let you know.”

After Schriver left, Meister opened the bottle, pouring himself a drink. The way rumors were flying, there was probably nothing to it. Still....

Rumors! How the hell was he supposed to deal with rumors?

After a week or so, Meister was able to put it out of his mind, except for a brief and totally unexpected comment from Tandy.

He had been making an effort to spend more time with her and they had grown close again. One evening, in an apparent attempt to reassure him, she confided that she knew that her brother had killed Tony Capullo.

"We've never talked about this, but I *am* in on the family secret, you know," she said. "About John... and Tony Capullo."

Meister said nothing. He just looked at her, wondering why she should bring it up now.

"I also know about Al Capone being after John—at least, at one time."

"So?" Meister finally said.

"So, that's not our worry, is it?"

Meister wondered now who she was trying to reassure. Him or herself? Probably both, he thought, taking her into his arms. "No, it's nothing. Long past. If Capone was going to do anything, he'd have done it then."

"I suppose so."

"You suppose right," Meister said firmly. He turned her face to his and kissed her deeply. "Do you have any idea how long it's been since we've made love?"

"Uh... last night?"

"Yes," he said. "So what are we doing sitting here when you know you've got a standing invitation to lie down?"

Tandy laughed delightedly. "A standing invitation to lie down?"

"One of my better lines," Meister said.

Tandy laughed again. "Oh, you do have a line, sir."

He picked her up in his arms. "Shall we?"
"Why not?"

Tandy said no more about her brother and Capullo after that one brief mention, and Meister again put it out of his mind. Schriver dropped from sight, as he often did for extended periods, and Meister made no attempt to try to track down his informants, Alfie and Quarts. He wasn't going to chase rumors that probably had their start in drunken saloon talk. When the blood started flowing, that's when he'd start worrying, Meister decided. He certainly wasn't number one on any hit list. There had to be many other candidates for that spot.

As it turned out, it was the Terrible Gennas. In a sudden, explosive bloodletting, Angelo, Michael and Anthony Genna were killed in a period from May to July.

The long-smoldering hatred that was triggered by O'Banion's assassination had finally erupted into what threatened to be an all-out gangland war. There was no telling who might be the next victim. It was also quite possible for someone on the sidelines to be cut down.

When they really started killing, what difference did an extra corpse make?

CHAPTER 42

Tandy was afraid now for Meister's life. With Torrio's protection removed, shouldn't Greg flee Chicago, as John had? She was kept awake nights by worry and couldn't see any other alternative. They had to leave, she decided. It was the only solution.

Meister would have none of it. He wouldn't accept the guilt-by-association that was being pushed upon him. Besides, he had too much to lose—his reputation, the club and all the money he was making.

The concern over whether to run or to make a stand became a constant source of argument between them.

Finally, in August, on a hot, muggy day, it blew up all out of proportion, with both of them saying things that they would always regret.

Tandy and Miranda, suffering from the heat, had retreated to the shade of the backyard, setting up a sprinkler for Alexander to play in. Frederick, stripped down to his diaper, was put in his playpen nearby so that he'd get the benefit of some of the splashing water.

Meister, hot and irritable himself, came home to find them that way, the house a mess and nothing done about starting dinner. He had been working at the club all day. Several of the help hadn't shown up, preferring the beach, apparently. This meant he would have to go back that evening for more work. Besides acting as host, he had to catch up on his accounts, go over the next week's food orders and interview replacements for three key employees who had been lured away by other clubs. He was jammed up, not enough hours in the day, and it struck him as unfair to come home for a too-brief breather to find another mess, nothing cooking in the kitchen and Tandy and Miranda sitting on their duffs in the backyard.

"It must be nice," he said sarcastically, joining them with a drink in his hand. Normally, the club being such a temptation with someone always wanting to raise a glass with him, he only drank on special occasions at home. Today, though, he felt he could use a glow, and the earlier the better.

"Daddy!" Alexander yelled, running through the sprinkler. "Watch me!" Screaming with delight, the child turned and ran through the sprinkler again, sending a spray into the playpen, drenching Frederick.

Tandy felt too miserable to even look up at her husband's greeting. "Please, no complaints today," she said from the make-shift hammock she was lying in. "If you're going to bitch, you can turn right around and go back to the club."

"Well, thank you," Meister said. "That's a nice hello."

Tandy still didn't look at him. "It's as nice as your 'It must be nice,' and you're welcome."

Miranda pushed up out of her beach chair like someone suddenly aware of a fast-approaching squall. "If you folks don't mind, I've got things to do."

"Yeah," Meister said. "I noticed."

Miranda stared at him, her dark eyes flashing with fire. Over the four years of her employment, she had become family and she was used to saying her piece. Nobody pushed her around and, until very recently, no one had tried. If anybody dominated, she did. "This ain't my fight," she decided. The rest was for Tandy. "Yell if you want me to take the kids."

"Daddy!" Alexander called. "This is fun! Put on your bathing suit!"

Meister ignored him, glaring after Miranda.

Tandy waited until Miranda was inside the house, the screen door banging shut sharply with a sound like the crack of a pistol. "You've got no right to go jumping on her," she said.

"Nor to come here, apparently," Meister countered. He took a long pull on his drink, which he'd made too strong. He could feel the whiskey burn going down.

"What's that supposed to mean?"

"What's it sound like?"

"A stupid comment," she barked.

Oh, hell, here we go again, Meister thought. He told himself that it was his fault, that he'd come into the yard looking for an argument. But the basic unfairness of it still rankled him. He was busting his bottom, all day, every day, late into the night, and she was lying around on hers. He had all the problems of the world on his shoulders. She had, at her convenience, two children in her arms. If anyone had a complaint, he did, he thought. And yet she was the one doing the complaining. All summer she hadn't let up, pushing him to sell out and leave. If he had come into the yard looking for an argument, it was because he had come to expect one, that was all. It was becoming a family tradition.

"Wasn't it?" Tandy demanded, still waiting for a reply. "Wasn't it a stupid comment?"

"Go to hell," Meister said. He took another long pull on his drink, then put the glass down and went to the side of the house to turn off the sprinkler.

"Hey!" Alexander complained.

Tandy sat up in her hammock. "Now what are you doing?"

"I'm trying to play with him," Meister said, looking at his watch. "I've got an hour, okay? Then I've got to get back to the club."

"You and your club. If you want to play with him, why don't you do what he asks, put on a bathing suit?"

"Yeah," Meister said. "Me and my club. If it wasn't for—"

"Hey!" Alexander yelled. "I was having fun!"

"Oh, you go to hell too," Meister told him. He turned the hose back on and went slamming into the house. "You can all go to hell!"

Tandy followed him into the house and on into the library. "Miranda, watch the children," she said over her shoulder.

Meister gritted his teeth and made himself a second drink. In his anger, he'd left the other one outside. "Do you ever watch them yourself?" he asked.

Tandy was just as furious. Her face was white with rage. "Yes, I do, and often," she said, barely able to speak. "I care for them very much. But I'm beginning to wonder ... do you?"

Meister glared at her. "Am I supposed to dignify that with an answer?"

"Do you?" she demanded.

He refused to answer, his anger growing. What kind of a question was that? How dare she ask it!

"You don't!" she cried, answering for him. "You don't care for them or for me or for anybody else. The only thing you care about is your precious club. That's all we ever hear from you anymore." She proceeded in a furious chant. "The club! The club! The club!"

"It's where I work!" Meister shouted, slamming his drink down. "That's more than I can say for you. It's how I earn the money for all this." He made a sweeping, disdainful gesture. "This palace you had to have, remember? An ordinary house wouldn't do, you being such a princess, with royal Crain blood."

"You're blaming me? We both wanted it!"

"I wanted it for you," he told her. "I bought it so you'd be happy. I've done nothing in this marriage except work for the things that please you. An elegant home, fine furnishings, the good life! Try to tell me that isn't what you want. Try to tell me I haven't provided them." The rest was a shout. "And you have the nerve to tell me I don't care!"

"You don't!" she shouted back at him. "What you're doing now, you're doing for yourself and you know it. You're fulfilling your own ambitions and dreams, not mine. I'm willing to give this up. It's you who wants to stay."

Meister retrieved his drink. That last accusation had stung deeply. Everything before it had been wild, furious, empty statements. Now, however, she was flinging the truth at him. "I'm not a coward."

"Fine," Tandy said. "Good. I'm glad for you." Angry tears filled her eyes. "But maybe I'm not quite so brave, all right? Maybe I'm afraid—for you, for myself, for our children. Has that ever occurred to you? That I might be afraid?"

He stared at her stonily.

"Well, I am," she said. "And the reason, if you're interested, is because I do care. I care about you and I care about Alexander and Frederick. This palace, as you call it, and everything in it, isn't worth a damn to me if I've got to live in constant fear of some gangster gunning you down. I'm more than willing to give it all up and return to New York."

"Like your coward brother?"

"Call him what you like, but I sometimes wonder who's the real coward, Mr. Meister, John or you, hiding behind lies. The house isn't what holds us here. We could get another just like it in New York. What really keeps us in this nightmare existence is the club and bootleg liquor and all the money you're making—not for me, but for yourself. So don't tell me you care. You don't."

Meister turned away. Was that the truth? he wondered, unable to face her. Was it the money?

"You know what you're asking?" he said. "Everything I've worked for—to just throw it away? You know I can't duplicate the Something Special in New York. You know I can't build up the same organization or make the same connections. What am I supposed to do there, join the Unione Siciliano?"

Her answer was like a knife in his back. "You could find a job, you're so fond of work."

Meister turned to face her. "Stop it, damn you! There's no danger. You're worrying about nothing. Just to satisfy your stupid fears, you want me to lose it all?"

Tandy looked at him. The anger was gone now and the tears, too. There seemed to be nothing left inside her. It had all been spent, leaving her empty. "You can also lose your family," she warned him.

"You're saying you'd leave me?"

"Yes—with your liquor and your lies."

Later, there was no repairing the damage. That night, when Meister tried to take her into his arms, she was as stiff and cold as a corpse.

"This isn't us, fighting this way," he said, letting her go.

"No, it isn't us," she admitted. "Things change, and people too." She turned away. "You're not the man I used to know."

Meister lay looking at her stiff back. He reached out, wanting to touch her, to turn her around, but it was like reaching for an indifferent stranger. He pulled his hand back. "You're not the same woman," he said, turning away himself.

"Then I guess we're even."

"Yes."

She didn't reply and he had the terrible feeling that this was the best they could ever hope for now, to simply be even.

Meister decided that the only answer was to meet with Al Capone and reach the same kind of understanding with him that he'd had with Johnny Torrio. If they could talk it over man to man and reach an agreement, live and let live, that should satisfy Tandy. But if they couldn't agree....

Well, all right, he'd give it all up, leave Cicero and return to New York. If that's what she wanted, if that was the price of keeping their marriage together, he would do it for her sake.

But he wasn't going to do it as an empty gesture, to satisfy a whim. There had to be good cause. He had to be told, flatly and directly, that he had a reason to run. He had to be told personally by Al Capone himself.

The next time Rags Ragulia came to the club, which was about a week after the blowup with Tandy, Meister told him that he wanted a private meeting with Capone.

"What for?" Rags asked.

"To talk," Meister replied.

"What about?"

"Private."

Rags shrugged and promised to deliver the message. No word came back, however, and Meister had to wait another week, until Rags put in his next appearance at the club, to learn Capone's reaction.

"What did he say?" Meister asked.

Rags replied with one of his familiar shrugs. "Nothing."

"You gave him the message?"

"Yeah, and he didn't say nothing."

"He must have said something," Meister persisted.

"Naw, he just looked at me."

Meister stewed over that answer all evening. It *was* no answer, he thought, and it was annoying. It was also a little frightening. What did it mean? That Capone thought so little of him he couldn't be bothered to reply? Or had Capone already made up his mind about him, meaning that there was no need for a meeting?

The son of a bitch, Meister thought. Capone certainly knew how to wield his new power. Of all the answers he could have sent back via Rags, nothing, absolutely nothing, was the most difficult to deal with. It conjured up all kinds of possibilities, few of them pleasant.

When the club closed that night, Meister asked Gang Clancey to stay behind and have a drink with him, deciding that it was time to reveal the extent of his problems with Capone and the pressures that Tandy was putting on him to return to New York. Until now, Meister hadn't thought it necessary to worry Gang Clancey, because in his own mind there weren't any problems, only silly fears blown all out of proportion by Tandy. Also, he'd had no intention of returning to New York.

Now, however, the situation had changed. It was as if he had picked at a scab, making an old cut bleed. Left alone, it would have been all right, it would have healed. But now?

What did "nothing" mean?

Gang Clancey was annoyed to learn that Capone had once threatened to murder John Crain to avenge the killing of Tony Capullo.

"I thought you said there was no bad blood between you and Capone?"

"There isn't," Meister insisted, still clinging to the conviction that this part of it was ridiculous. Capone might have good reason to dislike him, but not because of John Crain. "How could there be?"

"You don't know Italians," Gang Clancey told him. "They have a very strong sense of family. Look at any of them, how they stick together. They're fighting each other all the time, but let an outsider intrude, you've got *this*!" He bunched his fingers into a fist. "They're one."

Meister didn't see how that applied. "The Capullo thing happened while I was in Nebraska. Besides, John Crain and I aren't related by blood. We're brothers-in-law, that's all."

"That's all?" Gang Clancey shook his head. "No, you're wrong, lad. To Al Capone, you and John Crain are family. Born into or married into, you still have the same responsibilities and obligations."

"And guilt?" Meister said.

"In Al Capone's mind, maybe so," Gang Clancey answered. "How do I know what's going on in that hoodlum's head? But he obviously thinks of you two as more than just brothers-in-law. He also remembers you as partners, right? Back in the beginning, it was you and John Crain, partners together against the syndicate, selling that batch of Dunbar's Special."

To Meister, Gang Clancey's normally cheerful tone had become the voice of doom. "Thanks."

"You wanted my opinion," Clancey told him, still annoyed by so late a disclosure of all that was involved. "And if you'd asked me earlier, I'd have advised not to seek a meeting with the bastard."

Meister had no quarrel with that. Thinking it over, it had been a dumb move. To ask for a meeting was to suggest that there were problems to be ironed out. It would have been smarter to let the initiative come from Capone. Al wasn't shy. If he figured he had problems that could be ironed out, he'd call his own meeting.

And if they were the kind that couldn't be ironed out, well, in that case, there was no need for a meeting, was there?

"You understand what I'm saying?" Clancey asked.

"Only too well," Meister replied. "There's nothing I've done to Al Capone to justify him putting a bullet in me. So if he has plans to do that, it's on account of my connection to John Crain. And if he's that twisted, I'm sure as hell not going to talk him out of it, right?"

Gang Clancey nodded solemnly. "You want that drink now?"

Meister tried to laugh but couldn't. For the first time he had an appreciation of how John Crain must have felt, the target of a ruthless professional killer.

"I'll make it a double," Clancey said. He poured the same in his own glass, which he clinked against Meister's. "Well, here's to you, lad. I wish I knew what the hell to tell you."

"To me," Meister said hollowly. The whole thing was so damned ridiculous, he thought. He didn't know if he had a real problem or not. It had taken on the appearance of one because of Tandy's fears. It had been magnified by Capone's disdainful silence and now by Gang Clancey's concept of how Capone might define family. Yet, where was there any solid evidence that Capone actually intended to harm him?

There was none, and until he had some, it was ridiculous to give up everything and return to New York. Ridiculous.

"I've got to find out," Meister said at last.

Gang Clancey looked at him. "What?"

"What we've been talking about. I've got to find out if my presence here is such a thorn in Al Capone's side that he's planning to kill me."

"Don't mislead yourself, lad. There's no way of buying that kind of advance information. The only way you'll find out is when and if it happens."

Meister shook his head. "No, I'm not going to wait. I'm going to ask him."

"Hey," Clancey said, reaching out to grab hold of him. "You're not talking sense now. You think he's going to tell you?"

"He might. Anyway, it's better than just waiting, isn't it?"

"Come on! Don't be a fool. What did Rags say? Capone won't even meet with you."

"He'll have to—if I kick in his door."

"That's a good way of getting yourself shot." "Maybe, but it's still better than waiting."

Gang Clancey slowly released his grip. The truth was something he never argued with.

Ever since the fixed election that had won the syndicate control over Cicero, Al Capone had maintained his general headquarters in the Hawthorne Hotel, otherwise known as "Fortress Capone." It was reputed to be impregnable, but that was just newspaper talk, part of the misinformation that was beginning to spread in public print as word got around of Capone's succession as king of the Syndicate. The press was now bestowing the word with a capital letter.

Actually, Capone's protection, like Torrio's before him, consisted of a half dozen hoodlums posted along the route to his office. Any well-planned attack by an armed force of equal number could easily have cut down the baby-faced mobster. His real protection was the fear of retribution. You might be able to get Capone, but if you did, God help you.

Meister was thinking about this as he approached the Hawthorne the morning after his talk with Gang Clancey. He was intent on a direct confrontation with Capone. If, as he had heard, the palace guard operated in the same fashion as at Torrio's, he could make it as far as the inner chamber before being turned back. The outer circles functioned only to assure that a visitor was unarmed. It was in the inner chamber that audiences were granted or denied.

If he did get that far, there'd be just one more door to go through and, as he'd promised Clancey, he would kick the damn thing down if denied entrance. He wasn't going to spend the rest of his life, however short it might be, wondering and worrying about Capone's intentions.

Meister wasn't concerned about his immediate safety. For all its ruthlessness, the syndicate's palace guard was a disciplined crew, not given to sudden excesses. It wouldn't needlessly shoot down an unarmed man in its inner chamber. That would make for messy, unnecessary, unwanted publicity.

Foolhardy though he might be, Meister had learned enough about the syndicate's workings to know what he had a good chance of getting away with right now. And that was a one-on-one meeting with Al Capone.

In the Hawthorne's lobby he saw a familiar face, Manny Calvelli, who had formerly worked the gate at Torrio's mansion on Lakeshore Drive.

"Hey, Meister," Calvelli called out, as if greeting an old friend. He put his cigar aside and pushed up out of the sofa where he had been reading the paper. "Long time no see! What's new, huh?"

Meister thought that nothing was new with Calvelli. Neither rank nor dialogue had changed. Yet he was happy to receive the warm greeting. It indicated that he hadn't been designated *persona non grata.*

"How are you, Manny?" Meister said, shaking hands. "There's nothing new with me, but I see you've made a move, huh?" He glanced casually around the lobby, looking for additional guards. "It's kind of spiffy."

"Yeah," Calvelli admitted, displaying a certain pride of ownership. "The first time you been in?"

Meister nodded. "Uh-huh. I keep pretty busy with my own place. Now you're in Cicero, you've got to come by." He completed his casual survey, satisfying himself that Calvelli, for the moment, was the only guard in the lobby. He turned back to him. "Listen, I'm sorry about Johnny."

Calvelli shrugged, as if to suggest it was just one of those things. "You here to see Al?"

"I'd like to."

"Nobody told me," Calvelli complained. He looked around the lobby. "Just a minute. Let me find Lombardo. I'll take you up."

"Thanks." Meister was hardly able to believe his luck. It appeared that he was going to be provided with an escort to the master's door. He picked up Calvelli's newspaper and sat down on the sofa, thinking that the security for Capone was surprisingly lax. There were no guards in the lobby now.

Calvelli reappeared a couple of minutes later with a young, pimply-faced hoodlum, barely of drinking age, in reluctant tow. He was carrying a plate with a half-eaten sandwich on it. "Let's go," Calvelli said cheerfully.

Meister got up and left the paper for the young hood. He doubted if the kid could read, though.

"Kind of young, isn't he?" Meister suggested when they were out of earshot.

Calvelli answered with another shrug and Meister wondered again about Capone security. It wasn't as stringent as Torrio's. Did he know something his former boss hadn't known?

In the elevator, Calvelli subjected Meister to a quick but efficient frisk, which ended, as always, with a crotch squeeze. "I gotta do it," Calvelli apologized.

Now it was Meister's turn to shrug. The crotch, apparently, was a good place to hide a pistol.

Even with Calvelli providing escort, he was frisked twice more before reaching the inner chamber—once as they got off the elevator and again at a halfway point down the corridor. It was here that Meister discovered a possible reason for the lax security.

It looked like moving day. A door opened and a man in overalls backed out, struggling with one end of a heavy steel filing cabinet. His partner, too small for the job, was red-faced with exertion, unable to get the other end of the cabinet off the floor. Watching with undisguised disgust was a stocky, bullnecked hoodlum who looked as if he could have handled the cabinet all by himself.

"What a jackass," he muttered, glancing casually at Meister. He had his jacket off and he was holding his shoulder holster in his hand.

The inner chamber was a large, luxurious suite, and it contained the same kind of turmoil. The foyer was filled with randomly placed filing cabinets. Here again the guards had their suit jackets off, which was not normal protocol.

Meister looked around in disbelief. There were no doors for him to kick in; they were all open. He could walk in anywhere. And if he had wanted to snatch up a gun, he could have. There were enough lying around.

"What have we got here?" one of the guards demanded with obvious irritation. He was an older man with thin shoulders, a sunken chest and a bulging potbelly. If he'd been wearing a padded jacket, he might have been a menacing figure, for he had a cold, hard face and a jutting, blue-sheened jaw. In his shirt, however, he looked like an easy hit.

"He's here to see Al," Calvelli said.

"Now?" the guard demanded, as if this were the height of idiocy.

Calvelli reddened. He looked accusingly at Meister, the question implicit in his eyes: Didn't you have an appointment?

Meister said nothing.

"He—he's okay," Calvelli stuttered.

"You're a real stupid ass sometimes, you know that, Calvelli?" the guard told him. The rest was for Meister. "I don't know you."

At that moment, Paul Jacoby, the syndicate's planning director, entered the room, arms loaded with books and papers. He paused, staring over his half-frame glasses. "Meister, isn't it?"

"I told you he was okay," Calvelli said.

"Shut up," the guard ordered. His eyes had never left Meister. "On second thought, I don't give a fuck who you are, fella. You picked the wrong day." He pointed to the door. "Al's not seeing anybody."

"Take it easy, Shark," Jacoby complained.

The guard was still looking at Meister. "I said, *shut up*!"

The command was given so fiercely that everyone in the room stopped what they were doing. Meister, meeting the guard's steady gaze, had the uneasy feeling that Capone's troops, unlike Torrio's, might be given to occasional tantrums. The room was deathly silent, as if a live grenade had been dropped and was about to explode in the next instant.

"What the fuck is wrong now?"

The question, asked in a tired, exasperated tone, dissolved the tension as swiftly as it had developed.

"Aw, it's Calvelli," the guard said, still angry, but under control now. "He's such a stupid ass."

Meister, his own hard-pumping adrenalin subsiding, looked past the guard to the office that Jacoby had just come out of. Al Capone was standing in the open doorway in shirt-sleeves, like everybody else. His fashion-plate image was set aside to meet the day's demands, collar open and hair mussed.

"I seem to be surrounded by stupid asses," Capone said, not unkindly. Apparently he was too tired to really care that much about it at the moment. Eventually his dark, probing eyes fell upon Meister. "Who's this?"

"Calvelli brought him up," the guard explained. "Mister... Meister... I dunno. Who knows anything in this mess?"

"Meister?" Capone said. He frowned, as if trying to remember. "You're the guy who owns the Something Special." Now he smiled. "The one with balls."

"That's right," Meister confirmed. He found it hard to believe that Capone would have difficulty remembering him because their confrontation was so vivid in his own mind. But then it might have been a quite ordinary occurrence for Capone.

"So what are you doing here?"

"I'd like to talk to you, briefly."

Capone shook his head. "Not today, pal."

"It will only take a couple of minutes."

"I said—" Capone began, the frown returning. He stopped, thinking it over, trying to make up his mind. He looked at Calvelli. "Is he clean?"

Calvelli nodded, his relief showing. "He's a whistle."

"You got two minutes," Capone told Meister. He turned and went back into the cluttered office he had emerged from. "We can talk in here."

Meister started to follow but was stopped by the hard-faced guard. "Hold on, buster boy. I ain't had my squeeze yet."

With swift, practiced movements, he gave Meister the quickest and most efficient search he had ever experienced, the final grab at the crotch a little harder than necessary.

"Go."

Meister followed Capone into the cluttered office. He'd remember that. Shark would also have his crotch squeezed one day. But right now Meister had more important matters on his mind. Much more easily than he'd expected—too easily, perhaps?—he had his meeting with Al Capone.

Capone waited for Meister to close the door.

"Listen," he said then, trying to be affable at a difficult time. "That time-limit jazz was just for the boys, huh? I've been telling them all morning I can't see nobody." He looked around the shambles of the office. "Which, incidentally, is true. So maybe you'd better spit it out after all. What is it?"

Meister was taken aback. Capone was acting as if there had never been a problem of any sort between them, let alone bad blood that would prompt, for revenge's sake, the signing of a death warrant. "I've been hearing some rumors," Meister said, deciding it was best not to be too specific. "The talk is, now that you've taken over the syndicate, I'm living on borrowed time."

Capone frowned. "Rumors? Talk? What the fuck is this? You're coming in here with *rumors*?" He sighed, his whole body sagging. "Do you have any idea how many rumors I hear every day? If I checked them all out, that's all I'd be doing, you know?"

"Yeah, but I've really just got the one, which is maybe why it seems so important," Meister replied, refusing to be put off. He'd come for his answer and he would get it. "I want to hear it from you. Is there any bad blood between us?"

"Bad blood?"

"Yes."

Capone seemed genuinely baffled. "What for?"

"For the obvious reasons," Meister told him. "We had a run-in, I went over your head, talked to Torrio."

The puzzled expression slowly became a smile. "You think you're the only guy who ever did that?"

"I don't know. Probably not." Meister was beginning to feel foolish. He hadn't prepared himself for that.

Capone was laughing now. "Get out of here, will-ya?"

"What about John Crain?" Meister demanded, plunging ahead. "He's my brother-in-law—you know that?"

For an instant a murderous shadow seemed to darken Al Capone's face, but it came and was gone again so quickly that Meister thought he might have imagined it.

"Yeah, I know that," Capone admitted. The dark, probing eyes fixed on him. "So what?"

"Is it a problem for you?"

"No. It's not a problem for me. Is it a problem for you?"

"I don't want it to be."

"Then don't make it one."

Meister stood staring at the new king of the most powerful crime syndicate in the United States. Was this all there was to it? he wondered. Had it really been settled that easily?

"Listen," Capone said wearily, "I don't know who you think you are, but from where I'm standing you're a real small fish, Meister. You got one lousy club and some half-assed connections for good booze. You gave me some trouble once and it got settled by Johnny. The rest of it?" He shook his head. "What do you think? I'm some dumb fucking dago? I know where you end. I know where John Crain starts. I know there's no connection."

"Good," Meister said. "I just wanted to make sure I wasn't a problem."

Capone dismissed him with a tired wave of his hand. "You're not important enough to be a problem."

CHAPTER 43

Tandy wouldn't accept it. A mobster's word? Never.

Meister was equally adamant. He had bearded the lion in his den. What more did she want of him?

The arguments continued and nothing was settled. Tandy still wanted to return to New York. Meister still wanted to stay in Cicero.

The house became a constant battleground. They seemed to be always screaming at each other. Miranda refused to eat dinner with them and Alexander, obliged to, would sit with his hands covering his ears.

After a while, Meister took to living mainly at the club. He'd go there first thing in the morning, before breakfast, and he'd stay until late at night, returning only when he was sure everyone was in bed. He slept in the spare bedroom. If he did come home during the day, it was to see the children, not Tandy. By unspoken agreement, she would make herself scarce then, staying in her bedroom until he was gone.

What they had once regarded as a perfect marriage was now a mockery of even the most ordinary marital union. There was, in fact, no union. They were all but legally separated.

In Meister's eyes, Tandy, the wife he had once adored, had somehow been transformed into a spoiled, willful, destructive harridan. If she couldn't get her way, she was stubbornly determined to bring everything crashing down, leaving nothing but wreckage.

In Tandy's view, her once innocent boy-man had become a selfish, arrogant, overriding bastard interested in satisfying only his own needs and desires, and willingly endangering his family while he was at it He didn't care. If he did, he'd take her and the children back to New York and safety.

There was no compromise possible. One or the other had to give in and neither was prepared to do that.

By September, Meister didn't care anymore. He started staying overnight at the club, sleeping on a cot in his still-unfinished office. The only possible reason to go home at night would be to keep up appearances, and he was beyond that Tandy, in her willfulness, had destroyed their marriage, he thought, and why try to pretend otherwise? What sense did it make to sneak home late at night, sleep alone in a narrow bed, then hurry away at dawn? Whom did it help?

If a lonely bed was the reward for all his hard work, then the cot in his office would serve. If the place was unfinished, the studs not even covered yet, it was still preferable to an argument-filled home. Some peace and quiet, he'd settle for that, whatever the surroundings. If it meant everyone would know his marriage was on the rocks, he really didn't give a good goddamn.

The truth was, there were few people to know or care anyway. Gang Clancey was the one real friend he had made since coming to Chicago. Everyone else was a business friend. As for Tandy, she had women friends among the neighbors and a number of club friends, too, but if she had a confidante, it was Miranda.

They were alike in that way, Meister thought. He and Tandy had been so close for so long that no one else had mattered. They hadn't built up a strong, supporting network of friends. That process, normal for most young couples, had not been accomplished. Somehow there hadn't been a need, or time. All they had wanted was each other and the children.

Now, the bond cut, there was nothing. Meister was bitter. He hadn't prepared for this, but then why should he have? If a man believed in God, he didn't keep a spare idol in a drawer somewhere, just in case. If he worshipped his wife, he didn't hold auditions for replacements.

The irony, Meister thought, feeling ever more sorry for himself, was that he could have had his pick of a half dozen other girls. In the club's two years of operation, hundreds of waitresses had come and gone, among them a number of very attractive ladies and some with an eye for the boss. Had he wished, he could have bedded a few—and without complications. There had been Dorothy, a bosomy blonde bombshell; Lola, a smashing redhead, and Bonnie Burford, who had reminded him of Kate Jenkins. And, talk about passed up chances, what about Marvel McPherson, who had been booked to sing for a week and who had stayed for two months, the only reason being her interest in him, which she had plainly stated?

Meister shook his head. Marvel McPherson. He'd said no, he was married, but if she came in and asked him now, he'd say yes quick enough. That girl, she could make a love song out of "Yes, We Have No Bananas."

Too bad. He'd missed his chance. The last he'd heard, Marvel was married, too, living in Los Angeles. And in his present desperate need there was no one now ... except, of course, poor little Julie.

Meister shook his head again. If only she weren't such a child—what could she be, eighteen?—he could have found solace in her willing arms any time he wanted to. She was one of the new girls, and she had fallen in love with him, for no good reason. She had it so bad that it was a joke around the club. She'd once walked into a post because she couldn't take her eyes off him.

Funny kid, Meister thought, smiling. Poor, sweet, innocent Julie. Off the farm, just like himself, and so much to learn in the big city....

Gang Clancey came in with his newspaper. "You want to hear the latest?"

"No," Meister said, but there was never any stopping the Irishman. Gang Clancey had an insatiable interest in the outside world. He was following the Scopes "Monkey Trial" as if God himself were in the docket. When Ford, for the first time, offered a choice of colors in his car, Clancey had taken it as a personal affront. Ford had gone back on his word. The dictum before was that you could buy a Model T in any shade "as long as it's black."

"You'll want to hear this," Clancey insisted.

"Tell me," Meister said, giving up. "The Charleston has become fashionable, right?"

Gang Clancey shook his head. "No. Torrio's been released."

Meister took the paper from him. The news was in a late bulletin that took up just three paragraphs. Meister stared at the report, not really reading it, just picking words at random, enough for confirmation. Torrio had been released from jail. Capone had provided a three-car, safe-conduct motorcade from the jail to the railway station. Torrio was gone. Capone had it all.

"Well, that's that, huh?" Clancey said, taking the paper back. "The end of the old era, the beginning of the new." He looked at Meister. "Now we find out."

Meister nodded. Clancey's meaning was clear. Now, with Torrio really gone, would Al Capone keep his word, or would he come gunning for him?

"It wouldn't hurt to keep your wits about you for a while," Clancey counseled.

"I will," Meister promised, moving away. It wasn't something he wanted to discuss.

"You might consider hiring a bodyguard."

"No thank you."

"We're making enough money for it."

"I said no."

Meister left Gang Clancey to open the bar and went upstairs to his office. If he had one complaint about Clancey, it was his tendency, on matters concerning Capone, to side with Tandy. He persisted in seeing the man as a threat.

It was a mean thought, but Meister sometimes wondered about Gang Clancey's motive. The matter had been settled, damn it. He'd talked to Capone, man to man. He'd been assured there was no bad blood.

There also was nothing sinister in the fact that Capone had consolidated the syndicate's operations in Cicero. Yes, Meister admitted, he had made one mistake. He'd assumed on his visit to the Hawthorne that Capone was moving out. Actually, he was moving in the syndicate's files from Chicago. But having Capone close by didn't make him any more dangerous.

So why continue to worry him with the damn thing? Why rush in with the newspaper report of Torrio's departure? What did Gang Clancey want, to pick up the pieces?

Sometimes, in his dark moods, Meister wondered. If he did run, the club would go to Gang Clancey by default. With so many other clubs running full-blast in Cicero, the Something Special was no longer all that out of the ordinary and there was no ready buyer at the price it was worth. If he did run, he'd have to make a deal that favored Clancey, let him buy the club out of operating profits, an arrangement that would take forever before it was paid off.

Meister tried to push the mean thought from his mind. What was happening to him? He'd lost Tandy. Now, out of distrust, was he going to lose Gang Clancey? Was he going to reach the point where there would be just him and him alone? Was that where he was headed?

Meister looked around his unfinished office, bare studs staring at him from all directions and a conspicuous lack of furnishings. There was just the desk, a chair and a couple of filing cabinets, plus the cot he'd moved in the week before. He wondered why he'd picked that, a plain, cheap cot, when he could just as easily have bought a decent, comfortable sofa.

Was he purposely punishing himself?

At a loss, Meister paced his office, not sure of anything anymore… except that he was lonely.

It wasn't planned. It just happened.

Meister was locking up the club. Everyone had gone home, or so he thought, until Julie came rushing out of the ladies' room.

"Whoa," she cried, embarrassed.

Meister didn't recognize her at first. He had dimmed the lights and she had changed out of her uniform and into a smart dress. She was also wearing her hair differently, letting it hang in a loose swirl instead of confining it in its usual prim bun.

He stared at her in the darkened foyer. "Is that you, Julie?"

"Yes," she admitted, out of breath. "I'm sorry. I didn't think it was going to take so long."

Meister waited until she reached him. The "it" was the transformation, apparently. Besides changing clothes and letting her hair down, she had put on make-up, which she didn't normally wear except for a trace of rouge.

"What do we have here?" Meister said, surprised. His poor little farm girl was suddenly a woman, and an attractive one. "A date, is it?"

"Yes."

"Who with?" Meister wanted to know, innocently enough, and was at once sorry he had asked. It was none of his business.

"Lenny Hilton."

Meister frowned. He knew Lenny. He'd once employed him, briefly, as a bartender. He'd been fired for robbing the till. Several other club owners had later confided that they'd had a similar problem with him. At the moment he was working as a bouncer at a new after-hours joint, the Gold Room. It kept him away from the cash register.

"What's wrong?"

"Nothing," Meister said quickly. "It's just..."

He stopped. It really was none of his business, yet Julie deserved a whole lot better than the likes of Lenny Hilton. Despite his dark good looks, he was a no-good bum. His next position, the way he was going, would be syndicate hoodlum.

"I know," Julie said, noting his expression. "He's really not my type." She gave a helpless little shrug, lifting her overnight bag's strap onto her shoulder as she did. "Beggars can't be choosers."

Meister put out a restraining hand as she moved past him toward the door. "Hey! You can't mean that."

"Oh?" She waited for him to remove his hand, then looked at him squarely. "I've been in town almost a month and this is my first date."

Meister didn't know what to say. He knew of two young men at the club, both decent boys, who would have loved to ask her out except for her obvious interest in him. As a matter of fact, he had been wanting to tell them the way was clear, that they just had themselves to fight over Julie, but he'd been too busy with his own problems to take the time.

"First date, huh?" Meister said, glancing at his watch. It was only five after two and the Gold Room didn't shut down until four a.m., sometimes five. "That calls for a celebration. Do you have time for a drink?"

Julie looked at him, a question in her innocent blue eyes. "Yes, I suppose so," she said carefully. "Lenny's not off for a while."

"Then let's have one!" Meister said, a little more enthusiastically than he had intended. He switched on all the lights and then, realizing that that wasn't necessary, left them on only at the bar. "What'll it be?"

Julie hesitated. "I don't know. Gin?"

"Don't tell me this is your first *drink* too?"

She laughed. "No, but almost."

"Really?"

"Yes. I'm only eighteen, you know."

And look sixteen, Meister thought, taking her bag from her. He set it down in a corner and led her to the bar, lifting her onto one of the leather stools as if she were a child.

"Hey," she said, but it wasn't a complaint.

Meister went behind the bar and unlocked the liquor. He took out two bottles, one Gordon's Gin and the other Something Special. He got two glasses, a bowl of ice and some tonic water. He set everything on the bar and then went around to join Julie.

She had watched the preparations in silence. "Is this a drink or a party?" she asked when he slid onto the stool beside her.

Meister didn't answer. He wasn't sure. He kept thinking that she only looked sixteen and that her eyes were the color of high-mountain lakes. If a man ever fell in, would he want to swim back to shore?

"You're staring," she told him. Again it wasn't a complaint.

"I'm sorry," he said. He opened the Gordon's and poured a minimal amount of gin into her glass, following it with ice cubes and then the tonic, filling the glass to the brim.

"You're not trying to get me drunk?" Julie asked, laughing.

"No." Meister had just poured the weakest drink ever served at the club. "That is not my intention."

She was still laughing at him, but only with her eyes. "Then what *is* your intention?"

Meister didn't answer. He didn't dare. Instead, he opened the Something Special, pouring himself a very large drink. He dropped in two ice cubes and swirled the glass once.

"Cheers," he said, raising his glass. He downed half the whiskey in one gulp. Was it possible, he wondered, that his little farm girl wasn't quite the innocent he thought she was? Was it possible—God, what an imagination he had sometimes!—that she didn't have any date with Lenny Hilton?

"Cheers," she answered, taking a small, careful sip.

Meister looked at his watch again. Barely five minutes had passed, and already, like a schoolboy, he felt in a rush, anxious to get down to the real business. But what was the real business?

"We've got time," she said.

"Have we?"

"Yes."

For what? Meister wondered, the question persisting. He felt almost certain now that he'd been maneuvered. Not that he minded. Quite the opposite. It was a welcome diversion. The only thing spoiling it was to admit he was still gullible. It was all those years on the farm, he thought. Would he never, ever, escape them?

Julie took another small, careful sip of her gin and tonic. "Is it true what they say?"

"What? That I ate my mother?"

She laughed. "No, that you live here now." "Sometimes."

"Where? In your office?"

"Yes."

"Hmmm," she said, taking another sip of her drink. "Have you got it fixed up?"

He shook his head. "No, just a bed."

She shook her head. "That does sound like the minimum."

"Actually, it's a cot," Meister said, wondering why in the world he was making that distinction. He looked away. "I've also got a desk and a chair." And then he blurted out, "Would you like a tour?"

There was a long silence.

"You've got time," Meister said, turning back to her. "Haven't you?"

She was looking at him, the amusement gone from her eyes. They were serious now and the innocence had returned. She nodded for an answer and he reached out with his big hands, taking hold of her waist, lifting her off the stool, marveling at how small and slim she was, just a child really. "You *are* eighteen?"

She nodded again. Slowly, carefully, he put her down, reluctant to release her.

"I don't think we'll need the drinks," she said when he turned to get them.

"No," he agreed, looking at her. She was waiting to take him and she was more anxious than he was.

Going upstairs, they said nothing. Julie led the way, as if she had been to the office many times. Meister thought that she had, at least in her imagination. This was something she wanted. She had planned to have it, he was certain of that now.

Inside the office, she turned immediately, embracing him boldly, holding her mouth up to be kissed. Meister gave her a lingering kiss. Her full lips were soft and warm and tasted honey-sweet.

Bolder still, she took his hands, placing them on her firm breasts where her nipples had risen like little licorice candies. Meister could feel them through the thin dress, erect, thrusting.

Her body moved against his. God, Meister thought, kissing her again, her breasts lost in his big hands. How could he resist her?

"Be gentle, will you, please?" she whispered. "I've only been to bed with one other man, and I don't think it was the way it's supposed to be." Her hands moved down, taking hold of him. "God, you're big."

Meister unbuttoned the front of her dress, lifting a breast from the flimsy bra, kissing the little licorice candy nipple. One other man? he mused.

"He was just a boy," she whispered. "Nothing really happened. He couldn't get inside me." Anxiously, she fumbled with the zipper of his trousers. "He was too quick." She laughed. "Do you know what I called him? 'Sudden Tom.' "

Meister pulled away. No other man? Her first time?

"What's wrong?"

He took hold of her hands, both in one of his. With the other, he turned on the light, searching her face. "You've never had a man make love to you?"

"No," she said honestly. "Not really. It was just—" She tried to pull free. "Please... you're hurting me!"

"I *must* know," Meister insisted. "That's the truth?"

"Yes!"

"And Lenny?"

"He's just a date," she said. She began to cry. "I don't have to see him. Nothing's going to happen. He just said to come to the club tonight if I could. I don't have to go." Finally, she twisted out of his grasp. "What's wrong with you?"

"Nothing," Meister told her softly. "Nothing." He drew her back in his arms, turning her head up, gently kissing away her tears. "I'm sorry. I didn't mean to hurt you. I won't again ever, especially now."

She buried her face in his chest. "Would you take me then, please? I know a girl is supposed to wait, but I don't think I can. And even though you're married, I want it to be you. I know I can't wait and I want it to be you."

Like hell, Meister thought, holding her close. You're going home, little one... safe from me, safe from Lenny. You're going home... and so am I.

By four o'clock Meister was on his own doorstep, feeling better than he had in years and as anxious as the time he'd had chocolates and sunflowers in hand and was standing on the front stoop at 14 Washington Square.

Would she or wouldn't she? he had wondered then. He was wondering the same thing now. Would she take him back? Would she like to forever be his beautiful loving wife?

He raised his hand to lift the knocker. In his rush, he hadn't made it the same as before, not in the middle of the night. But he had wanted it to be as much the same as possible. He had dandelions, not sunflowers, and he wanted Miranda to answer and tell her, like Sadie had, that Mr. Greg Meister had come calling. He wanted to sit in the foyer, waiting and wondering. When she came down the stairs, as he knew she would, radiant in her haunting beauty, he wanted to stand up and offer the dandelions. He wanted to say, "I brought you these."

Down the street a car backfired. Meister turned, surprised to hear it. In the middle of the night there was seldom any traffic.

A black sedan was approaching at high speed, its lights off. Behind it was another, and then a third, a fourth.

Oh, shit, *no*! Meister thought. He tried the door, but it was locked, of course, and he didn't have time to get out his key. The clatter of machine-gun fire had already started.

Meister, an easy target against the white of the door, turned with his handful of dandelions, feeling the first slug rip through his chest like a stone. He slumped against the door, blood gushing from the wound.

No! But the clatter wouldn't stop. The stones kept hitting....

The doctors kept saying he should be dead, and for a week he thought each day would satisfy the judgment. He held on, barely. Lingered, and then, finally, to everyone's amazement, including his own, the crisis passed. He had made it.

He was going to live. Hit by six machine-gun slugs, two in the chest, one in the stomach, the rest in his right leg, which looked like a sieve, he had survived and he was going to live.

Not that he really cared that much anymore.

Meister knew his marriage was over. He could see it in Tandy's eyes the first time she came to visit, looking as ghostly as he himself felt.

If he wasn't dead, she was, or at least the part of her that had loved him. By his greed and arrogance he had destroyed that part of her. There was nothing he could do or say, no act of contrition, no vow, that would ever make her whole again. That part of her—the part that had loved him—was gone forever.

On her third visit she brought the children, and as soon as he saw them, he knew it was also going to be her last visit.

"You're leaving, aren't you?" he said.

She nodded. "Yes."

Meister looked at his children. Alexander, four years old now, a little man and tough enough, but like his father he'd always be a scarecrow. Frederick, the butterball, still a babe in his mother's arms, a child he hardly knew and now perhaps never would.

"I'm taking the children," she said needlessly. "We're going to Wicklow. They'll be safe there." She looked away. "You understand? I can't live with a hunted man I don't love or respect anymore. Nor can I leave my children with him."

"I understand," he said, looking away himself.

The rest of it was a blur.

"Say good-bye to your father, Alexander." "Good-bye, Father."

"Frederick says good-bye too."

"Do we have to go already?"

"Yes, Alexander. We have to go."

"Good-bye, Father."

"Good-bye, Alexander."

"Well ... I guess this is it. Good-bye, Greg."

"Will I see you again?"

"No."

Gang Clancey came that night, bringing a book as a gift, Fitzgerald's latest, *The Great Gatsby.*

"I don't know," Gang Clancey said. "I haven't read it yet, but from what they say in the reviews, there might be a bit of you in there."

Meister took the book, smiling bleakly. He didn't have the strength to read yet.

"Take your time," Gang Clancey counseled. "There's no rush. A few pages at a time. You'll be in this place for a while yet." He moved over to the window, staring out blindly, not looking at anything special but just not wanting to watch. "It's got a bookmark in it, a present from Miranda."

Oh? Meister opened the book to the first page. There was a dandelion there, pressed into it.

"You got it?" Clancey asked.

"Yes."

Meister closed the book, thinking he hadn't come very far from sunflowers to dandelions, but at least he'd tried. A man had to take a stand somewhere.

www.ingramcontent.com/pod-product-compliance
Lightning Source LLC
LaVergne TN
LVHW041059080826
845145LV00007B/1630

9781952138980